FROM THE HOOD WITH LOVE 3

BRIANN DANAE

Chapter One

Atlanta, GA

B etrayal hurt worse when it came from the ones
you loved most. The ones you trusted, thought
were loyal and would never stab you in the back. It
seemed like everyone was out to get him when all
Projex was trying to do was make sure everyone ate.
Never in a million years did he think his blood would
do some shit like become a rat. It didn't even make
sense, and before he could wrap his mind around why
Kordell had snaked him, Projex had pulled the
trigger.

"Ahh, man! Fuck!" Kordell shouted as the bullet pierced his shoulder.

"Shut yo' punk ass up," Projex seethed. He was ready to send a bullet that silenced him for good.

Grabbing ahold of his shoulder, blood oozed through Kordell's fingers as he struggled to get out of the path of Projex's gun that was trained on him. He knew the next shot would've for sure ended his life. At the front door, Sneaks and Bo's faces held the same confused expression. They had stopped to get some food before coming back to the Airbnb and just knew no niggas had the balls to follow them and run-up in their spot. Pulling their guns out, they eased their way into the living room and lowered their weapons when they saw Projex had been the one shooting.

"What you in here shooting for, nigga?" Bo asked.

Projex was so pissed off, he couldn't even speak. His nostrils flared as he watched his cousin groan like he was the one in pain. Didn't shit hurt more than being snaked by your own blood. With his chest heaving, Projex tucked his gun back at his waist. He wasn't trying to go back to prison, and he knew he'd be the first person the police would come looking for if Kordell came up missing. Instead of ending his life, Projex was gon' beat his ass.

Projex thought about letting him stand up for a fair one but changed his mind. Bullet in his arm or not, Kordell couldn't fuck with his hands. Sending a hard blow to his face, Kordell's head jerked to the left. Dazed, he had no time to gather himself before blows that felt like they would knock him unconscious, rained down on his face and body.

Drunk and injured, Kordell tried standing to his feet, but that only made the situation worse. Swinging with his good arm, he missed, stumbled, and fell to the ground, where Projex commenced in stumping him out. Projex had blacked out like he always did when fighting. The type of anger coursing through his body he'd never experienced before. Knowing he'd stomp Kordell to death, Sneaks pulled Projex away and urged him to calm down.

"Nah, cuz. Don't do this shit right here," he told him.

Projex's shoulders heaved as he panted, trying to catch his breath.

"What this nigga do?" Bo asked in an exaggerated tone.

"Was working with them people on my case," Projex breathed out, not even believing his own words. "My own fuckin' blood was trying to get me knocked off for a measly ten thousand dollars."

Bo drew his gun again and aimed it at Kordell. "Say what? Give me the go-ahead, and I'll end this nigga's shit right now."

Projex's jaw flexed. Bo was one of his shooters when he couldn't get at niggas himself, but this was personal. As bad as he wanted to give him the honors, he didn't. It was bad enough there was blood all over these folks' couch and floor. The last thing he wanted pinned to him was a body, knowing the place probably had cameras out front. He'd toss the owner of the crib some extra money for the cleanup but wasn't leaving a body behind. If they were back home, shit would've gone much differently. Kordell wouldn't have had the same fate.

Projex yanked out of Sneaks' embrace and stared with a menacing gaze at Kordell. Sneaks looked down at him and shook his head in disbelief. He'd been riding around with this nigga, making plays and all kinds of shit over the years. To find out he was the main reason why Projex went to prison had him wishing he hadn't stopped him from killing his ass. Snitches didn't make it where they were from.

"Damn," Sneaks mumbled.

"Just let me off this nigga, cuz," Bo urged.

Projex wiped at his nose. "Nah. Get yo ass up, Dell."

"C'mon, cuz. I can't move my arm."

"Nigga, you could move that mothafucka when you were writing them statements," Projex hissed, kicking him hard in the side. "Get yo' bitch ass up!"

Kordell's body immediately formed into a ball. He'd sobered completely up and was feeling every bit of pain Projex had inflicted.

"Help that nigga up, Bo," Sneaks said.

Bo sucked his teeth and frowned. "Nigga, you help his bitch ass up. I ain't doing shit if it don't involve ending his life."

Struggling, Kordell weakly stood to his feet as he coughed up blood. His face was swollen, ribs probably cracked, and his body beat up so bad he knew it'd be worse tomorrow. When he went to sit down on the couch, Projex pushed him away from it.

"What you trying to sit down for? You ain't staying here. You gotta get the fuck out 'fore I do somethin' reckless."

"Man, c'mon. I can barely move."

"Aye. On the real, you ain't gone have a heartbeat if you stay in my face. Walk yo' ass to this front door."

When he didn't budge, Projex pulled his gun out and aimed it at him. "Walk, nigga."

"Can I at least get my phone and clothes? Damn."

"Nah. You better use that other phone and call an uber or something."

"The flight leave in a couple hours, cuz. C'mon. You ain't gotta put me out."

Projex smacked him upside the head. "You ain't flying back with us. Let yo' ass show up to that gate."

Murderous thoughts clouded Projex's mind as Kordell limped to slowly open the front door. He didn't care that they were in another state. Kordell had to go. He had no sympathy for him and never would after today. How he was getting home wasn't his concern. Kordell was lucky to even still be alive.

"He really putting this nigga out," Sneaks said.

Bo was amused. "Shit, I would too. I can't believe he was snitching. While folks were going around saying it was us, that nigga was the rat. I woulda never thought."

Rumors were exactly that when it came to Sneaks and Bo's involvement with Projex going to prison. They had no affiliation, and it was crazy how people took false information and ran with it. For over three years, Kordell had been working with the police to pin something on Projex, and they'd finally caught up to him. He and Kelsi were both asked to testify against Projex, but Kordell declined. Kelsi happily accepted knowing or thinking she knew that Projex was the one to have killed Malcolm. The truth was, she didn't know, and neither did her ex-boyfriend, Austin. All they knew was that someone was going to be held responsible for killing him.

"Nah. Don't get comfortable on them steps. I'ont want you near this mothafucka period," Projex told Kordell as he tried taking a seat on the stairs.

Kordell looked at him like he was crazy. "It's six in the morning. The fuck I'm supposed to go?" he questioned, holding his shoulder. His breathing was slowing down, and his head was woozy.

"I don't give a fuck where you go, but if you trying to keep yo life, I'd suggest you get from 'round here."

The cousins stared each other down for all of ten seconds before Kordell turned away and started walking. He remembered there being a gas station not too far away and hoped he could make it before passing out. Once he saw him walking down the street, Projex went back inside the house.

"You good?" Sneaks asked.

Projex simply nodded his head upward. He wasn't good and wouldn't be for a minute. Digesting that type of betrayal was going to take time. Flexing his hand that was bloody, he shook his head with disappointment. He'd sat behind bars for three years for being related to a snitch. While he could've easily told his lawyer that Chevy was the one who killed Malcolm, even in death, Projex wasn't folding on his nigga. He for sure expected his lawyer to do his job, not knowing Kelsi and Kordell had the upper hand advantage with false information.

"What time we fly out?" Bo questioned.

"Ten something. Traffic gon' be stupid, so we gon' leave here in like an hour."

"Yeah. We gotta turn the rentals in and some mo' shit," Bo added. "What we gon' do about this couch?"

Projex shrugged. "They gon' probably charge the label's account."

"They ass better not send any pictures in."

When and if they did, Projex would just have to explain to Maxwell what went down. He was a street nigga. Sometimes, blood got shed. Projex was sure he'd understand. By the time Projex showered, tossed on a new fit, and packed his bag, it was time to head to the airport. Laurent had hit his phone on their way to their gate, letting him know he was staying a few extra days. Projex would've done the same had shit not gone down like it had. He wanted to get home and handle some more unfinished business.

Projex knew returning home without Kordell was going to raise some red flags, but he didn't care. The second Kordell stepped inside the gas station fifteen minutes from the Airbnb, an ambulance had to be called. He'd passed out from losing too much blood. When he was questioned about what happened, he claimed to not remember, and that was his best bet. His days were already numbered.

Kelsi hadn't been on his mind at all over the last three years, but she wasn't exempt from getting her ass beat either. Projex couldn't wait to have his cousins pull up on her and remind her who the fuck he was. Crossing a nigga like him was like playing with fire, and he didn't care about burning anyone.

While Projex had the weight of the world on his shoulders yet again, Loriana was stuck, standing speechless with tears in her eyes. Her chest ached with a familiar feeling she hadn't felt in years. It was heartbreak. Her brain couldn't comprehend why this was happening to her yet again. Seeing the tears in her eyes confused Joi.

"Wait. Why are you about to cry?" Joi asked with pinched brows.

Loriana swallowed the ache in her throat. "H-He's your baby daddy?"

This time, Symir frowned. "Her baby daddy?"

"Yes. Why else would you be coming out of her

mama's house and taking her to her doctor's appointment?" Loriana stressed, needing answers.

Nervously, Joi chewed on the corner of her lip. This was the main reason why she hadn't told anyone who her child's father was. It'd either cause too much confusion as if she was being sneaky, or it'd make it seem like she'd known who Symir was all this time. She tried to play it off by asking Loriana if she knew him, but Joi knew she did. Not until recently, though.

"I was carrying the bassinet in for Shamari. He in the car."

Symir nodded his head to his ride, and Loriana squinted her eyes to look through the windshield. Sure enough, Shamari was sitting in the passenger seat.

"So, Shamari is your baby daddy?" Loriana asked.

Joi nodded her head yes. "Yeah."

"Are y'all lying to save face, or is he really the daddy?"

"Lo, I don't have a reason to lie to you. Joi is young as hell, baby. Come on, now. I don't even roll like that."

Symir was offended. He could see why she may have thought that considering how the scene looked, but the baby growing inside Joi belonged one hundred percent to his brother. Until this moment, he didn't even know they knew each other. Shamari and Joi had been so close lip about their relationship to everyone except themselves. Symir had just recently, maybe a week or so ago, found out that Loriana and Joi were *sisters*.

Shamari had brought it to him on some, "Yeah, bro. We dating sisters." He was really vague about it. Symir never knew Loriana to have a sister, not a blood sister anyway, so he'd forgotten to mention it to her. The hurt expression on her face when she hopped out of the car let him know that Joi hadn't mentioned Shamari either.

A sigh of relief escaped Loriana's mouth. She'd been resilient and bounced back from a lot of trauma in her life and was sure there'd be more to come, but this was one situation she was glad hadn't turned out badly. Like only Loriana could, she asked a bunch of questions.

"Well, why didn't he get out and carry it in? He's the daddy, not you."

"Lori," Joi groaned, not wanting to get all into the details right now. She had a doctor's appointment to get to.

"What? I'm just asking a question. Clearly, you've been keeping him on the hush for a reason."

"Yes, I have. I'll tell you why in the car."

"You still want me to take you?" Loriana just knew that'd she be off the hook this morning. Especially now that she had a ride. "Why isn't Shamari driving?"

"He's hurt right now," Joi huffed.

Giving her a squinted, we're gonna talk alright gaze, Loriana shook her head. "I guess, Joi. This is all too much on a Tuesday morning. Is he too hurt to get in my backseat? Hurt or not, he needs to be at the appointment with you."

"I'll go see."

Loriana watched her trudge down the steps before facing Symir. He looked extra handsome this morning. Dressed down and out of his Royal Motors attire, which was usually slacks and a button-down, he was rocking jeans, a grey tee, and some grey Air Max Plus Nikes. She could finally appreciate his appearance because before now, all she saw was red.

Stepping down the steps, Symir stood in her face and shook his head. "You always thinking the worst." Pecking her lips, Loriana closed her eyes and releasing a deep breath.

"I know. I gotta stop doing that. I never used to."

After her life got flipped upside down with the death of her mother, then the spiral of events that took place right after, Loriana had long ago stopped thinking that certain things couldn't happen to her. It was a fucked-up way of thinking, but she couldn't help it.

"You gotta trust me. You really think I would have a baby on you?" Symir asked, needing to see where her head was at.

"I mean… we aren't necessarily together. So, no. But if you did, what could I do?"

In all of his years of dating, Symir had never come across someone as complicated as Loriana. She wasn't easy to figure out, guarded in a sense. Even the tiny part of her life he was in wasn't much. She'd expressed to him her hurt behind Projex going to jail, but it wasn't something she harped on out loud. Not to him, at least. Letting another man entirely in her world wasn't happening if she could control it.

"All I'm hearing is that you don't trust me."

"I do. But life is life. I can't expect for everything to be perfect. This isn't a fairytale."

She stopped believing in those long ago. When there was no prince charming sent to kiss her lips and wake her up from the nightmare of losing her mom, she knew right then to expect the unexpected. No one was exempt, not even Symir.

"It's not, but I hear you. You want me to drive them, or you got it?"

"I'll take them, then call you when I'm done. I don't have class until later on."

Symir wrapped his arms around her for a hug. She was still tense, and that didn't sit right with him, but he knew voicing it would change nothing.

"A'ight. I'll call you when I go grab some lunch."

When they walked to her car, Symir opened her door for her. Shamari had yet to climb from the passenger seat of his brother's ride, and Loriana wondered why. When Joi climbed into Loriana's passenger seat, she let out a heavy breath.

"He's not coming?" Loriana asked.

"No. I told him he didn't have to so me and you could talk. Plus, he can hardly move."

Loriana fastened her seatbelt. "He had surgery or something?"

"No. He had a fight last night."

Her head jerked her way. "A fight?"

"Yeah. He's an underground boxer but doesn't really want it to be known."

"Y'all sure do have a lot of secrets. So, tell me this. Did you know I was dating Symir?"

"Not at first, no. Me and Shamari really just got into a relationship, honestly."

"And you're pregnant already?"

Joi rolled her eyes. "Are we judging? I mean, let

me know if I can talk to you like my sister, or are you going to scold me?"

"You know you can. I just hate that you left me in the dark on this."

"I could say the same thing. You never told me about Symir. Is it because of my brother?"

Loriana sucked her teeth. "Hell, no. Projex has nothing to do with nothing."

Joi smirked. "Yeah, okay. Well, he was the reason I didn't tell you about Shamari. I kept mentioning you as my sis and finally showed him a picture of you. That's when he told me you were his brother's girlfriend."

"I'm not his girlfriend."

"And I'm not pregnant."

It was Loriana's turn to roll her eyes.

"Whatever. I'm not."

"Mhm. But anyway, I knew things wouldn't blow over so well with me being in a relationship and having a baby by Shamari, knowing Projex doesn't like his brother. Not just that, but you're dating the guy. It's messy, and I know how Shamari is when it comes to me."

Loriana smirked. "How is he?"

"Protective as ever. I used to think Projex was bad; Shamari is ten times worse."

Joi shook her head with a smile on her face. She wasn't complaining, but she knew when it came to her and now their child, Shamari would definitely fight Projex if it came down to it. Not because he wanted to, but because he knew it'd be some drama when it was revealed whose brother he was. He didn't give a fuck, though, and Joi knew that. She didn't need them on that.

"And how long have y'all been in a relationship?" Loriana questioned as she pulled into the lot of the doctor's office in Lee's Summit.

"Six months," she mumbled lowly.

"Damn. Y'all wasted no time, huh?"

"Shut up. It wasn't my fault."

Loriana glanced at her. "So, it was his?"

"No. I'm just saying. It's neither of our fault. My baby isn't a mistake."

"Of course not. I'm just saying neither of you tried to prevent you from getting pregnant either. No pull-out method or nothing?"

Joi smiled bashfully. "Um, obviously not."

Loriana chuckled and unlocked the doors. "Right. That's very much clear. Whew, girl. I feel like you just aged me. Now, all you have to do is explain all of this to your mama and brother."

Joi's lip poked out. "I know. My mama won't be

as bad, but I'm going to try to keep this from Projex for as long as possible."

"Why? Because of me and Symir? Don't do that."

"You really don't understand how much he loves you, do you?"

Loriana's heart fluttered in her chest. She did know. Well, she used to. That night he came to visit had fucked everything up. *She* had fucked everything up. Loriana would've been lucky if she'd even get a text from Projex now.

"I do."

"You can't if you think me telling him the guy who stole his real first love is also the uncle to his niece or nephew. That's not going to blow over with ease. If anyone knows how he is, it's you. Well, I thought you knew."

I thought I did too, she thought as they stepped inside the building. It'd been three years and some change since they were really acquainted. Time didn't change all people, and she saw that firsthand when he came to see her. Projex's temper was still short, patience for bullshit thinner, and heart still big. The only thing those three years did to him took time away. It also matured him, but he was still the same ol' Projex.

Nobody, not even his sister, was going to play in

his face. Especially with a nigga and his brother, who Projex thought he didn't have to worry about. Loriana understood where she was coming from now and had to agree. Maybe telling Projex wasn't such a good idea. Not this soon.

Chapter Two

Though she wasn't far along, only three months, Joi hated the way clothes fit her now. This was the fourth outfit she'd tried on, and at this point, it was just going to have to do. She'd always had a flat stomach and hadn't yet hit that grown woman weight she'd heard about. The weight she did see herself gain was all from the baby, and it showed. Dressed in a floral print mini dress with ruffles, her slight pudge made it seem like she'd overeaten. Rubbing her hand across her belly, Joi smiled.

"You're definitely not a food baby."

At nineteen, being pregnant was the last thing Joi thought she'd be. All about her education, she'd been focused on nothing but college and pushing herself to not slack off. Having graduated high school with half a semester's worth of college credits, Joi had nothing but extra time on her hands. Time to get well acquainted with Shamari and get knocked up.

They'd only been dating for six months, but they'd known each other since the end of January. It was almost the middle of September now, and Joi couldn't believe how fast their lives had changed in eight months. She didn't regret meeting him, but she did feel a way about who he was related to.

No questions asked Joi's loyalty would forever be with Projex. But Shamari was her child's father. She never wanted to feel like she had to choose between the two but knew it wouldn't be long before it came down to that.

Slipping on a pair of sandals and grabbing her purse, Joi headed out of her room. Shamari was on his way to take her out to eat, and she let him know that today would be the perfect day to finally meet her mama. Not use to having a boyfriend, Joi was trying to hold out on this greeting for as long as possible. Things were good between them, but she knew all good things didn't last long. Joi had witnessed it from a front seat view between Projex and Loriana. Having Shamari meet her family was big in her eyes. She didn't play when it came to her mama or brother.

A deep frown settled in the middle of her forehead

as she reached the living room. Joseline was arguing with someone on the phone, and Joi knew it was serious because she was speaking in Spanish. When she went back to speaking in English, Joi figured out who she was talking to. She could understand her in both languages, but Joseline's sister, Gina, only spoke English.

"Don't go speaking to me in Spanish! You know he was wrong for leaving him out there by himself," Gina fussed.

"Kordell is grown, Gina! You need to pop that titty of yours out of his mouth and let him be a man. If Projex left him out there, you and I both know it was probably a damn good reason why. Don't call me trying to check shit behind him. They are grown men."

"And that's my nephew, so I'ma call if I feel like he was in the wrong. Kordell was shot and everything, and you're acting like it's no big deal."

Joseline rolled her eyes. "I never said it wasn't. You just called me trying to jump down my throat like I know what's going on. I'm in the same boat as you. Maybe you should be asking Kordell who shot him."

"I did, and he's not saying anything!"

Gina's hollering was about to get her hung up on. Projex hadn't said a peep to his mama about what went down in Atlanta and didn't plan to until the timing was right. It'd only been a few days since he'd gotten back home, and he'd been on the go since. Revealing that type of information, especially about a family member, was up in the air for now. Projex was still contemplating on getting his cousin knocked off but was undecided. Their family would for sure be broken up and in disarray, if he'd gone with his first mind back in Atlanta. If he suddenly came up missing, all fingers would've been pointed at Projex, thanks to Kordell working with the cops.

"Well, I don't know what to tell you. I'm sure whatever it is, they squashed now, so relax. I'm already stressed out about your niece," Joseline said, eyeing her daughter.

Joi pressed her lips tightly together and thought, *now how I get in this?* Whenever her name came up in something that had nothing to do with her, she always thought of the Nene Leaks meme. Here she was minding her business, ready to eat, and her mama was blaming her for stress. Joi was sure she did play some part in it, but this wasn't about her right now.

"What I do?" Joi asked.

"She still hasn't told you who her baby daddy is?" Gina asked.

Joseline tooted her lips out. "Nope. I'm supposed to be meeting him today, so we'll see."

Joi grumbled under her breath while walking into the kitchen for a bottle of water. It was normal for her mama and aunt to sit up and talk on the phone, but she wasn't trying to hear them discuss her. Especially not when she'd decided to introduce Shamari today of all days. If her mama kept on, she was going to cancel her plans altogether.

Just as she was placing the cap back on her bottle, her phone rang. Nervous jitters swarmed her body as she dug inside her purse to retrieve it. Shamari had that effect on her. A simple phone call, text, or comment from him alone made her heart race. Her hormones were already out of order, and he contributed to their scatteredness.

"H-Hey," Joi answered, trying to sound unbothered.

"You nervous, bae? Your voice shaking."

When he chuckled, Joi did the same. Immediately, he calmed her.

"It's that obvious?"

"Yeah. Ain't shit to be worried about, though. We gon' get this out the way, and then I'ma feed you and my son."

Joi smirked. "You want a boy so bad."

"I want whatever God blesses us with, but I been praying for a boy."

Joi wasn't exactly sure what loving a boy entailed, but she was sure she loved Shamari. Not just because they were sharing a child, or because he was Joi's first real boyfriend, but because he was a believer and much more. It warmed her heart to know he had a relationship with the Man above.

"I know you have. Are you outside?" she questioned, going to open the front door.

"Yep. Pulling up now."

When she opened the front door, he was pulling into the driveway. With a clear view of her pushing the screen door open, Shamari frowned.

"Where yo' clothes at?" he questioned, peeping the short ass dress she was wearing.

All he saw were thighs and long legs that had him shaking his head. Joi looked down at her dress.

"What you mean? They're right here."

"A'ight, man. Here I come."

Joi told him okay and hung up. She saw nothing wrong with her dress but realized it was slightly windy outside. Figuring the only time she'd be outside wouldn't be for long, Joi didn't plan on changing. She had tons of cute outfits she was trying to wear before she couldn't fit them.

Inside his matte grey Dodge Durango, Shamari grabbed the white gift bag from the passenger seat and hopped out. Joi took him in. Each time she was in his presence, she became enthralled by him. Colossal compared to Joi's five-foot-eight frame, Shamari stood at six-foot-three. Pure muscles lie underneath a coat of the smoothest chocolate skin. His locs were neatly twisted in two-strand twists that hung down his back.

Shamari never had to try hard. He was fine effortlessly and that's what Joi admired most. He wasn't flashy though he had money. A gold watch adorned his wrist while a gold chain lined his neck. Simply dressed in jeans, a Vert Abrae white tee, and some Prada PRAX 01 tennis shoes, Joi smiled as he climbed the steps.

"You must be happy to see me," Shamari smirked, seeing her grin.

"Duh. I'm always happy to see you."

He licked his lips, appreciative of his view. Though Joi was slim, she had large breasts, sharp hips, and thick thighs. Genetically, she was shaped just like Joseline was at her age, and the definition of what slim-thick really meant. Her hair was combed out of her fresh doobie wrap, draping just past her shoulders with a part in the middle.

To the naked eye, Joi was innocent. Her baby face and doe-shaped eyes could get her anything she wanted. With Shamari, it did. He knew for a fact she wasn't innocent, though. He spoiled her without thought. As he got caught up in staring into her light brown eyes, imagining what their child would look like, Joi broke his concentration.

"Is the gift for me?"

Shamari bent down some to hug around her waist and plant a kiss on her cheek. Automatically, his hand went to the swelling of her stomach. Whether it looked like she was carrying a child or not, Shamari always acknowledged them both. His cologne made her eyes flutter and nipples tingle. When he stood up, he tugged gently on the hem of her dress.

"Nah. This for your mama. You can get yours later on."

When he smirked, she just knew he meant some dick. Lately, she'd been a horny mess and blamed it on the baby. Shamari was her second sexual partner, and at this rate, Joi was perfectly okay with him being her last.

"Get ya' mind out the gutter and let me in."

Joi smirked as he held the screen door open for her to walk through. Looking up from her phone, Joseline waited to see what type of young man her daughter had fallen for. Of course, they had talked about boys before, who she liked, and the birds and the bees. This was new, though. Joi had never brought a boy home to meet her mother. The reason why he was here made Joseline want to shed tears, but she held her composure.

Well, okay then. I know that's right, daughter, she thought as Joi and Shamari entered the living room. Taking in his appearance, Joseline appreciated how put together he looked on the outside. Handsome or not, Joseline needed to see what his intentions and plans were for her child and grandbaby. Whether he and Joi stayed together or not, he would always be their child's father.

An easy grin fell on Shamari's face as Joseline eyed him. Joi was literally her younger self and looked just like her. Nervously, Joi rubbed her clammy right palm along her dress. Before Joi could introduce him, Shamari did the honors.

"How you doing? I'm Shamari." Sticking his hand out, Joseline shook his while looking him in the eyes.

"Nice to meet you, Shamari. I'm Joseline. How old are you, baby?"

Joi groaned, "Ma."

"Don't *Ma* me. I'm just trying to get to know my grandchild's daddy."

She knew rolling her eyes would've gotten her knocked upside her head, so Joi just sighed. Shamari didn't mind the questions at all. It came with the territory. He already planned to be *that* daddy if his baby girl—if they had a girl—came home with a nigga. There'd for sure be some interrogating.

Shamari smirked. "It's cool. I'm twenty-two. I brought you a little something, too. Hope you don't mind."

Joseline glanced down at the gift bag in his hand, then back up at him. "I sure don't. What you trying to do, make amends since you got my baby pregnant?"

Shamari wanted to tell her he wasn't apologizing for knocking her up. He'd never regret that.

"No," he answered with a chuckle. "Joi told me your birthday is next week, so I copped you something."

Joseline smirked. Shamari was real smooth. The thing was, the way he spoiled Joi, he didn't mind spending some bread on her mama either. Joi had been nervous for weeks about this moment, and he wanted to ease some of the anxiety she had.

"It is. Thank you. So, tell me about yourself,

Shamari. You ready to be an active father in this baby's life? Do you have a job?"

The way her mama was rambling off questions, Joi decided to sit down. She should've known just bringing Shamari in to say hi wasn't going to fly.

"Yes, I have a job. I'm not gon' say I'm one hundred percent ready cause it's still early, but I'm gon' be in my child's life. No questions asked."

Joseline's facial expression didn't change, but Joi's did. She smiled, having heard him reassure her about his presence in her life even before she'd taken a pregnancy test. It wasn't that Joseline didn't believe him. She just hoped he could keep his word.

"Do you have your own place or live with your parents?" Joseline questioned.

Joi's eyes quickly cut to her mama. "Ma," she stressed.

"My own place. My mom passed some years back, and my dad lives in Miami."

"Sorry to hear about your mom. I didn't mean to be so intrusive," Joseline apologized.

"It's a'ight. My God mom knows about the baby and is excited. Y'all will have to meet one day."

Joseline gave him a soft smile at that. "Sure. Joi has a huge family, so it's best that we all get acquainted. You know it takes a village to raise a baby, right?"

"I do. Joi is in good hands. Especially with me and mine."

"I'm not too much worried about everyone else. As long as she's in good hands with you, then we won't have any issues." Joseline's brow raised, letting him know off bat that she didn't play any games.

Shamari chuckled. "Nah. No issues. You look like you don't play."

"I do not," Joseline sassed as her phone rang. "Especially about my kids. It was nice meeting you, though, Shamari. It's clear my daughter likes you, so I'm looking forward to getting to know you."

"Same. You ready to go eat?" he asked Joi, who rushed to her feet.

"Yes. I'm too hungry."

Joseline laughed. "You act like I don't feed you. Don't do that."

"You do feed me, and I'm sooo appreciative," Joi said, leaning over to kiss her mama on the cheek. "But I'm still hungry."

"I understand. Y'all have fun and be safe."

"We will," Joi told her as they headed toward the door.

Getting her emotions in check, Joseline followed

behind them. Seeing her youngest all grown up and starting a family was too much. Though she had hopes of Joi finishing her college career out before a baby came into the equation, Joseline had to remind herself that this wasn't her life. Yes, she was the parent, but Joi was an adult.

"That's a nice truck," Joseline complimented as they walked down the steps.

"Thank you," Shamari replied.

At the truck, he opened the passenger door for Joi before hopping in the driver's seat. Joi exhaled the minute they stepped out of the house. Getting her mama out the way was one thing. Shamari still had to meet her daddy and Projex. Just as they turned out of the subdivision, Projex pulled up a few minutes later. It was perfect timing, considering the mood Projex was in.

"What's wrong with you?" Joseline questioned as soon as he walked through the door.

The scowl on his face and entire demeanor screamed irritated.

"Yo' baby daddy."

"Who?" Joseline scoffed with a chuckle. "Stop playing with me."

"I'm for real. You know I ain't heard from that man in years, even before I went to prison, and he just called asking for some money. Nigga, what money? I'm broke like he was all my life."

Joseline wanted to check him about his language but let it slide. Projex hardly ever talked about Bryan, and she didn't urge him to. Since a youngin', Projex had made the decision to not depend on his father for anything. Even when he did look forward to something simple as a happy birthday and present, Bryan never came through. Projex had been over it but was pissed off and in disbelief that he had the audacity to ask for some money.

"How'd he get your new number?"

"Prolly my grandma. She wants us to have a relationship so bad like it'll change something."

Joseline sighed. She loved Juanita, but long ago had told her that there was no use in trying to convince her son to change for Projex. He was who he was.

"I'm not saying talking to him will or not, but that's up to you."

"I already made up my mind. You had a dude up in here?" Projex asked, smelling the pungent stench of Shamari's cologne.

Joseline chuckled. "Boy, I'm grown. If I did? You ain't my man."

"A'ight, Mama."

"Oh, get out them feelings. Don't be all fussy with me 'cause your daddy done pissed you off."

Projcx walked in the kitchen to see if she'd cooked. Seeing nothing on the stove or in the fridge, he grabbed a bag of chips out of the pantry and a Martinelli's apple juice. It was Friday, and Joseline only cooked on this day if it were a special occasion. It wasn't, so she wasn't touching a pot or pan. When Projex walked back into the living room, Joseline contemplated on asking him about what had gone down between him and Kordell. She knew if she didn't, Gina would more than likely be calling him.

"I talked to your Aunt Gina earlier," is how she started the conversation. "What's going on with you and Kordell?"

Projex's nostrils flared, and jaw tensed. His day had been shitty since it started. After reaching out to his lawyer and requesting to see the statements his cousin had signed, Projex was eager to pull up on him, air his spot out, and say fuck the family. Seeing Kordell's signature on them papers hurt his soul. For the love of that green paper, his nigga stabbed him in the back. Projex would've preferred he did it when he was facing him. That way, he could've seen it coming.

"Did you know he was the reason I went to prison?"

Joseline scooted to the end of the couch and grilled him. "What? He was snitching on you?"

Projex's nodded his head yes. "Yeah. Seen it with my own eyes, and he told me."

"Oh, hell no."

Joseline hopped up from the couch, forcing Projex to grab her hand. "Ma, hold up. Where you going?"

"To Gina's. She was hollering at me about why you left him and some mo' shit, and he was around here snitching. Your own blood!"

Disgusted that Kordell would do such a thing, Joseline cursed him out in her native tongue while Projex just shook his head. This is why he didn't want to tell her. The way Gina was carrying on, Joseline thought she was exaggerating.

"You should've done more than leave his ass stranded. So, the entire case was a lie? You did three years plus because your cousin snitched?"

Joseline couldn't wrap her mind around it as angry tears clouded her vision. She wanted to whoop Gina's ass for raising a fuckboy. The sisters had the same African American mother but different fathers, and Joseline was sure that snitch gene had to run on Gina's daddy side. Their mother didn't play that bullshit. Before anyone and anything, you were loyal to your family.

Projex would never utter what he told Kordell in Atlanta. Technically, he did three years for not snitching either. Telling her that Chevy was actually the one who killed Malcolm would've just been more shit he didn't feel like talking about or explaining. Instead, he nodded his head. He didn't even want to speak on it anymore. The last thing he wanted to do was let his emotions place him back in jail.

"You know what?" Joseline asked, stopping her pace. "Karma gon' get him, watch. You just wait and see. I don't need you getting into any more trouble. You have way too many good things happening in your life right now. You stay focused, you hear me?"

"Yes."

"You better have whooped his ass," she said, making him chuckle.

"I wanted to body that nigga, Ma."

When his voice cracked, Joseline rushed to hug him. The anger in his eyes let her know that if he could've and gotten off, he would've without no remorse. Joseline couldn't help but wonder if Gina knew. All this time, Kordell had been coming by the house, checking in on her and Joi when Projex was locked up, smiling and shit like he wasn't the reason her son was behind bars. Joseline wanted to fight him herself. That type of disloyalty deserved more than an ass-whooping.

As she held her son, her first baby, Joseline wished she could take the pain away. Projex's entire being was tense. His dreams since that early morning revelation had been one of him murdering his cousin. Each one was a different scenario, but in the end, Projex was the one pulling the trigger while staring him in the eyes. The same eyes that stared back at him during those visitations, telling him everything was all good. Kordell was hoping Projex never came home.

Unlucky for him, Projex was a free man, and Kordell would forever have a target on his back—his head rather. Projex wanted to blow his mothafuckin' brains out for his disloyalty. He wanted to do that nigga so dirty, he was unrecognizable. A closed casket, his Aunt Gina wailing at the top of her lungs, have to identify him by his teeth—unrecognizable. Not even the detest he had for his opps was stronger than the one for his blood. That was saying a lot because he'd been locked up for three years, gained some enemies while on the inside, and that still didn't amount to Kordell's treachery.

"Don't do nothing to land you back in jail, okay?"

Joseline said more than asked this time. She knew her son. He would forever get his lick back.

"I won't."

He wasn't lying, but it didn't mean someone else couldn't handle Kordell. And just like that, Projex was plotting again.

Chapter Three

"Oh, my gosh. I'm so tired." Loriana yawned while coming to a red light.

Nyree smacked her lips. "I told you to go home and take a nap. You always thinking you Super Woman."

"I am."

"Yeah, okay. When your ass gets sick because you don't listen to your body, don't be whining to me."

Being a college student with a part-time job, Nyree knew firsthand how it felt to have your body shut down on you. Many sleepless nights had gotten her through the semesters, but not in a healthy way. She'd binge on Starbucks, Red Bull, and snacks which quickly made her gain those freshmen fifteen pounds.

"Whatever. I had to come get my hair done. My head has been looking crazy for dang near two weeks."

"I hope you get them eyebrows tamed too," Nyree joked, making them laugh.

"I did that yesterday, thank you. While you talking shit. I'm pulling up to Moo's now, so I'll text you."

"Wait. Have you talked to Projex?" Nyree wanted to know.

"Girl, no. I texted him, and his ass asked what's up with a question mark like I was bothering him."

Nyree laughed on the other end. Loriana didn't see a damn thing funny.

"So, that's funny?" she asked.

"Girl, yes. That nigga said you ain't about to play with him."

"I'm not, though."

"Did you at least say you were sorry?"

Loriana's head drew back some. "Sorry? What am I sorry for?"

"Well, not say sorry, but I guess let him know you were in the wrong. That nigga, Juice, would've knocked my head between the washer and dryer had I did what you did."

"He be hitting you?" Loriana asked, not liking the way Nyree was talking.

"Girl, hell no. It's a figure of speech. But for real, Projex should've. You a bold bitch."

Nyree was laughing and shaking her head. In her eyes, it was mad disrespectful to tell Symir she loved him in Projex's face. Would Nyree have done the same thing? Most definitely not because, for one, she didn't love these niggas at all. So, those words would have never been spoken from her lips. For two, that fresh out of jail dick would've had her so delirious, she wouldn't have been able to form a sentence.

"What was I supposed to say?"

"You should've never called his ass to begin with, but lesson learned, friend. Now, you been pouting since yo' nigga came home when you could've been getting superb dick, knocked up, and a ring placed on your finger."

"Shut up. You really get on my damn nerves. That dick was out of this world, though. Damn."

Just thinking about it had Loriana shivering. Her entire body trembled as a flashback flooded her mind of Projex eating her out and long stroking her. Whoever he was fucking was lucky because baby, Loriana couldn't stop thinking about the way he made love to her body.

"I bet. But gon' head and get your hair done. I'll text you when I wake up from my nap."

"Okay. I love you."

"I love you, too."

Walking inside the salon with her purse tossed over her shoulder, Loriana stifled another yawn as she removed her shades. Her days were literally running together, and she should've taken Nyree's advice on getting some sleep. Not just sleep but resting her body. The extra credit hours she'd been piling on since she started college was only getting more intense as she ventured into her respective field. Loriana literally lived a no-days-off life. She was either in class, studying, or at work. There was no time to kick it if she planned to graduate by next spring.

"Hey, boo," Moo greeted as she and Loriana hugged.

"Hey. You look cute."

Moo was dressed casually in a nude biker shorts and tank set from *Mag Co.* with some Yeezy's on her feet. The six stitch braids in her head were neat as hell, and her lash extensions made her eyes pop.

"Thank you. You look tired. You were up late again last night, huh?"

Moo already knew Loriana's work ethic. It was

just as strong as her own. She was a faithful client of hers, and there'd been plenty of times where Loriana had to reschedule because she was too tired to get out of bed for her appointment. Moo didn't mind because it was her, but for anyone else canceling the day of without an emergency, they would've been charged. That was the perks of having been in a relationship with Projex. Plus, Moo had built a friendship with her.

"Yes. I'm almost done. These bags under my eyes are so ugly," Loriana griped as Moo began to detangle her hair.

"Your eyebrows are snatched. You can hardly tell you have bags, and when I get this head of yours together, you'll be just fine."

"You're right. I don't know what I want to get today, but I'll think about it while we shampoo my hair."

Moo told her okay, and they walked back to the wash station. Once she shampooed her hair, Moo put some deep conditioner in it before placing a plastic cap over her head and tucking her under the dryer. With her ginger-colored hair, it was imperative that Moo treated it with care each visit. Thankfully, Loriana hadn't gotten lazy with it and let the color damage her hair.

While under the dryer, Symir texted Loriana asking her where she was at so he could drop off her iPad. She'd left it over his house a few nights ago, and he was about to go out of town.

Lo: Getting my hair done. You can drop it off here if you have time.

Symir*: A'ight. I'll be there in like twenty minutes.*

B ack in Moo's chair, she rubbed some heat protectant through her stands and blow-dried Loriana's hair. Like always, Loriana didn't want anything fancy. Just her some luscious curls that she could wrap up at night and quickly comb down in the morning.

"Your hair gets thicker every time I see you," Moo told her.

"I know. It's that oil you gave me. You should definitely start selling it."

"That's the plan. Just waiting to finalize a few things, and it's a go."

Being a go-getter, Moo had her hand in more than one avenue. Still connected to her love for hair, she planned to offer a hair growth oil that clearly worked. One of her clients had done a big chop to her ears six months ago, and her hair was already back at her shoulder blades. Moo was just waiting for the business side of things to fall through, and it was up.

"Yes. That's what I love to hear. I know it'll sell out for sure."

"I hope so."

When Symir stepped inside the salon, Loriana's back was facing the door. All eyes ventured to the fine, chocolate as hell man whose cologne damn near overpowered the place. Finally, looking through the mirror, Loriana saw him walking up and smiled. He handed her the iPad, spoke to Moo, and checked Loriana's new hairdo out.

"Hey," she greeted. "Thank you."

"What's up. You're welcome. I'm headed out of town for the weekend, so I ain't want you to not have it."

"Where you going again?"

Symir had told her, but Loriana had honestly forgotten. These days, if it weren't super important information, she retained it, but not for long.

"Miami. I'll be back on Monday if things go as planned."

"Okay. Well, be safe. Tell your dad I said hi, too."

"I will."

When he leaned over to kiss her cheek, Moo's eyes widened. Not because of the kiss, but because her cousin was walking down the steps from the nail salon upstairs. Discreetly, Moo tried getting Loriana's attention, but it was of no use. Projex was already making his way over to her station.

Loriana's eyes damn near budged out of her sockets when she saw him. *Oh, shit,* she thought, seeing the sexy mug on Projex's face as he glanced Symir's way. He looked so good, Loriana didn't even hear Symir talking to her. The crisp cut, thick waves, and outfit were just subtle things that had her pussy pulsating. Prison had Projex's muscles on swole, but not in a manner that was unflattering. Everything about him had grown, including his cockiness.

"I know you ain't gon' walk by me without speaking."

Looking over his shoulder, Projex smirked at the little freak who was getting her hair braided. While he was locked up, she'd been one of many of the women who hit him up, wanting to keep him company. On them prison calls, Projex was selling a dream. His game had always been A1, so it was nothing to mack a bitch down without seeing them. In Danielle's case, she'd known him before he went in and was trying to know him—his dick rather—on a personal level now that he was out. She knew how the game went with a nigga on lockdown.

"I ain't even see you sitting here. What's good with you," he spoke smoothly, giving her a hug.

Danielle rubbed all over his muscles and smirked. "Mhm. I'm just getting this head of mine done. I see you got them hands done."

"Always. Gotta keep my shit clean. Never know when you might come across a dirty broad. Gotta decipher between the two."

Moo's station was close enough for Loriana to hear their conversation, and she frowned hard at his choice of words. Moo snickered, knowing he was throwing shots her way.

"Now, I know you don't be messing with no dirty hoes. That ain't you."

"It ain't, but you know how hoes be."

When he said that, he looked in Loriana's direction. Symir was talking, asking her how much longer she would be. His flight had gotten pushed back, and he wanted to grab a bite to eat with her before he headed out.

"Oh, um. That's okay. It'll be a minute. I have to stop by my aunt's when I leave here and the office. We can do something when you get back."

Symir didn't believe her, but he was going to let her make it. "A'ight. I'll hit you when we're about to take off and when I land."

"Okay. See you later."

When he walked by Projex, Symir gave him a head nod and said, what's up. Loriana held her breath. *Why did he do that?*

"Nigga, don't fix yo' mouth to speak to me," Projex said evenly.

The entire shop got quiet. Symir drew his head back.

"We know each other?" Symir questioned.

"Nah. So, ain't no need to speak to me, bruh. Keep yo' ass moving trying to be funny."

As a man, Symir thought it was customary to speak to another man when they were the only ones in a woman's setting. Clearly, he was wrong and didn't recognize who Projex was. Shamari had told his brother who Joi was related to, but with Projex being locked up, it hadn't clicked. Symir honestly didn't care enough to do any digging to figure out who he was. It didn't help that Projex's hair was now cut, either.

Symir chuckled. "A'ight, bruh." *Nigga must be having a bad day,* Symir thought as he walked out of the salon.

You could literally feel the atmosphere in the room shift once he was no longer present. Loriana exhaled, and Moo placed a hand over her thudding heart. She just knew she was going to have to repair her shop if they got to fighting.

"Girl," Moo laughed nervously, "you got these niggas tripping."

"That's your cousin," Loriana whispered.

Danielle poked her lips out and shook her head. "He was just speaking with your mean ass."

"You should've spoken to that nigga, then. The fuck he wanna talk to me for?"

"Projex, chill out." Moo laughed. "And get out that girl's face."

"Nah. He can stay right here. Ain't that right?"

Friskily, Danielle caressed his abs. Loriana was sure he'd slap her hand away, but he didn't. Her nostrils flared, and her eyes turned to slits.

Chuckling, Projex bent down to whisper in her ear. Loriana had no idea what he was saying to her, but it didn't matter. The act alone was pissing her off. When Danielle smiled widely, Loriana's teeth clenched simultaneously with her fist.

"Okay. I'ma hold you to that too," Danielle called after him as he walked over to Moo's station.

"Don't be coming in here trying to toss that weak ass game," Moo joked.

"We family. You already know ain't shit about me weak."

"Mhm. What you about to do?"

"I'd tell you, but mothafuckas ear hustling."

Loriana rolled her eyes and finally said something. "You're literally standing right in my ear, talking. Move."

Projex gripped her hair that wasn't flat ironed. "I should really fuck you up. On my mama."

Loriana's eyes widened. Not because she was in pain, but because she knew he was serious. "What you mad for?"

"Don't have that pussy ass nigga meet you anywhere I be at. Especially here. You ain't gone be satisfied until I body his ass and have you crying at his funeral."

"Knowing you, you'd probably make it to where I couldn't attend."

Projex smirked and let her hair go, then mushed her head playfully. "I'm glad you know. Moo, I'm finna shake, but I'll see you on Sunday."

"Wait. What's Sunday?" Moo asked, parting another section of Loriana's hair to flat iron.

"Granny's house. She having dinner for everybody. You ain't see it in the group message?"

"Ugh, no. I be so sick of them in there talking all day. Half of them got androids, and messages come in all out of order. I told your auntie to remove me, but she won't."

Laughing, Projex retrieved his phone just as a text from their family group chat came through.

"Here they go right now, asking what everybody doing this weekend."

Moo loved her family, but that was one thing she couldn't stand to be a part of. Projex's dad, Bryan, and Moo's mama, Tyra, were siblings. They had a host of other aunts, uncles, and cousins that consistently texted the group. Moo would respond to Projex in their own messages but not to the main one. She loved the family dynamic and all, but no.

"You know she ain't doing that. You better be there, too."

"I will. Call me when you own your way there, so I can meet you."

Projex told her alright and then stared at Loriana through the mirror. This was his first time seeing her since that night at her place. He didn't know if he wanted to snatch her ass up out of that seat or show her some love. He was at war with himself while battling his feelings for her, but it was clear that she still had him fucked-up.

Loriana was expecting for him to give into her easily, but she'd be better of wishing on a star. Projex was stubborn. The trait was literally embedded into his DNA. Once he felt disrespected, all bets were off. Whatever he said or how he made you feel didn't matter. With no words spoken, he shook his head at her before heading toward the door.

"You leaving already? I thought you were paying for my hair?" Danielle asked, bluffing.

Projex smirked. He wasn't a trick by any means, but Danielle had looked out for him while in prison. For that alone, he'd toss her some dick. He wasn't paying for shit.

"Long as you let me fuck it up."

The ladies in the shop smirked and laughed at his mannish reply. Even Danielle had to chuckle because how much damage could you do to some box braids? When he did end up walking out of the shop, Loriana sat still for all of two seconds once he was out the door before she hopped up and told Moo she'd be right back. Soon as he hit the unlock button to his whip, Loriana called after him.

"Projex, wait!"

He wasn't expecting her to chase him, but he wasn't going to show the shock on his face. With the black salon cap blowing in the window in the same manner as her hair, Loriana moved swiftly in his direction.

"The fuck you want?" Projex grumbled.

Loriana frowned. "Seriously? That's how you gon' talk to me?"

"Aye," he chuckled, "I could really dog you out for that shit you pulled the last time I saw you, but I'm tryin' to check my emotions and shit. So, yeah. This exactly how I'm handling you until I feel like I don't need to. Now, what you want?"

Loriana stared at him for a brief second before she turned sharply and walked away. Tears stung her eyes as she could literally feel her heart chipping away. Grabbing her arm, Projex stopped her, making her turn and face him.

"Man, I know you ain't 'bout to cry. Your cycle on its way?"

How he knew that and didn't care about asking was on the list of reasons why she still loved him. She brushed away the stubborn warm tear that slid down her cheek. "Yeah, but whatever. I'm just in my feelings, I guess."

"Ain't no need to be. You did this to us."

"And I'm sorry." She exhaled heavily. "I came out here to tell you that I was wrong for that night. I should've never even picked up my phone to call him."

"Nah. Say that nigga name. Ain't he the same

mothafucka who dropped you off that night after the pool party?"

Loriana nodded, and he licked his lips with a curt head nod. Projex didn't forget shit, especially a nigga's face. He had all the time while in prison to think about who Loriana was fooling around with. He knew it'd happen, just not with someone she told him she didn't even know.

"Yes, that's him, but I swear we didn't start talking until after you were locked up."

"And that's supposed to lessen the blow?"

He wanted an answer. It didn't matter that she was talking to him. It messed Projex up that she did it after telling him she didn't know him and after she'd broken his heart in his face. He could handle a lot of things but being disloyal wasn't one of them.

"No. I guess not, but I wanted you to know that I wasn't cheating on you."

"You broke up with a nigga anyway, so shit. It is what it is. If that's yo' nigga, I ain't gon' respect it, but do yo' thing."

She rolled her eyes. "He's not my boyfriend."

"Coulda' fooled me."

"Is that girl in there your girlfriend?" she asked, rolling her neck.

Projex grinned. "Nah. Just somebody who kept

me company while I was locked up. You know, nothing too serious."

"Mm. Coulda' fooled me. You offering to pay for bitches' hair."

He laughed at that. "Don't be salty yo' nigga didn't pay for yours."

Symir wasn't her man, but Loriana did feel a way about him not offering to pay for her hair. It wasn't like she expected him to, but the gesture would've been nice. Having been spoiled by someone of Projex's caliber, anything less was a slap in the face. Loriana missed his presence while he was away, but she felt it clear as day now.

"I don't know how many times I have to tell you, he's not my man. We're just friends."

"The same shit you wanted us to be but didn't even write me back."

"I did too! So, don't sit here and tell this lie."

"Man, you wrote me what twice? How many times I called your phone and you ain't answer?"

The guilt immediately settled in the pit of her stomach. When she didn't answer, Projex pulled his door open.

"Exactly, ma. It's good, though. I don't hold grudges. I just cut a mothafucka off. You did what you had to do for yo' mental or whatever, so I respect it. Just don't expect to be treated like you held shit down for me when that wasn't the case. Not mentally anyway. That's where I needed you most. You came through on the music tip, and I'll forever appreciate you for that. Thank you if I haven't told you already."

Regardless of their personal issues, Loriana made sure he was financially straight when he touched down. That was solid as fuck in Projex's eyes, but on God, he would've appreciated her more had she rocked with him mentally. Laurent was going to look out on the music tip for sure, so he needed his girl to keep his mind right. Everything else didn't matter.

"You're welcome. I didn't do that for recognition or anything. I did it out of love. Because I love you and want to see you make it."

"I know. And I appreciate you."

"So, do you still love me? It doesn't sound like it."

She stared him in the eyes, afraid of what his answer would be. Just as quickly as she switched up on him, Projex could've done the same with her. It didn't matter that he'd professed his love to her while digging her guts out weeks prior. This was a new day. Feelings could change at a drop of a dime and not have to be explained why.

"Is the sky blue?" he asked, and she goofily looked up, making him smirk.

"It is today."

"And even when it's not, I'ma always love you. I just hate the shit loving you makes me do. You see how I sound right now? Goofy as fuck," he said, shaking his head.

Loriana blushed. "No. You sound like you needed to get that off your chest. I'm not judging you. You know me."

"I know the old you. This new you got to reintroduce herself. I gotta see if she 'bout something before I be on some sucka shit again."

"So, that means we're good?" Loriana asked hopefully but should've known better.

"I ain't say all that."

Loriana huffed. "So stubborn, my goodness. I thought we were moving past this?"

"I never said that shit. I'm just letting you know where we stand. I love you, but I don't trust you all the way. Too much sneaky shit done went down, and until I'm ready to hear it all, we good where we're at."

"And where is that?"

"Friends. Ain't that what you wanted?"

Loriana opened her mouth to reply, but no words

came out. He'd called her out, and there was nothing she could do or say. Asking to be friends was comical; a joke Projex sat in his cell and played on loop in his head. He wasn't trying to be on no childish shit and use her words against her. Jumping back headfirst into something serious with Loriana after she'd bruised his ego would take a minute. Projex was being honest with himself, and he knew if they took it there now, he'd damage her and really break her heart how she did him.

"I mean, yeah. I guess we can be friends. Do friends pay for other friends' hair?" Loriana asked with a smirk.

"Nah. Not this one. Better call Nyree or somebody." Projex laughed and climbed in his ride. "Y'all still friends, right?"

"Yes, and that's so wrong."

"It's only wrong 'cause you used to me doing whatever for you. These big boy privileges, ma. You ain't there yet."

Smirking, Loriana backed away from his ride. Surprisingly, it was his same car he had before getting locked up. One of his uncles had maintained the upkeep, and it still drove like new. Until he met with an accountant, Projex didn't plan on spending any big money on anything yet. He was splurging on food, weed, and clothes at the most. Everything would come later, including a couple of whips he had his eye on.

The first thing niggas did when they got some money was go nuts. He didn't knock it cause coming where he came from, niggas like him didn't make it, so why not ball out? Projex was just moving smartly with his. He wanted to be wealthy where his money was making money, not spend it all, and struggle to make it back.

"I'ma get back there. We're going to get back there," she declared, meaning every word.

"We'll see."

Projex wasn't going to hold his breath on her declaration. He couldn't front like sitting here talking to her didn't feel right, though. They made sense, but he was now guarded too. If he let his guard down for Loriana again, he had to be one hundred percent sure she wasn't on no bullshit because the way folks had been snaking him, Projex was liable to treat her like a hoe from the hood. He'd gladly fuck her, duck her, and kick her ass to the curb like she meant nothing to him.

Chapter Four

Posted on the block in South Ave, Bo was sitting on the hood of a Lexus while rolling up a blunt. It was the weekend, and the hood was out. The dope fiends were too, as Sneaks, Draco, and a few other SAG members hugged the block and made plays. The summer had officially come to an end, but it was still nice out.

Draco, with his name fitting him so well, had his semi-automatic right by his side just in case something popped off. They'd had a few run-ins with some niggas in the last couple of years, but they weren't in any real beef as of late. Still, he sat with his eyes focused and head on a swivel.

"Man, I'm telling you. It was so many hoes at that

video shoot, dawg," Sir bragged. "That nigga, Laurent, be bringing the town out fasho."

"Hell, yeah. Half of em' be dick riding though," Bo added.

"That's what hoes do. Shit, I'm all for it."

"A'ight. Nikki gon' beat yo' ass again. Keep on." Bo laughed.

Sir's baby mama was a hothead, and he'd never regret his son but hitting her raw had been the worse decision of his life. She lived for drama, as did he, and was always ready to put on a show. If there was an originator of the saying *I love my baby daddy, I'll never let him go*; it was Nikki's ass. She couldn't stand Sir's ass but wouldn't leave him alone.

"Man. I ain't worried about her crazy ass. She knows what's up."

Peeping an old Ford Taurus bend the block, their conversation ceased. Bo tucked the blunt he had been rolling behind his ear and watched as the car pulled up on them.

"Y'all know who this is?" Draco questioned, ready for whatever.

"Nah. It look like a female driving, though," Sir replied as he squinted his eyes in a hooded manner.

When the car stopped and Kordell hopped out,

Draco was the first to aim his heat. Kordell tossed his hand in the air and froze up.

"Nigga, I know you ain't pull yo' snitch ass up over here," Bo spat.

"Nah, man. I ain't come on no bullshit. I'm just tryna see where y'all boy at."

All of their faces scrunched up as guns were now aimed at him in all directions. Bo didn't know who the chick was in the driver's seat, but he didn't give a fuck. Boldly, he walked over to the car, snatched the door open, and dragged her out.

"Bitch, who is you?" his voice boomed.

"I-I'm just his friend. Please don't shoot me."

"C'mon, man. You ain't gotta scare her like that. She good people."

"Nigga, shut the fuck up. You a rat. Ain't nobody affiliated with you good people, bitch!" Bo boomed. "You need to watch the company you keep," Bo told the girl but didn't let her go.

His hand traced her body for any wires. They were back on their turf and not in Atlanta. Bo wouldn't think twice about bodying her ass and getting rid of her. Baby girl was just at the wrong place, with the wrong mothafucka.

"The fuck you want?" Sneaks questioned Kordell. "You rolling up like you welcomed here, nigga."

"I thought my cousin would be over here. I just need to talk to him real quick," Kordell said with his eyes bouncing around.

Projex had let it be known Kordell wasn't welcomed anywhere they got money or kicked it at. Of course, word would spread fast about him being a snitch, so ultimately, anywhere else he pulled up to, people would've been leery of him. Kordell had officially been stamped as a snitch, and that wasn't a good look at all. Not for him or anyone he used to hang tough with. It was bad enough he was still breathing, let alone having the balls to drop by the hood like shit was all good.

Sneaks wasn't feeling how Kordell was moving, so he called Projex up. If he gave them the go-ahead, they were bodying him and calling it a day.

"What's good," Projex answered.

"Yo' peoples over here looking for you. Let him walk?"

Projex's jaw flexed. He'd told Kordell to not even show his face in South Ave, and he had the audacity to roll up on them? He had to chuckle. The nigga was getting bolder by the day, and Projex felt like he was testing him. He couldn't make any moves, though.

"Yeah. Let em' make it. He by himself?"

"Nah. With some dingy little bitch who 'bout to piss herself."

That pissed Projex off more. Kordell was dragging unnecessary people into his bullshit.

"Send that nigga on his way. I got it."

"A'ight," Sneaks said and hung up the phone. "Yo, Bo. Let that girl go. Get the fuck from around here, Dell. Come through here or anywhere else, we gon' light yo' ass up."

"So, y'all following that nigga Projex's commands now? Bunch of game goofy mothafucka's dawg. It's cool." He nodded his head. "I see how it is."

"Man, get yo' ass on 'fore I shoot you," Bo hissed, itching to pull his trigger.

Besides Projex, Bo was a certified shooter, one of three Projex could rely on to handle shit if need be. It wasn't that he was taking commands. He knew Kordell was a fucking rat and had any of them shot him, the block would've more than likely been swarmed with police. Them having their guns out on him was dangerous, but they weren't taking any chances with his ass.

Feeling a bit triumphant, Kordell smirked and moseyed around to the passenger's side. He'd only come through to ruffle their feathers and let it be known that he was looking for Projex. Easily, he could've pulled up to Joseline's crib but wanted to make a statement. He hadn't gotten touched yet and was still moving freely. It was sad and crazy to see what greed, envy, and jealousy could turn a person into.

Kordell's ill feelings toward Projex started way before he'd gone to jail and way before Chevy got killed. As his first cousin, Kordell always felt like Projex put every other nigga before him. Rather it be with getting money, putting him on bitches, or even kicking it, Kordell felt like he was always his last option. It wasn't until Chevy got killed that they hung out tougher, but by that point, Kordell had already planted the seeds to get his cousin locked up. It was a cold world.

When the Taurus pulled off the block, Bo stood in the middle of the street and scratched his scalp. Puzzled, his face frowned.

"I shoulda popped that nigga for just pulling up."

"And have your ass all in jail. That nigga was trying to get us caught up," Sneaks voiced.

"Hell, yeah. I'm 'bout to shake just in case them boys roll through on bullshit," Sir said, and they all agreed.

They all slapped hands and dispersed to their

vehicles. Never had a nigga gotten away with their life after pulling the shit Kordell had, but never had they dealt with a snitch either. Not this personal. They knew of a few, and that's all there was to them. If they were still alive, they knew not to step foot on any SAG turf. Clearly, Kordell thought he was exempt. He wouldn't be for long.

Across the city, Projex was fuming but humored as well. He knew his cousin. Kordell was doing shit to get a reaction out of him, but he wasn't going to feed into it. Instead, he was going to continue to piss him off, get money, and stunt on his ass every chance he got. Kordell was lucky he didn't have a main bitch, or Projex would've fucked her for fun just so she could run her mouth.

Knowing his cousin watched his every move on social media, though he was hardly on there, Projex decided to send a message. With his new gold and diamond bottom grill in, Projex cheesed with a stack of money sitting on top of his head and took a picture. He was never one to flash money, seeing that as corny and the quickest way to get robbed, but this was for fun. Niggas wanted his attention, and he wanted to let Kordell know he had it. He'd just delete it later if he felt like it.

The three hundred plus thousand dollars was fresh

out the bank. While Joseline was fine with the house she and Joi lived in, Projex wanted to cop her a new crib all cash. They'd just pulled up to see a house a Black realtor was showing them when Sneaks hit his line. This was the last bit of attention he was giving Kordell. Posting the picture on his Instagram, Projex didn't bother to add a caption. Real niggas knew what the fuck he meant.

"Were you just taking a selfie?" Joi asked as Projex hopped out of the car.

"Yeah. You wanna take one holding it?" he asked jokingly.

"Eww, no. That is so corny. I can't believe you even did that. You better not turn into one of those rappers who flash money all day. That's lame."

Projex couldn't help but laugh. "Damn. Tell me how you really feel. You gon' make me delete my post."

"Please do. You're so much better than that," Joi told him as they met the realtor at the door.

"Projex?" the middle-aged woman asked. She was professionally dressed in a black dress that stopped right above her knees, a pair of heels that she could comfortably walk in, and had a smile on her face.

"Yeah. This is my mama, Joseline, and my sister, Joi."

"Nice to meet you all. My name is Taletha. Will this be your first time purchasing a home?"

Joseline spoke up. "His first time, yes. The one we're in now is being leased. I'm here just to look."

Projex shook his head. He knew his mama wasn't being ungrateful. She just didn't want him doing the most for her. Projex wasn't going to listen. To him, he owed her the world. Copping her a crib was just a small token of his appreciation for her unwavering love and support as his mother.

"Well, that's okay too. As a first-time homebuyer, you want to have options, so I understand. We can take a look and discuss numbers if you're interested."

Projex looked at his mama as they stood in the foyer of the home. When he smirked, she rolled her eyes playfully.

"You really don't have to do this, Bryshon."

"Leave it alone, Ma. I'm buying you a crib, so go look around. You too," he told Joi.

While Joi tried holding it together, the fresh smell of paint had her nauseous as hell. There were certain smells she simply couldn't tolerate, and she'd just found out that paint was one of them. Seeing her eyes flutter, Projex stepped into her personal space.

"Aye. What's wrong with you? You been looking sick as hell lately."

"Bryshon, language," Joseline scolded.

"My fault, Ma, but she has. You got a fever or something? A stomach bug?"

Ever observant as if he were a doctor, Projex placed his hand to her forehead to gauge her temperature. When he dragged his hands down her arms and reached for her stomach, Joi pushed his hand away.

"Move. You don't need to touch all on me."

He drew his head back some and reached to touch her stomach again. The baggy t-shirt and leggings she was wearing hadn't thrown him off until now. When she scurried out of his way, Projex's eyes darkened dangerously. There was a lethal calmness in them that matched the tone of his voice.

"Joi," he called out, making her still and goosebumps coat her arms. "I'ma ask you something, and you bet not lie."

Gulping, Joi tried playing it off like she had an attitude. "What? I'm not sick."

"Nah. But you pregnant?"

When she glanced up at him, the guilt in her eyes gave her away. Projex didn't give her a chance to answer before he was up on her. Invading her privacy, he played tug of war, trying to lift her shirt, and won in the end. As soon as his hand felt her hard belly, Projex wanted to wring her neck.

"You fucking pregnant, man!" His voice was cold and sent chills down all the ladies' spines.

"Now, Bryshon. You're not about to holler at her," Joseline said, stepping between them.

"And you ain't said nothing!?" He looked at his mama like she'd just spit on him.

"And you're not about to holler at me. You better calm your ass down."

She didn't care how upset he was. He'd better remember who the fuck he was talking to before Joseline gave him a reminder. Feelings crushed because she'd undoubtedly hurt his, Joi wiped the tears that appeared under her eyes.

"Nah. Don't cry now. You weren't crying when you were spreading your legs open."

Joseline pushed him away from Joi but got right in his face. "You better watch your fucking mouth, and I mean it. Don't talk to her like that. Do you hear me?"

Ice grilling his sister with anguish coursing through his veins, Projex didn't bother to answer his mama. Joseline shoved him in his chest again.

"I said do you hear me?" she asked a second time.

Jaw clenched and heart shattered, Projex nodded his head. If he uttered another word, Joseline would've been slapping the taste from his mouth.

"I'm sorry," Joi cried, seeing the hurt mask her brother's face. "I didn't want you mad at me. That's why I haven't told you."

"Don't apologize to him. He better go cool off before I show my ass in here."

Joseline wasn't about to let him sit up here and talk to Joi any kind of way. Of course, he was upset, maybe even disappointed, but the damage was done. Once Joi turned eighteen, and even before, the decisions she made determined her future. In a society where people always had an opinion about other people's lives and how they should live them, Joseline wasn't about to let Projex make her feel bad. Yes, she had been upset at first, too, but she'd never turn her back on her.

Rather she told him before now or later, Projex was still going to be hurt. Joi was his baby. Though she had her own father, he'd practically raised her. They were way too close for her to hide something like this from him, and that's what bothered him the most. He knew she was damn near grown and probably out here doing her thing, but to get pregnant? Nah. Projex couldn't handle that. Especially knowing it more than likely occurred while he was away. He felt like he'd failed her.

Shaking his head, Projex had no words to say, and

that very seldom happened. Well, he had some, but they wouldn't be nice. He had questions, too, ones he planned to get some answers to. Going back to his car, he called up the one person he knew should've told him about Joi's pregnancy as well.

"Hello," Loriana answered.

"You knew!" his voice boomed with assumption.

Loriana's chest caved. She hated when he hollered at her. "Why are you hollering and knew what?"

"Man, don't sit on this phone and play dumb. You knew Joi was pregnant?"

She grew quiet, and that was all he needed to hear.

"That wasn't my place to tell you," she mumbled.

"Then what is your place, huh? Every time I think somebody looking out for me behind my back, they stabbing me in that mothafucka."

"She's grown, Projex. No one is stabbing you in the back. You just think everything is supposed to go your way, and it's not."

He sucked his teeth in annoyance. "Man, whatever. Fuck up off my phone 'fore you piss me off even more."

Without thought, he hung up in her face. He knew he'd probably hear her mouth about that move later on, but right now, he didn't give a fuck. He was in his feelings. The crazy thing was, he hadn't even found out the worst part of this all. He'd be sharing a niece or nephew with Symir and didn't even know it.

R arely was Laurent in town now, due to his busy schedule, but Projex had caught him at the perfect time. With the news he'd gotten earlier in the day about Joi, the first thing he did after smoking was slide to the studio. He'd been in there for hours writing, decompressing, and trying to figure out how his baby sister was about to have a baby.

Taking a pull from his blunt, Projex exhaled and nodded his head to a beat that Laurent was effortlessly rapping over. The contents in his Styrofoam cup shook as the bass from the music bumped obnoxiously. Projex hadn't planned on drinking, but when Yari and her homegirl pulled up on him with a bottle, he indulged.

"We should order some food," Yari suggested once the track stopped, and Projex passed her the blunt.

He nodded his head. "Yeah. I got the munchies like a mothafucka. What y'all want?"

"I'm good with whatever," Reign, Yari's home-girl, spoke up.

The duo had been there for at least an hour, and besides casual conversation with Yari, Reign hadn't spoken much. She was enjoying the vibes and chilling. She and Yari had been out shopping when she hit Projex up to see what he was on for the night. After telling her he was at the studio, Yari let him know she was pulling up on him. Reign tagged along since she had no plans for the night.

Glancing her way with low, red-rimmed eyes, Projex took in her appearance for the second time. When she first walked in, he'd been too deep into what he was writing to really assess her features. Wide hips and natural thick thighs sat comfortably on the couch and grabbed his attention first. Her waist-line was nonexistent, and Projex wondered if she'd gotten her body done.

Reign was naturally snatched and pretty. The golden blonde and black butterfly locs hung to her shoulders, framing her round face. Even though the place was dimly lit, Projex could tell she had some good skin. Her brown complexion was glowing and makeup-free. Her full lips were glossed, brows perfectly threaded, and a gold hoop nose ring dangled from her right nostril. She was dressed casually in ripped jeans, a blush-colored V-neck onesie, and Tory Burch slides.

Her attire was much different than the broads who'd come to the studio a few nights ago. Ayo, another rapper Projex was cool with, would have a packed studio during almost all his sessions. Women came scantily dressed like it was a club and even had the nerve to wear heels. Projex couldn't stand that shit. Of course, they were trying to impress the niggas in the room but ended up making themselves look silly.

"Dang, is something on my face?" Reign questioned, waving her hand in Projex's face with a chuckle.

He broke his gaze. "Nah. My fault. What was you saying?"

"You asked what we wanted to eat, and I said I'm good with whatever."

Projex drank from his cup. "You saying that now. Let me order some shit you don't like; you gon' be in this bitch complaining."

"Well, how'd you know what I don't like if you don't ask?"

With ease, Reign was a flirt. She meant no harm and sometimes got herself into situations and relationships that were never meant to go that far.

Projex smirked. He didn't care enough to ask. "I wasn't planning on asking."

Reign laughed. "Straight up, huh?"

"Yeah. If I do that, you gon' be wanting to tell me yo' favorite color, how them hoes at yo' job be stressing you out and shit."

Reign held her laugh in, making her cheeks rise, and dimples appear. *She pretty as hell,* Projex thought to himself. He'd met most of all of Yari's friends, but she was new and way less turned up than majority of them, including Yari.

"Cocky, aren't we?" Reign pressed.

"Not at all. I'm just stating facts."

"And what makes you think I'd want to do all that?"

"Why would you not?" he asked his question and stared at her intently. When she didn't cower away but instead stared right back, he smirked. "I'm a good listener."

"Mhm. Until I start complaining because *you* didn't listen and got me the wrong food."

Together, they laughed. Projex fucked with her vibe. He'd been so focused on making sure things were straight on the home front since he'd touched down that occupying time with a woman was the least of his worries. Especially since Loriana had pulled that weak shit on him. Projex had tunnel vision going on.

He'd knocked down Danielle a few times since being home, but he most definitely wasn't trying to wife her or get into anything serious. He was a man, though. One who appreciated the company of a woman on most days and didn't mind shooting his shot if he was interested. It was never mixed signals with him. If Projex wanted you, pressure was applied off top.

"You got me all wrong," Projex told her, snatching his phone up from the table. "Put yo' number in here and find out."

"Uh, oh. What is this? A new love connection?" Yari joked, watching the exchange.

Reign tittered, typing her number into the keypad and storing her name. "Not near."

"You all over here in our business," Projex told her.

"Boy, whatever. You're my best friend, so I can do that."

When Reign passed his phone back to him, Projex looked at the screen then up at her. She had a smirk on her face, and that right there let Projex know she was much more than what appeared on the outside. The purple umbrella emoji she added after her name had him ready to find out if she did, in fact, get as wet as her name. She added a crown, too, already staking claim to hold weight in his life as a queen. He could dig it. There was nothing sexier to him than a confident woman.

After ordering a gang of Chinese food, they chilled for a few more hours before Reign was ready to call it a night. Making sure they got to Yari's ride safely, he hugged her then did the same with Reign, only his hands drifted to the dip in her back as he pulled her into him.

"Thanks for the food," she told him.

"It ain't nothing. You welcome. I'ma hit yo' line to make sure you made it in, so don't ignore me."

She pulled out of his embrace and looked into his eyes. "I won't. You didn't even ask if I was single."

"Do it matter?"

She was single if he wanted her. Projex didn't give a fuck about her nigga, and if she did have one, neither did she.

Reign chuckled. "I guess not. Already, I'm sensing you like things to go your way. We're gonna butt heads."

"Nah. We gon' get along just fine. You already speaking ill over our friendship."

"You right, you right. Let me not do that." She

opened the passenger door to Yari's ride. "I'll be sure to reply when you text me."

"We'll see."

Projex went back inside the studio, and Yari wasn't a good twenty seconds out of the parking lot before she was asking questions.

"What was y'all talking about?"

"Him hitting me up when I made it in. Nothing serious. I was not expecting to leave here with a number. Especially his."

Reign wasn't as hip to who Projex was or what he did, but Yari was. She hyped him up to anyone who would listen and stayed letting people know that her best friend was a big fucking deal.

"Laurent's ole' faithful ass wasn't trying to do a thing. Niggas really be committed. Well, not all of them," Yari added as Reign sucked her teeth.

"Exactly. That's why I don't even feel a way about getting his number."

"You shouldn't. Projex is such a good guy and will treat you right."

Reign glanced her way. "Y'all ever messed around?"

"Girl, no. Never. That's literally just my best friend."

"Have you thought about it, though? You don't

have to lie. The nigga is fine as fuck and all those tattoos." Reign slid down some in her seat as if she were melting. "Whew. If I didn't have morals, I'd invite him over once he leaves the studio."

"No, bitch. If you didn't have a crazy ass nigga, you'd invite him over."

Reign sighed. "Right, but answer my question. You never thought about crossing that line? I've never had a male best friend, so I don't know how it is."

"Nope. Not once. We've been locked in for years, and it's been platonic. It's way too many other niggas out here to fuck up our friendship, and for what? You don't have anything to worry about."

Reign hoped not. She wasn't planning on getting serious with Projex, but she definitely didn't want to be on weird vibes with Yari if they had indeed fucked around. She'd seen it happen to other friends of hers and wanted no parts. If anything, all Reign wanted to do was kick it with him. They didn't even have to fuck, but she knew from tonight alone Projex wasn't the type of nigga you *didn't* put the pussy on. She'd be doing herself a disservice.

Chapter Five

"You gone sit in here and pout all night?" Shamari questioned before a yawn escaped his mouth.

Perched on the couch with her legs crossed, one of his oversized t-shirts draping her body and a bowl of Fruity Pebbles in her lap, Joi looked up at him. Minding her business in his crib, the TV was on YouTube as she watched the 85 South Show. In the middle of one of their mid-day naps, she'd gotten hungry and snuck out of his bed. On her second snack —the first one consisting of a turkey sandwich and chips—she was just chilling.

Joi swallowed a spoonful of her cereal. "I'm not pouting."

"What you eating in here for?" Shamari asked, plopping down next to her.

Affectionately, he nuzzled his face in the crook of her neck. Snuggling against her warm frame, he eased his hand up his shirt on her and rubbed her belly before venturing to her plump breasts. With ease, Joi's nipples hardened more than they already were as he gently caressed her frame. Shamari was always gentle with her. Despite the hobby he'd taken on, everything, when it came to Joi, was considerate.

"You were asleep, and I didn't want to wake you up."

He pinched her nipple, causing her to drop the handle of her spoon. "Mari," she hissed before a soothing sensation of him rubbing her nipple eased the pain.

"What?"

"Stop doing that. They're sensitive."

"My bad," he uttered, easing his hand from her breasts back to her belly. "You frontin' though. You know I sleep heavy."

That was the truth. Shamari could sleep through a tornado and not have a clue of what was going on. After his fight the night before, they'd gotten into a heated argument about her setting something up for Shamari to meet Projex.

Far from a lame, Shamari had long ago been ready to let him know what was up. Joi was just the one being scary. Even after Projex found out she was pregnant, Joi still didn't find the idea of telling him who her baby daddy was, appealing. Joi figured the longer she kept him unknown, the more time she'd have to come to grips with the entire situation.

What was simply supposed the be a cool kickback she attended with her best friend Dayci and homegirl Kania turned into Joi about to be a whole parent. Mind blown at how quickly things were moving, she'd sometimes distance herself from Shamari when she got in her head. It was a habit of hers, and she couldn't shake it.

"So, what's up? You still got an attitude?" Shamari asked, not letting up.

"No."

Shamari stared at the side of her face for a few seconds while Joi looked straight ahead. He knew she was still in her feelings. It was written all over her pretty face. He wasn't trying to stress her out but have her at her best, and the longer she prolonged this meet-up, she was going to stay in her feelings. Noticing he was still staring, Joi glanced his way.

"What?" she questioned. "Why you staring at me?"

"I can stare at you. You mine."

Shamari pecked her lips and lingered in her face. "You mine?"

Joi nodded her head slowly as a smile teased the corners of her mouth. "Yes."

At his age, Shamari never thought he'd be having a baby so soon, but he was happy as hell. When he and Symir's mother passed away in 2015, a piece of him had been feeling empty since. Honestly, he hadn't known peace since that day. Losing her as a teenager had turned Shamari into a hothead.

He'd consistently get into fights, be on high speeds with the cops for the fuck of it, and simply do reckless shit because he was grieving. For two years straight, Shamari was wilding out, and Symir was ready to ship him back to Miami with their dad. That was until their god mom stepped in and urged him to go to therapy. It helped for a good six months, then Shamari got bored.

His new outlet was boxing, illegally. The under-ground fighting hobby he picked up had been his saving grace. In the beginning, it was a stress reliever, then it became something he got paid to do. Shamari's hands were lethal, and on plenty of occasions, people had urged him to go legal with it. He was still undecided, not wanting something he loved doing to feel like work.

Drinking some of her vanilla almond milk out of the bowl, Joi placed it on the table in front of her. Still exhausted with an aching body from his fight, Shamari laid his head in her lap. This was where he found solace. The comfort Joi brought him from just being herself and relaxing with him on these types of days was one of the reasons he was ready to give her and their child whatever she asked and didn't ask for.

While his warm lips kissed along the inside of her caramel-colored thigh, she ran her hands through his locs and massaged his scalp. Her body shuddered at his simple touch. Bare chest with his locs strewed across her lap and couch, Joi took in Shamari's frame. With nothing but some boxer briefs on, his abs bulged with ease. His body was that of a god, a fine Black warrior. His neck was free of tattoos, while his upper chest was covered in them.

A comfortable silence surrounded them until Shamari turned his head and rubbed his nose along her panty-covered mound. Loving her scent, he inhaled deeply and made her place one leg over his chest. Joi looked down at him with amusement and a racing heart. Shamari was constantly testing the waters with her.

"Look at you. Wet already," Shamari said, eyeing the damp spot on her cotton panties.

When he pushed them to the side and kissed her slick lips, Joi's breath got caught in her chest. Her dainty hand went to caress his beard, but Shamari had other plans. With ease, he lifted her and positioned her right on top of his face.

"Mari," Joi gasped as he focused on sucking her clit into his mouth.

Shamari rubbed her booty and smacked it gently. "Relax, bae. You too tense. Let me eat this pussy for you. Get rid of this lil' attitude you still got."

"I don't — Oh!" she shrieked after being caught off guard by the rapid flicks of his tongue.

Not looking for any rebuttal, Shamari savagely ate her pussy. Forcing her to fuck his face, he gripped her hips and urged her to gyrate all over his tongue. Joi's body leaned over onto the back of the couch as she kept moving her body like a snake.

"Take this off," Shamari mumbled, trying to remove the t-shirt she was wearing.

Slipping it over her head, Joi tossed it to the ground. Gently, Shamari massaged her breasts with such tenderness, Joi couldn't help but moan. Between what he was doing with his tongue and his big hands, she was already on the verge of climaxing. When her legs tightened around his head, Shamari held the top of her thighs.

"Bae, okay," she whimpered, gripping his locs.

"Mmm, mm."

Shamari wasn't stopping. He didn't want to even if she begged. Early on in their relationship, Shamari saw firsthand how stubborn and spoiled she was. He had no issues with that, but he was breaking her out of that stubborn shit. Everything wasn't going to always go her way, and she needed to learn that. Especially with them about to have a child. This chapter in their lives was serious and only going to get more hectic as the days for her to deliver neared.

"Oh my gooosh," she cried as he slid two fingers inside her tightness.

Without releasing her pearl, Shamari made her cum so hard, her entire body trembled before toppling over. Wiggling her cheeks as she practically suffocated him, Shamari smirked underneath her. He took pleasure in pleasing her and knowing that she was carrying his seed made him want to accommodate every need she had. Even if there wasn't one, he wanted to be there. Whether that be physically, mentally, or emotionally, Shamari wanted to be and remain her person. Financially, she would forever be good.

Joi's body stayed hunched over his head with her face in the pillow. Heavy exhales escaped her lips as she squeezed her eyes tightly. That orgasm had stars dancing in her head. Lazily, Shamari placed kisses along her slickness before easing her down onto his lap. Joi felt the imprint of his erection and smiled.

"Chu' grinning for?" he asked as she leaned forward.

"This," she replied, reaching into his briefs while pressing her lips into his.

Sloppily, they exchanged a love-filled kiss. Before Joi could slide onto him, her phone vibrated on the glass table, making her lift up. Seeing her mama was calling, she sighed and withdrew her hand from inside his briefs.

"Hey, Mama," she answered.

"Hey to you, too, lil girl. I was just calling to see if you were coming home today?"

Joi paused and looked down at Shamari. His eyes were closed, and lips glossy from their kiss. She could see her juices coating his beard, and that made her wetter. *I should've just called her back,* she thought.

"Um, yes. I planned on it. Why you ask that? Is something wrong?"

"No. Nothing's wrong. I know you're pregnant and all, starting a family of your own, but you still live underneath this roof. You stayed out last night and didn't let me know, so I was just reminding you."

Joseline knew her daughter was grown, but as long as she still lived with her, she expected to at least receive a text or call letting her know she wouldn't be coming home. It was the little things she was going to miss when her baby moved out, and she wasn't trying to come down hard on her, but still. Common courtesy would always be appreciated.

"Sorry. The fight ended really late, and I forgot to text you. I wasn't trying to be disrespectful or anything."

"I know. I was just letting you know."

"Okay. But I'll be home in time for dinner. You are cooking, right?"

Joseline snickered. "Mhm, I am. You sound just like your brother. Is that all y'all think I'm good for?"

Giggling, she said, "Of course not, Mama. Maybe Projex does, but I know you're much more than an amazing cook."

"Yeah, yeah. Let you tell it. I'll see you later on. I'm about to run to this grocery store now."

"Okay. See you later."

Hanging up the phone, Joi slid it back onto the table. Looking down at Shamari, she ran her hand through his bearded jaw and pecked his lips.

"Now, where were we?"

Shamari peeled his eyes open. Licking his juicy lips, but not in a flirtatious manner, he stared up at Joi. Her hair was wrapped in a scarf underneath a colorful bonnet, and her face was bare. This was how he loved seeing her most; walking around his crib with hardly any clothing on, barefoot, hair tied up, and looking like she belonged there. Shamari couldn't wait until she was around there wobbling, asking him to bend down and tie her shoes, get weird snacks from the kitchen, and rub her swollen feet.

First, he wanted to get something established between them both. Last night their argument didn't come to an agreement, just a conclusion. Shamari was trying to argue, and Joi was tired. They fell asleep with unresolved issues, and he didn't like that.

"I'ma set something up to meet yo' brother," he let her know.

Joi swallowed hard and agreed. "Okay."

His brow lifted. "You good with that?"

"Yes. I don't have a choice. I mean, I do, but it's pointless to keep prolonging it. It's not like you're not going to have to meet him. I just don't want y'all to start fighting."

"I ain't on that, bae. But on my unborn, if he gets out of pocket, it's whatever. I'ma try to be cool. That nigga ain't yo' daddy. He wasn't even tripping like you say yo' brother was."

That was the truth. Joi's daddy, Deron, hadn't even tripped out like she thought he would. More than anything, he was excited for his baby girl. She was the second oldest of his and was giving him his first grandchild. Of course, he and Shamari had their own personal conversation off to the side, but other than that, everything was cool.

Things were different with Projex, though. Their situation was complicated, and Joi knew her brother. Just the way he'd spazzed on her had Joi wanting to say fuck them meeting. They could've met on acci-dent or at the baby shower some months down the line for all she cared. Projex's reaction was out of love and disappointment. Regardless of how old Joi got, Projex was going to forever struggle with her growing up.

"I know. It's just I'm his baby sister. If you had one, you'd understand."

"I do understand, but you gotta know I ain't no little ass boy. We about to bring a baby into this world, and I ain't trying to be into it with yo' people over my child. What that nigga gon' do? Stop me from being in y'all life?"

He wasn't asking to get an answer. Shamari

wasn't about to play behind Joi or his baby. He and Projex could either talk shit out as men, or they could go head up as men as well. Either way, Shamari was tired of putting this shit off. It was stressing Joi out, and that made her irritated with him. He didn't need that or like it.

"No. I'd never let that happen. I love you too much to let somebody come between us," Joi told him with nothing but conviction in each word she spoke.

Shamari smirked and pulled her to him by the back of her neck. "I love yo' pretty ass, too. Ain't nobody coming between us, though. I'll beat yo' brother's ass first and worry about that shit later."

Joi snickered and shook her head. "Shut up. Y'all are not going to be fighting. Let's focus on all of that later. Right now," she said, removing his dick from his briefs, "let's focus on this."

Sliding down onto his erection, they both moaned in unison. For now, Shamari was going to let it slide, but when it was time to meet Projex, he hoped he didn't have to take it there. For Joi's sake, he'd try to be on his best behavior.

I t was a rare occasion for Loriana to be in the house on a Friday night. Not *that* rare because she loved being home, but at the start of the weekend, Candace and Trell were usually trying to get her dressed and out on the town. If she wasn't hanging with Mhyale or making plans with Symir, the trio was kicking it.

With no plans, Loriana was comfortable on her couch and slightly buzzed from the mixed drink she made. Tequila was always her preferred liquor to indulge in, and it had gotten her right. Watching another episode of some true crime show, knowing she'd be spooked out, Loriana's eyes were glued to the TV. She was ten minutes into the episode and hadn't taken her eyes off it since. When her phone vibrated in her lap, she jumped so hard it fell to the ground.

Not expecting anyone to be calling her this late, she frowned when she saw Projex's number light her screen up. She hadn't heard from him since he called cussing her out about Joi being pregnant. Loriana felt like that wasn't her place to tell him, and he couldn't make her feel bad about it either. So, she wondered what he wanted at damn near one in the morning, especially with her.

Hesitantly, Loriana answered his call before it went to voicemail.

"Hello."

Projex cleared his throat. "Yeah, what's up. What you on?"

She grinned, hearing his low, husky tone. "Um, nothing. Watching TV. Are you okay?"

"I'm good," he said, then chuckled. "Why you ask that?"

"Because you're calling me and late at that.

He scratched his scalp. "I'm kinda fucked up. I ain't gon' lie."

"Oh, okay. Um, you been drinking?"

Loriana wasn't sure why, but she was struggling to find the words to say to him. Just hearing his voice was making it hard for her to formulate sentences, ones that had her second-guessing herself anyway.

"Yeah, and you know what's crazy?"

"No, what?"

"You the only person I thought about talking to, so I called your ass. I'm glad you ain't ignore a nigga."

Loriana smiled and got back comfortable on her couch.

"It's late, and I thought something might be wrong."

"That's the only reason you answered?"

Yes, is what she wanted to say. Instead, she told him her first thoughts.

"No. I kinda wanted to know why you were calling. I thought you were still mad at me."

"That lame ass nigga you fuck with must not be around," Projex said calmly.

It was his usual tone, but the way those words rolled off his tongue had Loriana wondering if Symir was a lame. There was so much conviction behind Projex's tone; he'd damn near made her a believer.

"No, he's not here. And that's not my nigga. We're just friends."

"You be letting that nigga fuck you?"

Loriana gasped a bit, not knowing why she was even surprised by Projex's insolent choice of words.

"I don't see how that's any of your business," was her reply.

"So, that's a yeah. That's crazy though, cause I thought we were friends too, and I ain't even smelled that pussy since I been home."

She smirked, trying to hold in her laugh. "Um, I'm not sure what you want me to say to that. Being friends and smelling my pussy has no correlation at all."

"It does. You just don't know it yet. Was you about to go to sleep?"

"No. Not for a little while, why?"

"Come down here and talk to me right quick. I wanna see you."

Her eyes bucked. "You're outside my place?"

"Yeah. I just pulled up. Throw something on and com'ere."

"Projex," Loriana said his name in a sighing manner.

"Nah. I ain't trying to hear no excuses. Bring yo' ass outside, cause if I come in… man. Just come down here."

"No, because you say all you wanna do is talk, and somehow, I'ma end up with your dick inside me."

"And what's wrong with that? I thought you loved this dick?"

Loriana rolled her eyes. "You get on my nerves. I'm not trying to go there with you. The shit we're doing is toxic, and you know it."

"So the fuck what. You about to piss me off with this whining you doing, like I asked you to travel around the world or something. If you not fucking with me, let a nigga know, and I'll slide out."

"Here you go getting upset cause you're not getting your way. That isn't attractive."

"And neither is you acting like a little ass girl. You either gon' come out here and talk, and we can fuck. Or I'ma come in, and we still gon' fuck. So, what you doing?"

"Those are not good options!" Loriana laughed, not even believing the conversation they were having.

"Them your only options. Now, hurry up. I ain't got all night, girl. This Henny gone wear off, and you gon' be mad."

Standing from the couch, Loriana shook her head as she went to her bedroom. "How you rushing me, and I didn't even invite you over here?"

"Don't matter. I'm here now, and you about to walk yo' ass outside. Bring me a snack too."

"Boy, bye."

Hanging up in his face, Loriana slipped her black *Sophisticated Tomboy* hoodie over her tank top and slid her sock-covered feet into some sandals. With her phone in her pocket, she headed toward the front door. To combat her nerves, she quickly poured herself a shot and tossed it back before grabbing Projex a bag of Cheetos from her pantry.

"Ugh! Damn, that's strong." She grimaced, holding onto her chest to ease the burn.

Thankfully, the early October wind helped some as she locked her key padded door and made her way down the flight of steps. Realizing she didn't know what type of car Projex was in, she went to grab her phone when bright headlights flashed her way. Practically blinding her, Loriana held a hand over her eyes as her mouth slightly dropped in awe.

Backed in under one of the unused carports, Projex was behind tint of his new whip. Not just any whip, but the one he'd been plotting on since he started hustling years ago. The black-on-black 2021 Range Rover Sport had been a gift he bought for himself because why the hell not? He deserved it, had earned it, and was proud of himself.

Besides his mama, Loriana was the only other person he wanted to show off his new purchase to. It was crazy that even though they hadn't spoken, Loriana was still that person —his person he wanted to share everything with. It was just the type of bond they had. Though it was much stronger before, Projex knew deep down they could get back to that.

"Okay! I see you." Loriana grinned as she climbed into the passenger seat. "This a rental?"

Projex smirked. "Quit playin'. This all me. Paid this bitch off in cash, too."

"Let me hold something then, baller," she joked.

"What you need?"

Though she was only joking, Projex wasn't. He

was naturally a giver, so it was nothing to make sure Loriana was good on whatever she needed. Loriana's heart melted, knowing he was serious.

"I'm fine. I was just playing. Congrats, though. This is really nice and fits you."

"Why you say that?"

"Cause, it's sleek but still has that masculine edge to it," she explained.

"I wanted the Lamb truck, but I told myself to wait. That mothafucka raw, too."

"I remember you saying you were going to get one of these when you came up. Seemed like it happened overnight."

A lot seemed to happen over the course of three years, but it didn't seem overnight to Projex at all. Those nights in his cell seemed to drag on, and he never wanted to see the inside of a prison ever again.

"Yeah. The money seemed like it happened overnight. Everything else just seemed to fall into place."

"As it should've. The universe just looking out for you."

Projex licked his lips. "Yeah? And who looking out for you?"

"Oh, you know. Me and the big dog upstairs are

real close. You know He doesn't play about me, so I've been good."

"Yeah. I had my talks with Him about you. My nigga was keeping secrets from me."

Loriana chuckled. "Don't start. Did you expect me to stay the same?"

"Nah, but I ain't expect for you to switch up either." Projex paused and drank from what was in his Styrofoam cup. Loriana got a whiff of it, and whatever it was smelled like straight liquor, no juice or anything.

"I was scared," Loriana told him honestly. "I didn't know what was going to happen with you or us. My mom had just passed. I was almost raped and robbed at gunpoint."

"When the fuck was you almost raped? Why you ain't tell me that?"

Projex wasn't trying to holler or be insensitive, but she'd just fucked his head up with that one. He knew about the robbery and asked around because niggas loved to brag, then had Laurent put some money on the nigga's head. It was just some dumb nigga testing Projex's reach, and he had to show him that niggas could still get touched from behind them bars.

"It happened before you went in. You know that

night I went out with Candace and Trell to that pool party?"

"You mean the same night that nigga dropped you off? Don't leave that part out."

Loriana rolled her eyes. "Yes, that night. Don't be petty. It was some guy. I don't know who he was, but um, Symir handled him for me. I didn't really know how to tell you, and you had your court situation going on. It was a lot."

This was the first time Loriana had talked about the night she was almost raped. Besides Symir, no one knew. She kept a journal of her feelings for the first year after it happened, having not quite grasped that it wasn't her fault. Sorting through her emotions and trying not to blame herself for the spiral of events taking place in her life took a toll on Loriana. Had she been weaker and not known the goodness of the Lord and how He would pull her through any storm, she wouldn't have been where she was today. She just kept reminding herself that if He did it once, He'd do it again. And here she was… still standing. Her testimony wasn't one to be ashamed of at all.

"C'mon, ma. You know you could've told me that. I'm sorry as fuck that happened to you. You went to counseling or anything?"

His concern for her made Loriana's chest ache

and throat clog with emotions. She did not want to start crying, so she forced her tear ducts to stay where thcy bclonged.

"Yeah. I'm better now. Enough of the sad stuff, though. I thought you were mad at me?"

"Nah. My mama made me realize that Joi is grown, and when she wanted me to know, she'd tell me. I still felt played. That shit is crazy. I'm really about to be an uncle."

"See. That's why I love your mama. She always gets you right on together."

Loriana wanted to change the subject. It was obvious Projex still didn't know that Joi's baby daddy was Symir's brother. Though the cat was out of the bag about Joi's pregnancy, Loriana still didn't feel comfortable forking over *that* information. She knew right away Projex would think she'd put Joi onto him when that wasn't the case at all. With as much snake shit going on around him, it was best Loriana didn't reveal their connection.

"Y'all both fake as fuck. Ol' jeffin' asses," he joked, making her punch him in the arm.

"Boy, whatever. She loves me. You shouldn't be riding around drinking. That's not smart nor safe."

Projex scratched at his patch of chin hair that he was letting grow into a goatee. Loriana absolutely loved it. He'd put on weight, grew some facial hair, cut his hair, and bossed the fuck up all in a matter of months. Loriana loved to see it and was telling herself not to climb over into his lap. She couldn't see his print in the basketball shorts he was wearing, but she knew it was there and waiting. Everything about him right now was giving off big dick energy, and Loriana wanted to ride his until she couldn't feel her legs. Even the way he was leaned back in his seat with his eyes low had her zoned out.

"I had a lot on my mind. Was ready to do some reckless shit, but I came over here instead."

Projex hated that he had to keep his head on a swivel and an eye out for Kordell. When those murderous thoughts of taking him out clouded his mind, jail time didn't cross his mental at all. He just wanted payback. Then, reality set in. He'd for sure go to jail and more than likely not get off if he moved off emotions. So, he checked them mothafuckas and came to the one person he knew would listen without judging him.

"I'm glad you did. You don't need to be moving recklessly, and you just got out. You into it with people already?"

"Nah. Not people, just Dell."

"Kordell? Your cousin?" Loriana asked incredulously.

Projex nodded his head yes, and Loriana's mind went on a rampage. Of course, Projex had kept her in the dark about a lot of things surrounding his case and the streets. Now that he was out, she was hoping that changed. The fact that he came over to talk didn't automatically mean that he trusted her, and Loriana knew that. Still, she asked when he didn't further explain.

"For what, though? You have so much more to be focused on right now."

"Tell that nigga that. He was the one snitching. I wouldn't have been in jail had it not been for him."

Loriana heard him clearly, but she couldn't comprehend why Kordell had been the reason he was in jail. As many times as he checked in on her, brought her money and acted as if he was so concerned, he had put up a major front.

"That is... I don't even know what to say. I'm mad for you. So, you basically did all that time for no reason?"

Projex shrugged. "Yeah, but, fuck it. Maybe I needed that time to sit down and chill out. Stop moving so carelessly and shit."

"Probably, but I hate it had to be through prison.

When did you find all of this out? I mean, if you don't mind telling me."

He didn't. That was the sole reason he'd slid through to see her anyway. He couldn't talk to just anybody about what was going on. Besides Laurent, no one else knew the specific details behind Kordell's betrayal. It was eating Projex up that he couldn't really get at him the way he wanted to, so he had to vent. Drinking only made him irrational and his mental cloudy.

When he was done explaining to her how he found out, Loriana was shocked, but not really. Women like Kelsi came a dime a dozen. For a bit of attention, some money, and moving with a scorned heart, no one was off-limits. That included Projex, who'd hurt her the most.

Loriana chuckled in disbelief. "Whew. And here I was thinking I had so much on my plate. This is beyond me."

"Shit, you and me both. It'll get handled, though." Projex grabbed the bag of Cheetos from her lap and went to open them, but Loriana snatched them back.

"Uh, you can say thank you."

He grinned her way and licked his lips. Instantly, Loriana's pussy jumped.

"Thank you for what?"

"For bringing your ass something to eat."

"What I'm really tryna eat is between them legs."

Loriana swallowed hard. "Okay," she mumbled. "We don't have to do all that out here. We can go in the house."

"Nah. We good out here. I'm tryna christen my ride. Com'ere."

Reaching for her, Projex lifted Loriana up with ease and planted her right in his lap. Adjusting his seat, he slid it all the way back and leaned it back some more. Comfortable, Loriana sat nestled in his lap like she belonged there. And she did. The thin leggings she was wearing made it easy to feel the bulge in his shorts.

"You look so fine with your hair cut," she openly expressed while running a hand over his deep-set waves.

"Thank you," he said, palming her booty. "Your ass so damn soft."

The sound of him ripping her leggings made her eyes widen. The fact that she wasn't wearing any panties made Projex smirk.

"You knew exactly what you were doing coming out here like this."

"I already had these on when you called."

"Yeah, a'ight. Tell me anything."

Loriana's steady breaths turned into needy ones. The way he was massaging her ass as she grinded on his lap was enough foreplay for her. Needing to touch him, she rubbed the sides of his face before kissing his lips and shoving her tongue in his mouth. Projex tasted the liquor on hers and wondered if that's why she agreed to come out and *talk*. Either way, he was appreciative of her presence and pussy wetting his lap up.

"Take this off," he said, lifting the hoodie over her head.

With her skin now exposed, Projex attacked her neck. Licking a trail up to her ear, he then maneuvered to her other side, where he sucked softly. All while his hand was playing in her wetness.

"I missed the fuck out of you, ma," he let her know straight up.

"I missed you too. So much."

"Show me then. Ride this dick like you missed me."

Lifting up some, Loriana allowed him to whip his dick out of his briefs and ball shorts. While he gripped an ass cheek, they stared at one another as she slowly slid down his length. It seemed as if she was sliding forever, but once settled, she exhaled a moan that was clearly satisfying. Her head dropped back, and Projex kissed the middle of her neck.

"This pussy so fucking good and wet," he groaned, gripping her hips and making her bounce on him.

Pushing him back into the seat, Loriana went to work. She didn't really need his assistance, and the liquor in her system had her on one. Lifting her tank top, Projex nastily sucked on her nipples as she rode him.

"What you all quiet for?" he asked, slapping her ass.

The way his dick was pounding into her, Loriana felt it all in her chest. She could hardly talk, let alone moan. Soft whimpers escaped her until Projex pulled on her hair and went deeper.

"Oooh, fuck," she semi-yelled, swirling her hips.

Taking every inch he had to offer, Loriana skillfully hopped up and down on him. Lifting her upper body, she planted her hands on his chest and grinded back and forth. Projex bit his bottom lip as his eyes filled with lust... or love. She couldn't decipher which of the two, but it didn't matter. Only this moment right now did.

Projex's chest heaved as she tightened her muscles

around him. Seeing her eyes roll back and feeling her legs tremble only made his dick harder. Pumping into her from below, their skin clapped loudly as he forced her orgasm over the edge. Crashing her chest into his, Loriana held him tightly around the neck as her entire frame shuddered with indescribable pleasure.

"I-I'm cumming," she moaned loudly.

"I know. Lemme feel that shit."

Loriana wasn't sure if he'd forgotten, but she was a squirter thanks to him. The harder his head tapped at her G-spot, the more essence she released on him and his brand-new truck. Projex wanted to christen his ride, and that's exactly what he got.

"Aw, damn." His teeth gritted as she squeezed the life out of his dick. He wasn't trying to bust yet, but Loriana was making it hard. Literally and figuratively. Holding her around her shoulders while long stroking her, Projex spoke directly in her ear.

"You gon' let me nut in this pussy? Have you give us some pretty ass babies?"

She shook her head no, and Projex spanked her ass.

"No? This pussy mine, ain't it?"

Possessive. He staked claim to something that unquestionably belonged to him whether she wanted to admit it or not.

Her head nodded this time. "Mhm," she moaned as he rotated his dick inside her.

"Mhm, what? Talk to me."

"This your pussy," she replied in a daze.

Head gone, Loriana caught her second wind and fucked him back. Now on her tippy toes in the tight space they were in, she galloped atop him with determination. While driving his length harder into her, Loriana slapped his window hard and screamed loud as hell.

"Aahhh, Bryshon! Ooh, right there. Right there!"

He smirked. "Quiet down, ma. Gon' have these mothafuckas think somebody killing you."

"You arrre!" she moaned as he chuckled.

The smirk on his face fell as she contracted her muscles around him. Somewhat obeying her wishes not to nut in her, Projex was barely able to pull out when he came. Feeling his semen shoot up her back and ass cheeks, Loriana sighed in content. In the moment or not, getting pregnant was not in the plans right now.

Breathing hard, Projex made his dick jump against her ass as she laid against him. Their breathing synced, and a calmness came over him. Feeling icky, Loriana lifted up and shivered as she climbed back over to the passenger seat. Before she sat down, she wrapped her hoodie around her waist and picked her tank top up from the ground, sliding it on.

"You wanna spend the night?" she asked out of the blue.

Projex wasn't expecting that, seeing as how she'd put up a fuss about him pulling up over there.

"Nah. I got an early morning and gotta go get my truck detailed, now."

"I'll wake you up. I have a hair appointment at ten."

The pleading in her voice reminded him of the old days. Loriana seemed almost clingy now that he was back in her presence, while Projex was feeling the total opposite. That post-nut clarity was a mothafucka.

"I'ma head to the crib," he replied dryly. Loriana frowned.

"What's wrong? You act like you can't spend the night or something. It's late, and you've been drinking."

"'Cause. I ain't trying to go there with you right now. Spending the night and shit gon' cause too much confusion."

Her head drew back some. "For who? Like you

didn't just come over here and toss me some dick and conversation. What's more confusing than that?"

Loriana didn't understand what he was trying to get at. One minute he was claiming to be done with her; the next, he was running back. She needed him to break it down to her.

"For you. Look how you about to spazz on me because I told you I'm good on spending the night. Ain't you the one who said what we were doing was toxic? I'm just trying to keep the peace."

A chuckle of disbelief fell from Loriana's lips. "You know what… I'm not even about to do this with you. If you wanted some pussy, that's all you had to say. I apologized for what I did, and I love you, but I'm not about to sit up here and let you make me out like I'm crazy. Like I'm the bad guy for living my life. You can get the fuck on."

"That shit overrated anyway."

Her head snapped his way. "What is?"

"You loving me. It sounds good, though, huh?"

She blinked a few times to make sure she was actually talking to Projex.

"I do love you. You know that."

"Is it conditional? Loving me is cool and all, but at what cost? A nigga really wanted your loyalty."

The tears formed in her eyes before she could stop them.

"What did you expect me to do!?" she hollered.

"To stick shit out!" he hollered back.

His chest ached while thinking back to how she'd broken his heart in that visiting room. For months, Projex questioned himself and second-guessed every move he'd made with her. Everything he did was from the heart, and he never expected her to give him anything in return, but damn. In the midst of his own storm, he was on the frontline battling hers as well.

Projex didn't want much, honestly. He knew holding a nigga down in jail, especially that young, was a lot, but he never thought she'd leave him hanging. The battle to jump headfirst back into something serious with her was a decision he wasn't ready to make yet. Spending the night, cuddling, and waking up to her would for sure bring on deeper feelings; ones he wasn't sure he could trust her with again so soon.

In his mind, sex was just sex. He should've known better, though. Their connection was so deep, it'd never be just sex between them. That's the reason he was parked outside of her crib now in his feelings.

"You bailed the second shit got tough, ma. Never

in a million years did I expect for you to fold on me, only to turn around and be with another nigga."

"So, this is about me dating Symir?"

"Nah. This about us and how you just said fuck what we had, like there was something better. Like we wasn't rocking solid in this bitch. That's what this is about."

The truth was his feelings were hurt. He'd bottled them up while in prison, not wanting to show any weakness. At night when it was just him and the darkness of his cell, his thoughts of her kept him up. It made no sense to him even though he understood what she was going through. He figured if he could thug it out with everything on his plate, so could she.

"Are we going to have this conversation every time we see each other? Fuck! I'm not about to let you make me feel bad for choosing myself. You knew what I was dealing with."

"And not once did I turn my mothafuckin' back on you."

The silence blanketed the car, ended their conversation. Loriana's head shook as her lip quivered.

"You're right. It's obvious you're not ready to forgive me, so fuck it. I'm not about to keep kissing your ass and pleading my case. We don't have to ever speak again after tonight since I'm supposed to be this perfect person who can't make mistakes."

"I ain't want you to be a perfect person; I wanted you to be *my* person. The one I could turn to, but you got it. We ain't gotta ever speak again."

Her nostrils flared, and her eyes swelled again with tears. She wanted to get violent and punch him in his shit but knew that'd get them nowhere.

"You mean that?"

"Do it sound like I'm playin'?" Projex questioned back.

Loriana's head bobbed as she opened the door. "Fuck you then."

"Nah, fuck you!" Projex spat harshly.

Before he could say anything else, Loriana slammed his door. As she strutted away, he let his window down and stuck his head out.

"That's why your leggings tore up! Take yo' ass in the house. Ol' dumb ass!"

"Nigga whatever!" she yelled, tossing her middle finger in the air. "Emotional ass little boy. Crying 'cause he couldn't get his way. Don't come over here again, or I'ma have my nigga beat yo' ass!"

"She don' loss her mind," Projex grumbled, ready to hop out on her ass.

When Loriana saw his door swing open, she took off running up the steps, damn near tripping over her feet. Her hand trembled as she quickly punched in her code and rushed inside. With the door locked and adrenaline on one hundred, she held her breath, waiting for him to come banging on her door. That'd be typical Projex behavior, and she was waiting for him. When thirty seconds passed, she laughed and shook her head. Projex would never put his hands on her, but she wasn't about to take her chances after talking slick like that.

Going into her bedroom, Loriana yawned while untying the hoodie from around her waist. Pausing her movements in the middle of her bedroom floor, her eyes squinted as if something were off. Searching for her phone in the inside of her pocket, she sucked her teeth loudly when she didn't feel it.

"Dammit! I must've dropped it in his stupid truck."

Rushing to her iPad, she FaceTimed her cell and waited for him to pick up. When he didn't answer on the first try, she called back.

"What you calling for? This my phone now." Projex laughed.

"Please don't be petty. Can you bring my phone back?"

"Now you wanna have manners? I thought it was fuck me?"

She rolled her eyes. "It is, but you have something that belongs to me, so can you stop being childish and just bring it here."

"Nope. You ain't getting this mothafucka back until I want you to. And when I see you, I'ma fuck you up too. Talking all that shit while running in the house."

"You get on my nerves! I'ma call your mama. Nah, let me call Ms. Juanita. You know she doesn't play about me."

"Call her," Projex laughed, "I already told her how you broke her grandson's heart, so she don't fuck with you how you think, but gon' head."

Loriana sighed. She wasn't about to do this with him. It was too late, her pussy was sore, and she had to be up early. Rightfully so, Projex did let his grandma know that Loriana had played him, but it was still love on his end. So, in return, Ms. Juanita gave the same. She checked up on her from time to time, so Projex was really just talking for his health. His family loved her regardless of what they went through.

"You know what, keep it. You're lucky I have a work phone. Ol' thieving ass."

"Yeah, yeah. Get off my line. I need to focus driving, and you distracting me."

Loriana waited for him to hang up in her face, but he never did. Ever since that day years ago when she let him know to never do that, he hadn't.

"Man, quit breathing in my ear and hang up. Weird ass girl."

She giggled and unintentionally told him bye like they were cool. How they went from talking on the phone to fucking in his truck to arguing and back laughing again was that toxic shit she was talking about. Loriana couldn't lie, though. She missed the excitement, and if there was anyone she'd want to be toxic with, it was him. Bryshon Petty Ass Emery.

"This man better bring me my phone back," she mumbled, walking to her bathroom. Ten o'clock would be there before she knew it, and she was not missing her hair appointment, phoneless or not.

The following day after getting her hair done, Projex still hadn't dropped Loriana's phone off, nor had he made plans to. That left her to make personal calls from her work phone. It was no issue, but she didn't feel like explaining why she was calling or texting from it.

"Had you not been being fast, you'd have your phone." Nyree laughed as she drove to Target.

She'd called her so they could laugh about the situation like only they could. Nyree was still away at school, and Loriana couldn't wait until they both graduated next semester. With Loriana having taken off for a semester, she picked up extra hours during the summer, spring, and fall. To others, her workload seemed like a lot, but Loriana had no issues. She was used to working hard and pushing through tough obstacles—schoolwork included.

"I was tipsy, thank you," Loriana sassed.

"Girl, what the hell ever. You knew why that man pulled up to see you. You don't gotta fake it for me. If you just wanted some dick, say that."

Loriana snickered. "Lowkey, I did, and then he got all serious talking about I did him wrong, and I don't love him for real. Ruined the moment."

"I mean…"

"You think I did him wrong?" she asked incredulously.

"Not to the point where he has to hold it over your head, no. But I do feel like maybe you could've been there for him more than what you were. As close as y'all were, I think it surprised everyone when you just stopped talking to him."

"He cut me off too! I couldn't even visit, and he never called."

"You broke the nigga's heart. What'd you expect him to do? Keep false hope, wishing you'd change your mind?"

Loriana sucked her teeth. "No, but I'm not the only one to blame for us, and honestly, I'm tired of talking about it. The shit is in the past."

"Clearly, it's not by the looks of it, but okay. You ain't about to have an attitude with me cause you and that nigga can't work shit out. Y'all were supposed to fuck and make up. Not go right back to beefing. Yo' pussy must be whack."

Loriana cackled loudly, making Nyree do the same.

"Bitch, please. I had that nigga asking if he can give me a baby."

"Oh, hell nah. He was trying to trap you!? See, that's just like a nigga. Be all in they feelings, then put a baby in you cause they caught you slipping. No ma'am. I'd be sending that lil' mothafucka right back to its owner."

Screaming, Loriana wiped tears from her eyes. "Shut up! Would you get an abortion if you got pregnant by Juice?"

"If? Ain't no hypotheticals around here and there sure ain't gone be no pregnancies 'cause I make him strap up. Plus, I don't think he'd intentionally try to get me pregnant. That's not something we need right now."

With her away at school and Juice still making trips to see her, Nyree knew better than to believe she was the only one he was sticking dick to. In fact, she never once thought that was the case, and she let it be known she wasn't exclusive to him. They were rocking how they were rocking, and Nyree wanted to keep it that way. Too much was on the line for them to be in a serious relationship and having babies.

"Neither do I. I don't think I'd get an abortion, though. Nah. I know I wouldn't."

"Even if he trapped you?"

"Even if he didn't," Loriana let be known.

On plenty of occasions, she thought about what her and Projex's child would look like and how raising them would be with the lives they lived now. She smiled at the thought then rolled her eyes after thinking about last night. Projex would've been the baby daddy from hell but love the fuck out of their child and her, for sure. She could see it now.

"Oop. I heard that. You better be careful then. And what about Symir?"

"What about him?" Loriana asked as if he were an issue.

Earlier that morning, he'd texted her phone, and

of course, Projex didn't reply. When Symir called, Projex thought about not answering out of respect for Loriana, but he couldn't have cared less about respecting him.

"Yeah," he answered while getting his truck cleaned.

Symir pulled the phone away from his ear to make sure he called the correct number. "Who this?"

"This Projex, nigga. Who is this?"

Symir chuckled at the grit in his tone. "My name popped up when I called, so you know exactly who this is, cuz. Where Lo at?"

Lo? Projex thought with his lip turned upward. Generic ass nickname. "She occupied right now. I'd say I'll have her call you back, but she ain't. Don't call or text our phone no more."

Disrespectfully, Projex hung up in his face. Symir didn't have Loriana's work number saved even though she called from it sometimes if hers was dead, and he had no way of contacting her. He could've gone through social media, but he was going to wait until she reached out to him. As of now, she hadn't yet, but when she did, he was going to give her a piece of his mind.

"You really just gon' mess around with both of them?" Nyree questioned.

"I mean, if it comes down to it, yes. I'm single. There's no reason I should feel obligated to be tied down to one man."

Nyree shook her head. "And they both love you. Do you know how messy this can get?"

"I'm not even thinking that deep into it, honestly. You know what they say about expectations."

"No, what?"

"Don't have them. I'm going with the flow and living my life. After Projex practically cussed me out last night, I realized taking these niggas seriously and giving my heart away isn't for me right now."

"Or you only want to give your heart to one person, but y'all can't get it right. I think that sounds more like you, but hey! What do I know?" Nyree chuckled.

"I can't stand you sometimes." She grinned. "Am I wrong for loving both of them?"

"Shit, you gotta ask yourself that. Miss Loriana Luckett, torn in between the two."

The duo shared a laugh as Loriana found her a parking spot near the front. As always, Target was packed. There was always something Target would tell her she needed once inside, so she hadn't bothered to make a list like she usually would. She loved it there. Trader Joe's was her next stop.

"I am not. I'ma just have fun for a while. Maybe think about settling down once we graduate."

"Mhm. I hear you. It's all fun and games until somebody's feelings get hurt, and I'd prefer it not be yours again. That nigga Projex is out of prison now. I can whoop his ass."

Nyree spoke in a joking manner, but she was dead serious. Yes, she'd said Loriana was in the wrong for leaving Projex hanging, but that didn't mean she didn't have to watch her deal with his lockup alone. Projex was so butt hurt about her just wanting to be friends but failed to acknowledge his role in their separation as well. Phone calls to her didn't happen for a while, letters stopped appearing in her mailbox, and there were tons of restless nights Nyree had stayed on the phone while she cried to her.

Never one to be a hater, Nyree was happy he was home, and they were rekindling their love, but at what cost? Sometimes, Loriana could be too nice and feel bad about protecting her feelings. Nyree knew that off bat, so Projex blaming her for their ending wasn't something she liked, and at the end of the day, she was riding for her girl.

"I wish you were here now so we could ride up on him and get my phone back."

"Girl, you might as well hold your breath on that one."

"Right," Loriana huffed. "I'm 'bout to go in this store, though. I'ma text you when I get home."

"Okay. I love you."

"I love you, too."

Exhaling, Loriana unlocked her doors and climbed out. She only needed a few things from inside and planned to be in and out within thirty minutes, tops. After browsing the graphic tee section, she headed to get her groceries. Most weeks, specifically Sundays, she liked to meal prep. Her days were long, and eating out once or twice a day always made her feel sluggish. So, she tried to cook at home and take her food with her.

Turning down the chip aisle, her eyes squinted as a familiar face came into view. It'd been a long while since she saw Akira, but she'd never forget what she looked like. They were best friends at one point. The little boy in the front of the cart swinging his feet looked exactly like the pictures she'd seen on Facebook. Exactly like his daddy.

"Loriana? Hey, girl," Akira spoke way too cheerfully for Loriana.

When she went to hug her, Loriana frowned and stepped back some. "No need for all that."

Akira chuckled and brushed the confusion off her face. "Oh. Right. My bad. How have you been? It's been forever since I've seen you."

"I've been good, and I know. I guess Kansas City isn't that small."

"Right. This is my little boy, TJ. Say hi, baby."

The little boy waved, and Loriana gave him a smile. He was handsome and had the cutest twists in his head.

"Aye, bae. You get them chips I like?" a masculine voice called from behind Loriana. When he came into view, her eyes widened a bit.

While Akira's son undoubtedly belonged to Tre, she was shocked to see Keith stroll up on them. Over the years, Loriana didn't have time to keep up with who was doing what. She didn't care to and especially not enough for someone who was no longer her friend.

"Loriana?" Keith said her name the same way Akira had. As if they were shocked to see her. "Damn, what's up?"

When he went to hug her, Akira snatched him back by his shirt. Loriana snickered.

"Really, Keith?"

"What? I was just saying hi."

TJ waved his hand again, making Loriana smile.

He was innocent in all of this, but she couldn't help but wonder how their relationship came about.

"She don't need a hug."

That quickly, Akira had switched up. Loriana had seen her true colors way before now, so she wasn't tripping. She didn't need a hug from either one of their asses.

"Whatever, man. How you been?"

"Good. Your son looks just like you," she said with a smirk.

His brows furrowed. "Who, TJ? Aw nah. This ain't my—"

Akira elbowed him in the side, and Loriana couldn't help but wonder if she was abusing him. Not on no funny shit either.

"Thank you," Akira spoke up. Well, it was nice seeing you."

"See you later!" TJ yelled out, grinning.

Keith didn't even bother to speak as he followed behind Akira. She hadn't heard it, but word on the street was that Tamika, Tre's ex-wife, was running his pockets while going through a messy divorce. He tried to make it work, but Tamika was not about to let him having a child on her slide. She didn't care how young or old the girl was. An outside baby was an absolute no in her book.

With Tre struggling to pay lawyer fees, providing for his son happened less often. Financially, he may not have been able to provide to the full extent, but he always had his son and was trying to do right by him. Keith had stepped up to the plate and helped take care of her son. As her boyfriend, he felt it was only right. Akira, on the other hand, had simply settled for him since she couldn't have Tre. Young and dumb, she thought he'd leave his wife when in the end, his wife left him.

Seeing them together again was comedy and reminded Loriana that sometimes, you just had to laugh at life. Not because it was a joke, but because it tested you at all levels. You'd be doing your own thing, then boom, it'd remind you just how far you've come. The old, younger Loriana would've been hurt. The new her simply spoke and kept it pushing. She had groceries to get and a phone to retrieve.

Chapter Six

Annoyed that she even had to pull up on him, Loriana whipped her SUV through the hood. She pulled into South Ave, where Projex told her to meet him to retrieve her cell phone. He wasn't meeting her, so he made her come to him. He'd kept her cell through the weekend, and it was now Tuesday evening. Tired of holding it hostage and wanting to see her face, he promised to be on his best behavior when she came through.

Slowly, Loriana cruised through the block until she spotted his silver Firebird parked on the side of the street of a teal house. Pulling behind it, Loriana placed her ride in park and exhaled. Dialing him on her work phone, he picked up on the second ring.

"You ain't gon' get out?" Projex asked, opening the front door.

"No. Can you just bring it to me? I'm tired."

"Nah. Come get it."

She glared at him through the passenger window and rolled her eyes before hanging up. Climbing out her ride, she hit the locks while adjusting her dress. What seemed like the fiftieth yawn since she'd gotten out of class fell from her lips. She was beyond tired and hated that he'd made her drive all the way to the city.

Posted on the porch in the doorway, Projex looked just as tired as she was. One hand was tucked in the front of the grey joggers he was rocking, while a plain, white tee showcased his cold physique. On his feet were some Nike slides, completing his relaxed fit. When she made it up the steps, he smirked down at her and licked his lips.

"You got an attitude?" e wanted to know.

"No. I'm tired."

"Shit, me too. Come in right quick," he said, stepping to the side.

Instead of putting up a fight and telling him no like she wanted to do, she listened. Loriana's body shuddered at his close proximity and masculine smell. Even if she did have an attitude, being in his presence weakened her resolve. Once she crossed the threshold of the neatly decorated home in shades of grey and yellow, Projex closed and locked the door. Walking up behind her, Projex playfully put her in a headlock.

"Now, what was that shit you was talkin' the other day?" he whispered lowly against her ear. "You gon' have who beat my ass?"

Smirking, Loriana didn't move as he pressed his dick firmly against her ass. She felt the gun he was holding too. "I don't know what you talking about."

"Yeah, I bet. I could end yo' life with one snap of yo' neck right now. You better act like you know who you fuckin' with."

"Trust me, I know. Crazy ass, boy."

Projex released his grip on her and pushed her away from him. "I got your boy. You coming from work?"

She nodded her head yes. "Yeah, and classes. Whose house is this?"

"Bo's baby mama."

"You real comfortable just chilling over here. Where he at?" Loriana scanned the place as if he'd pop out. Projex chuckled at her jealousy.

"He ain't here."

Her brow raised. "So, what you doing here then?"

"Minding my business. Come on."

He walked off but didn't hear her walking behind him. Feet planted, Loriana stayed where she was.

"You just gone stand there?" Projex asked her.

"Yep. This might not even be Bo's baby mama's house. Probably some broad you mess with."

Projex shrugged and scratched his stomach. "A'ight. Stay in here then."

Leaving her be, Loriana fidgeted with contemplation for all of ten seconds before following behind him.

"I'm in here," he called out from a bedroom that smelled of lavender and lemons. "Close the door."

Shutting the door, Loriana now understood what he was doing. Not completely, but the table covered and piled high with money lead her to believe that he was finishing up some business. The only furniture inside the wood floor bedroom was a leather couch, a metal chair in the corner, a black dresser, and a glass table that belonged in a living room. She noticed small bags of some colorful pills, some weed, and other drugs she couldn't name. The pleasant scent she smelled was coming from a lit candle on the dresser.

"This a trap house?" she asked, making him smirk.

"Nah. It look like it?"

She shrugged. "Kind of. I mean, you got all this stuff back here."

To her knowledge, Projex had only sold weed. Seeing him count up thousands of dollars and wrap rubber bands around them with ease had her seeing him in a different light, one that was making her wet. Projex looked exactly like those types of men she'd read about in urban fiction books. Only, he really lived that life.

Even though he'd touched his first million, Projex was still a hood nigga to his soul. He was a true fucking hustler and got to the money no matter what. He, Bo, and Draco had caught wind that Kordell was now hanging with some niggas from another hood. He had to get in where he fit in, and that was cool with Projex cause the nigga was never welcomed back to their hood.

One of the niggas Kordell was hanging tough with ran a trap house that stayed flooded. Some young cats were supposed to be watching after it earlier that day, but Bo sent some hoes through as a distraction and made their lick way too easy. The stash Projex was counting up was just his. Since Kordell couldn't get touched yet, Projex was bringing hell to anybody he was associated with.

He finished counting before looking up at her. An

easy grin curved his mouth as he took in her appearance. The navy-blue dress clung to her ever-present curves while Chanel runner shoes had replaced her pair of heels. Going from work straight to campus led her to keep a spare change of clothes in the trunk.

"You look pretty," he complimented with ease.

Loriana blushed. "Thank you. What's with all this stuff?"

"A little come-up. Huh," he said, handing her some money.

He just knew she'd question him but was shocked when she simply took the money and tucked it in the pocket of her dress. Loriana liked to ask questions. She never wanted to be out of the know if she didn't have to be. Lately, though, she was learning to just be observant. A lot of things could be found out on her own if she just paid attention.

"Thank you. Is this compensation for stealing my phone?"

"Did I steal it, or did you drop it in my truck?"

She smirked. "You stole it *after* I accidentally left it in your truck."

"That's yo' fault. That mug been ringing off the hook too. Let me find out you out here bopping," he said seriously.

"Yeah, right. I don't have time for any of that."

"Bet not. You gotta stay focused, so I can see you walk that stage."

Her heart swelled at his words. Always the encourager, Projex had rooted for her even when they weren't on good terms when he was locked up.

"I don't have long. Just one more semester."

"That's what's up, ma. I'm proud of you for thuggin' that shit out. I'ma have to get you a nice ass gift. Take you on a trip or something."

He was thinking out loud, and that made Loriana grin.

"I thought you said we don't ever have to speak again? What happened to that?"

He gave her a yeah-right look. "I was mad and agreeing with you. You crazy as hell if you think I was gon' go through with that."

This back-and-forth shit between them was confusing her. One second, she couldn't stand him. The next, he was discussing taking her on a trip. Loriana wasn't sure if he'd caught a mild case of amnesia or had become slightly bipolar, but he needed to stick to what he said. She did too. She was seemingly wrapped up in what he was saying and going with the flow. She hadn't forgotten the words he'd spoken to her that night in his truck. They seemed to be on loop whenever her mind quieted down long enough.

"You never know with you. You keep switching up on how you feel about me."

"It's always love with you, but you be having me fucked-up."

Her lip curled and arms crossed. "I could say the same thing about you. Do you even remember how you talked to me that night?"

His head bobbed forward. "Yeah. And I meant that shit too."

"That's exactly why I said what I said. If loving me makes you second guess how you feel for me, then I'm cool on us. Seriously. I can't deal with this wishy-washy mess."

Her throat clogged a bit as those words left her mouth. She meant them, though. Projex was taking her through an emotional toll for no reason. His misplaced feelings for her had him tripping out, forcing chaos between them whenever they spoke.

"Why you keep trying to cut me off?" Projex questioned. Loriana's eyes stretched.

"Are you serious right now? You literally make me want to smack you, sometimes. Did you not hear anything I said? We're not healthy for each other, and being friends doesn't seem to work for neither of us."

Projex yawned. "You really just talking for no reason, ma. We in this shit for life. I told you that."

"You're really crazy. Let me get my phone so I can go home."

With her hand outstretched, Projex looked her over and smirked. He loved getting on her nerves. The pout on her lips and crease in her forehead was cute to him.

"Come get it," he said, sliding her phone from behind the pillow and into his pocket.

"You're so aggravating. Grow up," she mumbled, stepping into his space.

Reaching her hand into his pocket, Loriana had to dig deep in his joggers for it. He made his dick jump with a smirk on his face before grabbing ahold of her wrist.

"Why you always gotta be difficult with a nigga?"

"Says the person who's doing all of this over *my* phone. Can you let my wrist go?"

"Can I eat your pussy?"

Loriana's eyes closed. Projex knew what he was doing by inviting her in. He had plans to eat her pussy in his ride, but things changed. There was nothing but space and opportunity now. He asked for consent, but by the look of Loriana's pebbled nipples and heavy breaths, he didn't need it. He knew her body better than she did. When she didn't say no, Projex pushed her dress up over her hips and tossed a leg over his shoulder.

"This pussy so fat and pretty," he whispered, inhaling her scent. His entire nose was pressed into her slit.

In one motion, her thong was slid to the side, and his warm tongue explored her pussy lips. Knowing he had just counted money, Projex was trying his best not to touch her with his hands. A pro with it, he flicked his tongue along her clit, making it appear from its hood. Loriana's jaw dropped as he cuffed her ass, stuffing his face further between her legs.

The mission was to make her ass lose all control and beg him to stop. Paying her back for all the shit-talking she'd done on Friday, Projex sucked on her pearl, making her leg buckle.

"Uggh!" she moaned, gripping the back of his head. "I'm about to cum already."

He knew that. It never took long when his mouth was on her. Fucking his face, Loriana sensually rolled her hips, chasing after her orgasm. Her eyes crossed as Projex hit her with a suck and lick combo that had her running.

"Un, un," he mumbled, spanking her ass. "The fuck you going?"

Her heart raced as he kept applying pressure. Checking her flexibility, Projex pushed her leg upward in a leg hold position like she was a dancer. Licking from her pussy to the crack of her ass, he made sure not to miss a drop of her. Projex devoured her and didn't stop until he was good and ready to.

Loriana had both arms wrapped tightly around his head as her body shook. "O-Okay. I can't take anymore," she whined as Projex chuckled between her legs.

Lazily, he rolled his tongue over her folds one more time before easing up. Struggling to catch her breath, Loriana fell directly into his lap once he lowered her leg. Projex held her close as her body twitched with aftershocks of a damn good nut.

"Goddamn," she wheezed, wiping her forehead. "I gotta stay away from you."

"No, you don't. Gimmie a kiss."

Not waiting for her, Projex tongued her down. Loriana was two seconds away from whipping his dick out and riding it, when hard knocks came to the door.

"Who is it!" Projex yelled out.

"Me, nigga. You got company?" Bo asked.

"Yeah. I'll be out there in a second."

Bo told him a'ight, and Projex went back to

kissing on Loriana. His hand eased between her legs, gripping her thigh.

"You got lucky. I was about to fuck the shit out of you."

She giggled against his mouth and slowly stood up. "You be trying to embarrass me. You know I'm loud."

"I love that shit."

Lust clouded his vision as Loriana slid her thong off and adjusted her dress. Dangling them on her index finger, Projex snatched them up and shoved them in his pocket.

"Thanks for the souvenir," he joked, adjusting his dick and standing up. "Let me clean this shit up, and I'll walk you out."

Nodding her head, Loriana went to lean on the dresser. She couldn't wait to get home and soak in the tub. The inside of her thighs was soaked, and she hoped the back of her dress wasn't wet. Five minutes later, they were walking out of the bedroom and into the living room.

"Well, look who it is," Bo said. "What up, Loriana?"

"Hey."

Projex took in the extra person besides Bo's baby mama, Drita, and he grinned. Sitting comfortably with her eyes trained on him, Reign smiled in his direction. Peeping their interaction, Loriana glanced at Projex before her gaze fell onto Reign. She didn't like the look she was giving Projex, but she wouldn't voice that right now.

"Chu' doing in my hood?" Projex questioned her.

"Am I not welcomed?" Reign smirked, easily flirting like always.

Drita spoke up. "Girl, don't listen to Projex. He don't run shit. You gon' introduce us to your friend?"

Bo shook his head and mumbled, "Messy ass. You just heard me say her name, and you know who she is."

"So, nigga. That wasn't an introduction. She in my house."

"And I was just leaving out of it. No need for the pleasantries," Loriana let her know.

Off bat, she could tell Drita was trying to be messy, and Loriana wasn't about to feed into it. Drita tooted her lips out and mugged her as she headed to the door. Reign was her cousin, so she'd already been put on game about Projex and her talking here and there. It was nothing serious but seeing him coming out the back of her house with another woman rubbed her the wrong way. Reign, on the other hand, was cool as a fan. Projex wasn't her nigga to be sweating.

She didn't even sweat the one she was in a relationship with.

"I'ma walk her out right quick and make some moves," Projex let Bo know.

"A'ight. We supposed to be sliding to go bowling and get some tacos later on. You riding?"

Reign smiled and then heard Loriana suck her teeth.

"I'ma see," he let him know.

Projex dropped the bag off at his car before walking her to her ride. Loriana unlocked her doors and almost forgot why she came over there in the first place. Holding her hand out, Projex reached in his pocket to retrieve her cell.

"Thanks. Have a good night," she said, trying to climb in her seat.

Projex gently grabbed her arm. "Damn. Can I get a hug? Fuck you trippin' for now?"

"I'm not tripping. I'm good."

"Gimmie a hug then," he urged, testing her.

Smacking her lips, Loriana gave him a quick hug and pulled away. Projex shook his head. He knew why she was annoyed all of a sudden, but she had no reason to be. He didn't know Reign would be with them when they came back. It didn't matter if he knew or not. Loriana had picked up on the vibes and was ready to go.

"You gon' call me when you get home?"

"No. For what?" Loriana questioned.

"So, we back on that. I thought we just discussed this."

"No. You talked a bunch of bullshit, and I listened. I never said I agreed with you. My mind hasn't changed."

He frowned. "A'ight, bet. You ain't gotta call me, but I know you better answer that mothafucka when I call."

Loriana looked him upside the head. "Or what?"

"Try me and find out. Slide through that bitch and get you evicted for noise disturbance."

"Childish. Don't you need to be in the studio somewhere? Leave me alone." She laughed, unable to stay fully mad at him. He made it hard to do so.

"Don't worry about me. I'm good."

"Mhm. I hear you. You better get back in there to your little friend."

He laughed for real this time. "I should, huh? Don't want her wondering what's taking so long."

Her jaw clenched. "Move," she hissed, trying to shut her door.

"I'm playing." He laughed, easing into her space.

Gripping her chin, Projex licked her lips before kissing them. "Text me when you get home, a'ight."

"Okay."

"Okay, what?"

Loriana giggled. "Boy. I'ma text you when I make it home."

"You better."

"*You* better be safe wherever you're going."

Projex patted his hip where his gun resided. "Always. Can't get caught slipping. I got too much to live for. Life just getting started, ma."

She grinned at his words because life surely was just getting started. Not just for him, but for them both. They'd been down and out long enough. Projex wanted her right by his side to experience it all, but the way they were carrying on, he wasn't sure if Loriana still wanted the same thing. Only time would tell, and he hoped it'd come with more clarity on both of their ends.

"Come on, sis! Take another shot!" Nyree shouted in Loriana's ear.

Her arm was tossed over her shoulder as plastic shot glasses in front of them began to get filled with tequila. It was homecoming weekend at Nyree's school, and Loriana had driven down with Trell and Candace to kick it. This was the last official home-coming they could celebrate before graduating, and Nyree was going all out.

They attended the football game earlier in the day and were now pre-gaming for the actual party being thrown by the Alphas on campus. People from other colleges, their hometown, and even some alumni had come in town to kick it. Loriana was trying to hang, but she knew if she took one more shot, she wouldn't make it to the party. It'd happened to her before during her early college days, causing her to miss out on a few functions.

"I'm good," she slurred a bit. "Give me some water."

Going to the fridge, Nyree grabbed her a water and twisted the cap for her. "Huh. Sit down and sober up because you going to this party."

Thankfully, they had already snapped pictures up. Some of Nyree's homegirls from school were in attendance, as well as a few of her homeboys. One, in particular, was her little boo, Maverick, that she'd been messing around with since freshman year. He attended a college about an hour away and always came in town when his brother was playing. They met at a house party after a football game and had kept in touch since.

Whenever either of them was free, they made time for each other. It was nothing serious, just some casual sex and good conversation, and that's how they liked it. Propping her phone up on the bottle of liquor, Nyree slid her thumb over the bottom of the screen on Instagram, choosing the hands-free option. With Trell playing music on the aux, they'd been jamming all night. *Pussy Talk* by the City Girls was blasting, and Nyree tapped the circle on her screen.

"Boy, this pussy talk Birkin, Gucci, Chanel. Boy, this pussy talk, Louis, Pucci, YSL," Nyree rapped, meaning every word.

Yesterday when they were at the mall, Juice called her while they were out shopping. Their conversation went from what she was doing, her telling him she saw these cute ass Louis Vuitton heels, to racks being deposited into her Zelle app within ten minutes. The money he gave her wasn't hurting his pockets at all. On a daily, Juice was touching so much money. Getting Nyree whatever she wanted was something he looked forward to doing.

From when he first took her shopping to deck her dorm room out, Juice learned one of her love languages—some shit he knew nothing about back then—was receiving gifts. As long as she'd let him, Juice was going to provide them with a bow.

Seductively, Nyree twirled her hips to the beat and snapped her fingers. She was feeling the liquor while putting on a show for her camera that'd soon be a video posted to her close friends. Maverick watched her do her thing before he boldly stepped behind her and gripped her hip. He knew exactly what that pussy talked like and was ready to take her into her room for a quickie before they left.

"Okay! Fuck it up, Ny," Candace cheered, recording her.

Maverick was tall like she preferred, had milk chocolate skin, the prettiest set of white teeth, and long locs that hung past his shoulders. In sync, Nyree backed her ass up on him and stuck her tongue out. Removing his hand from her hip, he let Nyree show out. She popped her back and put that arch in it that made his dick harder.

When she lifted up, Maverick whispered in her ear, making her laugh. Drunk, Nyree shared the video to her story and locked her phone.

"No. We don't have time. We already about to be late," she told Maverick as Loriana lifted her head up from the table.

"Bitch, get uuuup!" Trell yelled as they all tossed back their shots that had been sitting for too long.

"I am," Loriana groaned, finishing her bottle of water. "I gotta pee."

While she ambled to the bathroom, the rest of the crew prepared to leave. In her bedroom mirror, Nyree applied a fresh coat of gloss to her lips. Her beach wave curls with a middle part were still intact and looked cute with her attire for the night. They'd all decided to wear some shade of nude, and the color meshed well against her toffee brown complexion. The one-shoulder tube top and high-slit-wrapped skirt showed nothing but flawlessly oiled skin.

"Who driving?" Maverick asked as she buckled her heel.

"Candace, probably. She decided to be the DD for the weekend."

He nodded his head. "A'ight. Y'all be safe. I'll see you later on."

When he leaned her way for a kiss, Nyree turned her head, so his lips smashed into her cheek. Maverick didn't know what it was, but Nyree didn't like kissing him in the mouth. In her mind, that was much too intimate. It'd take what they were doing to another level to her, and this wasn't that. She was simply having a good time with him.

"Drive safely," she told him, standing to her feet.

Shaking his head, Maverick headed out of her room. She didn't know why he was acting like that when boundaries between them had been set long ago. Just because a little liquor was in their system didn't mean anything. She reserved those special privileges for Juice only and didn't feel bad about it. Kissing Juice always left her breathless and wondering what'd transpire if they elevated their relationship.

Nyree knew that wouldn't happen anytime soon, so instead, she focused on her frame in the mirror. Already standing at five-foot-seven without heels, the nude So Me 100 heels had her towering like the stallion she was. Still slim in the waist but with some meat on her bones, specifically her thighs and ass, Nyree was stacked. She had the body of a track runner and thanked her mama for good genes, walking campus, and working out for her figure.

"Okay, hoes! Let's get ready to go. Somebody go check on Loriana's drunk ass!" Nyree yelled from her bedroom while removing her phone from the charger. Going to the fourth drawer on her dresser, she opened it and pulled out a baggie of pills, placing them inside her purse.

Posing, she took some pictures in her floor-to-ceiling mirror before flipping the camera around. After snapping some selfies, she looked them over bcforc texting four of them to Juice. They'd Face-Timed earlier in the day, and he told her to have fun tonight. She was sure he'd be in town to kick it with her, but apparently, he had other plans. It wasn't a complete lie, but not the entire truth.

Posted up at one of his patna's cribs in the college town, Juice's phone pinged with four attachments from Nyree. His pink tongue rolled over his lips as he swiped through each one, admiring her. The one of her squatting with her pussy damn near winking at him was his favorite, next to the one of her cheesing. Her eyes were sultry, a bit glossed over, and low from all the liquor, and he knew she was feeling good.

Juice hearted his favorite ones and typed out a quick text back.

Juice: *You look good lil' baby*

Nyree couldn't help but blush. Juice swore she was his lil' baby, and she wasn't going to deny it. While Juice had mentioned them being together in a relationship on more than one occasion, Nyree was fine with just being friends. The extra benefits that came with it didn't hurt either. She'd thought about it but knew being anything more would cause distractions, and that's not what she needed right now. Plus, a relationship came with too many demands and certain boundaries. Nyree didn't want to be tied down, period. When she was ready, she promised to be all in. Until then, she was doing her and focusing on school.

Responding with a thank you and a kissy face emoji, she walked out of her bedroom to see everyone ready to go. Loriana was obviously the drunkest as she swayed from side to side. As the designated driver, Candace headed out the door first while Trell helped a grinning Loriana down the steps.

"Bitch, you better make it inside this party I know that," Nyree told her as she sat beside her in the back-seat. Nyree's roommate and some of her friends hopped in another car.

"I am, friend. I promise. Let me just rest my eyes for a second," was Loriana's reply.

With the music blasting, she did just that. The ten-minute drive to the party went by fast and was just what Loriana needed to regain some energy. Now inside the party, she and Nyree turned up like the college girls they were. This was their second to last semester, so it was only right they went out with a bang for the last homecoming weekend.

"Them niggas be looking so fine when they

stroll," Candace semi-yelled in Loriana's ear. It was loud enough for Trell to hear, and he agreed.

"Hell yeah. One of their asses needs to pick me up the way they keep wagging their tongues out."

The girls fell over one another laughing, but Trell was serious. The Ques always got the party hype. Had Loriana not been scared during the Pretty Nasty party she came down to during her freshmen year, she would've let them pick her up too. It was a different time now, and the tall, chocolate Que with a mean swagger in his stroll and long tongue had his eyes glued on her.

"Oh shit," Candace whispered. "He's looking right at you."

Boldly, Loriana stared back. He was shirtless, showing off well-defined, perspired abs that made the heavy gold chain around his neck glisten even more. Loriana couldn't help but gawk over his thick arms. His beard was full, lips juicy, and the purple bucket hat on his head made him look even better.

When she smirked, he moved in on her. While Loriana thought he simply wanted a dance, she was quickly reminded why they were called nasty. Lifting her up with ease, the Que placed his head directly between her legs while Loriana held on for dear life.

"Oh, my gosh, bitch!" Trell squealed.

Loriana's eyes were wide open as she grabbed his hat off his head and placed it on hers. *Nasty Song* by Lil Ru was bumping loudly, making her rotate her hips and enjoy herself. Thankfully, she had on panties, but the thong had done nothing to conceal her goodies. Her entire ass was out as the Que freakily rolled his neck and got hyped up by his bruhs.

"That's my bitch!" Nyree laughed as he lowered her from his shoulders and to her feet slowly.

A bit woozy, Loriana stumbled a bit, but he caught her around the waist. She caught a generous whiff of his cologne and got even dizzier. With them being in a hot ass party, he still smelled good.

"I know that pussy tastes as good as it smells," he whispered huskily in her ear before continuing the stroll with his line.

A chill shot up Loriana's spine as she watched him walk away. She wasn't used to hearing another man besides Projex and Symir talk vulgarly to her like that.

"He got yo' lil coochie wet, huh," Trell said in jest, making her shove him in the chest.

"Boy, no. Move," she laughed. "I hope no one was recording that."

"Why?" Nyree asked. "It's not like you got somebody watching your every move."

"I might. I don't want to be on random people's social media with my legs around some man's head."

Nyree shrugged. "Too late for that, pooh. At least you looked fine as hell up there."

The group of friends laughed, further letting Loriana know there was no use in worrying now. The deed was done. With her buzz coming down, Loriana asked Trell to walk to the bar with her. She had cotton mouth something serious and was dehydrated. Dressed in the themed color for the night, Loriana's corset-style mesh mini dress accentuated her curves. Clear, open-toe mules with chunky heels were on her feet. Thankfully, the heels were easy to walk in because if not, she would've been busted her ass on the slick, tile floor.

What was supposed to be her grabbing a bottle of water turned into Loriana being urged to take another shot with her friends. It was a half one, but she was definitely done for the night. She was an emotional drinker, and before the party was even over, she was FaceTiming Projex while deep in her feelings.

The party had done what it was intended to do, and that was turn them up one last time. While everyone was ready for the after-party, which was being held at a house a few alphas shared, Loriana was ready to go back to Nyree's and be caked up on the phone. Walking out of the building, Loriana huffed in frustration when Projex didn't answer.

"This nigga gone make me slap him," she mumbled.

Her eyes scanned the parking lot in search of the vehicle that was bumping music so loudly, it was literally rattling her nerves. The bass was clear, letting every lyric flow through the speaker with ease.

"Aye, there you go!" some guy called out, walking up on her.

Loriana frowned before realizing it was the Que who had picked her up. "Oh. Hey. What's up?"

"You got my hat still?"

Loriana tensed up. She most definitely put his hat down somewhere. Where at? She couldn't recall.

"I'm sorry. I think I left it at the bar or by the stage."

"It's all good. Put your number in my phone, and we'll call it even."

She smirked. "I don't go here."

"Shit, neither do I."

Just as he was handing her his phone, Projex called back on FaceTime. Without hesitation, she answered in anticipation to see his face.

"You drunk, ma?" Projex chuckled sexily. His

eyes were low as he was super faded in the studio with Ayo.

"I am, and I miss you. Come get me," she whined into the camera, forgetting all about the Que beside her.

"Where you say you put my hat, lil' baby?" he asked, making Loriana jerk her head in his direction.

"I just told you."

"Yeah, but it's probably gone now. Let me get your number, and we're good, though."

"Yo, L-Boogie. Handle yo' business, ma. I'ma hit you later."

Her attention was now back on him. "No. I wanna talk to you." She pouted. The mug on his face let her know he wasn't feeling some nigga all in her face.

"Then talk to me and not them mothafuckas around you. You know I'ont play that."

Sensing Loriana wasn't going to give in to him, the Que walked away. It was his best bet because she wasn't sliding him her digits anyway. Loriana's eyes squinted, trying to peep who was all in the studio, but Projex was sitting somewhere by himself. Nine times out of ten when Ayo had a studio session, he could never just come by himself. He always told a few people to slide through, which in turn led to an entire function.

"You giving niggas your number now?" Projex tried to say jokingly, but Loriana knew him.

"No. Did you see me give him my number?"

"Aye. Don't get smart. I'ont know what you gon' do when we get off this phone."

She rolled her eyes. "Whatever. I wish you were here. I wanna suck your dick so bad."

Projex smirked at his little baby talking that hot shit. "Yeah, you drunk for real, ma. Who driving? Where Nyree at?"

"She right here, why?"

"I need to make sure you get to where y'all going safely. Lemme holla at whoever sober."

Protectively, no matter where she was or the terms of their relationship, Projex was always going to look out for her. He made that promise years ago and meant it. While Loriana tried getting Nyree's attention with Maverick all in her face, Reign had caught Projex attention as she walked up to him. Loriana only caught her hair in the camera and not her face as she bent down to whisper something in Projex's ear. When he smirked and nodded his head with a lick of his lips, Loriana saw red.

"A'ight. Gimmie a minute," Projex told her.

"You got me fucked up!" Loriana shouted, catching the eyes of people walking by.

"Chu' screaming for? Calm yo' ass down."

"No! Cause you got bitches all in your ear, grinning and shit. Wait until I see you."

Coolly, Projex lit a fresh blunt and blew smoke into the camera. "What you gon' do, ma?" When he smirked, Loriana wished she was in his presence.

"Just wait and see stupid ass. You all in your feelings about some dude I don't even know when you stay giving these bitches attention."

"Am I not supposed to?"

His question was spoken so nonchalantly, Loriana was mad she even called him. If no one in this world could piss her off, you better believe Projex could. By simply being himself at that. When she didn't answer, Projex took the initiative to get her off his line.

"Let me call you back."

"No! You better not hang up this phone, Bryshon. I swear to God!"

"Girl," Nyree stressed, walking over to her. "You don't need to be caked up anyway. You see all these niggas out here? Hang up on him."

"Oh my gosh," Loriana stressed.

"Listen to your friend if you want to." Projex chuckled. "Make me do that drive for real."

"You ain't running shit, Projex. Let my girl have her fun. She'll see you when she gets back in town."

With that, Nyree hung up in his face. Had she not, they would've never gotten off the phone until Projex made her hang up on him. He wasn't going to hang up in her face; they had a rule behind that. No matter how annoyed or mad, he never just hung up on her.

"Why would you do that? We were talking," Loriana fussed.

"No. You were whining, and we not doing that tonight. Call that nigga later. We about to hit the after-party."

"I'm not going. You can drop me off at your place."

Night ruined thanks to her being in her feelings, Loriana was ready to get out of her heels and lay it down.

"Nope. Get out them feelings, little baby, and worry about him later. You think he over there pouting about you? No. So, bitch, you don't need to be worried about him. Now, let's go."

Loriana rolled her eyes but knew she was right. It took everything in her not to blow his line down, but long ago, Mhyale had gotten her hip to letting a nigga do him. She hated being in her feelings behind him but wouldn't want it to be over another nigga at all, so she chucked it up and headed to the car.

"Isn't that Juice?" Loriana questioned as the loud

music from earlier became clearer the closer they got to Nyree's car.

Posted up in a heavily tinted, black SRT Durango with the doors open, Juice bobbed his head in the driver's seat to King Von. A bunch of girls was surrounding the truck shaking ass while niggas animatedly rapped the lyrics to *Crazy Story*, wondering who Juice and all his niggas were.

"Yeah, that's him. Ol' scheming ass." Nyree smirked.

To her knowledge, he was back in KC, but of course, a hustler like Juice wouldn't miss out on the type of money being spent tonight, nor did he let Nyree know his every move. He had to keep her on her toes. While she had no idea Juice had been watching her since she walked out of the party, Nyree strutted over to him. The confidence in her walk as she ignored the girl bent over in front of the truck with the headlights directly on her had niggas breaking their stare to focus on her, ogling her being as if she were the only woman to exist.

"I know that's right! Fuck it up, friend!" one girl yelled, hyping her friend up as she bent over, wobbling her ass.

She like, "Von you already know, just put your girl on
fleek"
I'm like cool, I can do that boo
What you want some shoes?
Jimmy Choo, with a handbag too, red or baby blue?
She get to smilin' cause she ain't used to this, 'cause
she ain't used to shit
I'm just laughin', coulda been a pimp the way I move
my lips

"Goddamn. Who that?" Some guy gawked, eyeing Nyree as she strolled by.

When he tried grabbing her hand, Nyree shook him off and kept it pushing. Juice smirked, knowing had she not spotted him, she probably would've given ol' boy some play.

"Hey, y'all," Nyree spoke to Juice's homeboys, who she'd become cool with over the years.

Neeko, Naaz's brother, gave her a head nod. In his hand was a coffee cup filled with something that had him leaning. Mack and Chayse, two SAG members, were taking it light tonight, staying on their toes just in case some shit popped off. They were in a different city, but their guns still bust the same if niggas got out of pocket.

As she invaded his space, Juice studied her. The pictures she sent in their text thread were mediocre compared to the live version of her. Nyree never had to try hard, and that's what he liked. Giving him a smirk, Nyree grabbed the blunt he was puffing on and hit it a few times. Only she had those types of privileges.

Retrieving his blunt from her outstretched hand, Juice looked her over. Warmth filled his chest, knowing that the sly grin on her face was because of him. She was pleased to see him. Then, he thought about the nigga who'd been all in her ear minutes prior. The sensation fizzled but only slightly because Nyree always left a fire burning when near him, which he could never quite extinguish.

"You doing pop-ups now?" Nyree wanted to know.

His presence or behavior wasn't out of the ordinary. Yet, she asked anyway.

"If that's what you wanna call it. Them the shoes you copped?"

She glanced at her feet and stepped back some. "Mhm. You like?"

French painted toes were his favorite. They

looked even better in the seven-hundred-dollar heels wrapped around her ankle.

"They cool."

Nyree playfully rolled her eyes. Juice was too chill. If she liked it, he loved it. Whatever made her happy, he was with. That's all that mattered.

"Boy, whatever. These heels are fire, and my feet are literally on fire, too."

"You and that boy word. Talking to me like I'm one of your homeboys."

"You not?"

Their eyes challenged one another. They both knew what it was and what it could've been. Yet, somewhere in the midst of just kicking it, lines were blurred. Wanting more but not knowing how to move on left them where they were.

"Keep on playin' with me," Juice told her, eyeing a chick who was walking up.

"Hey, Juice," she said in a singsong, flirty manner.

Nyree's head swiveled to the left. A mug easily etched across her face. With no regard to Nyree standing there, she carried on a conversation once Juice hit her with a head nod.

"What's up wit' it."

"I'ma see you later on?"

"Nah. Prolly not. I'ma catch up with you later on, though."

She gave him a pout but accepted his answer. "Okay. You better hit me up, too."

"I gotchu'."

Openly, he watched her and her friends walk away before glancing down at Nyree.

"Baby, the disrespect," Nyree said in full animation. Her skin grew warm, and her heart was beating erratically.

"You getting upset for no reason. Chill out."

"Nigga, don't tell me to chill. What was that? I'ma catch up with you later on," she mocked, causing Chayse, who was close by, to smirk. He peeped the argument about to happen soon as ol' girl walked up.

Not finding humor in the way she was acting, Juice stood from his seat ready to shake the scene. "You doing too much. I'm 'bout to leave."

"Oh. Cause you wanna be Mr. Fucking Friendly and get mad cause I said something, you wanna leave? A'ight, bet."

She spun to stomp away, and Juice grabbed her arm. Pinning her to his chest with a hand firmly on her ass, he pecked her lips.

"Stop that shit. Giving these mothafuckas something to run they mouth about. You know what it is."

"Do I?"

Bullheaded, neither admitted what it was right then and there but knew.

"I'ma slide through later, so stay yo' ass up," he let her know. "You got me?"

Nyree rolled her eyes. "You know I do."

"And I got you. Remember that."

"Whatever. Be safe."

"Always. Aye!" Juice called out to his boys. "Let's shake."

Walking over to her friends, Nyree was stopped a few times by a couple people wanting to know if she was going to be at the afterparty. She let them know she would be, and they headed back to her apartment to freshen up.

"These niggas really be for everybody," Loriana blurted on the drive back. "I'ma start doing me, for real."

"Girl, boo. Like you ain't been on that since your man was locked up," Trell divulged.

"I wasn't on none of that. But wait until I get back to the city. I'm on everything moving."

Candace snickered, knowing her friend was telling lies but let her make it. "I like that energy, Lo.

Let me find out you trying to give Projex a dose of his own medicine."

"The whole fucking cap full," Loriana said as she and Trell high-fived. "You good, Ny?"

Looking up from her phone, clearly detached from the conversation, she uttered, "Huh? Yeah. I'm good. Just seeing what everybody on."

"I don't know what everyone else is on, but my buzz is completely gone. We taking some shots when we get in the house," Trell let them know.

"No, we are not. *You* can take them by yourself. Ain't nobody trying to be in the ER for alcohol poisoning tonight," Candace said.

"Ugh, fine. You hoes is lame!"

They hadn't been in the house for a good twenty minutes, and Trell was back on his level. With the balcony door open, allowing the night breeze to enter the home through the screen, Trell sat out there smoking hookah. Loriana was laid out on the couch, half-asleep, while Candace and Nyree's roommate and friends chilled at the table talking.

Before she could even step foot inside the apartment, Nyree's phone was ringing off the hook. She was used to it, but it had been jumping a lot tonight. Slipping into some leggings, a simple tank top, and some Crocs, Nyree headed out of her bedroom.

Stepping onto the balcony, she grabbed Trell's attention.

"I'm 'bouta go to that red car right there. I'll be right back."

"Okay. I got you."

For the next hour, when her phone pinged, Nyree was out the door. On one occasion, she and Trell left but came right back. When they did, he and the other girls headed to the after-party while Nyree and Loriana stayed behind. Having to make another run, Loriana rode with her while trying to stay awake. When they pulled back into the complex, Nyree had someone waiting on her.

"My bad, girl. I didn't realize what time it was," a girl from her yoga class told her as she met at her passenger window.

"It's cool. Be safe."

As the driver backed out, Nyree's eyes squinted as scintillating headlights headed their way. Backing into a vacant spot, Juice parked and hopped out. Seeing who it was, Loriana headed up the stairs as Nyree waited for him to cross the lot. He approached her with silence while his eyes held a loudness of disapproval in them. In his hand was a bag of food from a local burger spot he fucked with. She grabbed one of the drinks he was carrying and walked ahead of him.

"Lo, you want one of these burgers?" Juice asked her.

"No. I'm good. Thanks, though."

He gave her a head nod and continued removing food from the bag. Inside was Nyree's go-to. A single burger with only mustard, bacon, mayo, and lettuce. They shared a large order of steak fries, contently eating in silence.

While Loriana grabbed her things to shower in the other bathroom, Nyree and Juice went to her room when they were finished eating. Getting comfortable, he slipped off his Royal Jordan 1's, then removed the contents out of his pockets.

"You don't wanna be here or something?" Nyree questioned, not feeling the silent treatment he was hitting her with.

"What I tell you 'bout having mothafuckas pull up to where you lay at?"

She sighed hard and loud.

"Nah. Don't be doing all that. That shit too risky, and y'all the only ones here? You be doing that shit all the time?"

"Not all the time, but sometimes. I can't meet everyone everywhere. It's convenient."

"It's an easy lick. That's what it is."

Walking into her bathroom, Nyree reached under

her sink for the medium-sized jewelry box that held everything but jewels. Inside was a bundle of money, neatly wrapped, and a bag of pills. Stepping back in the room, she held it out for Juice to take.

"Here then. Since I don't know what I'm doing."

"You so damn dramatic. Go put that shit up."

Ignoring her, Juice slipped his shirt and tank top over his head, leaving her to gawk at his back. Intricate, black, tattooed ink of where he grew up was stretched across his sculpted back. It was so detailed, Nyree knew the exact location of where he'd spent his childhood and young adult years. But of course, she wanted to know the background as to why he'd gotten it.

"What made you get this on your back?" she asked one night as they laid up in his bed.

One of her many trips home as a freshman was spent at his place. It was her first and last destination. Straddling his back with only his t-shirt draping her frame, she delivered a much-needed massage. Her finger trailed over one of the apartment buildings etched into his cinnamon-colored flesh. Nyree was working kinks out of his body that he'd unintentionally gotten and would all over again from eating her pussy. She kept running, so he chased her, placing himself and her in the most strenuous positions until she came in his mouth. The chase was worth it.

"I love my hood," Juice answered, vocal cords thick with sleepiness.

"That much to get it tattooed on your entire back?"

Her voice raised some, full of wonderment.

"Yeah. Them my people. My family. I'll do whatever for em' cause the love always gets returned. When I was hustling young as fuck, I'm talking ten, eleven years old, folks looked out for me. I always had a place to rest my head if I got locked out, something hot to eat, a way to make money. When I started seeing some real cash, I remembered who was always there for me and been looking out since."

Though Juice was slanging drugs through his hood and surrounding areas, he put people in positions to get to the money, too. In his eyes, everyone could eat if there was food out there. His family, like others in their neighborhood, struggled. It was no secret. They resided in the slums. Poverty-stricken families went without on a daily basis. As a community, they did what they could with what they had and looked out for one another.

When Juice was up, he literally put his hood on

his back. Even when he wasn't, his positive outlook on life kept his people inspired and motivated to get on their shit like he was. He had siblings to care for and a mama who barely did, so Juice never half-stepped. Pressure behind making it out of the trenches had been applied since he knew the value of a dollar and the power behind the moves he made.

Nyree knew he was a certified SAG member, but she didn't know the details. Of course, she wouldn't, seeing as though that type of information was never discussed. Through the grapevine, she'd heard how good of a guy Juice was, how he took care of his people and was one of the biggest hustlers with an even bigger heart.

"Wait. How are old are you, again? Just twenty-three, right?"

"Yeah. Why?"

"It just seems like you have a lot of people depending on you, and you're young. I know that can be stressful."

Nyree didn't know the half.

"Yeah, but shit, it's life. That mothafucka gon' stress you out regardless, so why not thug through it? You gon' either make a way out of no way or find yourself in the same position you asked God to get you out of but ain't put no action behind it."

Her hands stopped moving. Moments like this made her wonder if all men were as mature and bossed up as Juice was. Though only four years older than she was, Nyree saw him as being wise beyond his years. Having to grow up in the conditions he had, Juice had no choice but to conform.

"Nyree," Juice called out when she hadn't moved an inch.

"What? Take this shit back and have somebody else do it."

"You fishing for something to fuss about, and I ain't even on that tonight. Why, when I tell you something, you can't just listen? Whatever I'm saying is for the betterment of your safety. You think these pill heads care that you cool, got a pretty face, and carrying heat on you?"

The gun on her waist hadn't been removed yet, but she kept it close by. Especially when making plays. She hadn't had to use it yet but never wanted to be caught slipping.

"No," she mumbled.

"Exactly. So, move like you got something to lose, instead of sitting here pouting 'cause a nigga gives a fuck about you. Now, go put that shit up and come here so I can rub your lil' ugly feet."

Grinning, she rolled her eyes. "My feet are not ugly. You don't want the money I made?"

"Nah. Keep it. That's yours."

Nyree went back into her bathroom and put the pills away before counting the money. She'd made a nice little come-up since Thursday. Juice giving her money wasn't new. Him telling her to keep all the profit was, though. Instead of questioning it, Nyree hopped in the shower. Five minutes later, Juice was pulling the shower curtain back and getting in with her.

Turning to face him with her breasts pressed against his chest, an unspeakable expression washed over Nyree's face. She wanted to say something but couldn't muster up the words. His sleepy eyes burned into hers as she cupped his face in her hands. His head lowered, placing a deep kiss on her lips, her chin, and lastly, her neck.

"Why you gotta look at a nigga like that?"

"Like what?" she questioned in a breathy manner.

"Like I mean the world to you. Like you wanna tell me your deepest secrets and shit."

Her heart flipped in her chest. "Because you do, and I don't have no secrets to tell."

Juice pulled her closer. "We all got secrets, baby. Some ain't worth keeping to ourselves."

Nyree had no response. She let the silence settle between them before lust took over. With her hands around his neck, Juice lifted her with ease with one hand while the other assisted in guided his dick into her wetness. The gasp Nyree let out always made his dick harder. His intrusion always caught her by surprise.

"Oooh, right there," Nyree moaned softly as he stroked her in an unrushed manner.

Juice always joked that she was fun-sized compared to him, but he loved that shit. Nyree was the perfect kind of petite with some weight on her that made it easy for him to bounce her atop his meaty dick.

Placing her back against the wall, Juice went deeper, hitting a spot that had her screaming his name out.

"Uuuugh! Jovani!"

"Jovani, what huh?" He grunted, snaking his tongue across her neck before sucking on it. He left no room between them or any for her to run.

"Y-You gon' make me cum!"

"I want you to cum all over this dick."

Nyree didn't have to be told twice. She was going to do that anyway. With the combination of his commanding tone, hand around her neck, and dick stretching her out, she had no choice but to release. Her legs trembled as he whispered, "Good girl," in her ear, causing the flood gates to open even more.

That was always the goal, his number one mission right now, and he'd passed it. Now, it was time to start all over from the beginning. By the time he was finished with her, Juice was going to make sure her ass slept like a baby. His baby because she deserved that shit.

Chapter Seven

Shamari wasn't accustomed to losing... at anything.

Whatever skill he wanted to learn, he studied it, practiced, and became a master at it. You only become great at and of something when you put the work behind it every day. Even when he felt like he was about to lose, he trained his mind to push harder, swing quicker, keep his balance, and duck at his opponent. He kept fighting no matter what.

The crowded gym was packed with people. Mostly filled with men who were there to watch the fight and make bets. Half the money was on Shamari. Sighs of frustration buzzed around the room as Shamari's opponent took a hard hit to the ribs.

"Gotdamn, Juke!" a man with his money on

Shamari yelled out. "Gon' break that nigga's fuckin' ribs. Get em' some milk!"

Boisterous laughter filled the air, along with spat curse words and shouts for Kane to get his shit together. A lot of money was on this fight, and with it being the last of the night, niggas were riled up. Anxiously, men stood around the ring, watching them go blow for blow. Women stood nearby, somewhat interested in the fight but not as nearly as interested in them trying to be seen. For the love of attention, they were scantily dressed with their hair done up and high heels on while having to endure the dense musty atmosphere, sticky heat, and ultra-rowdiness.

Zoned out in his head with chants of his own, Shamari stayed focused. One distraction and he knew it'd be over. This had been one of his toughest fights in a while. Up for the challenge as always, he ducked a few swings Kane sent his way. He coined the nickname Juke for being swift on his feet, always misleading his opponent. Tapping into another side of himself, Shamari heard his dad's voice loud and clear.

Physically, Neil wasn't outside the ring coaching him. He'd called right before Shamari came out of the locker room and pissed him off. He liked to keep a clear head before a fight, but that hadn't been the case tonight.

"You think some illegal fighting gon' take care of a baby? Ain't no money in that, son."

Shamari threw a vicious punch, landing it along Kane's chin. His head jerked as he stumbled a bit. The mention of his unborn brought out the beast in him.

"Your best bet would be to move to Miami and get a real job in the family business. It's a guaranteed check. Ask your brother."

Shamari wasn't asking Symir shit. He had nothing against him, but he was his own man. He'd already helped out with Royal Motors here in KC. He didn't see the point in moving just because his dad wanted to expand. That was on him. As much money as they were bringing in, Shamari was sure he could hire as many employees as he needed. He'd better because he wasn't moving to Miami. The conversation was over before it even began.

"I ain't trying to talk about this shit right now. I'm 'bouta get out in the ring. I'll hit you later."

That was only part of the conversation. Neil had tried his best to convince his son that there was better out there. That running the family business would set him up for life. It sounded good, just not coming from Neil. He'd down-talked Shamari's decisions to risk his life in the ring, hardly supported him, and about had a stroke when he found out he had a child on the way.

Just the thought of his dad not being there for him when he and Joi's child was born fueled his anger even more. Jaw clenched, Shamari delivered swift combo's in Kane's direction, backing him into a corner. Not letting up, blood leaked from Kane's mouth as his body took a beating.

"That's enough!" a woman shouted, cringing at the sight before her.

It was never enough until Shamari physically saw the fight vanish from his opps' face. Crouched over, Kane's exhausted limbs took weak swings at Shamari's legs. The fight was clearly over, but until Kane was completely down on the ground, Shamari wasn't letting up.

"You niggas better run me my mothafuckin' money," a guy spoke to his partners as the ref pushed Shamari away from Kane.

Onlookers who had watched Kane fight for years were in disbelief, some even disappointed. Shamari was considered the new kid on the block. He didn't move like one, though. Talking too much about how lethal his hands were wasn't his thing; he let them speak for him. The proof had been sealed tonight as he huffed and stared out into the rowdy crowd who was chanting his name and showering him with praises. Not everyone was on his side, though.

"And just like that, ladies and gentlemen, the winner of the night's last fight goes to Juke!" the paid announcer called out into the mic.

"That's what the fuck I'm talkin' 'bout, my boy!" Shamari's homeboy, Draymo, shouted.

Shamari's chest heaved as he went to dap up Kane. It was a damn good and fair fight. The two simply gave each other head nods of respect, too out of breath to speak. Climbing out of the ring, Shamari was greeted by pats on the back and the type of support from strangers he wished he received from his dad. It was all good, though, because proving him wrong would be the sweetest victory.

His coach, Kit Steel, had a proud smile on his face as he approached him. "How you feeling?"

"Good. Real fucking good."

"As you should. That fight just got you a nice check, youngin'. Get cleaned up and come rap with a few folks here to talk business. You got time, right?"

Shamari nodded his head. "Yeah. I got a few minutes."

"A'ight. We'll be by the front."

Heading to the locker room, Shamari caught the glares of envious niggas who were clearly on Kane's team, but that's all they gave. It wasn't as if he cheated his way into another win, so the animosity was for no reason. Brushing them off, Shamari located his locker, grabbed his bag out, and changed into a jogging suit after wiping a few cuts and bruises down. With his duffle bag on his shoulder and a Gatorade in his hand, he headed for the door, ready to get his earnings.

"Aye, cuz."

Knowing Draymo would never address him like that, Shamari frowned and looked to his right at the person who was trying to get his attention. Knowing exactly who Projex was, his defensive posture didn't waver, but his face relaxed some.

"What's up?"

"Good fight. I hope you ready to throw hands like that behind my sister and the baby she's carrying."

"Without question, my nigga. I've been trying to have a talk with you for a minute. Let you know what type of time I'm on with Joi and our child. I love and respect her, so I hope it ain't no tension behind that cause it's whatever, for real."

Projex smirked. "Nigga, you talking real tough."

"Nah. I'm just letting you know."

"Well, know this," Projex said, stepping in his

direction so he could hear him fully. "I don't play when it comes to Joi. Never have. You seem like a cool dude, but I don't give a fuck about being cool if you hurt her, put her in some bullshit with these hoes out here, or bring her any unwanted stress while she pregnant. As long as you handling your responsibilities as a man, we good. It won't ever be static between us. I ain't the type of nigga you wanna try to fight. Feel me?"

Shamari's nostril's flared, not liking how Projex was trying to lil' boy him. "You got a problem with me being with your sister?"

"My problems get solved. You'd know if there was a problem, cuz."

"I mean, I feel like there is. I don't know if the beef you got with my brother is fueling that, but me and Joi ain't got shit to do with that."

Projex's top lip curled. "Who yo' brother?"

"Symir."

Playing it cool, Projex kept his poker face on after hearing his name. *Ain't no way this bitch been lying like this.* He'd never call Loriana out of her name, but that was the first thought to go through his head. Putting two and two together, Projex realized Shamari was the link connecting them all. That was how Loriana knew about Joi's pregnancy, and now he needed to find out why she had failed to mention it to him. Homegirl hadn't made a peep.

"I ain't beefing with yo' punk-ass brother. You can tell him I said that shit, too, if that nigga feel some type of way."

It was Shamari's turn to smirk. "Yeah, a'ight. I'll let him know. What was your name again, cuz?"

Humored by the youngin's sarcasm, Projex replied, "Uncle Projex, nigga."

Shamari couldn't help but laugh. "Yeah, I guess you are. Shit's crazy."

"As a mothafucka. Be safe out here. You got hands, but niggas like to shoot when they too pussy to fight. Don't get caught lacking."

Shamari's head bobbed, already knowing. That's why he had his gun tucked in the waistband of his joggers. Niggas out here were either mad, broke, or both and would do whatever to ruin the next man's life. It was sad, but the truth.

When Projex walked off, Shamari stood where he was for a few seconds before heading toward the front. While Joi had wanted them to sit down and talk once she arranged for them to meet, Projex had other plans. He was tired of her dancing around the subject of who his niece or nephew's daddy was, so he did a little research. Obviously not enough, seeing as though he didn't know Symir was his brother.

Projex couldn't believe it. The one nigga he ever felt some animosity towards behind the first woman he loved was going to be an uncle to his sister's baby.

"I'll beat that nigga's ass," Projex mumbled, hopping in his truck. "He fucked my girl and got his lil' bro on my sister? Yeah, niggas is out they mind."

He had no real beef with Symir yet, and for his sake, it'd better stay that way.

Tucked away in her office, Loriana grinned at the screen of her iMac. She should've been finishing up an assignment for class, but instead, her eyes were glued to the YouTube tab. On it was an interview one of their artists had recently done, and she couldn't have been prouder. While her job description didn't necessarily require her to assist in interview etiquette, she didn't mind helping out where she saw the need. Plus, Dre was from where she grew up. Seeing him flourish and make it in an industry that he always dreamt of being in made her proud.

"Knock, knock."

Peeking around her screen, pinched brows dented her face. "What're you doing here?"

"Dang. That's the greeting I get?" Symir questioned with a chuckle.

In his hand were a dozen roses and a noticeable gift bag from BVLGARI. His pop-up was unexpected, but Loriana always appreciated them. Standing from her chair, she gave him a smile as he kissed her cheek.

"Sorry. You normally text or call me if you're stopping by. Thank you. I love these," she gushed, inhaling the roses.

Symir placed them along the empty spot on her desk and pulled her into his embrace. With him working what seemed like overtime times two, he missed her. The disconnect between them was evident, and that's why he was there.

There was nothing more pleasing than a good-smelling man. Symir smelled heavenly as her face was planted into his firm chest. The white button-down, dark grey slacks, and black dress shoes were his attire for the day. His close-cut beard tickled her as he kissed her cheek again while rubbing up and down her back.

"You're welcome. How's your day been?"

Loriana broke their embrace. "Boring. I haven't

had much to do today, which is surprising. So, I know the rest of the week will be swamped."

"Perfect timing then. Let me take you to lunch," Symir told her.

For a beat, Loriana hesitated but didn't know why. Actually, she knew exactly why but didn't want to admit it to herself. Having lunch with a friend was harmless. Only Symir hadn't quite grasped that that's what they were. Instead of making a fuss about why she couldn't go, Loriana locked her computer, grabbed her purse, and removed her jacket from the coat rack it was hanging from. The temperature was in the low sixties for early November, yet the sun still provided a certain amount of warmth to not need a full-blown coat.

Symir eyed her lustfully and licked his lips. "Or we could stay here, and you be my lunch."

Loriana blushed but forced herself not to giggle. Sometimes, the things he said could be so corny, but she liked it. He was always himself with her no matter what. The form-fitting burgundy sweater dress had a scoop-neck, showing off just a bit of cleavage while outlining her curves to a T and stopped right below her kneecaps. On her feet were a black pair of knee-high boots that color-coordinated with her purse of the day.

"If my stomach hadn't just growled, I'd take you up on that offer."

"Faking," Symir called her bluff as he let her walk ahead of him. "You too scary for that."

Only if he knew she'd fantasized about getting fucked in her office, with a hand over her mouth while trying not to get caught. In her imagination, Symir was never the one delivering the dick, though. It was the only other man who she was never scared to get nasty with and for.

"Right." She smiled and hopped on the elevator. "Where are you taking me for lunch?"

"What you got a taste for? I'm good with whatever besides seafood. After being in Miami for them days, I ain't even trying to smell any."

"Why ask then tell me what *you* don't want? Maybe I wanted some crab legs and shrimp."

He ran a hand over his waves. "If that's what you want, we can get that."

"I was joking. We can go somewhere quick. I forgot I have a meeting at two-fifteen."

Symir looked down at his watch as the elevator opened. "It's only twelve-thirty. You in a rush to get away from me like you don't miss me."

"I do, but whose fault is that?"

"No ones. We both have lives, but I feel like I'm

the only one putting in the effort to spend time with you."

Loriana rolled her eyes as they approached his truck. If she knew he was going to be doing all this whining, she would've declined his offer.

"So, us going out to lunch, talking on the phone, and spending time when my schedule allows me isn't effort?"

Symir sighed and opened the passenger door for her to climb inside. "It is, baby. All I'm saying is it seemed like you were trying to rush our lunch date. You don't miss me?"

Navigating between her legs, Symir gripped her bare thighs as her dress rode up them. As her breathing hitched, Loriana shivered as his lips grazed her neck. Feather soft kisses decorated her skin, causing her to release a moan.

"Mm, I do. B-But… we can't do this out here," she said, weakly pushing him back some.

Symir was so fine, with his dark skin and perfect smile. His genetic makeup was ridiculous and flaw-less. Regardless of looks and the way he'd easily made her center drip, Loriana was not about to indulge in anything sexual in broad daylight. Espe-cially not right out front of her job.

Placing her feet inside the vehicle, Symir shut her

door and walked smoothly around to the driver's side. Once inside, he started the ignition, cranked the heat up some, and sat there.

"Loriana. Let me ask you something," he said, causing her to slowly glance his way.

His tone of voice rubbed her the wrong way. She swallowed hard with anticipation of what he had to say, pestering her nerves.

"Do you love me?"

"Of course, I love you."

He chuckled lowly. "You know, something told me that'd be your answer." He looked at her in the eyes. "Do you really love a nigga, or am I just taking up space in your life?"

"Where is this even coming from?"

"It's just a question, baby."

"Yes, I love you. You know that. I know sometimes it may seem like I don't, but I'll do better. You mean a lot to me, and I don't want you to ever feel like you're just occupying space for no reason. I want you here."

She grabbed ahold of his hand for extra reassurance.

"I want you here too. Forever. I see us building a life together, starting a family, passing down wealth to our children and generations to come. My pops asked about you when I was just there, and he's ready for some grandkids."

Loriana wanted to pull her hand out of his grasp so badly, she cringed on the inside. How them going to grab a bite to eat pivoted into a conversation discussing kids was beyond her.

"Well, thank goodness Joi is due soon." Her chuckle came out dryly, but he hadn't caught on.

"One more won't hurt. You still want kids, right?"

Her head bobbed. "Yes, one day. Not right now."

They had discussed the topic of having kids after Loriana found out Shamari was Joi's baby daddy. There was no mention of them specifically sharing a child, but clearly, the wires had been crossed.

"Right, right. You're still young. Maybe a wedding first, then a baby. Gotta go in order knowing you."

Loriana gave him a tightlipped smile. "Yeah. Marriage first doesn't sound bad."

"That's what I was thinking, too. We're both still in our twenties, so it's time. I was just trying to see where your mind was at. If we were on the same page."

"For the most part, we are. These are serious subjects, and I don't take either lightly."

With her parents having been divorced, seeing

Akira have a baby with a married man, and couples openly cheat on one another, Loriana was good for a while on all that. Her sole priority right now was herself. School and work were all she had time or patience for. This conversation alone was draining her and making her make a mental reminder to go missing on Symir for a few days.

"Neither do I. That's why I had to ask if you loved me. I knew you did, but hearing you say it sounds better."

He grinned her way, and Loriana plastered the fakest smile. She did love him; that wasn't a lie. She just couldn't love him the way he deserved. Her heart belonged to Projex. He'd captured it years ago and held that mothafucka captive. There was no key to unlock and unleash it to another man.

"Your birthday around the corner, too," he acknowledged out the blue. "You haven't mentioned doing anything yet."

"I know. I'll probably just do something simple. Have Mhy plan a birthday dinner or something. Between classes and work, I don't have time to take a trip."

If she wanted to graduate with her prospected class, Loriana had to stick to the script. School, work, home. Maybe a bit of networking in between the week and on the weekends, but besides that, her schedule was jam-tight.

"I know. We'll save the big trip for when you cross that stage. Tell your cousin to put together something nice for you. I'm sure people will come out."

"Oh, they will." Loriana laughed.

Her friends loved her and wouldn't miss an opportunity to turn up. She'd be twenty-two, the youngest in their group of friends.

"Let me know where at, and I'll make sure you get reservations while Mhyale sends invites."

Loriana nodded her head, liking the idea already. Something classy and intimate with her closest friends and family this year, and next year she'd do it big. The only issue was if she wanted to have both Symir and Projex in the same room. She wasn't going to not invite him but quickly thought to leave the guest list up to Mhyale. She'd leave the task of inviting him up to her.

Chapter Eight

Birthdays hadn't been the same since her mother passed. On the night before and mornings of her special day, Loriana always anticipated a gift from Linette. She always tried to figure out what she'd gotten her but never could. While it was never about the gift, Loriana knew it made her mama happy to see a smile on her daughter's face. One year the only thing she'd gotten was a homemade strawberry cake, but it was the best cake she'd ever eaten and shared with her favorite person.

On her birthday four years ago, Linette purchased her a citrine heart-shaped pendant linked to a gold chain. Ironically, the color of her birthstone just so happened to be her favorite color —or a hue of it. To this day, Loriana still wore her necklace along with the iced-out one Projex had gifted her.

She promised to not let her mom not being here dampen her mood. Instead, Loriana thanked God for the years they shared. The first birthday without her was hard. Every first of something without her mother's presence crippled Loriana. Slowly but surely, she was able to do things in her absence without feeling like she was suffocating. Today would be no different.

After an early morning hair appointment, Loriana was primmed and pampered, thanks to Symir. He'd booked her a spa treatment earlier in the week, had stylists come out with designer clothes for her to choose from, and had lunch delivered to her while she was under the dryer. While she appreciated him, Loriana thought it was too much. People going out of their way for her still overwhelmed her.

It didn't matter, though, because she was loved, and Mhyale made sure she felt every bit of it at her dinner party. Taking her duties as the event planner seriously, Mhyale didn't skip a beat. Knowing her cousin asked for something small at her favorite restaurant, Mhyale wasn't having that.

"Mhy," Loriana whined as she stepped inside the private room in the restaurant. "I told you something little. Why you go and do all this?"

"We don't do nothing lil' around here, boo. Everything big." Mhy smiled as she recorded her.

Right by her side was Symir with an even bigger grin on his face. Seeing her happy was all that mattered. Thanks to the manager of *Seasoned*, Mhyale was able to hire a friend of hers to come in and decorate the room. This was on a much smaller scale than the parties Kema was used to planning, but her creative touch didn't waver.

Orange, white, cream, and gold balloons in different sizes were blown up to form an arch. Happy Birthday, Loriana was written in orange cursive along a cream backdrop, while the table was set in the same color scheme. When Loriana told her she wanted a dinner and that Symir was footing the bill, Mhyale wasted no time jumping into event planner mode.

Tears of happiness settled in her eyes as she glanced around the room. The two rectangular tables comfortably sat fourteen people, leaving an aisle in the middle to walk down. A gift table had already been filled with bags, making her poke her lip out. When she gave Mhyale her short list of people she thought may come out and celebrate with her, Loriana was sure at least half of them wouldn't show. She had to have a bit more faith in those who loved her because almost every seat was filled.

"You like it?" Symir whispered in her ear, and she nodded before turning to face him.

"I do. Thank you. You too, Mhy. I can't believe this."

"Well, girl, believe it and enjoy. You only turn twenty-two once."

Making her way around the room, Loriana hugged and thanked everyone for showing up. A few of her cousins were in attendance, as well as some of her co-workers that she spoke to outside of work. One of Symir's friends and his wife waved her over, giving warm wishes while her dad Greg, Elana, and Ethan sat at the opposite table. Of course, Aunt Peaches popped out for her niece while Nyree, Candace, Trell, and Moo showed up as well.

Who she wasn't expecting to see was Shamari. He was sitting alongside Joi, who looked so pretty pregnant. Beside her was Ms. Joseline, who had a smile on her face. Loriana was like a daughter to her, and when Mhyale hit Joi up about the dinner, she, of course, told her that her mama was invited.

"You look so pretty, sis." Joi grinned as they hugged. "This dress is fire."

"Thank you. Look at my lil' baby poking out."

Loriana rubbed her visible six-month stomach, and her heart melted. Regardless of who her child's father was, Loriana would never treat her some type of way. Joi was her little sister no matter what. Saying hi to Shamari with a quick hug and thank you, Loriana hugged Ms. Joseline. As always, her hugs felt like home.

"Happy birthday, sweetie. You look gorgeous as always."

Loriana blushed. "Thank you. I'm glad you could make it. I know it was short notice."

"Of course. Juanita sends her love. You know she was hot she couldn't come show her face."

They chuckled at that. Projex's grandma loved Loriana and had called to send her love. She was out of town on a girl's trip but made sure to let her know to come and see her when she was back in town. Their relationship had gotten a little rocky when Projex was in prison, but they were fine now. After she'd broken his heart, Projex didn't want anyone in his family dealing with her. If she cut him off, he was cutting her off too— family, friends, and all. He didn't give a fuck. Thankfully, Ms. Juanita came around because Loriana had some rough days that she prayed her through.

"Niece, I know you see me!" Peaches yelled from across the room.

Loriana's eyes darted to find Mhyale. They made contact, and Mhy shook her head in annoyance.

"I swear she better not act a fool tonight," Mhy whispered in Naaz's ear.

He rubbed her thigh to calm her down. "She good, Mhy-Mhy. Let her kick it."

"No, because then she gon' start showing out. This is not about her."

"If she does, I'll walk her outside, a'ight?"

Mhyale sighed heavily but agreed. "Fine."

They'd just gotten there, and already Peaches was lit. Mhyale didn't know what she'd been sipping on before they picked her up, but clearly, it had her on her level already. Before she could make her way over to her auntie, Loriana's feet came to a halt as Laurent and Maliya entered the room. In each of their hands were large gift bags.

"Oh, my gosh! I thought you were out of town," she squealed, rushing over to them.

Maliya hugged her first and smiled. "We were, but of course, we couldn't miss your dinner. Happy birthday, boo."

"Thank you! I can't believe Mr. *Sis, my schedule too packed*, came home for me," Loriana laughed.

"You know I couldn't miss this, or I'd never hear the end of."

"I'm glad you know." She chuckled. "The gift table is over there."

"A'ight. Why yo' auntie looking at me like that?" Laurent questioned with humor as their focus shifted to Peaches.

Loriana snorted on a laugh. Peaches was staring him the fuck down and didn't care about who saw her. "Please excuse her. She's tipsy already, and you're famous."

"I ain't nobody special. I'm just a street nigga who happens to sing and rap," Laurent replied humbly.

Loriana waved him off. "You are special, so stop. Y'all can sit wherever there's space."

Letting her walk ahead, Laurent pulled out Maliya's chair for her. Venturing to another section of the room before her feet began to hurt, Loriana chatted with her dad, stepmom, and brother before dragging Nyree to the restroom with her. She'd been on go for the last couple of hours and needed to relieve her bladder.

"This dress so short, I almost didn't have to lift it," Loriana said, coming out of the stall to wash her hands.

"It's cute as hell, though, and got you looking real thick, honey."

Always her hype man, Nyree coached her through FaceTime on what outfit to wear. The patterned sequin dress matched the decorations of the party to a T. With the sleeves long, her upper back exposed, and caramel thighs on display, Loriana was killing it. Moo had hooked her up with a long blunt-cut black wig that looked to have grown from her scalp. The gold YSL heels set off the entire ensemble.

She stepped out of her comfort zone with this outfit and had been doing that more than often. Nyree loved to see it. Loriana dried her hands, applied some lotion, then glossed her lips.

"So," Nyree began, "you already know what I'm about to ask you."

"I know. That's why I made you come to the restroom with me."

They snickered, and Loriana playfully rolled her eyes.

"I know Mhy invited him. He better not act like that."

Loriana shrugged. "If he does, oh well. I guess I really know where we stand if he doesn't show up."

Her shrug was a nonchalant one, but Nyree knew better. If Projex didn't show his face, Loriana's feelings would for sure be hurt. If nothing else in this world pissed her off, it was someone who she considered close to her, acting as if her birthday meant nothing.

"You don't care about Symir people being here too?"

"Nope. I mean, what can I do at this point? He's going to have to find out anyway."

Nyree nodded her head as they headed out of the restroom. "You're right," she murmured, fixing a strand of her hair.

When they bent the corner, heading to the back, Loriana stopped walking, causing Nyree to bump into her. Greeting her with his handsome grin that had her fixated on him, Projex sauntered her way. As if he had the cheat code to what'd she be wearing for the night, Projex matched her fly.

A black button-down was slightly open at the top, showcasing heavy gold chains around his neck. Distressed black jeans fit perfectly with a pair of burnt orange Off the Grid Gucci sneakers, while a gold Cuban link bracelet weighed his wrist down. Without effort, he captured the salacious stares from the array of women in eyesight. As many times as she'd seen him since he'd cut his hair, Loriana was still getting used to his waves. They were fucking sickening and held the deepest ripples, while his lineup was razor-sharp.

Loriana stood in awe of his presence, almost missing the gang of niggas he'd brought along with him. Well, not a gang, but his gang.

"Birthday girl," Projex said with a smirk and lick of his lips. "Happy birthday, ma. You look fine as fuck."

His hug wasn't one that showed he hadn't been thinking of her all day. She'd waited around since her eyes opened to see his name pop up on her phone, wishing her a good day, but it never did. Projex had to let her mind wander. Popping up late at her dinner was how he chose to make his entrance. Of course, he came with a gift in hand. The others she'd receive later on.

Engulfed in him, Loriana's pussy thumped as they shared a hug. She didn't get this feeling when she and Symir embraced, and that alone should've let her know what was up. If the nigga doesn't make your pussy palpitate when y'all hug, he isn't the one for you. When they released one another, Projex dragged his index and thumb over a piece of her hair.

"I like this. You colored your hair?"

She snickered. "No. It's a wig."

He frowned, examining her forehead with a slight squint of his eyes. "This shit looks like yours. That's crazy."

"I know, right. Moo got your girl right on together. You're late and brought extra people with you."

Peeping who was with him, Loriana smiled while seeing Bo, Sneaks, and Ayo. They'd stepped out dressed nicely and smelling even better. They all told her happy birthday before she thanked them. Nervousness settled in the pit of Loriana's stomach as Projex tried to walk toward the back.

Immediately, he peeped her hesitance. "What's good?"

"Um. There's someone here I think you should know about."

"That lame nigga?"

She nodded her head yes and then hurriedly shook it no. "I'm not calling him lame."

Projex chuckled. "Shouldn't be calling that nigga at all, but I'ma let you make it cause it's your birthday. Anything else?"

He was testing her. Joi and his mama had already let him know they'd be attending tonight's festivities. So, naturally, Projex knew Shamari would more than likely be there as well. He wanted to hear it from Loriana, though. She'd been lying long enough.

"Yeah, he's Shamari's brother."

"I know."

Casually, Shamari had let Joi know he'd met Projex at his fight. She played it cool, but when he went to shower, she hurriedly called Loriana. They both were relieved that it hadn't turned into them fighting.

"You know? Okay, okay. Good. That means you'll be on your best behavior then?" Loriana asked in a hopeful tone.

Leaning toward her, Projex kissed her cheek. "What's that?"

She should've known better. Releasing a sigh, she headed back to her dinner with the guys following behind her. Projex spoke to his mama, sister, Greg, and his family, before slapping hands with Laurent.

"My nigga. What's good?" Projex greeted.

"Shit. I can't call it. You sure you supposed to be here?" Laurent said in jest.

Projex hit him with a yeah right smirk. "I was gon' be in this bitch if she invited me or not."

"Cuz looking like he ain't feeling your presence."

With a head nod in Symir's direction, Projex diverted his gaze. He and Loriana looked to be in a heated argument right outside the double doors of the room. His eyes stayed glued on her as her hands moved animatedly and annoyance crossed her face. Projex's jaw clenched when she tried to walk away, and Symir grabbed her hand. It wasn't aggressive, but Projex didn't care. He was ready to turn her birthday dinner into a crime scene in three seconds. He went to walk out there and check him, but Laurent stopped him.

"Nah. That ain't yo' business. Not right now, at least. Sis, good. Look."

Walking back inside the room, Loriana was adjusting her dress before she took a seat at the table. The annoyed expression was still present, but she ultimately grinned when Trell whispered something in her ear. In his true fashion, he was talking shit about both of Loriana's men being in attendance.

"She better be, or I was gon' ruin this entire thing."

"Projex!" Joseline called him, noticing his mean mug. "Come here real quick."

The tension in the room lessened as food was ordered and conversations carried on. For the remainder of the night, a smile was present on Loriana's face. It felt good to enjoy her special day after being swamped with no time to herself. As the evening winded down, one of the waitresses rolled her cake out with lit candles atop it. Like every other detail of her dinner, the two-tier cake was made up of white icing and adorned by orange and gold edible flowers.

"You went all out, huh?" Loriana cheese, facing Mhy, who was already smiling.

"Of course I did. I mean, I am the best big cousin ever."

"Girl, boo. We know y'all cousins," Trell voiced, making the room laugh.

With ease, they harmonized as they sang the Stevie Wonder version of *Happy Birthday* after the regular song. While blowing out the flames, Loriana briefly closed her eyes and made a wish. It was a quick one but worth it.

"What you wish for?" Nyree asked jokingly.

"I can't tell you, or it won't happen."

"Tell me. I'll keep it between us," Projex told her.

The intense stare he was giving her made her chest heave some. He had been saying little slick comments to her all night, hoping for Symir to get beside himself and say something, but it never happened. Projex would never intentionally ruin her dinner, but he was checking that nigga's gangster. Obviously, he had none 'cause let that had been Projex, Symir would've been escorted out the fine establishment before this point.

When Symir stood from his seat and cleared his

throat, all attention went his way. Trell nudged Candace's arm and leaned down to whisper in her ear.

"Not this nigga about to give a speech about how he loves Loriana." They snickered.

"She doesn't even like him for real," Candace whispered back.

Sshh," Symir's friend's wife hushed.

Both their heads swiveled her way as they mugged her.

"Girl, who you telling hush?" Trell sassed before Candace made him turn away from her.

"Stop," she fussed.

While one half of the party was team Symir, the other half was undoubtedly rooting for Projex. The few people who were on no side simply wanted what was best for Loriana. Coolly, Symir licked his lips and gave Loriana a smile.

"I just want to take the time out and thank everyone for coming to celebrate my love's birthday tonight. She wanted a simple dinner, and I think me and Mhyale came through on that."

Loriana nodded her head in approval, feeling all the love in the room.

"She's been working her ass off finishing up school and working at Aspire, so it was only right she gets treated like the queen she is on her day."

"I know that's right, niece!" Peaches blurted out, sipping on her third Jack and Coke.

When he reached for her hand, Loriana hesitantly stood to her feet. She hadn't told him she wanted anything for her birthday, so she hoped he wasn't about to surprise her with a new car or something. She would've been grateful, but that was doing a lot. Buying a car was nothing compared to Symir lowering himself to one knee before her while pulling out a black velvet ring box.

"Oh, my gosh!" Mhyale gasped in utter shock. Eyes wide and mouth wider, her eyes darted around the room at everyone else's face. While Symir's friend had his phone out recording, everyone else was too much in astoundment to move. Loriana included.

So caught off guard by his action, her hand trembled inside of his. When they had that talk about marriage and kids in the car, him proposing surely wasn't on her mind. Not in the slightest.

"Loriana, I—" was all Symir could get out before boisterous laughter from Projex echoed throughout the room.

Practically in tears, he was leaned back in his seat, cracking up. His boys looked at him like he was crazy, with silly grins on their faces. Loriana's heart broke for Symir. The embarrassment on his handsome face morphed into a deep scowl.

"Aye. You see me trying to do something!" Symir spat.

Projex slowly sat up straight in his seat. "Nigga, do it look like I give a fuck? You better off getting yo' lame ass up and taking this L. She ain't saying yes to you, cuz."

"Now, Projex," Ms. Joseline tried to intervene. "All that was not called for."

"It really wasn't. You ain't put no ring on it, so what you pressed for?" Shamari wanted to know, not feeling this dissing coming his brother's way.

Joi immediately grabbed Shamari's hand, placing it on her belly. He needed to remember that they had a child on the way.

"That's the thing. I can, and she'd say yes right now." Nonchalantly, Projex shrugged because he knew what it was. Everyone in that damn room was reading it correctly except Symir. It was sad.

Symir's gaze fell back onto Loriana, who had a look of uncertainty in her eyes. Not because she didn't know what to say but because she hated she had to do it right now. Being put on blast made her cringe. Had Symir known that, he would've asked for her hand in marriage in a more private setting. Somewhere where she could decline his engagement ring without feeling as if she were about to pass out.

Pleading with her eyes, she hoped he got the message and just stood up. When he didn't, she slowly shook her head no and mouthed *I'm sorry*. Symir wanted to protest and ask her why, but what would be the point? She'd made her decision before he could utter the words, and they were final. An awkward silence filled the air as he stood to his feet and brushed a hand down his dress pants.

"Got yo' old ass knee hurting for no reason." Projex laughed, making Trell yelp.

"Chile. The embarrassment," Aunt Peaches muttered. "Can we at least still cut the cake, hell? It's still my niece's birthday."

"Mama," Mhyale sighed as Symir stormed out of the room. Loriana fixed her feet to go after him but was immediately stopped by the sound of Projex's voice.

"Aye. I wish you would," he spoke in that tone of voice that made her rethink her next moves.

Not for long, though, because she simply sat back down in her seat as her friends rushed over to her. Projex was playing it cool but had she let that nigga slide a ring on her finger, he was going to show her what not being on his best behavior looked like for real. The tightness in his chest eased up some when they locked eyes.

Loriana was his baby. His L-Boogie. There was no way he was about to sit back and watch her get proposed to by a nigga other than himself. The fact that Symir even felt comfortable enough to do so had questions swarming through Projex's brain that only Loriana had the answers to. He planned to get them up out of her too. There was no more of that keeping secrets shit unless it was between them. Projex promised that.

———

After work, there was always a little fun involved. Being cooped up in the studio practically all day, Projex, Ayo, Sneaks, and a few other men decided to slide off into the strip club. For it to be a Thursday night, Stroker's had a packed crowd. With the newfound fame and name he was making for himself, Projex and Ayo alike had a few women in their section, vying for their attention.

It was crazy how his name was buzzing. Projex moved lowkey, handled business with who he preferred, and had a list of artists trying to work with him. Since being home, he added producer to his list of titles, and this was only the beginning.

While one chick sat to his left, who was indeed pretty in the face, the stripper in front of him making her ass wobble, garnered his full attention. While he wasn't trying to draw too much attention, it was a fail, thanks to Ayo's stunting ass. Not stingy at all with their money, the men had their section flooded with bills as bottles of over-priced liquor occupied the tables.

Admittedly, Projex was a bit faded as he was leaned back on the couch with a half-empty cup in his hand. When the stripper bent over, giving him a shot of her pussy through the thong she was wearing, Projex knew it was time to head home. They'd been there well over two hours.

"You good?" Sneaks questioned, leaning near his ear.

Projex's head bobbed slightly. He was straight but in no condition to be driving. Polishing off his cup, he gave a firm smack to the stripper's ass who'd earned every cent, before letting his eyes roam the club. Though dimly lit, he peeped her familiar face outside of their section right away.

The bouncer at the rope looked over his shoulder to grant her access, and Projex nodded his head. A lazy grin covered his face as she approached him. Her friends, including Yari, were right behind her. Through Projex's hazed vision, her physique didn't go unnoticed. The grey, long-sleeve full bodysuit, with a low cut back and extended pant legs, fit her thick frame snuggly. His eyes didn't make their way to her feet, but he was sure she was wearing heels due to her added height. Or maybe it was the mass of curls covering her head in a flirty manner.

"Hey, best friend," Yari spoke, leaning down to hug him.

"What's up with it."

"I see you out living life," Reign acknowledged.

Projex gave her a sly grin. "Might as well be. Look at you."

His eyes danced over her frame without shame, making the girl who had been trying to bag him all night get up and excuse herself from their section. When Reign went to take her place, Projex drunkenly pulled her onto his lap. Giggling, Reign looked at him over her shoulder.

"What?" he pressed.

"Nothing. Surprised to see you out. I thought you were at the studio."

"I was, now I'm here. What you doing out?"

"Just chilling. You know my sister works here, so we decided to come see her dance."

Sky, Reign's older sister, was a well-seasoned stripper at Stroker's and a crowd favorite. Though she had no intentions of coming to the club tonight, Reign wasn't about to let Projex know the only reason she was in his presence was because Yari saw him on Ayo's Instagram story. While in the house with her off day falling on tomorrow, Reign was complaining about her boyfriend, who she'd been trying to break things off with for months now. Yari was tired of hearing about their issues and told her to get dressed so they could hit the town. Now, here she was in the presence of the one man she couldn't keep her thoughts off.

Having a down-to-earth personality was nice. Reign loved how easily she and Projex vibed. He carried himself, with her at least, much older than twenty-four. She wasn't coming across that with niggas years older than him. Tallying his looks up with the dick he'd blessed her with, and Reign was a goner.

"I'm tryna see you dance. Let me see you bounce that ass for me," he instructed with a pat to her soft ass.

With no unsureness or care as to who may have

been observing her, and there were eyes all over them, Reign wind her hips in his lap. Just as skilled as her sister, Reign could dance her ass off. Honestly, she could've been a stripper too, but couldn't see herself showing that much skin in front of strangers. She didn't knock the naked hustle at all, though. Like the DJ knew exactly what she needed to hear, he transitioned to the perfect song.

"Yeah, bounce that ass," Projex encouraged as Webbie's voice came over the speakers.

Bounce that ass like that like that
Bend over, let me see it from the back
Like Beyonce, like Trina, like a big booty ass black
diva, like a stripper
Up and down like flippa, bend over let me see it from
the back.

She vibrated her ass to the beat, keeping Projex in a trance. Beside them, Yari was hyping her up, rubbing all over her booty too.

"Yeah, friend! Okay, bitch. You better look back at it!"

Reign's sex appeal was crazy as she tossed her curls to one side and stared Projex down over her shoulder. Reaching forward, he grabbed the bottle of Remy and drank straight from the bottle before handing it to Reign. Accepting it, she took a swig and placed it on the table, all while still shaking her ass.

Snaking his hand around her waist, Projex held her firmly in his lap. His hand traveled between her legs while heavy, warm breaths tickled her neck. Palming her pussy, Projex spoke freakily in her ear.

"This pussy so fat. It feels like she missed me, too."

Reign was so thankful for the somewhat dim lights because clearly, he had no care in the world. Squeezing her legs tightly together, she clasped a hand around his wrist and twisted her body to face him.

"She does. You ready to go?" she questioned.

"Yeah. We can—"

A commotion from the entrance of their section caused Projex to stop talking. Already on alert, Sneaks was on his feet, seeing why some nigga was trying to make his way into their section. Projex stood next, maneuvering Reign off his lap.

"Reign! Hoe, you out yo' mind!" Her crazy as hell boyfriend, Rodney, screamed. He was no match for the security and was about to get his shit knocked if he didn't calm down.

Projex looked her way. "Handle that nigga 'fore me and mine do."

Regardless of how much he'd been drinking, wasn't no nigga about to step to him or her crazy. Reign stood slowly, in no rush to de-escalate the situation for Rodney's sake. How he figured out where she was didn't even bother her. The way he clocked her moves was annoying as fuck. As she headed to calm him down, Rodney got beside himself, talking recklessly to Projex.

"Bitch ass nigga, you bet not let me see you 'round her again!" he spat, pointing his finger with venom in his eyes. Seeing his girl, who no longer wanted to be his damn girl, hugged up with him had Rodney seeing red.

Projex couldn't help but sneer his way. He was never about to beef over a woman, especially one that didn't belong to him. Reign was cool, her pussy was better than good, but Projex had enough on his plate. Some situations just weren't worth catching a body over. He wasn't letting the disrespect toward him slide, though.

"Aye, let's shake," he told Sneaks and Ayo, who were ready for whatever.

Walking out of the section, Projex sobered up just enough to punch Rodney in the jaw, knocking him out cold. His body bounced off the tile floor, causing the music to come to a halt.

"Gotdamn!" someone yelled dramatically.

"You straight?" Projex asked Reign, who nodded her head. "A'ight."

Stepping around Rodney, they walked out of the club to the cool, fall air. The breeze was much needed, considering how hot Projex was. He wanted to strip from his damn clothes and lay under the fan and AC.

"You know that nigga gon' be on yo' head after this," Sneaks told him, climbing in the driver's seat. Projex slammed the passenger door. Ayo was pulling up right on the side of them.

"It's whatever," he said, yawning. "Damn. I was trying to fuck on little baby tonight. Niggas be hating."

Sneaks laughed and rolled his window down to chop it up with Ayo. "Be safe, cuz."

"Y'all too. Don't let that nigga be on no wild shit. Take y'all ass home."

"This nigga," Projex mumbled, pulling his phone from his pocket.

There was a text from Reign already, but Projex

was off that for the night. The unwanted drama wasn't his speed. If anything, the only person he cared to make a scene with was Loriana. She was the only woman to get that type of energy out of him. Thinking of his boo, he called her up as Sneaks pulled out of the parking lot. When she didn't answer the first time, he called right back.

"You too fucked up to drive?" Sneaks asked. Projex's car was parked at the studio, about twenty minutes away.

"Shit. I feel like it. Hello? Aye, ma. Wake up."

Groggily, Loriana rolled over in her bed. She wasn't even sure how she answered the phone. "Why are you hollering?"

"I ain't hollering," he spoke louder, making her wince. "You sleep?"

"Not anymore. What's wrong?"

"Aye," he laughed before calling her on Face-Time. "Answer that mothafucka."

"Oh my gosh," she fussed but answered anyway. It was pitch black on her end, while the cities lights brightened his screen every few seconds.

"Aye, ma."

"Hmm?" Loriana hummed.

"I'm drunkathanabitch." He laughed, combining words that shouldn't have been.

In the driver's seat, Sneaks shook his head with an amused grin on his face. His boy was tore up and seeing him openly talk to Loriana always humored him. Especially because he never mentioned anything about her or their situation to him or any nigga besides Laurent. Even then, it was the bare minimum.

"I see. I hope whoever is driving isn't drunk, too."

"Nah. My nigga good. What you doing?"

"What does it look like, Bryshon?"

"Girl, don't be saying my name like that. Crazy ass. You hungry? My fucking stomach touching my back. Get up and cook me somethin' right quick."

Loriana laughed. "Boy, no. Do you see what time it is?"

"I can see just fine. Come on, ma. Do me this solid. Ain't shit open but nasty ass Taco Bell. You know I don't eat that fake shit."

"Who said you could come over here anyway? I have company."

"On big God himself, I'll air that bitch out if you got that dumbass nigga over there. You better quit playing with that man's life 'fore it gets took."

The seriousness in his voice made Loriana smirk. Jealousy was sexy as hell on him, but she also knew better than to play with him like that.

"So violent. Ain't nobody over here. I have class and work tomorrow, though."

"That's cool. I'ma sleep in til' you get done."

She yawned. "Okay. How far away are you?"

"Shit," he thought, looking out the window, "yo, Sneaks. Slide me to Loriana's crib. Aye. I'm like twenty minutes out. Stay yo' ass up. Matter fact, get up and start cooking. I'll be there in fifteen."

Another yawn escaped her mouth as she rolled over. "You swear you running something. Be careful."

"Fasho. I love you, ma."

Her heart swelled in her chest. "I love you, too."

She stayed in bed with her eyes closed for another ten minutes before getting up and sliding on her house shoes. She went to the bathroom, peed, washed her hands, and headed to the kitchen. Thankfully, she wasn't as sleepy due to her calling it an early night around eight. She'd fallen asleep doing an assignment, woken up to complete it, showered, and gone right back to bed.

Knowing she wasn't about to make a full-blown meal at damn near four in the morning, Loriana warmed up what was supposed to be her lunch for the day. A turkey burger with turkey bacon, onions, lettuce, and cheese would have to do. Popping some fries in her air fryer, she waited for Projex's arrival.

Right on time, knocks came to her front door. Pushing herself away from her island, Loriana went to let him in, and Sneaks pulled off.

"Damn," Projex groaned, stumbling across the threshold. "You got it on hell in here."

"Don't come in here complaining. You could've gone home or somewhere."

Grinning, he eyed her booty in the shorts she was wearing before slapping it. "Shut up. It ain't even that cold outside yet. Yo' bill gon' be through the roof."

"Pay it then."

He pulled a stack of ones he hadn't thrown at the strip club from his jeans. "I gotchu'. What else you need?"

Observantly, Loriana eyed him. She knew he kept money on him, but never a bunch of ones. And he was super turned up. When he called, her initial thoughts were that he was coming from the studio. Now it was clear he'd been out kicking it.

"You have fun tonight?" she asked, looking him up and down. Projex eyed her frame in the booty shorts, half-shirt, and scarf tied around her head. Walking by her, he ran a hand over her stomach and kissed her cheek before washing his hands at the sink.

"It was straight. Shoulda' kept my ass at the studio for real."

"Why? You look like you had a good time," she pressed, fixing his plate.

If this was the sober Projex, he'd know she was fishing for answers instead of keeping casual conversation.

"Niggas was on some tough guy shit and got smacked. I just be trying to chill, and niggas always wanna try me. Like I ain't no real nigga. Like I ain't with the shit."

"You want some mustard?"

"Yeah. Hook my shit up how you be doing yours. I want two of them hoes."

"I gotchu'," she said, sounding just like him.

"You sure this time? If I go to prison again, you not gon' fold like last time, are you? I got enough snake mothafuckas around me, ma. You gotta be my solid thing in this world. I don't even trust niggas how I used to. Everybody got they own agendas. You got lame niggas proposing to my wife and shit."

Loriana rolled her eyes. "No one told him to do that."

"Somebody should've told his ass *not* to do that. Nigga was tripping. Had you even acknowledged that shit, I was catching a case. I don't know why you be playing with me like I won't."

He was rambling but speaking facts. Loriana

wasn't mad that she caused him to lack trust in her. She knew it'd take some time to gain that back, but how long was too long to keep throwing it in her face?

"You won't go to prison again, so don't say that."

"But answer the question, though? I'ont even wanna be around you if I feel like you can't hold me down. You know my own auntie ain't speaking to me behind her snitch ass son?" He scoffed.

"Really? That's messed up when he was in the wrong."

"Yeah, but fuck it. Family will do you dirty just like a random mothafucka that don't know you. Kordell lucky we ain't crossed paths. That's crazy, man. I'm real-life beefing with my own cousin behind some money. Nigga ratted me out for some damn paper."

Loriana didn't have anything to say, so she just continued to listen while pulling the fries from the air fryer.

"And you know what's wild, ma? I got so much fucking money now, the nigga could've been eating with me. But he got greedy and turned into a snake. Shit really fucked me up."

The hurt in his voice made her chest cave some. Projex had never spoken on the situation with

Kordell. It was of the past, and he'd done his time, but it still pained him to know his own blood had crossed him over some shit he had no clue about.

On purpose, Projex tried to make sure he didn't run into him. The way he was up right now, going back to prison for murder, was for sure out of the question. In his mind, he was hoping karma came around like the bitch she was and did him, Kelsi, and whoever else involved dirty. They were straight grimy for what they did to him.

Loriana sat his plate down in front of him. "You know, people who wrong you in the world and move about like nothing happened, never live a peaceful life. No matter how long it's been, nothing good ever comes to them. I don't know what you're feeling because Kordell was family, but I do know how it feels to be stabbed in the back by someone. Just know he's going to wish, if he isn't already, that he never did that to you. I wouldn't be surprised if he tried to make amends."

He'd tried but failed. Pulling up on the block that day was Kordell's weak attempt, one that almost cost him his life. As the months went by, Projex's hatred for him simmered some but not completely. So much good was happening in his life, he didn't have time to focus and give his energy to negative situations.

Keeping busy and making money was all the motivation he needed to stay out of the drama, but he'd never run from it if presented to him.

Once he was done eating and showered, Projex fell right to sleep in the comfort of Loriana's bed. He complained about it being hot but was damn near trying to crawl in her body the way he slept all over her. Knowing she had to be up in less than five hours, Loriana was right with him in a peaceful slumber. Thankfully, when her alarm went off, she didn't feel tired at all. A good night's rest with the person who felt like home was everything.

Easing out of her bed with her phone in hand, Loriana went to shower and get dressed. The time she spent to herself in the quietness of the morning was essential to her day. Relieving her bladder on the toilet, she did a few inhales and exhales, gave praise to God for allowing her to see another day, and then continued on with her routine. The vibration of her phone across the counter, once she was clean, caught her attention.

Symir's name flashed across it, and her first mind told her to ignore him. She'd been doing it more frequently now, preferring to hit him through text. The last time she talked to him in Projex's presence was part of the reason they were rebuilding their relationship now. Loriana wasn't sure what he wanted to talk about so early when she'd said all she had to say.

It was the day after her birthday, and Loriana had a serious hangover. She groaned lowly as she maneuvered on her couch. Passed out on the floor with a blanket over him was Trell while Candace and Nyree occupied the sectional across from her. Squinted eyes searched for the time on the stove, indicating that it was well into the afternoon.

"I feel horrible," she moaned, sitting up on the couch. Her body flinched when knocks from her front door resounded throughout the apartment.

"Who the hell," she mumbled, standing to her feet. Had she known where her phone was, she could've seen who it was through the Ring app.

A sigh and an eye roll came from her after seeing Symir standing there. After walking out of her dinner, he only came back in to tell her he was leaving, now here he was hours later. Loriana reluctantly opened the door and just stared at him. Like her, he looked like he had a long night of drinking, only sobering up long enough to come and talk to her.

"Can I come in?"

"I'll step out here." She didn't care about the slight breeze. "What's up?"

"That's all you have to say after last night?"

Loriana tried to disguise her annoyance, but it was written all over her face. "You mean after you did something we hadn't even talked about? What is there for me to say?"

"Something. You know how embarrassed I am?"

"You?" Her voice elevated. "When have we discussed getting married? Matter of fact, we're not even in a relationship, so I honestly do not understand how you thought proposing to me was cool. What. Was I just supposed to say yes to save face?"

"We're not in a relationship?"

Loriana stared at him like he was dumb, and she was starting to believe maybe he was. "Symir. We were dating. Nothing between us was exclusive for you to go out of your way and buy a ring. That is crazy."

"You saying were like we're not anymore."

"At this point, we're not. You didn't even ask my dad for my hand in marriage but invited him to my dinner? Does any of this sound right to you? I mean, please let me know if I'm tripping."

"Nah. Maybe I was. If that nigga Projex proposed, you'd say yes in a heartbeat."

"Always worried about the next nigga." She chuckled, totally over this conversation. "It doesn't

matter what he does, but clearly, he's the reason behind this."

Once you feel like you're in competition with the next person, that's when you lose. The way Symir kept bringing him up pissed her off because they weren't even rocking like that either. Not enough for Projex to propose. And even if he did, that was none of Symir's concern.

"I thought we were on the same page," he said lamely.

"Obviously not. Look, I'm sorry for not accepting your proposal, but that's just not where I'm at in my life right now."

He frowned. "What kind of apology is that?"

"The only one I'm giving!" she spat.

"Well, you can keep that shit. I should've known something was up the minute you started acting different. You love that nigga more than me?"

Her hand came to his chest as he stepped up on her. "You need to back the fuck up."

"Answer my question. Be real with a nigga for once in your life."

"What I really want to say will have you out here crying, so I think it's best you just leave."

His jaw clenched tightly. Loriana's brow raised as

her hand found the handle of her door. Symir took a step back, and his chest deflated.

"You really love him. That shit is crazy, but you got it. I got my answer."

His head bobbed as if he was finally coming to the realization that what they shared didn't mean much. And it didn't. Loriana was thankful for him during the season of her life, where he played an important role, but seasons change. He wasn't meant to come into this new one with her, and damn sure not as her fiancé.

Sympathy lingered in her eyes before she stepped back inside her apartment. There was no use in answering his question because it shouldn't have even been one. Loriana didn't just love Projex. She was in love with him. Deeply. Submerged in all things Bryshon Emery. Symir was a fool for thinking otherwise.

When her phone stopped vibrating, she sighed. She needed to close that chapter of her life for good. While Loriana did feel kind of bad for letting things progress with him in Projex's absence, the love she had for him wasn't fraudulent. Some things in life just weren't meant to last forever, and their relationship was one of them. It was no hard feelings, but on her

Donell Jones shit, Loriana knew where she wanted to be.

After brushing her teeth, doing her facial routine, and oiling her body down, she opened the door. Projex was still knocked out in the bed with the comforter now thrown off his body, with the white sheet in its place. A body that Loriana's mouth couldn't help but water over. She wasn't sure how he spent most of his days when locked up, but it was evident he worked out. Ripples of hard abs framed his body while his lengthy, thick dick rested along his thigh. A chill surged through her, thinking of him sliding inside her, but Loriana had other plans this morning.

Easing onto the bed, positioned on her knees between his legs, Loriana licked her lips and pulled the sheet back. She was always eager to touch him, amazed by how big he was. A hand gripped his muscular thigh as she lowered her head. Puckered lips kissed up his pole before reaching the tip. Twirling her tongue around him, she took him inside her warm mouth. Feeling him go from completely soft to hard as steel within seconds made her proud.

A groan came from above her as Projex's heavy lids slid open. Loriana's eyes met his, and he smirked.

"Damn, ma. Good morning."

Her good morning reply was hummed around his dick. From the base of his pole to the head, she sucked him gingerly, showing nothing but apprecia tion for him being so blessed. Wet slurps sounded off in the room as his hand came to her neck. Projex massaged it gently, encouraging her skills.

"Aw, fuck ma. Ssss… Damn," he hissed in a guttural tone.

Loriana went lower, expanding her throat, so he had complete access down it. Freakily, she massaged his balls, too. The grip on her neck went to her hair covered in a bonnet that would sure be off once her mission was complete. She was trying to suck his soul out of his body.

Smack!

The spank he delivered to her ass caused Loriana to moan louder. That only made Projex closer to his climax. He wanted to ask her who taught her how to suck dick like that, but he knew that was all him. His baby was a star student. She'd mastered how to take complete control while slobbering all over his pole, giving him prime fellatio.

"Fuck! I love your ass," Projex proclaimed, sounding as if he was stressed out about doing so.

That was far from the case though. He had no worries as Loriana pulled that nut right up out of him.

Lifting her mouth some, Loriana wanted him to witness his kids coating her tongue. Jerking him in a quick manner, she looked him in the eyes with her mouth wide and tongue stretched out. Projex's stomach sank, breathing became choppy, and eyes fluttered.

"Fuuuuuck," he groaned sexily as she wrapped her lips around him.

The sweet taste of him had Loriana smacking her lips and licking them clean once he was done filling her mouth up. With a smile on her face, she lifted and placed her hands on his thighs. Projex's body shivered, and she chuckled.

"Good morning," she said sweetly.

He pulled her to him so quickly, Loriana yelped in surprise. Kissing her lips, with morning breath and all, Projex slobbered her down. The towel she had wrapped around her was snatched off, and the wetness between her legs was all his doing. It was a turn-on to see him so vulnerable while she made love to him with her mouth. When he eased her onto his still hardened member, gripping one of her ass cheeks, they moaned in unison.

"Man, this pussy so good. Why this shit so good, huh?"

"Because it's yours."

He bit her bottom lip as she rode him slowly. "I know it is."

In a trance, bodies moving in sync, they made love. It was slow and sensual, bringing tears to Loriana's eyes. She wrapped her arms around him as he buried himself deeper, never wanting to remove himself. Planted, grounded, in the depths of her walls, connecting to her soul, is where he wanted to dwell. For life. There was no getting rid of him.

"I love you so much, Bryshon," Loriana confessed with her entire heart.

As badly as she wanted to stay in bed and go another round, Loriana got up and took another quick shower. Now rushing, she hurriedly got dressed before she was late to class. Content with a grin on his face, Projex was still laid out in her bed, watching as she moved about the room. He'd gotten up to pee and brush his teeth, then hopped right back in the bed. When he yawned loudly, getting extra comfortable, Loriana looked his way.

"What?" he asked.

"Just rub in my face how you're about to go back to sleep."

"Nah. I'ma get up and make some moves. That BC powder you gave me worked quick as hell."

She slipped on a pair of leggings. "They're magical. Where you going?"

"To the crib and take Joi to get something to eat. She texted me on some *hey, brother*," he said, doing his best imitation of her voice. Loriana snickered. "I'ma have her come pick me up."

"She misses you, I'm sure. You been acting funny with her. Don't do my sis like that. She needs all the support and love she can get, especially from you."

Projex sucked his teeth. "No, I haven't. She spoiled, that's all. All the women in my life spoiled as fuck, dawg."

"And who might all those women be because I been feeling real neglected."

"You fronting," he laughed, "like I ain't just drop mad bread on you for your birthday."

"I'm not talking about being spoiled materialistically. I want to spend one-on-one time with you. How we used to be."

Projex scratched at his chin hair. "Back then, we had a lot of free time on our hands. We in grind mode right now, ma."

"So, you saying we can't spend more time together?"

Loriana clearly heard what she wanted to hear.

"Nah. I'm saying we going with the flow. Stop

putting pressure on some shit that you know gon' happen automatically with us anyway. You see where I'm at right now, right?"

"Yeah, but you could've been anywhere else."

Projex stared at her for a beat. She was right, and had Reign's dude not popped up at the club wildin' out, he was sure he would've been waking up to her instead. Loriana didn't need to know that, though.

"But where I'm at? You tryna start some shit already and gon' be late for class."

"Whatever. You know I'm right. That's why you trying to change the subject."

"Right or wrong, you was the one getting proposed to. If a nigga wanted to be somewhere else, I got every right."

Loriana huffed in frustration. "Stop bringing that up. *He* did that on his own. And go be somewhere else then, Bryshon. I know the next time you come over here trying to fuck, I'm making you wear a condom. I don't know who you been tossing dick to."

"You funny," was all Projex said as he got out the bed clad in some Polo briefs.

"You gon' think I'm hilarious when I go ghost on your ass."

Striding in her direction as she zipped up her

over-the-knee boot, Projex smacked her booty. "That ass getting fat."

"Move!"

He held her around the waist and nestled his face in her neck. "Who you going ghost on? Huh?"

"You, 'cause you think I be playing with you," she fussed.

"Nah. I know you serious, but what I gotta stop wearing a condom for? You don't want my babies?"

"Yep. Down my throat." When she laughed, Projex bit her neck. "Oww, stop!"

"Quit talking crazy then. Condoms ain't ever been our thing for real. Why start now?"

She moved his hand from around her. "Because like I said, I don't know who else you're having sex with. I was reckless this morning, but I'm not trying to catch anything or get pregnant right now."

"A'ight. We just won't have sex then."

Her head snapped upward. "Now, why are you being dramatic? Just wear a condom." The thought of him depriving her of that dick had her in a panic.

"Nah. I'm good, ma. You basically saying until we exclusive, I gotta strap up."

"Yeah. I see nothing wrong with that. I mean unless you're not trying to go that route."

When he didn't reply right away and scratched his

hair that was quickly growing back, Loriana's eyes blinked in astonishment.

"Oh. Okay. I see what it is now. You want to do your thang. I get it."

Projex huffed. "Who being dramatic now?"

"Am I wrong, though?"

"Nah. You ain't, but don't think too much into it."

Loriana waved him off and grabbed her charger out of the socket. "Right," she scoffed. "Be sure to lock my door when you leave out."

"Damn. I can't get a kiss bye, a see you later, no I love you, baby?"

In a rush, Loriana stepped to him, pecked his lips, and gave him a quick hug. "I love your annoying self. See you around."

Laughing, Projex yanked her to him. "Yo, quit fucking playing. Give me a real kiss, or I ain't letting you leave."

"Oh, my gosh. You really get on my nerves. Here," she fussed, poking her lips out.

Tonguing her down, Projex playfully humped her before letting her go. He had a grin on his face that made her blush. "Now, you can leave. Have a good day and shit. Don't let none of them professors piss you off."

"I won't. Tell Joi I said hi."

He walked her to the door, loving this college girl look she had going on. He hated how he'd missed her earlier years, knowing she was probably in full nerd mode, being early to class like the scholar student she was. They had missed out on some important parts of each other's lives, but there was nothing but space and opportunity to make up for the time lost.

While Projex started his day and had Joi pick him up, Loriana's seemed to go by quicker than she expected. By the time she had to go to work, she was in need of a nap. Walking out of her lecture hall to her car, her phone rang as she scrolled through emails on her work phone. Her face lit up seeing Nyree's name and contact picture flash across her screen.

"Hey, Ny," she answered.

"Hey, girl, hey. What you doing?"

"Leaving campus about to go to work. I don't know who signed me up to be an adult, but this shit is for the birds. I just wanna go home and take a nap."

"Girl, yes. This is very much ghetto, but it's okay. It'll all be over real soon."

The two were counting down the weeks until graduation and couldn't wait. Thankfully, their ceremonies weren't on the same weekend.

"Right, right. What're you doing? I can't wait to see you for Thanksgiving break."

"I'm headed to this study group, girl. I don't like working with people, but I guess I have to."

Loriana laughed. "Exactly."

"I'll be there on Wednesday. That ain't why I called you, though. Have you talked to Projex?"

"Mhm. I left him at my place this morning. Why?"

"This morning?" Nyree questioned slowly. "Chile. Why did that man punch some nigga in the club last night?"

"You for real? How you know?"

"It's all on social media. They saying it was behind some bitch he fucks with."

Loriana immediately felt ill. Just as Nyree was saying she was going to send her some screenshots, Mhyale was clicking in on her other line. While Loriana hadn't been on social media that much today, word had clearly gotten around about Projex knocking Rodney out. Of course, people in the comments were making up assumptions, but most had proof.

Declining Mhy's call, Loriana stopped walking and watched the first video Nyree sent her. In it was Reign dancing on Projex. Her chest tightened, watching how intimate and cozy the two appeared to be. The next video was of Projex walking out of the section and punching Rodney in the face. Loriana tossed a hand over her mouth as he fell to the ground.

"This is the same girl I was telling you about," Loriana vocalized.

It was cold as hell out, but her body was on fire. She knew she hadn't just been talking for her health earlier this morning. Projex had been out here doing him, that she was sure of.

"The one who was at Bo's house a while back?" Nyree questioned, remembering Loriana calling her as soon as she pulled off.

"Yep. Wow. This nigga straight lied to my face this morning."

She was mumbling to herself as she unlocked her car door. Sliding in, she cranked the heat up, removing the beanie from her head. Projex hadn't necessarily lied, but he hadn't told her the truth either. He kept it as real with her as he knew she could handle. Telling her that he was feeling Reign and had knocked her nigga out for disrespecting him wouldn't have served a purpose.

"Wait. He came over last night after all this?" Nyree wondered.

"Girl, yeah. And was drunk as hell. See. This is why I told myself I was good on him."

Her voice cracked, and she shook her head in annoyance.

"Awww, boo. Don't start crying. Just ask him what's up. You know how shit can get misconstrued on social media. Especially with everybody thinking they know people's business."

Loriana sniffled, pissed she even got that deep in her feelings over a couple of videos. She'd given him the chance to mention something this morning, so no, she wasn't going to ask no questions.

"I'm good. I guess this is my karma. For real, I have no reason to be tripping. We're both single."

"You have every reason to ask him what's up. Don't downplay it cause that's what we're not about to do. If he fucks with her, then cool, let a bitch know something, but don't be all in your face and bed like she's a nobody to him. These hoes be moving just as sloppy as these niggas out here, and you don't need to get caught up in that drama."

Loriana sighed. "True. But for real, Ny, I don't even have the energy to keep going back and forth about this. He's single, so I'ma let him live his single life. Just know from here on out, I'm moving the same way. No more sparing feelings, 'cause he sure ain't give a fuck about sparing mine."

"I know that's right! We ain't pacifying these niggas feelings no more."

"Man. Here you go fronting," Juice said, walking up on her.

"Boy! Don't be scaring me like that." Nyree laughed before giving him a kiss. "Lori, don't let that nigga ruin your day, okay?"

"I'm not. I promise."

"Good. Have a good day at work, and I'ma text you later."

Loriana told her okay, and they hung up. The urge to send Projex a hateful text message had Loriana's leg shaking. Everything he did now while out in public would be captured by the right people and thrown to the wolves of social media. That liquor had him slipping big time. Instead of handling the situation like she wanted to, Loriana locked her phone and exhaled. Some arguments weren't even worth it. At least not right now.

She wasn't playing about going ghost on him, and now it was time to show and prove just how serious she was.

Chapter Nine

No matter how many times Projex read over the text messages Loriana sent him, he didn't see what she was tripping over. Joi had mentioned the videos to him that afternoon when she came to pick him up. Not on social media to scroll and keep up with everybody, Projex wasn't aware he and Reign had been posted on a few blog pages. He expected Loriana to blow his line down that day, but she hadn't.

Instead, she waited until days later when he was in the studio, in his zone, to fuck up his mood. He'd been sitting in the same spot for the last ten minutes, annoyed as fuck with her and himself. Not because of the situation with Reign, but because people thought he had beef behind her. It was never that deep.

Loriana didn't care how deep it was or not, she was cool on him, and that's exactly what she told him.

"Aye, you good?" Laurent asked, walking back into the studio.

Projex looked up from his screen. "Yeah. I'm straight. Trying not to pull up on this girl, man."

"Who, that Reign chick?"

"Hell nah. Loriana's ass. She just texted me some wild, disrespectful shit. Talking mad crazy to a nigga like I'm pussy."

Laurent couldn't help but laugh. Projex was really upset, and the mug on his face was pure evidence.

"Sis about to be done with your ass; watch."

Projex waved him off. "No, the fuck she ain't. How she tripping on me when weird cuz proposed to her and shit? Now, I'm the bad guy 'cause I got a lil' dance."

"Aye. On everything, I was nervous for you. What if she would've said yeah?" Laurent asked, not able to mask the smirk on his face.

"I woulda knocked that mothafuckin table over and beat his ass. Tossed that cake on that nigga and all. Fuck you mean?"

Projex was so serious, Laurent didn't even know why he asked. Catching his breath from laughing, he shook his head.

"That had me uncomfortable for him."

"You! Nigga, my mothafuckin' heart was beating so fast. 'Bouta have a damn heart attack." He chuckled, thinking back to that day. "You was gon' have to bail me out of jail, on my mama. I was gon' do that nigga dirty."

"She still fool with him?"

Projex shrugged. "Shit, I'ont think so. After this shit with Reign, I wouldn't doubt she be on some get back with me. She been moving real petty like that."

"Whatever way she moving, you need to keep yo' head clear. You got too much on the line to be out here on some reckless behavior. You know Maxwell talking about we might be nominated for a Grammy."

With bulged eyes, Projex hopped up from his seat. "Swear?"

"On SAG, nigga." Laurent laughed after seeing his broad smile, showing all teeth.

They slapped hands. "Yo, that's wild as fuck. A Grammy nomination? Two lil' niggas from South Ave? I don't even know what to say, bro."

Bereft of speech, Projex felt an unexplainable sensation course through his body. He knew his hard work would pay off in more ways than one, but never this soon and at this magnitude. Projex wasn't sure how true Maxwell's assumptions were, but the man hadn't steered him wrong since they met. As the owner of MM Record Label and a Black man, he made it his mission to put other Black men in positions to win. No matter their past, there were enough jobs and money for them to all eat.

Attached to Projex's first million-dollar-plus check were plenty more to follow. The price had gone up, the bag increased, and access to him was much harder now. Even if they weren't nominated, Projex was happy as fuck that his name was mentioned anywhere around that type of success.

"I didn't either, but we worked hard for this. All them late nights and early mornings weren't in vain."

Projex nodded his head. "Fasho."

Their song *The Perfect Time* had dropped in February before Projex was released and had sat at the number one spot for months. It'd just recently dropped to number two and fluctuated every day. Projex wanted to personally thank whoever at the Recording Academy who had voted for them. He'd written plenty of songs for lots of artists, but this one was different. It meant more to him because, at the time, he was locked up and losing faith. Laurent was always his voice of encouragement, sending nothing but positivity his way. Projex held that shit down, and now it was up... in all aspects of his life.

Super motivated now that he'd gotten that news, Projex stayed in the studio for three more hours creating. If they'd been nominated for a Grammy, it was clear his name was really in the mouths of people who mattered, and he wanted to keep it that way and give their asses something good to talk about for the long haul.

When he was leaving out, trying to decide if he should slide by his mama's crib, Reign called. They texted briefly when their videos were circulating, but she wasn't tripping. Not at first anyway. She wasn't in the blind about who Projex was anymore, but she surely wasn't prepared to be attacked on social media behind a man she thought was single. He quickly cleared the air for her, and they'd been good since.

"What's good," Projex answered.

"Hey. What you got going on?"

"Leaving the studio. What you doing? You sound asleep."

She yawned. "I just woke up not too long ago. Work stressed me out today."

"Yeah? Tell me about it."

Reign snickered. "Remember when we first met, and you said I'd be wanting to tell you about my day?"

He smirked. "I ain't lie. You 'bout to run your mouth," he said, making her laugh.

"Whatever. Let's go get some food, and you can tell me about your day, too."

"A'ight. We can do that. You want me to pick you up, or you driving?"

"I'm not driving if you're offering to come get me."

He shook his head, already knowing that would be her answer. Women didn't like driving anywhere if there was a man present.

"Lazy ass. I'll be there in a minute."

Reign told him okay, hung up, and hopped up to get dressed. She'd showered when she got off of work, so she simply freshened up. Tossing on some high-waisted jeans, a cropped teal sweater, and her tan UGG boots, she was ready to go. Twenty minutes went by quick, and Projex texted letting her know he was outside.

Projex eyed her hips as she strutted to his car. They were poking out effortlessly, and the clenched bottom of her bubble coat made them stand out more. As soon as she climbed inside, her soft scent invaded his space.

"Hey," she spoke, leaning over to hug him. "It's too cold."

"And you wanted to get out in this. You could've just cooked us something."

"I didn't feel like cooking, or I would've."

Projex turned at the corner and asked, "What you trying to eat?"

"Nothing too fancy. Something we can grab and come back to the crib and eat if that's cool with you."

"Yeah, that's cool. Call *Juvie's* and order some chicken and fried shrimp. It should almost be ready by the time we get there."

Pulling her phone out, Reign called in their order. When she was off the phone, Projex turned his music up and bobbed his head. It was nothing like that classic *Crenshaw* album to put him in a good mood. Coincidentally, the song playing described his and Reign's situation to a T, making her believe he played it to get a reaction from her.

"Look, now, if I was yours, and you was mine
Would you do me like you do him and have someone on the side?
So, keep yo' nigga, while I stay on my grind
Just hit me up and we gon' spend some time."

G lancing his way when the song ended, Reign smirked. "What you trying to say?"

"I ain't say nothing. I have been meaning to ask what was up with you and yo' nigga though."

"Nothing at all. I've been trying to be done with him for months now," she spoke with irritation. Rodney just didn't give up.

"Yeah? How's that working out for you."

"Perfect now. He went to jail yesterday."

Projex would never root for another Black man going to jail, so he didn't say anything to bash him. As the hothead he was, Rodney rode around with his gun as a known felon. When he got pulled over, he thought about running from the boys but knew that'd end up worse than just sitting down and doing his time.

"Damn. That's fucked-up."

"No, it's not. He violated his probation and knew better, so that's on him."

"So, you ain't gon' hold him down?"

Her head swiveled his way. "Hold him down for what? I've been telling you for months now how he won't leave me alone. Maybe him being in there will."

Indifference settled in Projex's chest. He fucked with Reign tough, but he ain't like how she was coming off. Granted, he didn't know their background or history, but still. Before he could let the situation between him and Loriana play a role in their conversation, he changed the subject.

"Yeah, we'll see. Tell me about yo' day, though. What them hoes do now?"

Reign laughed and proceeded to give him all the work tea. As a bilingual healthcare insurance agent, her days of talking on the phone dragged. The pay was nice, and she lived comfortably, so it wasn't too bad. Today had just been one of those days.

"Every week, I think about quitting, but I know I can't," she explained when she was done venting.

"Why can't you?"

"I'll need something to fall back on, first. I could probably go a year max without working, but I don't want to do that. I just need a vacation. Even a small one would do."

He nodded his head, knowing exactly how she was feeling. "Yeah. That don't sound too bad."

When they pulled up to *Juvie's,* they decided to eat inside and catch a vibe. The lounge on a weekday was laidback, and the atmosphere was real chill as R&B crooned through the speakers. Reign couldn't front; she was happy Rodney was locked up. He'd been a pain in her ass for years now, but she'd never been ready to be completely done with him until this year. What she and Projex had going on was just for fun.

She wasn't trying to get her feelings involved and didn't really want any drama between him and Rodney either. They were kicking it, and if it turned into something more, cool. If not, Reign was fine with that too. Being cuffed or locked down was not on her agenda. Right now, Projex was the only man she liked spending her time with, and he provided a much-needed escape from Rodney's ass.

"You didn't tell me about your day," Reign said, dipping a fry into her honey mustard.

Projex didn't mind sharing the good news with her about possibly being nominated for a Grammy, but he felt that he should've been sharing it with Loriana first. Even if she was mad at him and had cursed him out earlier, he saved that news exclusively for her.

"It was mad productive. Got some good news through the record label that's gon' take things to a new level."

She smiled proudly. "That's good. It's crazy that you're on the rise as this big producer but don't act like it."

"What you mean? How a nigga supposed to act?"

"I'm not saying it in a bad way. I've just seen plenty of folks from the hood switch up once they reach a certain level of fame, is all. Try to stunt on the ones who came up with them. You're not boastful at all."

Projex licked his lips. He was proud as fuck of himself. So boastful, yes. Did he brag about the shit he had and the money he was making? No. That was no one's business but him and his accountant.

"I ain't a nigga who always had shit, so I ain't downplaying my accomplishments. None of this was handed to me. There's a time to stunt and a time to stay low and get that shit out the mud. When it's my turn, I ain't gon' act like I ain't work hard for it, so some stunting on niggas might just happen."

He chuckled as she did the same.

"And that's okay. Show these men out here that they can get to it just like you have."

"Straight up. If anything, seeing a nigga from where we're from make it even just a little bit should motivate and inspire."

"Yeah, but you know how that goes. Some people can't get that envious spirit up off their back long enough to celebrate the next man. It's sad."

Projex shook his head, knowing first-hand how that went. "I'm already knowing."

They finished eating, and he paid for their bill while she went to use the restroom. Now back at her place, Projex had no intentions of going inside, but Reign asked if he wanted to chill. Not minding, Projex came in and did just that until the movie they were watching began to watch them.

Slowly, the two kissed before Projex was maneuvering them into a new position on her couch. With him hovering above her now, he slid off the shorts she'd changed into. Her bare kitty greeted him, slick with wetness that had him contemplating on if he should taste her or not. Projex loved eating pussy, specifically Loriana's. Her taste was one of a kind and though he was a pleaser, eating Reign's pussy wasn't the end all be all. He hadn't done it yet, and they'd fucked before, so he didn't see what the point was now. The second he thought of Loriana, he made his mind up, slid on a condom, and tapped her thigh.

"Turn over," he demanded.

On her knees, Reign arched her back, giving Projex the most perfect view. Gripping her ass cheeks with both hands, his dick needed no assistance as it pushed inside her gushy walls. Her arch deepened as he fucked her slowly. With one foot on the ground for leverage, Projex hit corners inside her that had Reign scooting away from him.

"Nah. Where you going? Gimmie this pussy," he grunted.

Reign moaned softly, throwing her ass back. She was reaching her peak already and not mad at all about it. Projex's eyes closed for a brief second but shot open when his phone vibrated in the pocket of his jeans. Ignoring it, he focused on the way Reign's ass jiggled and bounced back against his thighs with each thrust.

"Mmm, yes. Fuck me just like that," she hissed.

When his phone vibrated again, Projex got annoyed and paused his movements. "Hol' up right quick."

He didn't bother to slide out of her as he bent down to retrieve it. After seeing Loriana's name, Projex knew he couldn't answer right now. Not like this. He figured he'd call her back when he left, but Loriana had other plans for him. When his phone rang a third time, Reign huffed and slid off him.

"Just answer it, or they're going to keep calling."

He picked it up before it could go to voicemail. "Yeah?"

Projex didn't mean to sound annoyed, but he was. After the text she sent him earlier, he didn't care to know why she was blowing his line down.

"A-Are you busy?" Loriana slightly stuttered, immediately putting him on alert.

Climbing from the couch, he removed the condom and pulled his briefs and jeans up. "I was, but what's up? What's wrong?"

"He followed me home and won't leave."

His jaw flexed. "Who?"

"Symir did. I was leaving work late, and I thought maybe I was tripping, but then I got here, and he's been outside my apartment since. I didn't want to call the police."

"He outside your door?"

The Ring app on her phone was pulled up with a clear view of Symir pacing outside her door.

"Yes. If I don't call the police on him, I'm sure my neighbors will. But I'm scared. I've never seen him act like this, and I didn't have anyone else to call. But if you were—"

"Baby, relax. I'm on my way. Stay on the phone with me."

Loriana sniffled. "Okay."

Muting the phone, Projex walked back inside the living room to Reign, who was dressed and sitting on her couch. She didn't hear his conversation, but by the looks of it, knew he was about to leave.

"I got an emergency, but I'll hit you up later on, a'ight?"

"Okay. Drive safely and let me know when you make it home."

"I will."

Hopping in his car, Projex sped to Loriana's place, not giving a single care about the rules of the road. What would've normally taken him twenty minutes took him thirteen to get there. As he pulled around to her side of the complex, he hit his lights like the true street nigga he was.

"He still there?" he asked.

"I don't see him, but his car is still here."

Loriana had been peeking back and forth between her Ring app and her curtains. By the way Symir parked, she couldn't tell if he was inside his car or not. Projex's question was answered when he was in front of her building. In haste, Symir peeled out of the complex like a mad man. Projex was in a different car, so he was sure he hadn't peeped him.

"When'd you get that?" Loriana asked, watching him reverse an Audi coupe into a parking spot.

"Like a week ago. Unlock the door."

Hopping out, Projex jogged up the steps, and she opened the door for him. She bit the corner of her lip as he approached her. Sliding his hand through her hair, he placed his lips to her forehead as her arms wrapped around him. She was damn near trembling as he held her.

"It's a'ight. I got you."

When she inhaled with relief, Reign's feminine scent triggered her senses. Brows pinched, Loriana pulled away from him.

"You were with her?" she questioned, looking him in the eyes.

"Yeah."

She blinked and nodded her head slowly. "Okay. He's gone now, so you can leave. I'm good."

"Man, don't do that."

"I'm not doing anything. I didn't mean to interrupt, so go back to enjoying your night."

She walked away from him, pissing Projex off. "You gon' walk off while I'm trying to talk to you?"

"I don't care to hear what you have to say, honestly."

"Bruh," he chuckled in a heated tone, "you gon' really piss me off with this dumb shit. Grow the fuck up, cuz."

"No. You grow the fuck up!" she shouted, twisting her neck his way. "You the one keep playing games. I'm just learning to play them better."

He ran a hand over his face, not even in the mood

to do this with her. "What you really mad for, huh? I thought you were cool on me. Told me to live my life and to leave you alone. Ain't that what you sent in that text earlier?"

"Yep," she sassed, popping her lips. "That's exactly what I said, so bye. Go do you."

"You so fucking irritating. I don't even know why I deal with you, man."

Loriana laughed. "I know why, but like I said... you can stop. It's not hard to stop fucking with me, clearly. You got these hoes lined up waiting to be on your dick."

He sucked his teeth. "Loriana, shut up for real. You think you know everything and just making yourself mad for no reason."

"So, you ain't just come from fucking her?"

She propped a hand on her hip and dared him to lie.

"Nah."

"Let me smell your dick then."

He choked on a laugh though this shit wasn't funny. "Girl, what? You tripping."

She moved toward him. "Nah. If you ain't just come from having sex, let me see for myself."

"Man, move," Projex spat, shoving her hand away from his crotch. "You doing too much."

Loriana punched him hard in the chest. "Cause you lying! Just leave! I swear, I'm good on you!"

Walking up on her, Projex trapped her against the island. "Man, quit all that hollering. You tripping out for no reason."

"No, I'm not. How you gon' come over here smelling just like that hoe? That's so disrespectful. Get out of my face, Projex. For real."

"Projex? Man, don't call me that shit. It's Bryshon to you, and what you mean? You told me that nigga was over here bothering you, so I pulled up."

"And now I want you to leave," she hissed.

Grabbing her face, Projex squeezed her jaws, forcing her lips to pucker out. "Make me. You want a nigga out yo' life so bad, make me get out of that mothafucka."

Venom swarmed her eyes as he didn't let up. Loriana went from scared, to relieved, to angry in a matter of minutes. Her emotions were scattered; she couldn't place them where they needed to be. Her chest heaved against his, and he couldn't help but kiss her lips. Frustratedly, Loriana jerked her head away from his mouth.

"Fucking stubborn. I can kiss you."

"No, you can't when you probably had your nasty

mouth on that bitch. You better not let me catch you with her."

He smirked. "What you gon' do, Ms. Tough Ass?"

"Let me see you out with her and find out."

Loriana told him to do him, but if she caught him, she was liable to break his jaw, bust his windows, flatten tires, and some more shit. She'd go straight D'Wana from *Next Friday* on his ass.

"You always trying to fight with me, and all I wanna do is love you," Projex let her know.

Loriana rolled her eyes. "That's hard to believe. Let my face go," she fussed, tossing his hand away from her.

"Me loving you is hard to believe? Nah. It's clear as day, but you keep trying to fight it, and for what?"

"I'm not competing with no woman over you. These hoes can have you before I ever stoop that low."

He chuckled. "These hoes don't want me."

"Tell me anything."

"I do gotta tell you something."

"What, Projex?" He gripped her face harder this time. "Ooouuu," she muffled out.

"Quit playing with my name."

"You gon' quit squeezing my jaw like that. Damn, you're rough."

He gently massaged each cheek with the back of his knuckles. "My bad. I do have to tell you some news I got today, though."

She sighed. "I'm listening."

"Me and Laurent might be nominated for a Grammy."

Her gasp, bright eyes, and squeal of excitement made him smile as his heart expanded in his chest. "Oh, my gosh, bae! I'm so happy for you."

Her arms tossed around his neck, forgetting that she was mad at him. This was why he wanted to tell her first and in person. Seeing how happy she was for him made his night. When she pulled back, the smile was still on her face and in her eyes. Tears had gathered there as well.

"I'm so proud of you. Seriously. You about to make me cry."

He chuckled. "Shit, that's how I felt when Laurent told me. That's crazy, huh?"

Her head bobbed as she nodded. "Yes, but no at the same time. A Grammy nomination is huge, but you are so deserving. I don't know anyone who works as hard as you. No goal is unobtainable or crazy when God is involved. Remember that."

"And you wonder why I can't stop fucking with

you no matter how annoying you are," he joked. "That's exactly what I needed to hear."

"Why'd you ever doubt that you could reach this level?"

He shrugged. "I ain't doubt it. I just ain't expect it to happen so soon. On the real, I don't know if I'm ready for all this."

With her, he could admit his true feelings. Since he was released from prison, his life had been on go. Putting in the work wasn't where he felt unprepared; it was the fame that came along with it. He'd already seen some sides of the industry that he wanted to stray away from and have no dealings with.

"Well, you better get ready because it's your turn. What? You wanted me to give you some sympathy? Aht, aht. You ain't come this far to only come this far. It's time to do what you've always wanted to do. That moment is right here, and I'm not going to let you get cold feet and miss out on it."

He gave her a smile that warmed her insides. "Bruh, I love your ass. On my mama."

"Please don't put that on Ms. Joseline. That's my girl."

"She don't even like you, for real. She be jeffing."

"Oh, please. Your family loves me." She laughed, and they got quiet soon after. They stared into each other's eyes, searching for the words to say. Loriana spoke first.

"Thank you for coming over here tonight. I'ma have to get me a gun."

"You mean another one. What happened to the one I got you?"

Right after he'd realized she and Mhyale were living by themselves, he copped her a gun. Scarily, Loriana never brought it in from her car, which would defeat the purpose of having it if someone did run up in the crib.

"Someone stole it out of my car on the Westport a few years ago."

"Broke ass niggas," he spat. "It's cool. We gon' cop you another one. Some shit that'll sit that nigga on his ass if he pops back up over here."

Her eyes widened. "You want me to shoot him?"

"Nah. I just want you to act like you are. Yeah, ma. Or do you want me to do it? Just know if I do, his people gone be making some funeral arrangements."

"No. I don't want you to kill him. That's a little extreme."

"Harassing you is too. Following you home is enough to make an example out of that nigga. Matter fact, just give me his address. I'ma go have a talk with him about learning some mothafuckin' boundaries."

Her shoulders dropped as she sighed. "I will, but you're not going over there tonight."

"That's coo. There's other days this week for me to have some fun," he said with a grin.

"Right. You going home when you leave here?"

His head tilted to the left. "You putting me out?"

"Um, yes. We're cool, but we ain't that damn cool right now. I'm standing on what I said about letting you do you."

"But you were just—" He stopped himself. "You know what? A'ight. I guess I'ma head to the crib then. Damn. A nigga come be Captain-Save-A—"

"I know you aren't about to call me a hoe!" she spat, pushing him away from her.

Projex laughed hard. "Nah, nah. I was gon say Captain-Save-A-Lo. Like your name."

She gave him a blank stare, not finding what he said funny at all. "Yeah, okay. Keep on testing me, Bryshon."

"Aww, there she go. You know my name now? I'ma have to make you scream that mothafucka so you won't forget it again."

"Please. I won't be screaming anything for a while. That dick is tainted."

"No, it's not. It belongs to Loriana Emery."

Her heart skipped a beat as she eyed him. "I'm not your wife just because you add your last name to mine."

"You gon' be my wife one day. I told you that a long time ago. Have us a bunch of badass kids and shit. Watch."

"Eww, no." She faked gagged.

"Quit playing. You know you wanna have my babies, girl."

She laughed as he hugged her tightly. "Mooove. You always wanna be on me. Act like you have to touch me all the time."

"I do. Remember that when you wanna be all in my face," he said, slightly shoving her away from him. "I'm 'bout to go home."

"Awww. You mad?"

"Nah. You the one gon' be mad when you gotta use that vibrator tonight." He chuckled.

"Me and my vibrator get along just fine, thank you. At least it doesn't talk back and piss me off."

"It can't suck your toes and cuddle with you, so I'ont care what you talking about."

Loriana snickered behind his back as he walked to the door. It for sure couldn't do all that. Projex had her spoiled with that, and she loved it. He went to open the door but paused and looked back at her.

"Loriana."

Her eyes brightened some. "Hmm?"

"What's that address?"

Without protest, she rattled off Symir's address and sighed. "Remember, he's the uncle of Joi's baby."

"Nah. *You* remember who I am. I don't give a fuck who uncle he supposed to be. You mine, and I'm not ever about to play no games about you."

She nodded her head as he kissed her forehead. "Okay."

"I'ma text you when I get to the crib. I love you."

"I love you, too."

Watching until he made it to his car, Loriana then closed and locked the door. She could only hope that Projex didn't hurt Symir too much. While they were trying to find balance in their life, doing something that would cause a rift in their family would definitely set them back more than they already were.

Chapter Ten

The one thing Nyree hated more than being woken up out of her sleep, or room temperature water, was being sent on a dummy mission.

"This my last time meeting with any of his people," she fumed, ready to pull out of the secluded area she'd parked in.

Her eyes scanned the parking lot she was supposed to be meeting one of Maverick's homeboys in for what seemed the hundredth time. According to Maverick, he should've pulled up ten minutes ago. The only reason she was sticking around was because he wanted to cop a hefty amount. Money was money, but now she realized doing business with some people wasn't going to fly.

Just as she began to place her car in drive, the make and model of the vehicle Maverick had described to her, pulled up next to her. Sighing, Nyree grabbed the pills. The man's appearance made her stomach coil as he looked much older than a guy who would hang with Maverick and his boys. Then again, not everyone in college was in their twenties, so she shook off her weird energy and rolled her window down.

"Nyree?" the man questioned.

She nodded her head. "Yeah. They're all here."

When he reached in his pocket, she assumed he was pulling out the money, but instead, the guy displayed a police badge. The color drained from Nyree's face as she tried to put her car in drive and pull off. That was her first instinct, but she failed. The officer yanked on her door, stopping all efforts of an attempted high speed because that's surely what'd they be on with her.

"You're hurting my arm!" Nyree shouted as he roughly pulled her from the driver's seat.

The extra officer, who seemed to appear out of nowhere, had her heart thudding wildly in her chest. Nyree had read the news articles, watched clips, and marched to protest against the killing of Black people, specifically women, at the hands of police. She prayed she wasn't another statistic.

"Ma'am, just relax and cooperate. That's all we're asking," the second officer spoke.

Afraid of losing her life behind a drug transaction gone wrong, Nyree did as she was asked. After being placed in handcuffs that elicited sharp pains to her shoulder, she was placed in the back of the discreet squad car. Anger soured through her chest as one of the officers began to search her vehicle.

"That mothafucka set me up," she hissed.

Then, she thought about how she was going to explain this to not only her mama but to Juice as well. He'd warned her about moving so sloppily yet hadn't taken heed to his forewarning. Worry began to settle as they pulled off the lot twenty minutes later. Nyree was a tough girl, but she'd never been involved with the law. Not to the point where she got arrested anyway.

Calling Nakita was out of the question when she was given a chance to call someone. Hoping her Uncle Chris could get her out of this jam, she dialed his number. Her breathing was labored as the phone seemed to ring extra loudly in her ear. It was late in the evening, and she hoped he wasn't busy at work.

"Uncle Chris," she said with relief once he answered.

"Nyree?"

"Yes. It's me. Um, I was arrested, and I need you to come get me out, please."

Nyree heard him moving around and then a door close. "Arrested for what? You in town?"

"It's a long story. I'm here at school. I didn't want to call my mama, so you were my only other option."

Uncle Chris sighed. "I'll be there. It's going to take a few hours; you're not right up the street."

"I know. I can wait."

"Are you okay? Did any of them mothafuckas handle you roughly?"

Tears formed in her eyes. "No, not really. I guess they were doing their jobs."

"I'ma see for myself. Sit tight, baby girl. I'll be there as soon as I can, okay?"

"Okay. Thank you so much."

Uncle Chris told her she didn't have to thank him, but Nyree did. That two-and-a-half-hour drive through the night wasn't going to be an easy one, especially not knowing what he was up against once he reached her. Nyree didn't even have a clue what she'd gotten herself into. Selling pills to the students on campus was supposed to just be some easy money, not have her looking at doing some jail time.

With the sun coming up and more than a few hours later, Nyree's bail had been posted. Uncle Chris greeted her with a hug before examining her frame. As a policeman himself, Chris thought he could use his position to get her out of there without a hassle, but that didn't work. Nyree was treated like the drug-dealing civilian she was.

"You alright?" he questioned, and she nodded.

"Yes. I need to see where my car is towed."

Her thoughts ran wild. It was Tuesday morning now, and she knew Juice had to be losing his mind. Monday nights belonged to him. Every night did, really, but those specifically. When he couldn't be in town to lay up with her, they'd stay on FaceTime as she studied or did her homework. The lie she told him about running to get some food with friends instead of what she really had planned was her bad karma.

I should've listened, she thought, sliding into the passenger seat of her Chris' car.

"You mighty quiet. Tell me what happened," he urged, not pulling off yet.

Nyree knew there was no use in lying, so she didn't. "The cop was undercover, and I tried selling him some pills."

"You what?" Chris thought he'd heard her wrong. "Selling pills? What the fuck are you doing selling pills, Nyree?"

"I've been doing it. I just got caught slipping last night."

"Caught slipping?" Chris scoffed. "You could've lost your life! That's not getting caught slipping. That's called being irresponsible as fuck!"

He was so loud, Nyree's body shook. "I know!"

"You must not. Who got you selling pills, 'cause I know for a fact you ain't just doing it on your own?"

"Nobody has me doing anything. It was my decision."

"For what, though? Help me understand what the purpose of this is. It can't be for no money. You don't want for anything."

Nyree shrugged her shoulders. She hated being chastised by her uncle. He took his role in her life very seriously, so to see him visibly upset with her hurt her feelings.

"You do know. Don't sit there all hush mouth now."

"Just because. It wasn't for a specific reason. I just wanted to do it. It was easy, I saw a need for it, and I provided."

Chris couldn't help but chuckle. "You saw a need

to sell drugs when you're supposed to be down here earning a degree. Yeah, maybe these professors of the classes you're enrolled in aren't doing their jobs. So, what you gon' do next? Drop out and be a queen pin?"

Nyree sucked her teeth. "No. I graduate next semester."

"You sure about that? Once this gets back to the university, you better hope and pray they don't expel your ass."

Her heart sank. She hadn't even thought about that. Getting expelled this close to graduation would literally kill her. Those tears she'd been desperately holding in slid down her face. Nyree didn't even bother to wipe them.

"I can't believe you, Nyree. After all me and your mama been through to get you this far, you go and do something foolish like this?"

She sniffled. "I'm sorry."

Chris simply shook his head. She was sorry now, but it was too late. Before they pulled off, Nyree called the tow company's number on the card she was given. Her car was there, and they only accepted cash if she wanted it back.

"I have cash at my apartment," she told her uncle.

"I bet you do."

He could only imagine what else she'd been doing in college. The weekly updates she gave him never mentioned her pushing pills. Her not having a specific reason for doing so didn't sit right with Chris, and before he left, he promised to get the truth up out of her.

Pulling into her apartments, Nyree's eyes widened when she saw Juice's truck backed in where he normally parked. When she didn't answer her phone, and no one knew her whereabouts, he hopped on the highway. Juice knew she had to come home at some point, and he wanted to greet her when she got there. This wasn't the perfect time, though.

Juice knew it was her. His concerned gaze fell into a squinted one as he inspected who was driving. As tired as he was, seeing Nyree in the car with a man gave Juice crazy energy. He didn't bother to wipe the sleep from his eyes as he hopped out with his gun by his side.

Knock! Knock! Knock!

"Get the fuck out the car," Juice spat.

The butt of Juice's gun damn near broke the driver's side window. Not knowing who he was, Chris went for his gun as well.

"No, no! Wait!" Nyree shouted.

Panic funneled through her body at the speed of light.

Hurriedly, she unfastened her seatbelt and hopped out. Rushing around to Juice, she pushed him back as Chris hopped out of the car with his gun drawn. So blinded by rage, Juice hadn't realized Chris was in uniform. He was on the clock and came straight to Nyree's rescue.

"Who is this!?" Chris shouted, ready to end him.

"Nigga, who is you?" Juice pressed.

Nyree was about to lose her mind. With all her might, which wasn't much due to hours without water or food, she shoved Juice back some more. Her arms wrapped around his waist as she stared into his face.

"Jovani, that's my uncle."

His dark eyes stayed trained on Chris until Nyree forced him to look at her. "What?" His mind refused to accept the words she just said.

"He's my uncle. You don't need this," she said, grabbing ahold of his wrist. She had to calm him down and quick.

Juice's chest heaved as he watched Chris like a hawk. He didn't think Nyree was lying. Chris' protectiveness overshadowed his. Both men were willing and ready to go to war behind her. What fucked him up was that she had never told him someone this close to her was a cop. Juice pushed her away from him and tucked his gun at his waist.

"So, this was yo' secret, huh?" he questioned.

Nyree's chest tightened. The disappointment in his tone made her sick to her stomach.

"I-It's not like that."

Her voice cracked right along with her heart at his next words.

"That's exactly what a disloyal mothafucka would say. You got it, though, Ny. Ain't no need to send for backup, cuz," Juice sneered at Chris.

"You better watch how you talk to her, my guy."

Juice sniffed and rubbed at his nose. "Yeah, a'ight."

"My niece here seems to be way in over her head and got herself locked up. You got anything to do with that?"

Some of his anger evaporated, leaving him even more confused. Nyree stared at him with pleading eyes. She wanted to explain. She could explain, but not right now. The tension surrounding them was too thick. She had to clear the air between her drug-dealing friend, who was much more than that, and her uncle, who locked guys like him up for a living. This wasn't going to end well, and she knew it. She felt it deep in her bones as Juice's nostrils flared. His concern for her well-being shined through but wavered.

"I'ma tell you," Nyree told him.

"Not right now you aren't," Chris let be known.

"Uncle Chris," Nyree whined. "Please. Just give me a minute."

"Nah. You good, Ny. Handle yo' business. 'Cause after today, all this shit is a wrap."

Nyree's face scrunched up. "You don't mean that."

"I mean every word. Try me and see."

"Are you threatening her?" Chris' jaw clenched.

"Man, quit fucking talkin' to me, cuz. I'ont associate with 12." He mugged Nyree up and down, further making his point clear.

Nyree drew in a sharp breath. "Jovani. This is my family. I would never do anything to jeopardize your freedom."

"But you'd jeopardize yours?" Chris wanted to know.

Nyree had made it very clear without saying who she'd gotten the pills from. Chris could read between the lines very well. He just hated that it was this late in the game. The way she was going back and forth with Juice let him know baby girl was deep in; her head barely above water.

Juice could only shake his head while backing away from her. "Handle yo' business."

"You are my business!" she shouted. "Don't do this. You're taking everything the wrong way."

"Am I? I see why I ain't ever met your people. I get it now, baby. Ain't no need to explain."

Nyree never begged a soul, but she was ready to at this moment. She needed Juice to understand that she wasn't being sneaky like he assumed.

"But I want to. I have to. I know it looks bad, but it's not. I can't control what his profession is."

"Quit trying to explain yourself and let him leave. He'll listen when he's ready." Chris had to intervene. Hearing his niece whine to Juice was pissing him off.

Nyree's throat ached with defeat. Letting Juice walk away from her was for the better. There was no getting through to him right now. Him or Chris. She bit her bottom lip as it trembled, until it throbbed like her pulse. Nyree had promised not to get in her feelings behind their situation and had failed miserably.

With no other option but to go inside the house and grab the cash to retrieve her car, Nyree pulled her eyes away from Juice's truck pulling out of the complex. She rushed up the steps and was bombarded with questions by her roommate. Promising to catch her up when she got back, Nyree left right back out after grabbing the money. Inside the car, her leg bounced as her nerves still hadn't settled.

"You gon' tell me who he is?" Chris asked.

Nyree shook her head no. "Not right now. I just want to get my car and go back home to take a shower."

Chris accepted that for now. It was two days before Thanksgiving, and he was more than thankful that his niece wasn't locked up. Things could've gone much worse than they had, and he hoped this was a lesson Nyree learned from because this was only the beginning.

Projex missed the thrill of placing fear inside a nigga who was pussy. Preferably the ones who fucked with someone that belonged to him. No matter how anybody looked at it, Loriana was his. She was made specifically for him. Just because Symir called himself being there for her wasn't enough to make Projex let him slide for the disrespect.

With his gun in his lap, Projex pulled the blunt from behind his ear and sparked it. Inhaling deeply, he stood from the chair he was in and walked over to the bed. He took a few more pulls before he let the ashes decorate Symir's face. Stirring in his sleep, Symir's eyes popped open, and he immediately reached for his gun that was no longer in his nightstand. Projex had removed that the second he stepped inside the room.

"What you reaching for, nigga?" Projex spat. His gun pressed up under Symir's chin as he put out the blunt on his bare chest.

Symir's jaw clenched. At a disadvantage, he sat stiffly as his chest heaved. Evident fear danced in his eyes with a hint of anger. Projex was bold. No one had ever pulled a gun on him, let alone snuck into his crib undetected.

"I'ma only tell you this shit once. Leave Loriana the fuck alone. You see how easy it was to get up in here? I'd hate for all those businesses you got to magically burn down. Don't come to her job, her crib, none of that. You damn sure better not follow her again."

Symir tried to speak, and the gun flew across his jaw, instantly drawing blood. Projex gripped his neck so violently, he began to choke.

"Bitch, I ain't tell you to speak. Nod your head 'fore I put a bullet through this mothafucka."

Hurriedly, Symir nodded his head. His orbs held the type of fear that fueled Projex back in the day.

This wasn't how he moved now. Prison had changed him for the better. The life he was adjusting to couldn't afford to be tainted by reckless behavior. Loriana was the exception. She was always the exception, and Projex was going to make it clear to anyone who stepped out of line with her. Niggas, bitches, whoever. They all could get checked behind her.

With a shove, Projex released him. Clinging onto the air that graced his lungs, Symir leaned over, sucking in deep breaths. His head spun as oxygen resurfaced to his brain. Disgusted that he had even been able to breathe in Loriana's direction, Projex mugged him.

"Now, you can speak. Say, 'I'm sorry for touching what's yours.'"

Symir glanced up at him like he was crazy, and he was. "W-What?"

"You heard me, cuz. Say, 'I'm sorry for touching what's yours with my weak ass.'"

When he didn't budge, Projex inched his gun back underneath his chin.

"A'ight, a'ight," Symir agreed. His jaw was aching terribly. "I'm sorry for touching what's yours."

"Nah. What else?"

"With my weak ass," Symir mumbled, embarrassed as hell.

Projex smirked. "Pussy mothafucka. Remember what I said. I'd hate to have to revisit this conversation."

After walking out of his house through the front door, Projex hopped in the blacked-out suburban waiting for him. He had a flight that boarded to Atlanta in two hours, but business had to be handled first. He hoped Symir would've taken his L like a man and left Loriana alone, but he hadn't. The only reason he still had his life was because of Joi. Symir had better thank her. If it was up to Projex, her child would only have one living uncle.

"We should go to the all-black party tonight," Loriana suggested, looking up from her phone and over at Nyree.

Perched on her best friend's couch, Nyree held a wine glass in her hand that needed to be refilled. It was the day after Thanksgiving, and they were both in their feelings. Fronts were put on while they visited family the day before. Now that they were alone, they could be vulnerable. Nyree wasn't in the mood to party.

"I don't feel like being around all them people," she let Loriana know.

"Okay. We can just sit in the house and be two sad bitches then."

Nyree smirked before the duo laughed. "We are sad, huh?"

"Miserable at this point."

"Now, see no. Miserable just sounds weak. I ain't no weak hoe."

"Neither am I!"

They were trying to be serious but kept laughing. Nyree drained her glass and sat it on a coaster.

"Have you talked to Projex?"

Loriana shook her head no. Tuesday was the day of the Grammy nominations, and he and Laurent had been nominated for Best Rap Song, which was a songwriter's award. She never doubted that they wouldn't be. When she FaceTimed him to congratulate him, he was all smiles. A few drunk texts were sent to her later that night, letting her know he was having a good time.

What Loriana didn't expect to see when she got on Instagram was a picture of Reign hugged up with Projex. Loriana wasn't sure if he'd flown her and Yari out, but that's all she could come up with. It's what made the most sense because why else would they both be in Atlanta at the same time as him?

Yari's post was congratulating him as her best friend, with a long caption about how he worked so hard for this moment. Loriana couldn't help but roll her eyes as she read over each sentence. The way he and Reign were hugged up gutted her. It wasn't one of those friendly hugs.

Projex looked invested. Like he wanted her there to celebrate with him. That's where Loriana should've been. Right by his side, rooting for him while recording his smile as he and Laurent popped bottles. She deserved to share the moment with them and not be at home, contemplating her next move. One minute they were good, and the next, it was as if Projex was doing shit on purpose to end them for good.

"Nope. I'm so tired of arguing about the same thing with him. Maybe we should just call it quits," she muttered, not wanting that, but she didn't know what else to do.

Coming second to another woman wasn't happening, period. Some bonds you just had to let go of. No matter how bad it may hurt, that pain doesn't last long. It just hurt less. She wasn't going to force herself to be okay with the sucker shit Projex was on because he'd never let her be on that with him. Him moving about with Reign like she didn't have his heart didn't sit well with her at all.

Loriana wanted the type of love they shared before shit got chaotic. It was for sure worth fighting for, but damn. How much fight did she have to put in? If it was payback Projex wanted, he was getting it with no remorse. That wasn't the case, though. He was simply living his life until she was ready. As always, the ball was in Loriana's court with him. The only difference now was Projex was the coach. There weren't no plays being made unless he called for them.

"If you're serious, then do what's best for you," Nyree told her. "You think he gon' let that happen?"

"I don't care what he thinks should happen between us. He's the one playing games. He'll express his feelings like he wants us to be together, then turn around and do shit like fly some hoe out."

Nyree laughed. "How you know she a hoe?"

"I don't, but that doesn't matter."

Projex was steady sending mixed signals. If he was trying to settle down with Reign, he could've just said that. Lying about it was petty. One thing she wasn't about to do again was be placed in another love triangle. Symir's crazy ass was enough.

"I love y'all together, but I get it. Some shit is just draining. You should at least ask him. Y'all have been through a lot to just end it."

Loriana waved her hand dismissively. "Exactly, so if anything, he should want to get his shit together. You see, I did."

"Girl, please. You ain't have no choice fooling with that weirdo. Shamari acts nothing like his brother, does he?"

"No. Not at all. Symir started flipping out of nowhere. I probably shouldn't have led him on."

"Girl, fuck him. Don't matter if you did or not. That nigga hurt his own feelings playing rebound to Projex. He knew what it was, and so did you."

Sighing, Loriana couldn't do anything but agree. "Right. What's up with you and Juice? Are you going to go see him while you're in town?"

"I thought about it, but I don't know. He was so nonchalant when we talked on the phone the other day. Like he didn't care if we talked or not."

"You been in town since Wednesday night, right?"

Nyree nodded her head yes. "Yep."

"That's probably why he's acting like that. That man ain't trying to talk over the phone, Ny."

She plopped back onto the couch, resting her head along the cushion. "I know, but I'm kinda nervous to see him in person. You should've seen the way he looked at me when I told him about my uncle."

"I mean… he has the right to feel some type of way. You do, too but look at it from his perspective. He's a street nigga. Not knowing his *girl* was related to a cop can look a bit suspect."

"You know I'm not even on that type of time, though."

"Yes, I do, but he doesn't. He only knows just as much as you tell him and trusts that it's not something to have you looking like an opp."

Nyree chuckled. "Girl, you been around Projex for too long. Talking about an opp. Never that. I get where you're coming from, though. I should go over there and have a face-to-face talk."

"Yep. That's what I'd do. Go plead your case."

Laughing, Nyree stood up from the couch. "Girl, shut up. We both in the doghouse."

"Nah. You on your own with that one." Loriana chuckled.

Thankful she'd only had a small amount of wine, Nyree freshened up some before hopping in her car. She thought about calling him to let him know she was pulling up but didn't want to get rejected. That's why she'd been avoiding him since she got in town.

Traffic was thick as she drove through the city

with Tink in rotation. When she pulled up to his place, she exhaled after seeing his car in the driveway. While on the phone with his younger sister, Juice noticed motion on one of the TV monitors from his cameras. He was standing at the counter eating left-overs from yesterday. His FN sat right beside his cup of apple juice.

"Asha, let me call you back."

"Okay, brother. Love you."

"I love you, too, sis."

Juice's eyes stayed trained on the cameras as Nyree made her way up to the door. He was surprised to see her in person but knew he was going to let her in. He unlocked the door and opened it as Nyree fidgeted in place, waiting for him to say something.

"Can I come in?" she asked.

Juice moved to the side, letting her bypass him. "Why you wearing that?"

"Wearing what?" she questioned, facing him while removing her coat.

"That perfume. Where you been?"

Si by Giorgio Armani was one of Nyree's favorite perfumes. It'd become Juice's favorite on her as well. She'd been wearing it for years now, and he made sure she stayed stocked up on it. Juice was trying his best not to give her a hug.

"Nowhere, really. I was out shopping earlier then went to Loriana's."

He gave a head nod and walked around the island back to his plate of food. Contently, he ate a piece of turkey before shoving a forkful of greens in his mouth. He caught Nyree licking her lips when he looked up.

"Can I have a bite?" she asked, and he shook his head while sliding her his plate.

"I shouldn't give you shit. You on my bad side right now."

Smirking, Nyree picked his fork up and ate some turkey, a little mac and cheese, and greens before sliding it back to him.

"You shared your food, so I can't be on it that bad."

"Had you taken your ass back to school without me seeing your face, we was gon' have problems fasho."

Her heart skipped a bit. "You were acting like you didn't want to talk to me when I called you yesterday."

"I didn't. You weren't saying shit I was trying to hear."

Nyree sucked her teeth and leaned against the island. "Communication is key with me."

Juice's head cocked to the side. "I can't tell. You be ready to tell me everything else but failed to mention yo' folks was a cop. How's that communicating?"

"I didn't know how to tell you without me looking like a fraud."

"Bruh, nah. I ain't accepting that weak excuse. You know me, lil' baby. You could've kept that shit uh hunnid with me. We solid. It's you hiding it from me that got me feeling like you was on some setup shit."

"Never," she said sternly. "I don't even rock like that."

"Was you ashamed of me or something?"

His question held a hint of uncertainty as if Nyree was embarrassed about who he was or how he lived. She wasn't at all and wanted him to know that. She needed him to feel that she was all for him. Coming around the island, she wedged herself between him and it, placing her arms around his frame.

"No, bae. Never. I just didn't want to be at odds with you about something I can't control. My uncle is not worried about you doing what you do. He just hates that I got mixed up in it."

"Speaking of that, I need to make a visit to see that nigga, Maverick, huh?"

Nyree exhaled. She knew it was coming. Maverick hadn't intentionally set her up, but he was the sole culprit. His homeboy's dad was the cop who faked like he was trying to buy some pills from her. As an athlete, there were a lot of things they got away with in college, but failing multiple drug tests and getting caught with them was different. So, of course, to stay on his dad's good side, the homeboy gave up Nyree. Maverick wasn't the one to blame, but he for sure looked suspect.

"It's not necessary. You said what I was doing is a wrap, right?" Nyree smirked while looking up at his face.

A piece of cornbread was on his lip, and she licked it off with her tongue. "Freaky ass girl. I was talking about us and that, but you ain't going for that, I see."

"Sure ain't."

"What yo' uncle saying they gon' charge you with? That's why I always told you to move like you got something to lose, Ny. You tried selling to an undercover. Ain't no telling what they gone try to hit you with."

"I know," she groaned. "What if they ask who I got it from?"

"You tell me."

"I'll never snitch on you, daddy. I'll hold a brick for you, daddy," she rapped, making him grin.

Juice gripped her ass. "I'm being serious."

"I am too. Hopefully, it's nothing too serious. My uncle is trying to pull some strings. That's not my fault the cop's son is a pill popper. He shouldn't be an addict."

Juice shook his head. "Nah. Take accountability for yo' actions. I'm responsible, too, cause you was too eager to push that shit. It was a good lil' run, but that's a wrap."

Nyree kissed along his neck. "Fine. That's the only thing that's a wrap."

"You gon' make me fuck with you?"

"You really ain't have no choice. You thought you did?"

Pushing his plate to the side, Juice picked her up, placing her on the counter. Running his hands up her thighs covered in some thick leggings, Juice thought about their relationship. He hated the way he felt being at odds with her, and it'd only been a few days. Her presence in his life was one he appreciated, but he wasn't going for no flaw shit.

"Aye. If they talking about more than some community service hours or something, you bet not take that shit."

"Jovani." Nyree sighed. "No. You just told me to be accountable for my actions. Why would I let you go down for it?"

"I wasn't asking you, Ny. I'm not letting you do no time for that petty shit. End of discussion."

Her lip poked out in a pout as he sucked it into his mouth. From there, their tongues twirled as Nyree tried meshing her body against his. When she moaned, Juice pulled back. He wanted to let her know something else before he fucked the disobedience out of her.

"This next holiday, you meeting my people, and I'm meeting yours," he told her straight up.

"Okay."

His brow lifted. "What? No pushback?"

"Nope. It's time anyway. I can't have you and my uncle beefing."

"I was gon' beat his buff ass."

Nyree's head fell back as she laughed loudly. "Boy, please. You got hands, but I don't know about all that."

"Yeah, a'ight. So, you trying to be my woman?"

She blushed while running a hand over his thick waves. "Oh, no more friends with benefits?"

"No more of that."

"I mean, I guess since you asked. I figured you'd just tell me. That seems to be your thing."

"I got a thing with running shit. You can't tell?"

"Mhm. I can. Now, run me that dick. I missed it and you."

"Nah. Come suck this mothafucka first," he ordered, slapping her thigh while scooting away from the counter. "You owe down for being on some sneaky shit."

With pleasure, Nyree hopped down from the island and pulled his shorts down while lowering into a squat. His dick bounced out so beautifully. She looked him in the eyes while dragging her tongue along every pulsing vein. Juice helped glide his member into her warm mouth, instantly coating it with saliva, before withdrawing.

Nyree freakily swirled her tongue around the tip before Juice slapped his dick against her tongue and her plump lips. Easing him back inside her mouth, her head bobbed slowly. Juice stared down at her pretty chocolate face so intensely, perplexed by how she was able to swallow him completely.

"You sorry, lil' baby?" Juice asked her.

Innocence traced her eyes as she nodded her head. Next came a loud slurp as she removed him from the back of her throat. "I'm sorry, Jovani."

She said it so sweetly; Juice had no choice but to forgive her. He was planning on doing that anyway, but her admission made it that much easier. Some bomb ass make-up sex was right up their ally to forgiveness and the perfect way to start off their relationship as a couple.

Chapter Eleven

As she walked around her house, blowing out her *Scent'd by KC* and *T&S Living Essentials* candles she had lit, Mhyale held her phone in her hand. She could never just light one at a time, so she had a bunch going. She was getting ready to head to her mama's house but was running some business ideas by Rhyli first.

"I think getting a vending machine is perfect. All the money will come back to you and right back into the salon."

Mhyale agreed. "That's what I was thinking too. Okay, cool. I'ma call the guy I been in contact with and let him know it's a go. What you over there doing?"

"Girl, trying to hide from Blayze. I spent so much money over the weekend, I made myself sick."

"Like he tripping. As long as you copped my boy something, you should be good."

"I did. He wanted a new grill for the summer. I snagged a really nice one that was on sale online. He'll be happy about that."

Mhyale put on her Dr. Martens poly casual boots. "I know he will. Tell him gon' head and throw some ribs on there. I didn't even get to do any shopping for real. I was at the shop all day. Then, by the time I got off, I was dog tired. Naaz did grab me some shoes, though."

"That was sweet of him. Men swear they don't be knowing what they like on you until you wear something that they don't like."

The two laughed because that was nothing but the truth. Even if Mhyale didn't think some stuff Naaz picked out for her was all that, she still wore it because he liked it on her. It was compromising. Yes, he had style and could get fly with the best of them, but Mhyale had to question his suggestions sometimes.

"Right. I'ma text you later, though. I'm about to go see my mama," Mhyale told her.

"How's she doing?"

That question always conflicted Mhyale. She didn't want to lie to her and say she was doing good because she wasn't. Peaches wasn't doing horrible either, but she'd changed and not for the better. Mhyale gave her the best answer she could.

"She's doing her best and has her days. I'm hoping today isn't one of them. I really can't keep doing this with her."

Rhyli sighed, feeling for her friend. "I know you can't. And I'd never tell you to deal with it because you know how damaged it had me. I'm still in therapy."

They were quiet for a second as their minds drifted down memory lane. Rhyli seemed to have the picture-perfect life now, but it took more than a few frames to get here. She'd been through hell and back, burned by people she loved the most, and looked out for by people she least expected. Mhyale knew first-hand how hard she'd had it, and at the age she was at now, she didn't expect to be going through the same troubles with Peaches.

"We'll be good, though. Just gotta stay prayed up," Mhyale said.

"Always. I'll talk to you later."

Mhyale told her okay and headed out the door. She had some free time in her schedule today to run by her mama's and hoped she didn't have to stay for long. With booked hair appointments, searching for the perfect salon space, and juggling day-to-day life, Mhyale was on the go almost every day of the week.

She was paying booth rent at a popular shop in the city and had been for the last two and a half years, but it was time to spread her wings. It'd been time, but she was waiting until she felt like she was in the best position to do so. Not just financially but mentally as well. Running a business wasn't for the weak. She learned that from assisting and watching Amiya and Maliya run *MAG. Co.*

The second Mhyale pulled into her mama's driveway, a scowl covered her face. Taking a minute to calm her nerves, Mhyale practiced the deep breathing exercises Rhyli had suggested. She'd get so worked up and overwhelmed with situations that it made her just want to break down. Giving up wasn't an option, so Mhyale did the next best thing, and that was center her focus on relaxing. There was only so much she could do.

Climbing out of her car, Mhyale shook her head at the damage to Peaches' car. The front bumper was hanging off, large paint marks from a red car were on the side, and the dome light was on. By the looks of it, Peaches had barely made it home and sideswiped someone else en route to getting here.

"At least she locked the door," Mhyale grumbled, using her key to open the front door and let herself in.

Had Mhyale not been used to seeing her mama's place in the condition it was, she would've sworn someone had come in and robbed her. It was a complete mess with evidence that a party of some sort had taken place the night before. Possibly the night before last as well.

Empty liquor bottles decorated the floor while half-eaten plates sat on the living room table. Pillows were thrown about, butts from cigarettes and blunts were piled in ashtrays, and it reeked of an odor so unpleasant, Mhyale gagged. She didn't even want to know what the kitchen looked like.

Heading to her mama's room, she was shocked to see her awake and in her bed. Still in the clothes from last night — this morning rather — Peaches was rolling her a blunt. She glanced at Mhyale in the doorway and continued rolling up.

"Mama, what happened to your car?"

"Shit, I don't know. What happened to it?"

Peaches voice was raspy, full of sleep or the lack thereof. She was honestly still drunk and had a hangover but needed to hit her weed before she went back to sleep.

"Did you hit somebody last night?"

"Girl, nah. I was fucked up leaving from over Kiki's 'nem. I should've stayed my ass there, but you know she got thirty kids and shit." She sealed her blunt. "Wasn't nobody trying to hear all that crying. Hand me that lighter on the dresser."

Sighing, Mhyale grabbed the blue lighter and tossed it onto the bed. "Well, you hit something. You shouldn't even be drinking and driving. The bumper is hanging off the car, and you just got it not even six months ago."

Inhaling, Peaches slowly blew the smoke out of her mouth. "Okay, Mhyale. Tell me something I don't know. You coming in here working my nerves too early now. Gon' with all that."

"No. Because you're tripping. Why would you put other people's lives at risk like that? Especially when—"

"You better not even go there," Peaches spat.

When Linette died, Peaches tried her best to not let liquor become her crutch. With each passing day, that task became harder to stray from. It was a temporary fix, and she knew that, but in the moment made her feel her best. Grieving for her wasn't some walk in the park.

It didn't help her process any when her boyfriend was killed a little over a year ago. A drunk driver had hit him head-on while he was on his way to Peaches' crib. The upward journey she thought she was on while dealing with grief only intensified. It placed her in a chokehold and hadn't released her since.

Mhyale was trying to be as understanding as she could, but it was rough. Especially when Peaches talked to her like she was dirt on the bottom of her boots. The verbal abuse always took her back to a time when she and Memphis were younger. Their mother used to be so angry all the time. They couldn't understand it. Their minds were too undeveloped to see that she was the product of a generational curse.

When they got older, she eased up some, but the trauma Mhyale endured would never be forgotten. It was a trigger for her, and Peaches didn't even know it. For years, they'd been good. More than anything, Mhyale wanted a relationship with her mom. Peaches was her girl, and she tried to sweep her wrongdoings under the rug, but that had stopped. Their relationship became even more strained when Mhyale called her out about how she was behaving.

"Why you come in here fucking with me, huh? I'ma change the locks and then what?"

"Don't do that. I'd hate to not be able to see if you were alive or not."

Peaches scoffed. "Right. Like you give a fuck."

Tears sprang to Mhyale's eyes. "I do. I don't know why you always say that. Why do you treat me like I'm the bad guy? I haven't done anything to you."

Putting her blunt out in the ashtray on the bedside dresser, Peaches sucked her teeth. "Here you go getting in your feelings. Thinking everything is about you. What about me, huh? I'm the one who lost my sister and man back-to-back. Cut me some damn slack, Mhyale."

"And that's an excuse for you to be a shitty mother towards me?"

Peaches laughed. "Shitty? All the shit I went through to make sure you and Memphis had a decent life, and this the thanks I get? Child, you better leave me alone."

"You're our mother! You're supposed to go through shit to provide for us. We didn't ask to be here."

"You right. My ass should've swallowed or something. Used that damn money your daddy gave me to get an abortion instead of my hair done for the club. Guess I learned my lesson."

Her words stung Mhyale to the core, ricocheting off the dingy colored walls and stabbing her right in the chest. Mhyale knew her mama was off in the head and said some wild things, but this had taken the cake.

"You're sad," Mhyale told her.

"You the one standing there with tears in your eyes. I'm not sad at all. You and Memphis sit up here and just expect for me to be okay. I'm not!" she hollered.

"And we get that, but don't take your hurt out on us! You've done that enough already!"

They stared one another down with the utmost animosity. If Mhyale could, she'd beat her ass for talking to her like that. She knew how to fight thanks to Peaches. They'd gone head up a few times when Mhyale was a teenager, but she wasn't on that right now. She was grown and just wanted her mother's love, not the tough love she thought she needed.

"Okay, Mhyale. Make sure you lock my front door on the way out."

Mhyale shook her head. "Whatever. You need to get up and clean this house up. This ain't what Memphis pays your rent for every month."

"Yeah, yeah. Tell that nigga come clean it up since you so worried."

Peaches snuggled under the comforter, not having a care in the world about what Mhyale was saying. Mhyale wanted to say more, but she didn't. She couldn't, or they'd be in here fighting. With heavy steps and an even heavier heart, she left out of the house, being sure to lock the door. Inside her car, she tried doing her breathing techniques, but they didn't work. It didn't matter how old she was. Hearing her mama talk to her like that crushed her feelings.

With her hands atop the steering wheel, Mhyale cried hard. Her shoulders bounced with every breath she struggled to let out. A mixture of emotions took over as she released her tears. She couldn't believe their relationship had gotten to this point. If she was honest with herself, she didn't see them coming back from this point either.

Her body jerked upward when someone knocked on her window. The lash extensions she was wearing were ruined now, but she didn't care, nor did she care for Jasheer to see her this way. It wasn't the first time. Knowing she didn't want to verbally speak, he pulled her door open and pulled her out of the car. Hugging her tightly, Mhyale sobbed into his chest. Soothingly, Jasheer rubbed her back.

"Ssshh. It's a'ight. I got you. Let that shit out."

Mhyale did just that. She hadn't cried in so long. When she lifted her head once done, she felt lighter already. Sniffling, she let Jasheer wipe her tears. Her nose was now red, matching her eyes.

"Thank you. I needed that," she told him.

"It's nothing. You good now?"

"No, but I'll be okay."

"Follow me to the crib right quick. Can you do that?"

Mhyale nodded her head and got back in the car to follow him. Jasheer had pulled up across the street and a few houses down to see his grandma when he spotted Mhyale's car. Never one to miss the opportunity to speak when in her presence, he walked up to the house but spotted her in her car instead. Her shedding tears brought back too many memories. He knew she wasn't okay, and he didn't like that.

Pulling into his driveway fifteen minutes later, Jasheer hopped out of his car and waited for her. She'd been over there plenty of times, but for some reason, this time felt different. Mhyale stepped inside as he turned the alarm off and got comfortable, taking a seat on his couch.

"You hungry?" Jasheer asked.

"No. I'm good."

"A'ight. Roll up for us."

Digging in his pocket, he handed her a bag of weed and grabbed the pack of rolling papers off the counter.

"When you stop smoking Backwoods?"

"A couple months ago. I got some if you wanna roll that instead."

Mhyale shook her head. "No. These are cool. They're better for you anyway."

Jasheer smirked and sat on the couch. "They are. You wanna talk about it?"

"Not really. You know how she gets. Today just really did it for me, though. It's like what's the point in trying with someone who consistently hurts you?"

She wasn't necessarily looking for him to answer, but more so thinking out loud. It'd been the same question she had for years, and she couldn't even answer it herself.

"Thinking they'd change."

"You'd think she would with how many chances I've given her, just to end up giving her another one, hoping she saw where I was coming from. I'm tired of this shit."

"I hate seeing your feelings hurt, Mhy. That shit be fucking me up."

Mhyale licked her lips and passed him the joint to spark. "You hardly see me anymore."

"Whose fault is that? I ain't went nowhere."

She eyed his living room, noticing the toys and playpen. Jasheer was an active father in his son's life, and Mhyale loved it. It didn't help that the little boy looked just like his daddy. He was literally his twin as if his mama hadn't carried him for ten months. Whenever Jasheer posted a picture of him, Mhyale didn't hesitate to react to it.

"You got a whole family now," she stated, brushing his question off.

"Yeah. That lil' boy is my world."

An easy silence fell over them as they got high. This was how they coped back in the day. For Mhyale, it was anyway. Those breathing techniques Rhyli taught her didn't have shit on a perfectly rolled blunt stuffed with potent weed. It was a high Mhyale never minded taking, especially with Jasheer. With the way Peaches behaved, she was surprised she hadn't tried something stronger.

"I miss kicking it with you," Jasheer told her.

Mhyale glanced his way, trying not to get caught up in his looks. Jasheer was the type of fine that made you do a double-take and smile when he caught you eyeing him. His locs were pulled into a disheveled bun atop his head, giving you the best view of his chiseled face that would've been symmetrical had it not been for the tattoo along his right eyebrow. You would've missed it if you didn't pay close attention, thanks to his rich, umber skin. Black jeans, a black AMIRI logo hoodie, and coke white Ones were his getup.

"We've kicked it recently. Don't act like it's been months since you saw me," Mhyale stated.

"I ain't talking about out on the town. I'm talking about me and you, on some chill shit like this."

She passed him the joint, already feeling the effects of the weed. "Mhm. I hear you."

"Do you, though?" he asked, leaning into her space.

Knowing exactly where her spot was, Jasheer kissed her neck. Mhyale's eyes fluttered as she swiveled her neck to the side, only intensifying his need to touch her.

"Answer my question," he told her, clutching a boob in one hand and massaging it.

Mhyale wasn't even sure what the question was. She missed his presence, and his touch alone reminded her of how long it'd actually been since she felt it. She and Jasheer connected on a level that many didn't understand. Beyond sex, he got her. He'd been that home away from home for so long, Mhyale didn't see the wrong in their actions. That's until her phone vibrated in her lap, snapping her out of her lustful high daze. Guilt settled in her belly as Naaz's name popped up on her screen with an incoming call.

Jasheer saw it too. Mhyale let it go to voicemail, knowing she'd never further disrespect him by answering while in another nigga's face. When he sent her a text right after, Mhyale felt shittier than she already did.

Naaziq: I'ma slide to the grocery store when I get off. You want something specific for dinner. A nigga got a taste for some spaghetti.

He double texted, warming Mhyale's heart.

Naaziq: I hope you having a better day today too. Here's a lil something to get yo nails done.

The apple cash displayed three hundred dollars. That was more than enough to get her nails done. Naaz was always gifting her just because gifts. If he liked it, he copped it for her. When Mhyale did ask for something from him, he played it off like he wasn't going to get it, but she always ended up with whatever she mentioned to him. It was the little things. The things that set him and Jasheer apart and a reason why she needed to get her ass up from this couch.

Scooting off the couch and standing to her feet, Mhyale fixed her joggers. "I'ma head out. Thanks for making sure I was good."

"I ain't know y'all were together."

They weren't, but Jasheer didn't need to know that. What they had going on was their business.

"Yeah. You know how that goes," she told him, walking toward the door.

Jasheer couldn't help but chuckle. He knew all too well. At one point in their lives, Jasheer was the one texting to see what she wanted to eat. It was clear things had changed, but not by much.

When she reached for the door, Jasheer grabbed her hand, making her face him. Her concerned eyes met his determined ones.

"Don't ever feel like you gotta be somewhere you don't want to be, a'ight? It's always room for you here."

Mhyale nodded and squeezed his hand. "I know. Thank you again."

Jasheer let her walk out of the door, and he promised that'd be the last time without making her his for good. Fuck what she and Naaz had going on. They had history too; the kind Jasheer wanted to revisit.

"Who'd you say we were meeting again?" Loriana asked.

She was sitting shotgun in Mhyale's whip. The two hadn't spent time with each other in some weeks. When Mhyale called her up to go grab some food and run errands, Loriana was all for it. She was on Christmas break from classes and knew this would be the last real one before things got serious. Graduation was literally a semester away, and she couldn't wait nor slack off.

"Carlo. He owns a vending company I want to use for my shop."

"You do his wife's hair, right?"

"Yep. They so fly. That's how I'm trying to be when I'm ready to settle down."

Loriana smirked. "With whom is the question."

"Girl. Tell me about it. I don't even wanna tell you what almost happened between me and Jasheer the other week."

"Knowing you, I'm sure y'all almost made up for lost time."

Mhyale shook her head, almost embarrassed with herself for how easily she'd let Jasheer become routine in her life again. It happened so organically;

she was questioning how their relationship would look in the future. She had always appreciated his friendship, and that's what she wanted to keep the most, but temptation was hitting her hard.

"Had Naaz not called, I would've had that man's head buried between my legs," Mhyale let her know.

"Naaz is such a good man, Mhy. Why you be moving like that with him?"

"Past traumas. It's not something I don't know. I just hate that we're still in limbo with what we're doing. He won't let me go, I won't leave him alone, yet we can't settle down. I be in that man's bed almost every night or he in mine, then go about my day like I'm single."

"That's just crazy to me," Loriana mumbled, not understanding what the issue was, but she had no room to talk. Mhyale let her know that too.

"No, what's crazy is Projex parading ol' girl around like she's his or something. You need to go get your nigga back ASAP. She making him look bad."

Laughing, Loriana pulled her phone from her purse to reply to Nyree's text. "He's not worried about me."

"Yeah, but you're worried about him. You really gon' just let him live happily with another woman?"

Loriana shrugged, not wanting to get in her feelings with this conversation, but she knew it was coming. Anything concerning her and Projex in the same sentence made her nerves rattle and heart ache.

"I guess. I don't know what you want me to say, Mhy. We talk here and there, fuck on occasion, and I guess that's all we're doing."

Mhyale sucked her teeth. "Because that's all you're demanding. You need to put your foot down and let that nigga know the real. He having his fun because that weirdo, Symir, is no longer in the picture but let you start talking to another man and showing interest in him. All that nonchalant attitude and treating you like a sidepiece will be a thing of the past."

Loriana was quiet, knowing for a fact that's just how Projex would be. She'd been done with the tit-for-tat long before it could begin. There was no reason to give him the runaround, lead another man on, and possibly get him hurt. She'd given him a taste of his own medicine and was throwing in the towel. Symir hadn't even been a good get-back nigga to flaunt anyway, in her opinion.

"I don't want to or have time to talk to another man just so he can realize where home is. Why do I have to be the one to still try and make amends when I've tried?"

"Because…" Mhyale paused. She was about to say some real shit that applied to her as well. "Sometimes men aren't the ones who fuck up a good thing. Us women do too."

Loriana rolled her eyes. "I guess. If me fucking up means I have to keep kissing his ass for the rest of our lives, then I'm good."

"Well, be good then. Don't say I ain't try to put you up on game," Mhyale stated, done with the conversation since Loriana clearly was.

"I won't. You know I appreciate you. I just gotta figure out how to move on my own."

"As you should. Let's go in here real quick."

Parking out front of the warehouse, Mhyale zipped her coat and shut her car off. Loriana followed suit and walked behind her up the steps and into the building. Glancing around the concrete pavement with rows of vending machines and shelves filled with other items Carlo sold, Loriana nodded her head. She saluted a man who was about his business.

"Mhy, what's good? Glad you could swing by," Carlo said, walking up to them.

Loriana had to tuck her lips, or she was going to be way out of pocket for what she wanted to say. *Damn, this man is handsome.* When women called a man handsome, that meant he was beyond fine. Carlo was exactly that. His jet-black hair reminded Loriana of Projex's as well as the tattoos on his hands and arms. Dressed in grey slacks that held a tucked in white button-down with the sleeves rolled up, Loriana knew exactly why he'd been deemed one of the finest men in Kansas City.

There were a lot of them, but Carlo was in a lane of his own, one many women couldn't swerve in no matter how hard they tried. Misani had that on lock. Literally. The huge rock on her finger and even bigger belly she was sporting as she wobbled to his side had women hot. They could stay mad, though. Carlo wasn't going anywhere.

Mhyale smiled big as she saw Misani. "Hey, Carlo. This is my cousin, Loriana. Misani, girl. I swear you were not this big when you came to see me two weeks ago."

Misani huffed as Carlo eased his hand onto her lower back. "I know. This little boy is taking over my body."

"Aww," Loriana cooed. "You're having a boy. You look beautiful."

"Thank you so much. I'm ready for him to come on out."

Lovingly, Carlo kissed her cheek and rubbed her

belly. His son went wild, making Misani's face frown up.

"Don't be trying to rush my king, ma. He good."

"You try carrying him then," Misani said, making him smirk.

"I'll leave that up to you. Come on, so you can get off your feet. Y'all can follow me," he told them, ushering Misani to his office first.

He didn't care if she hadn't been on her feet that long; Carlo wanted her to relax. In another part of the warehouse, they followed him to some vending machines that were wrapped with people's specific custom designs. Immediately, Mhyale knew that's what she'd order.

"Yep. This is it," she told him.

"A'ight bet. How soon you need it, and how many?"

"Just one for now. I'm definitely going to be placing some around the city now that I know how much money they bring in. My shop should be done within the next three months, hopefully."

She'd finally found one in the perfect location and with the perfect layout. Now, it was time to go into grind mode with no days off to make sure she met her deadline. If the contractors she hired stayed on their shit, Mhyale was planning to open up at the beginning of April. With Christmas having just passed and the inclement weather they'd been receiving, she hoped that was enough time.

"That's plenty of time. Things do come up, but we should be good on timing. You want to pay for it today?"

"Sure do. Let this be one less thing I have to worry about," she told him with a chuckle.

"A'ight. My wife should have that paperwork ready for you up front."

"Okay. Thanks again. It's so good seeing a Black man running his own businesses."

"I 'preciate that. Same to you. Every time Sani mentions your name, it's always good praises behind it."

Mhyale smiled. "That's my girl. It's women like her that motivate and inspire me to keep going. If she can make it from where she came from, I know it's possible for me to be in the same position or better one day."

Carlo nodded his head and couldn't agree more. His wife had a more than rough upbringing, but she thugged it out. She'd hit a few hurdles along the way, almost lost him and her life, but she was here. God had bigger plans for her life, and she was going to see to it that she followed through with His promises.

"Fasho. Just keep yo' head on straight, and don't worry about what everybody else got going on. That's the quickest way to lose sight of what's most important, and that's the goals you have for yourself. Everybody ain't as committed or got that drive like you, so remember that and what you started for."

As always, like only he could, Carlo spit some knowledge to her, which Mhyale soaked up. Loriana too. The reason he'd made it far in life was because he stayed focused on the next day and goal, not what happened yesterday because that time was gone. Misani, as his backbone, further pushed him to set a foundation their kids would be thankful for. He didn't want them getting shit out of the mud or struggling to make it like he and Misani had.

After making her payment and signing some paperwork, Mhyale and Loriana went to grab some lunch. While they caught each other up on what'd been going on in their lives, which seemed to be so much with every passing day, Loriana's mind ventured elsewhere. The conversation she and Mhyale had on their way to the warehouse was weighing heavy on her. It didn't help seeing Carlo love on Misani so effortlessly. The love they shared was potent, making Loriana go deeper into her feelings.

She wanted that. The long gazes, kisses to the

cheek, protective hand rubs to her belly, and much more. Maybe not right now, but one day. She wanted a family of her own to come home to and relax with. A man she could get money with while helping run his businesses and carrying his child. There was only one man she wanted to experience that with.

Hours before, Loriana wasn't sure how she wanted to go about handling Projex, but she was sure now. Today's conversations were the true eye-opener for her. That's why when they were done eating, Loriana got dropped off back at home before hopping in her truck and heading to the studio where Projex was at. She'd texted him to see what he was doing, and of course, he was working. She told him okay but should've let him know she was coming by.

Reign had pulled up on him twenty minutes prior and would've more than likely still been there when Loriana arrived.

While she was on her way to see him, Reign was on the phone with Yari. It was already bad that her ex was locked up and catching wind that'd she'd been out with Projex again, and here Yari was working her nerves even more about their situation.

"All I'm saying is, don't look at it like you're using him. He fucks with you the long way," Yari told her.

"I understand that, but this wasn't even supposed to go this far. I was trying to be grown; now look."

"Well, that's life, honey. If I were you, I'd milk the fuck out this situation."

Reign frowned. "You saying this like Projex isn't your best friend. That's weird, girl."

"He is, but I'm just keeping it real. What bitch you know gon' give him up just 'cause she wasn't looking to be all serious with him."

"Uh, me," Reign laughed, "it's not ever that deep."

"To you, it's not, but do your thing. Call and tell me how it goes or come by to see me."

"Mhm. I will."

Reign hung up the phone, feeling a type of way. She'd met Yari through her sister, Sky, and they'd become close over the years. Sky had been telling her sister from the jump that Yari was a little off and be on some weird shit, but Reign brushed it off. She was the type of person to always try to see the good in everyone. Now, she knew why her sister had given her a heads-up.

Not letting their conversation deter her from what she needed to do, Reign pulled up to the studio. She was granted access to come up by the security guards and hopped on the elevator. She talked to

Projex last week and had made her mind up about them already.

Stepping inside the room, Reign grabbed Projex's attention as he looked up from his composition notebook. Regardless of how many years it'd been or how much money he was making, those notebooks were his favorite to write in. By now, he had well over fifty of them. An easy grin settled on his face as he stood up to greet her.

"What's good? You look nervous," he joked as they hugged.

"I am."

"No need for all that. Just let me know what you trying to do, and we'll go from there."

Reign nodded and swallowed her anxiety before showing him her phone screen. "I want to end things. You're a good person, and I feel like dragging you into me and Rodney's bullshit is wrong."

"And, what about this," Projex asked, placing a hand on her belly. "You ending that too?"

"Unfortunately not," she said, playfully rolling her eyes. She wasn't far along but knew she was keeping her baby. She didn't care that she was ending things with its daddy or not.

"I figured you wouldn't. Don't do a nigga like that."

"Boy, please. This was my decision, and hopefully, it's for the best. No hard feelings, right?"

"Nah. None at all, baby mama," he joked, making her hit his arm.

"Shut up. Thank you for being so understanding, for real. I know what we were doing wasn't supposed to be all this, but you make it easy for a girl to fall in love."

"Look at you trying to game me down. Ain't no need for all that. You already had me."

"Ugh, still going to be your cocky self."

"Aye. I don't know how else to be. You trying to stick around for a lil' bit?"

Reign shook her head no. "No. I just wanted to stop by and break the news to you face-to-face. I'm about to go get me some food."

"A'ight. Good luck with everything. I'd say let a nigga know if you need something, but I'm officially cut off."

She waved him off as they embraced again. This time, longer and now with an audience. Loriana stilled at the door while watching them hug like long-lost lovers. Her lashes damn near flew off her face as she blinked her watery eyes to keep from crying. Instead, she cleared her throat, forcing Projex to look up. His heart fell to the sole of his Yeezy slides while his arms slid from around Reign.

"What's up, ma?" Projex asked, trying to play off his nervousness.

He recalled Loriana telling him not to let her catch him with Reign, and that day had come. The scene playing out looked suspect as hell, and he didn't want her thinking it was anything except what it was; them ending their relationship.

"Hey. Am I interrupting something here?"

Reign turned to face her, giving her a smile. Loriana's mean mug stayed on her face. *Bitch, don't smile at me while you all in my nigga's face,* she thought but kept her cool.

"Oh, no. I was just leaving out. I like those shoes," Reign complimented genuinely.

Projex looked at her feet and smirked. She was rocking a pair of neon pink Chanel tennis shoes he'd gotten her for Christmas. They exchanged gifts, Projex outdoing her like always, but it was the thought that counted. Loriana knew he hadn't gotten home appliances for his place, so she splurged on that, a couple pairs of shoes, and a new comforter set. The new mic she got him was way out of her budget, but she didn't care. The smile on his face when he unwrapped it meant more to her than some money he gave right back to her anyway.

"Thanks," Loriana mumbled, making Projex shake his head. She wasn't about to be all friendly because she gave her a compliment, so he could shake his head all he wanted to.

"I guess I'll see you around," Reign told him.

Projex simply nodded his head, looking on as Reign bypassed Loriana and headed out the door. He released a deep breath and smiled at his boo.

"Damn. You look pretty as hell, ma. Where you coming from?"

Loriana glared at him. "What was that about?"

"Nothing you need to worry about."

The sound of her sucking her teeth let him know this wasn't a conversation he could blow off.

"For what I came up here to tell you, yes, it is."

"Tell me what you came up here for, and I'll tell you what that was about."

Loriana was stubborn, but she had to put that behavior to the side for now. Her heart was on the line, and she was tired of playing with this man. Seeing another woman all in his face like that made her decision to come up here worth it. It gave her a clear picture of what'd she have to witness without him in her life. She wasn't going for that.

Sighing, she placed her purse down on the table. "Fine. I know we've been through a lot and not really seeing eye-to-eye right now, but I love you. I've never stopped, and it has never wavered. Even when you piss me the fuck off, I'm still yours. My entire heart belongs to you. It has since I was eighteen, and I can't see my life without you in it. I don't want to be without you, and I hate that I'm not the one getting to experience and share your biggest moments with you. I fucked up, I know, and I'm sorry for bailing on you. I've learned my lesson, and I just want my friend back. I miss you. I refuse to go another day without talking to you or getting on your nerves."

She inhaled, and Projex let her keep going.

"The love we share is unmatched, Bryshon. You've made me look at life so differently since you came into mine, and I appreciate you more than you know. Like, you're literally my favorite person ever. You're so selfless and make me feel safe. I literally thank God for you every day because, without you, I don't know how I would've made it. You helped me grow into the woman I am today, and I want you by my side as I continue to navigate this crazy world. I can't do this shit without you."

Projex's heart thumped so wildly in his chest, he had to tell himself to relax. Tenderness lined his throat as her words got the best of him. He had to clear his throat to keep from shedding some thug tears.

"Damn," he coughed, "that sounded like some wedding vows, ma."

"I know," Loriana whined. "But it's how I feel. It's how I've always felt. I'm tired of fighting with you, acting like I don't miss you because I do."

"I miss the fuck out of you, too. On God. Shit has been crazy, and I couldn't even share it with you."

She could hear the regret in his tone. That made her feel a smidgen better, knowing he felt the same way she did.

"You could've. You were just being an asshole. Flying hoes out to events they shouldn't have the privilege to attend."

"Fly who out? I ain't bought nobody no damn plane ticket." He felt disrespected for her to even think that.

"So, she and Yari just magically appeared in Atlanta last month when you were there?"

"Yeah. Yari called me like they were in town, so I invited them to where we were. I hope she wasn't making it seem like I flew her out."

Loriana tried to hide her grin. "No. I just thought that was the case."

"Never. They flew in town on their own and got back home the same way."

"That doesn't erase the fact that y'all looked real cozy together. Is she your girlfriend?"

He stared at her with no expression on his face. "Loriana."

"What? I'm just trying to understand where she fits in 'cause you're not making it known."

"Nowhere. What you walked in on was us ending shit."

Relief flooded her veins. "Cool. So, we can see where our relationship goes now?"

"Yeah, but I gotta tell you something that might not let that happen."

Her chest tightened, and her stomach plummeted. "O-Okay. I'm listening."

"I might have a baby on the way."

Loriana lost all sense of sound. The fogginess rushed her ears like it did when she'd fainted at cheerleading practice in the sixth grade. Linette had rushed from the sideline in a panic after seeing her baby fall out. She'd been dehydrated, deprived of something that she needed to survive. That's exactly how she felt in this moment. She was about to pass the fuck out. There was no way Projex had given another woman what belonged to her.

Her heart split in two as she reached out to grab ahold of something. Anything to break her fall. Projex was right there. With his hand around her waist, he called her name loudly. She squeezed her eyes shut. Images of the future flashed through her mind, and in them, she wasn't present. It was Projex, his family, and a baby that should've been carried by her. When a tear slipped from her eye, Loriana came back to reality.

Shoving him away from her, her voice cracked as she whispered, "A baby? You have a fucking child on the way. How could you?" The disappointment in her tone crippled him.

Projex reached for her. Desperate to clear up what he meant. "Ma, I'm joking."

"That's not something to fucking joke about!" she yelled in frustration. "Grow up! Why would you think telling me that is cool? You must have a child on the way, and I wish you would lie."

The grit in her tone made his eyes widen. He couldn't even be mad because had she told him some shit like that, he'd be doing more than hollering.

"I swear, I don't. I thought I did a few days ago, but the doctor confirmed that I'm in the clear."

She listened with bewilderment in her eyes and

etched across her face. "So, you fucking these hoes raw? I should kill you," she spat, rushing him.

She swung like she was on the streets, landing a few hits to his body. Projex let her get a few licks off before trapping her arms behind her back. Chest-to-chest, Loriana huffed, trying to break free from him. She dug her chin into his chest, forcing Projex to cave his body away from her.

"Yo! Chill out, ma. Damn. I'm trying to explain."

"There ain't nothing to explain, stupid. I know how babies are made."

"Well, shut the fuck up and listen 'cause I don't have one on the way. I told your ass I was playing."

Loriana stomped on his foot with all her might, causing him to lose the grip on her wrists. With that advantage, Loriana wasted no time swinging on him. She was taking all her anger out on him. More than anything, she was hurt.

"I hate you!" she screamed, swinging and missing.

Projex snatched her to him and pushed her down onto the couch. In a bear hug, he lay atop her, needing her to calm down.

"Baby, please chill. Just calm down for two minutes."

He could feel her heart going crazy against his

chest. His was too. Projex didn't think telling her like this would turn into a brawl, but he should've known better. Loriana let him keep her in place. Hovering over her, Projex saw the tears coat her eyes.

"Stop crying, ma."

"Nooo. I-I can't believe you. Why would you do that?" Loriana cried, no longer putting up a fight. Her arms fell lazily to her side.

"It wasn't on purpose. The baby is not even mine. I swear. She too far along for that baby to be mine."

Loriana knew the *she* he was talking about was Reign. It didn't matter who it was. Knowing he'd had unprotected sex with her and could've possibly had a child on the way crushed her to her core. No matter how good the dick felt from Symir, Loriana always made him strap up. There was no time to be caught in the moment because then shit like this happened. Loriana was sick.

"I'm so fucking stupid. You out here really doing you and look at me; foolish confessing my love to you like a dummy. Let me up!"

"Lay the fuck down," Projex hissed, pushing her shoulders back into the couch. "I ain't letting you up, so chill before I sit on your ass."

"You so stupid! You got her pregnant, knowing she had a nigga. You like sloppy seconds, huh? Just run up in anything without a rubber. Eww. I can't even believe you right now."

"Man, shut up. You talking crazy. It wasn't even like that."

"Then how was it, Bryshon? Please let me know, because right now, once I get up from here, I'm done with you. A baby? Nigga, I would never."

He sighed. "I know, ma. Just let me explain."

Though she was beyond pissed off, Loriana listened to him. At least he was willing to explain. The nigga owed her that. Projex made sure to strap up every time with Reign. It was out of habit. He wasn't into hitting nothing raw that he couldn't see raising a child with. Reign was cool, but Projex knew who he wanted to carry his babies.

When she and Yari came down for the Grammy nominations party, Projex was drunker than he'd ever been. He hadn't really celebrated his accomplishments, so all bottles that night were turned up in honor of them. Partying back home on the block was lightyears away from partying with folks in the industry. There were no expenses spared, and Projex took advantage of that a little too much.

When he woke up the next day, Reign was laid out naked beside him. She, too, had indulged in way too much liquor. With a banging headache, Projex went back to sleep. When he woke up a second time, Reign was dressed and waiting for Yari to leave from out of some nigga's room. Their wild night wasn't brought up until Reign noticed her period had been MIA.

With it being the holidays, she had to schedule an emergency doctor's appointment. Just purchasing a test from the local Walgreens wasn't going to cut it. Before Rodney went to jail, they were having sex up a storm, even though she was trying to be done with him. Her and Projex's slip-up was a mistake. When the test came back, showcasing her being eight weeks, Reign cried.

The way she'd been partying, she was sure she'd harmed her unborn. She cried harder because it was just like a nigga to trap you when you were done with their asses. Reign was sure Rodney had knocked her up on purpose.

Last week is when she let Projex know it was a possibility between him or Rodney being the daddy. At the time, she had only tested positive for being pregnant but wasn't sure how far along she was. Thanks to her amazing doctor, she was able to get in and ease her nerves of wondering who her child's father was. Right away, she knew dragging Projex along wasn't the plan. So, that was the reason for her pop-up today.

She'd texted him her results, and he told her to slide through so they could talk. He wanted to see them in person, too. Projex figured they hadn't used a rubber when he didn't see one or a wrapper while straightening up the room. He just hoped like hell the baby wasn't his, and luck had been on his side.

Loriana's head shook as he finished telling her every detail. Projex left nothing out, not wanting any secrets between them. If they were starting over, he wanted a clean slate. He didn't want anything they could throw in each other's faces because he was tired of that shit too.

"I just… I really don't even know what to say to all this," Loriana said, finally sitting up.

Projex licked his lips, praying he hadn't fucked up for good. "You still wanna work shit out?"

"Honestly, maybe we should just chill."

"Nah. No, man. I ain't with that," he protested.

Her head cocked to the side. "And I ain't with you almost getting someone pregnant. Now what? Where do we go from there?"

"God told me to ask you for forgiveness."

"Bryshon. Quit playing with me and using His name in vain."

"I'm serious, ma. I asked him what I should do because I knew I had to tell you. I'm sorry for joking about it, but on the real, I can't lose you behind that. If it makes you feel any better, she the only one I was fucking."

Loriana rolled her eyes. "No, it doesn't make me feel any better. My fucking heart is hurting. I guess this is my karma."

"Nah. Not for real. It kinda skipped you and slapped me."

The smirk teasing the corners of his face annoyed her, but she couldn't help but grin as well. "She hit hard, huh?"

"Hell yeah. So do you. I'ma have to put you in some gloves and get my money's worth."

"You had me all out of character in here. That's embarrassing."

"So what? It was just us. You had every right to lay hands on me, but don't do that shit no more."

"Or what?"

"Or nothing. We don't play them fighting games. I'll walk away before I ever think about laying a hand on you. That shit is lame."

She scratched her scalp. "Yeah. I can't say the same. Depends on how mad you make me, but I'll try my best."

"Violent ass girl. So, what's up? What we doing? I ain't trying to be in the doghouse with you, ma. I miss the fuck out of you."

"It's that easy for things to go back to normal for you?" She wanted to know. Her feelings were still raw, and her mind was still comprehending what'd just gone down.

"Yeah. Let this shit go. We either rocking or we not. I ain't being insensitive to your feelings. I'll try to give you some space for a few hours, but we not going days without seeing or talking to each other. That shit ain't happening."

"A few hours?" she questioned.

"Yeah. You need more time than that?"

The seriousness in his tone made her laugh. "If I did, I clearly wasn't going to get it."

"Space causes confusion and doubt. I don't need you ever doubting my love for you. And don't sit up here and say I would've never fucked somebody else if I loved you cause you had a whole nigga on me. I tripped, but we were good. You got yo' lick back, and I got mine."

"I don't really feel like I did enough, though," she said, with a pondering expression on her face.

"Quit playing with me, Loriana. For real. Ain't no doing nothing. That lame out yo' life and she out of mine. So, what's up? I ain't gon' keep asking your big-headed ass."

Smirking, Loriana scooted over and into his lap. That easily, Projex's tense frame relaxed. He rubbed on her booty, missing the feel of her all over him.

"You gotta tell me you're sorry in another way."

"A'ight. Whatever you want," he said with no hesitation. She could get any and everything from him, and she knew that.

"Don't retaliate against your cousin."

His jaw clenched. "Man, get off of me."

"No. I'm serious. Look at me," she urged, grabbing hold of his chin. "Let it go. You see how karma works. It does its job. I know you're hurt and disappointed, but taking his life will ruin yours. You don't need that on your conscience."

Projex knew she was right and had made up in his mind that he wouldn't go after Kordell, but if he saw him out, he couldn't make any promises. He was going to try to keep his cool, though. These days, he had to move smarter. A lot was on the line, so for her, always for Loriana, would he promise not to touch Kordell.

"You right. He ain't worth me killing, but that don't change the fact he needs to die."

Loriana sighed. There was no winning one

hundred percent with him. "I'm sure when it's his day to go, it'll come. Not by you, though. And not by anyone you send his way. Promise me that."

He gritted his teeth. "I gotchu'."

"No. Say I promise, and then give me a kiss."

Projex kissed her first, delivering a hard smack to her right ass cheek. "I promise, ma. Anything else you want from me?"

Loriana smiled. "Nope. I got the one thing that's keeping you alive, so I'm good."

"Yeah. This mothafucka belongs to you. It's just in my body. I'm sorry for real, though. We ain't gon' have no issues from here on out."

"I hope not. I don't think I can deal with any more drama after this. It's about to be a new year. We have to start fresh and let dead ends fall off. You need to start moving in a way that honors what we're trying to build. The more careless you move, the more you fuck up our union, and I'm too young to keep getting my heart played with."

Projex gazed into her eyes, making a vow to himself to protect what they had, no matter what came his way.

"Fasho. I'm with that. I ain't on no more bullshit. That means you can't bring this situation up once the clock strikes twelve on New Year's Day."

"That's fine. You can't mention Symir's proposal or say anything about me leaving you while you were locked up."

"Unless…"

"Unless what?" She coked her head to the side.

"We're talking about it."

Loriana shook her head no. "No. We can't mention it at all anymore. Act like it never happened. Didn't you just say to let things go?"

"You right. I did. So, a'ight. January first is when we start clean. What we doing until then?"

"Boy." She laughed. Her head tilted back, giving him the perfect opportunity to kiss her neck. "Mmm. We're living life."

"Yeah? You know what we haven't done before?"

She was distracted by his hands sliding inside the band of her leggings and gripping her ass cheeks.

"No, what?"

"Fucked in the studio."

Her eyes peeled open. "It's not happening today. I need to see some negative test results before we do anything."

"A'ight. You got that. Just know once I slide this dick up in you, I ain't going easy on you at all. I'ma make sure you can't move until the new year."

Her body shivered. It was only Monday, the

twenty-eighth. Loriana wasn't sure if she was trying to be bedridden for the next three days, but she was up for a challenge. The way Nyree gloated about her and Juice's makeup sex, she was for sure trying to see what that was about.

Grinning, she pecked his lips. "Ooh. I like a challenge. How much you wanna bet I make you tap out?"

"I ain't betting you nothing," he laughed, "stay trying to finesse me."

"You saying no because you know I'ma win. You can't control yourself when you in this pussy. I know it, and you do too."

"See. You talking like that about to have your face stuffed in this couch. Get off me."

He tried lifting her up, but Loriana clasped her arms around his neck.

"Stop. I'ma chill, I'ma chill." She giggled. "Gimmie me a kiss."

Obliging to her command, Projex kissed her slowly, savoring the taste of her on his tongue. He missed her like crazy and was happy as hell they were back on good terms.

"I love you, ma," he spoke against her lips.

"I love you more."

Chapter Twelve

The first step to recovery was admitting you were an addict. Loriana had already done that. It only took one hit of Projex's dope dick to have her feigning, ready to sit in a circle and tell her story. Surely there had to be other women who felt like she did.

Ducked off inside one of the bathrooms inside the mansion party they were attending, the couple was fucking like it was the end of the world. Tilting the bottle of Clicquot upward, Projex drank the champagne down before slamming the bottle onto the countertop.

Smack!

"Throw that shit back and stop runnin'," he gritted out, spanking Loriana's right ass cheek. That seemed to be his favorite one. Lifting his shirt, he held it between his chest and chin.

"I'm nooot."

Her sexy moans only fueled him to sway deeper in the pussy, making her wetter than she already was. After being held up in the house with him since Monday, Loriana wasn't even sure how she was walking right now. True to his word, Projex didn't let her out of his sight once those test results came back. He fucked the doubt and insecurity about their relationship right out of her, then licked her pussy until she sobbed.

Gripping her hair, he clasped a hand around her neck, forcing Loriana to look at them in the mirror. Her eyes were low and mouth slightly ajar, displaying the sexiest fuck faces Projex had ever witnessed. Planting his foot on the toilet beside them, he yanked on her hair. That leverage made her walls tighten.

"You was gon' give my pussy away?" he queried, pounding into her. "Huh?"

"No! No! I swear I wasn't!"

"I'ont believe you."

Her eyes rolled as she bounced her ass back on him. His grunts and their skin slapping were all you could hear over the loud bass coming from the other side of the door. Loriana's grip on the counter loosened as she stretched her arms out, forcing the arch in her back to deepen.

"Damn. Yo' shit so fucking wet, ma. You gon' make me nut all in this pussy. That's what you want?" he asked, leaning into her ear, switching his strokes up. His dick planted so deeply inside her, there was no way she could run.

"Yeees," she moaned as his fingers circled her clit. "Cum all in this pussy. I want to feel it allll."

Projex made her get out of her body by saying and doing things that only he could. Only with him would she ever do. The night before, delirious and on a high, she'd agreed to try anal. Projex had freakily let saliva fall from his mouth onto her asshole before rubbing the tip of his enlarged dick over her hole. Loriana wasn't used to ass play, but the feeling of his thumb inside her made her curious to see what else would have her busting back-to-back like she had.

Panting, she wrapped an arm around his neck, forcing him to kiss her lips. Loriana didn't want them to ever be disconnected again. A gasp escaped her as her legs quaked. Projex kept his pace, loving how her gushy walls contracted around him.

"Yeah, baby. Let me feel it. Fuuuck," he moaned in her ear as she came.

Her orgasm hit her so powerfully, Loriana

couldn't even shout his name, let alone catch her breath. "Uuuuh! Ssssshhh. Yes!"

Feeling his dick twitch as she rode him until her release subsided, Projex tapped her butt. She knew what he wanted and would gladly do so. The party was still in full swing, and the last thing she wanted to be doing was walking around with his cum dripping from her. Pulling out of her, Projex kissed her cheeks before spreading them, allowing his tongue to glide across her slick folds. He had the right mind to slide back up in her, but Loriana had other plans. She didn't even take a breath as she lowered to the ground, taking him fully into her mouth. The taste of her only made her go harder. Her mouth was wetter, and her throat expanded as she polished his pole.

"Fuck!" Projex spat.

Her hands rotated counterclockwise as she sucked him off. Slurping loudly, Loriana didn't care who came looking for them. She was on a mission. Projex's stomach caved as she hummed around his length. He was touching the back of her throat, and she was moaning like it brought her pleasure. It did. Pleasing him turned her on. It made her bob her head in a quicker manner to get him off.

His eyes crossed as he watched her enjoy herself.

Loriana was looking right up at him with those drunken eyes of hers.

"You so fucking pretty with my dick in your mouth. Fuck," he huffed out.

Loriana pulled him from her suctioned jaws to say, "Cum in my mouth, bae."

Jerking him with one hand, Loriana applied straight pressure that had him busting a nut so big, it dripped from her lips as she slurped up every drop, all while looking him in the eyes. She made sure to lick him clean, pulling him back inside her warm mouth to ensure no nut was left behind.

Projex's body spasmed. "Oooh, fuck! You's a nasty lil' bitch."

Trying to catch his breath, he leaned onto the counter just as Loriana stood up. Falling into her, she smirked as he planted his face in the crook of her neck and held her close. Then, her brows pinched as she thought about what he'd just said.

"Bae," she called out.

"Huh?"

"You called me a bitch."

He lifted his head so he could look at her face. "A nasty one, though," he acknowledged, running his thumb over her swollen bottom lip. "You don't like that?"

Loriana blushed. "I do a little. Just don't say it any other time."

Projex smirked and kissed her lips. "I gotchu'."

Once they were cleaned up, they headed out of the bathroom. Projex tugged on the black distressed booty shorts she was wearing, making sure her ass wasn't hanging out. As if she could stop it. Loriana smirked and glanced his way as he strolled beside her, taking her hand in his.

"They're not going anywhere." She chuckled.

"Yeah, they are. Straight in the trash once we get to the crib."

"I wish you would."

"Don't worry. I'ma grant that mothafucka."

She shook her head, making a mental reminder to hide them from him. The only time they did leave his house was to hit the mall up for their outfits tonight. Long ago, Loriana had learned to never dress for the weather but for the occasion. So, she was blacked out in her shorts, a black mesh top that had her boobs looking just right, and leather shark lock Givenchy pant boots. Around her neck was an iced-out tennis necklace, matching the bracelet on her wrist.

Projex hadn't half-stepped either but kept it simple, letting Loriana steal the show. The white Givenchy tee with black script was paired with black denim jeans and Jubilee Retro 11 Jordan's. He wore no jewelry except a bust-down AP diamond watch Laurent had gifted him for Christmas. The only other thing shining on him was the top row of his teeth. Those VVS diamonds greeted you before he could.

"Run me my money!" Mhyale yelled to Nyree. She could only shake her head as the duo stepped into the room.

"I thought y'all went to talk?" Nyree smirked.

Projex licked his lips. "We did, with y'all nosey asses."

"For the new year, I want y'all to get some business," Loriana told them, wrapping an arm around Projex's waist.

"Girl!" Mhyale and Nyree shouted before they all laughed.

"Y'all was about to miss the countdown being nasty. Here," Nyree said, handing them each a flute of bubbly.

Surrounded by nothing but family because that's what Projex considered everyone in the room to be, they held their glasses up to toast. It'd been a long year. A successful one that had opened up all of their eyes to reality. It had its downfalls as well, but they weren't harping on that. Loriana bounced on her toes as they counted down, giddy to move on and start fresh. The smile on Projex's face as he watched her made her stomach flutter.

"Five, four, three, two, one! Happy New Year!" they all shouted.

Neither of them bothered to sip from the flute as their lips connected. He held Loriana close, thankful he was able to bring this year in with her. The last three were lonely as fuck, so he cherished this one more than anything. Joseline locked eyes with her son when they broke away, and he gave her a head nod while lifting his glass. Coolly, she mimicked his moves, making him grin.

"Happy New Year, baby. I'm so happy we're spending it together," Loriana told him sweetly, then got nasty with it. "I can't wait to sit on your face when we get home."

His hand slid to her ass, and he gripped it softly. "I'm looking forward to it, ma. You ain't gon' be too drunk, are you?"

"Drunk or not, you eating this pussy."

"Sshh. A'ight, girl." He laughed. "You want everybody to know I be doing all that?"

Loriana giggled. "Trust me. They know. You and Laurent's song ain't sitting at number one for no reason."

Projex couldn't do anything but smirk. With their

name buzzing, they took advantage of the spotlight and released an R&B single titled *Feel You* that the radio, ladies, and clubs couldn't stop playing. It was more of a freaky, add this to your sex playlist, type of song, but it's what Laurent needed. Of course, Projex had come through with his beast of a pen. The label was one hundred percent behind them, letting it be known they pretty much had free reign to do them. Projex and Laurent were strategic with it, though.

When DJ Teeleché played their Grammy-nominated song, the party turned up even more. Rushing to grab her phone, Loriana pulled up her camera to record them. Rapping word for word, with arms tossed over each other's shoulders, liquor bottles in their hands, and genuine smiles on their faces, the men performed as if they were on stage.

Projex beaming wide and throwing his hood up had Loriana cheesing. The drunk, happy, carefree him was her favorite. They weren't just celebrating making it to a new year, but for his freedom as well. All of theirs. Bo, Sneaks, and Ayo had put in mad work within the last year. So much so that Projex hired on Bo and Sneaks as his security. It had gotten to that point in his career where people were walking up to him, and Projex was a street nigga. It was going to get some getting used to not reaching for his gun when someone, who was a fan of his work, approached him.

"Aye! I love you niggas, man!" Bo shouted, letting them know he was clearly drunk.

Nyree looked over at Loriana and laughed. "You know when niggas start confessing their love, it's time to go."

"Right. We don't need them in here reminiscing, running their mouths."

"You ready to go?" Juice asked Nyree, sneaking up on her.

"Not yet. Maybe in like fifteen minutes. That cool?"

His head bobbed. "Yeah. Let me go roll up right quick."

Absolutely smitten by all of him, Nyree watched him saunter away. "Whew. He knows he's fine," she said, grinning.

"You're so in love."

"Eh. I wouldn't call it all that. I do really like him, though."

"That's how it starts, friend. Then, you're like me wanting to live in that nigga's body."

Nyree cackled as Loriana kept a straight face. "You're serious, too."

"Deadass. Look at him."

They focused their attention on Projex. He was standing in front of Joi and whispering something to her belly. She was getting bigger by the second and was so happy her baby shower was coming up because all she wanted to do was relax.

"He is going to spoil the hell out of that baby, watch," Nyree declared.

Loriana gazed with dreamy eyes and a swelling heart. "Yeah…I'm already knowing."

As the party winded down and everyone began to head to their respective homes for the night, Joseline made sure none of them were driving. Everyone except Sneaks, who was Projex and Loriana's chauffeur home.

"Text me when you make it home," Joseline told her son while giving him a hug. "See you later, my girl."

That's what she called Loriana. She had been since her tutoring days. "See you later. Love you."

"I love y'all too."

On their way to Projex's crib, Loriana talked real boldly, letting him know what she was going to do to him once they got inside. Those last few shots she took with the girls had put her over the edge, and Projex wasn't going to call her bluff, so he let her talk. When they did make it inside, he had to carry her in, undress her, and put her bonnet on.

"Talking all that shit." He chuckled, pulling the comforter up over her.

"Bae, wait," she whined, reaching for him.

"What's the matter?"

"I'm drunk."

"I know, ma. I'm a lil fucked up too."

"Then get in the bed with me. What you doing?"

His phone vibrated in his pants pocket but went undetected to Loriana.

"I'ma be in here in a minute. Lemme set the alarm."

"Okay," she yawned, "hurry up."

Walking out of the bedroom, Projex retrieved his phone from his pocket and froze in his tracks when he looked at it. The unknown number on his screen had delivered a text that Projex wasn't expecting at all.

(816) 500-0012: I'm sorry for everything, cuz. I hope you got it in you to forgive me one day. Shit wasn't even supposed to go like this. I'm proud of you. Keep flexing on these niggas.

A name didn't need to be attached to know who it was. Projex knew who the sender was and was conflicted if he should reply or not. He stared at the message for so long, wondering why Kordell had even done what he had. Wanting to leave that negative shit in 2020, Projex decided to leave the message on read. Kordell was the nigga he was flexing on unintentionally, so his fake praise wasn't needed. Projex was sure forgiveness would come one day, but it wouldn't be tonight.

L oriana hated that a big ass window brightened up Projex's entire bedroom. The second she opened her eyes, needing to relieve her bladder, her head started spinning.

"Damn," she hissed lowly as her temples throbbed. Mixing champagne, D'Ussé, and tequila was a bad idea.

If the rays from the sun hadn't annoyed her, the ringing of Projex's cell phone surely would've. Knocked out cold next to her with his mouth open, Projex was getting the best drunk sleep of his life. She had no energy to search for his phone, so when it stopped ringing, she silently said thank you and closed her eyes. That only lasted for so long because it was ringing again the second she closed them.

"Oh, my gosh. Where is this dang phone," she fussed, climbing over him and to his side of the bed.

Her head spun as she leaned over to grab it off the dresser. Seeing that it was his mama calling, Loriana didn't hesitate to answer for her.

"Hello," she answered groggily, not recognizing her own voice.

"Hey, my girl. Is Bryshon awake?"

"No. He's knocked out."

"Wake him up for me, please."

Urgency laced her tone, making Loriana wonder what was wrong. Instead of asking, she did as she was asked. Shaking his shoulder, Loriana called out his name.

"Bae. Bae, get up. It's your mama."

Projex frowned, trying to blink the sleep out of his eyes. Grabbing the phone, he mumbled, "What's up, mama."

"Bryshon," she sighed, "they found your cousin's body this morning."

His body tensed, and his mouth became watery. "K-Kordell?"

"Yes. Gina called me not too long ago."

Hardly had Projex ever been rendered speechless, but he was in this moment. An array of emotions hit him at once, making him not know how to feel or even believe what his mama was telling him. Just hours before, Kordell had hit his line, asking for forgiveness, somewhat trying to make peace with him.

Projex cleared his throat. "A'ight. Y'all going to Aunt Gina's?"

"Yes. I'm up getting dressed now. I know how things ended between y'all, so I'm not going to force you to come. But think about your auntie, okay?"

"A'ight," was all he could say.

"I'll see you in a little bit. I love you."

"I love you, too."

Joseline had to let him know she loved him. She said it whenever they got off the phone but hearing it this morning hit differently. Her words clung to Projex's heart, bringing about an aching sensation out of nowhere.

"What's going on?" Loriana asked, grabbing ahold of his hand.

"They found Kordell's body this morning."

Tears sprang to her eyes as she wrapped her arms around him. "Aww, man. I'm so sorry."

Soothingly, Loriana held him and rubbed his back. Projex sat there stiffly, mind on a million. He had no urgency to make amends with his cousin, and even if he could, it'd have to be one-sided. Loriana wasn't shocked to feel liquid drip onto her shoulder. Before the betrayal, Kordell was his nigga. His blood.

They were family. Never did he think it'd come to this.

"I'm here, okay. Just tell me what you need me to do," Loriana said, wiping his face.

Only in the comfort of his bedroom with the one he loved the most could Projex be this vulnerable. Those would be the last tears he shed over Kordell. His death hurt, but it didn't hurt worse than him snitching.

Some hours later, posted in the kitchen of his Aunt Gina's crib, Projex was leaning up against the backdoor, looking on as everyone moved about in a desolate manner. Sadness clung to the air while throws of people came to give their respects. Projex was high as a kite. He had to be under the influence to be around all these people.

He hated how death was the only time some family came around. That shit seemed phony to him, so he was staying out of the way. It was only because of his mama that he was even present. His Aunt Gina was cool, but after word had gotten out about the real reason Projex stopped fucking with her son, she distanced herself from not only him but Joseline as well.

They weren't going to kiss her ass and hadn't. Family was family, though, and Joseline knew if the shoe was on the other foot, she'd want her to be there for her. Losing a child—no matter how—that pain was unbearable. Gina was moving about robotically, trying to save face for her guests when she shouldn't have been.

"You want me to make you a plate?" Loriana asked, coming to his side. She'd been sitting in the dining room with some of Projex's cousins.

"Nah. I'm straight. We gon' head out in a lil' bit, a'ight?"

"Okay. I'm ready whenever you are. Just come get me."

He nodded his head as she placed a kiss on his cheek. Projex's phone rang for what seemed the hundredth time that day. Word had spread quickly about Kordell's death, and his wasn't the only one. Kelsi had been with him when his car was riddled with bullets. They were sitting in the car at a park, unaware of the danger ahead of them. They should've been, though.

For months, the two had been hitting licks on people, not caring about the consequences. They'd even set a few niggas up, so the way they went out wasn't a shock to most who knew what they'd been up to. For those that didn't, their emotions were showing all over social media. Loriana's entire timeline was filled with sadness when it shouldn't have been. It was the first day of the new year, and it had already started off bad.

"Was he on drugs or something?" Joseline whispered as they stepped outside.

Projex shrugged. "I'ont know, Mama."

"That's just crazy to me. And that girl he was with was just caught up in his mess," she said with a shake of her head.

He told his mama just as much as she needed to know. Telling her Kelsi was moving just as reckless as he was served no purpose, so he kept that information to himself. He was sure when his aunt was ready to give out the details, Joseline would be the first to hear about them.

"Yeah. Life is crazy. We about to head out, though."

She squeezed him tightly while they hugged. "Okay. *Please,* be careful. You already see how this year is starting off, and I'll burn this city down if something happens to you."

"I'm good, Mama. We going back to the crib."

"Okay. Text me when you get there. I love you."

Projex told her he loved her too and headed to his truck. Loriana was already inside on the phone with Nyree, sharing details about what they'd found out so far. As if her words to Projex in the studio came to fruition, karma had paid Kordell and Kelsi both a visit. Though the situation was sad, she was glad Projex had nothing to do with it. They'd crossed enough people and had way too many enemies for him to even be considered responsible.

"Yeah. We're about to head home now. Mhm. I'll call you later," she said as he pulled away from the house.

Loriana didn't know what to say, and instead of saying the wrong thing, she grabbed his hand and held it. Lifting it to his mouth, Projex placed a kiss on the back of it as he exhaled.

"Thank you, ma. I know being around death is probably a trigger for you."

She gulped. "Yeah. But it's fine. I'm okay, and I want to make sure you're okay as well."

He didn't say anything for a few minutes, still holding her hand as he navigated the wheel with his left. She knew it was wrong to be thinking about how fine he looked doing something so simple at a time like this, but Loriana couldn't help it. The veins in his tattooed-covered hands were wildly attractive, along with his clean, manicured hands.

"I'ma be good long as you by my side."

She leaned over to kiss his cheek. "I will be."

It didn't need to be mentioned, but Loriana felt like she owed it to be there for him. Whether he'd been her shoulder to cry on when her mom passed or not, Loriana made a vow to hold him down. He may have been good now, but on those days where he wasn't, because those days would appear, she wasn't going anywhere.

Chapter Thirteen

Barefoot with a fluffy white towel wrapped around her, Loriana stood at Projex's bathroom sink, brushing her teeth. After spitting, she yawned and rubbed at her eyes. Yesterday was Kordell's service, and it had mentally drained her. While some people considered funerals a celebration of life, she couldn't wrap her mind around death. She was well aware that everyone didn't live forever, but it still put a damper on her mood. Thankfully, they were celebrating the life of Joi and Shamari's baby today.

It just so happened the service fell on the same weekend as her baby shower. Some of their family stayed in town an extra day and helped her and Joseline prepare. While Kordell was a known snitch, that didn't stop his family from turning up for him. Projex stuck around for as long as he could tolerate before locking himself in the studio all night.

He let his mind zone out and penned words the world probably would never get to see or hear. Getting it off his chest and onto paper was the first step to releasing all the animosity he had towards Kordell. When he came home to Loriana in his bed, wide awake waiting for him, Projex took the remainder of his frustration and pain out on her body. In a good way. His second release came after he fucked her roughly, then slowed down so she could feel his loving. He had to remind himself to be gentle with her; she was his safe space.

Loriana's body ached in a way she didn't mind. She could tolerate this type of bruising. With her eyes closed, her head rolled from side to side as a pleased look covered her face. Projex stepped behind her, placing a kiss on her neck then collarbone. He massaged her shoulders as her lids opened slowly.

"You good, ma?"

She nodded, staring at his handsome face through the mirror. "Mhm. A little sleepy."

"My fault. I did have you up all night."

"It's okay." She smiled softly. "You needed that."

"I did. What you wearing?"

There was no specific color theme for the baby

shower. Joi told them to wear whatever they wanted because the baby's gender would be revealed there. Loriana side-eyed him as he stepped to the side of her and grabbed his toothbrush.

"What?" Projex questioned.

"Why you wanna know what I'm wearing?"

"Cause, you be getting fly. I'm tryna match that."

When he smirked at her, Loriana playfully rolled her eyes. Since they'd gone shopping on New Year's Eve, dressing almost identically in Givenchy threads, Projex fucked with it. Loriana was used to dressing in budget-friendly pieces growing up. When she got into her career field, she figured it wouldn't hurt to buy high-end designer shoes at least. She could make that work with her lower-priced clothing.

From the moment he was released from prison, Projex had upgraded her wardrobe. There wasn't anything at the malls he didn't fund. She could buy it herself, but he liked spending money on her. Spoiling her. He saw how hard she busted her ass in school and at work, so tossing some racks her way when she had a stressful day or week was nothing to him.

"We are not an old couple who has to dress alike." She snickered.

"Yes, we do. We gotta represent. Just pick my shit out for me, ma. Don't be like that."

Going inside the bedroom while he hopped in the shower, Loriana searched through the shopping bags scattered across his closet floor. They'd hit the stores up twice this week, and it made them feel somewhat better. Grabbing their outfits out, she went back into the room so she could iron Projex's shirt. She found it funny how they'd fallen into a routine with one another in just a few weeks. Not because the chemistry wasn't there, but because Loriana felt real domesticated.

"Look at me cooking, cleaning, and ironing clothes. Who I think I am?" she asked herself, chuckling.

Loriana made sure to be fully dressed when Projex got out of the shower. Knowing him, he'd try to squeeze in a quickie, and they didn't have time for that. The baby shower started at one, and it was almost noon already. Once he was dressed, Projex twisted his hair that he was letting grow back out. He fucked with his cut but missed his twists.

"Give my shit a few more months, and I'ma have Moo twist me up," he said to Loriana, who was applying some gloss to her lips.

"Guys be looking so funny looking with those little twists in their head."

He narrowed his eyes her way. "You shouldn't be

looking at them niggas that hard no way. Keep yo' focus here," he said, gesturing his fingers back and forth between them.

Loriana cackled as he ran a hand down his crisp white Stafford t-shirt. Joseline used to keep him in a fresh tee for school, and Projex still wore them to this day. It was fresh out of one of the packs he had while a wife-beater rested underneath. On his head was a Burberry bucket hat. He rocked navy blue jeans that matched Loriana's navy leather pants and white Forces on his feet.

He said he wanted to match her fly, so Loriana did just that while picking out his fit. She had on a white lapel collar crop blouse and some brown ankle boots that hit just right with his hat.

"You're so annoying. Let's go before your sister starts calling us to hurry up."

"You driving?" Projex asked, spraying some cologne on.

In a daze, Loriana stared at him as he placed the bottle back on the dresser. Her chest rose and fell slowly. Her eyes turned lustful as she felt her nipples pebble.

"What time is it?" she asked in a weird tone.

Projex looked at the time on his phone. "Time to go. Why you looking like that?"

"It's the cologne. It makes me want to hump on you," she said before doing exactly that.

With her arms wrapped around his body, she thrust her hips against him while sniffing his neck.

"Mmm. I shouldn't have bought you this. It makes me want to take my panties off and give them to you."

He spanked her ass with a silly grin on his face. "It don't feel like you even wearing any. This shit do smell fire, though."

Another one of his gifts from her for Christmas was a bottle of Baccarat Rouge 540. The unisex fragrance smelled better on men, in her opinion. Loriana was ready to take Projex down; fuck them being on time. Joi would be there.

"You can only wear this in the house. I'm not playing."

"Man, bring yo' ass on. We still gotta stop and get some tissue paper."

Grabbing her red *Haus of $y* round bag, she draped it over her shoulder. "Okay. Let me take a picture really quick."

Posing in front of the mirror she'd added to his bedroom, Loriana snapped a few of herself before Projex joined her. Standing slightly beside her with his hand on her hip, she captured their photos. She kept tapping her thumb as he kissed her cheek, gripped her ass, and smiled big. Yesterday had been heavy, so she was glad to see him in a much better mood.

"Yeah… send me those," he told her.

Loriana told him okay, and they headed out of the bedroom. While many of Shamari's family thought Joi was having a girl, Joi was set on her baby being a little boy. That was Loriana and Projex's reason for wearing blue instead of some shade of pink. Regardless of gender, Projex was hype for his baby sis. He'd long ago gotten over the fact that she was pregnant and had stepped into protective uncle mode.

Pulling up to the building Shamari had rented out for the next five hours, it was clear the party planner knew her assignment. The owner of Dare to Design Event Planning had aced her test with flying colors. The floating blue and pink balloons outside led them into what Loriana could only describe as a winter wonderland. While the room was nicely decorated in shades of light blue, silver, and white, she'd tossed in some hints of pink as well.

The table designated for gifts had already began to fill up. Large, white letters that spelled out the word ROYAL held a glass table. Loriana took it all in, in awe of how the designer was able to transform this room.

"This fly as fuck," Projex stated, picking up one of the 3D crown cookies from the table.

"Right. I'ma have to hire her for an event."

That made Projex think of something. "You want a graduation party?"

"Un, un. I don't need all that. Wait," she chuckled, holding her hand out, "I'm saying that now, but we'll see how I feel when it gets closer."

He added that to his mental Rolodex, reminding himself to ask again in a few months. After sitting their gifts down on the table, they walked over to where Shamari and Joi were. Loriana's heart fluttered while seeing Shamari handle her so gently as he palmed her belly.

"Relax, baby. You look fine. Fine as hell," Shamari said, running his index finger over her nose. It was the feature on her face that seemed to get oily the most now.

His words boosted her confidence. With her body going through so many changes as a first-time mother, Joi didn't feel pretty on most days. This was the most she'd gotten dressed up in weeks. While she whined about the extra pounds in her face and thighs, Shamari loved it and always let her know it too.

"Am I showing too much cleavage?" Joi asked, tugging on the fabric of her dress.

"No. Them titties sitting nice and pretty. Your skin glowing, lip gloss popping, and you're rocking the hell out of this dress."

Joi blushed and sighed. "Okay. Thank you, baby. You always know what to say."

"Joi!" Loriana called out. "This dress is too cute. Look at your belly. Bae, look at her belly."

Projex laughed. "I see her, ma. It ain't hard to miss."

"Boy, whatever. Hey, sis. Not y'all came in here trying to match." Joi smirked. "That's cute."

"You know your brother always trying to be like me. Hey, Shamari."

"What's up. 'Preciate y'all for coming through on everything today," he said as he and Projex slapped hands.

"Always. It's whatever for her and the baby. Know that."

Just because Projex didn't care for Symir, he wasn't going to hold no imaginary beef with Shamari. He peeped how he was on his own wave, doing his own shit, and could only respect it. As long as he was there for his sister, Projex had no problem with him.

"Where'd you get this dress from?" Loriana asked.

"Shein. I just be ordering stuff on that dang app, but this was perfect for today."

Loriana nodded her head. "Mhm. It really was. Let me take some pictures of y'all before everybody gets here."

Scooting back, she pulled her phone out and opened the camera. Dressed in all white, Joi looked like a goddess. Her hair was in spiral curls with a deep part on the right side. The floor-length off-the-shoulder dress with mesh sleeves was breathable and very much so comfortable. She wasn't going for the cutest nowadays, but what made her feel relaxed and was loose-fitting. Shamari was decked out in all white as well, making their pictures come out perfectly.

Once the guests arrived, plates were fixed, games were played, and family members from both sides had become acquainted. Ms. Joseline was making sure everyone was enjoying themselves when Symir entered the room. Loriana spotted him first as she came from the restroom down the hall. She had no intentions of speaking to him, but of course, he opened his mouth the greet her as she tried to squeeze by.

"Damn. It's like that?" he asked, grabbing ahold

of her hand.

She yanked it away from him. "Please don't touch me."

"I'm saying. You acting like you can't speak."

Loriana frowned. "Speak for what? We don't have anything to discuss."

"We don't? You don't want to apologize for yo' nigga breaking into my house and holding me at gunpoint?"

He was angry. Loriana could see it all in his face. She almost laughed, knowing Projex had done exactly what he was supposed to do in handling him without going too far.

"Now you're just making up lies. If that did happen, that's between you and God."

Symir sneered. "How?"

"Because He's going to be the one you have to pray to the next time you harass me."

With that, Loriana walked off. Projex had watched the entire altercation go down, telling himself not to get up. If he had, he was going to ruin the baby shower and paint those white flowers Symir was standing by, red.

"Fuck that nigga want?" he asked when Loriana sat down.

She stabbed one of the meatballs on his plate with

her fork. "Asking why I didn't speak. He's so weird."

"That nigga ain't gon' stop until I have his ass in ICU eating through a fuckin' straw," he fumed.

Loriana sighed and rubbed his back. "It's fine. This is his first time saying something to me since you visited him."

"I ain't visit nobody, ma." His glare dropped as he smirked. "I was just sliding through the neighborhood, and his door was open."

"That's crazy; people leave their doors open like that," she went along with him.

"Hell yeah. Next time, I'ma have somebody rob that bitch."

She choked on a laugh before covering her mouth. "Do not. Leave him alone. Let him enjoy this day as an uncle."

"Man, fuck cuz. My baby only got one uncle."

She could only shake her head, knowing he meant that. After opening a few gifts, the party headed to another part of the building where there was a boxing bag pinata. Shamari had no clue this was how they were doing the gender reveal, so when he looked over at Joi, hitting her with that breathtaking smile, she knew she'd done a good job.

"Yo, baby. This cold." He chuckled, sliding gloves on his hands. "I ain't even think of this."

"I knew you wouldn't."

"Come on now, so I can prove y'all wrong," Ms. Joseline said, recording with her phone. She wanted a granddaughter.

Shamari's god mom, April, snickered. "Watch it be a boy."

She'd flown in town the night before and had been checking in with Joi since she found out about the baby. She was just as excited as everyone else since she had no children of her own.

Squaring up with the bag, Shamari wasted no time connecting his fists. For anyone who didn't know he was a trained fighter, they were stunned at how he moved and the intensity behind those punches. They were swift and direct, causing the bag to bust in less than fifteen seconds.

"Oh my gosh!" Joi screamed as she rushed over to him.

Pink confetti flew from the bag, covering the white tile floor. With a smile a mile wide, Shamari caught her in his arms.

"We're having a girl," she cried as fresh tears coated her flawlessly made-up face.

"My princess." Shamari grinned. "You happy?"

"Yes. Even if she was a boy, I'd be happy. Thank you, my love."

He pecked her lips while everyone tried grabbing her attention. "Nah. Thank you."

Ms. Joseline did a little twerk and snapped her fingers as she got them on camera. "Say, I told you so. I knew you were having a girl!"

"You've been saying it for so long, I think you jinxed us." Shamari laughed.

"Nope. It was just meant to be. Now everybody can take all this boy shit back to the store."

That comment had everyone who heard her laughing. The only person who knew what she was having was Joi's best friend, Dayci. She'd kept that secret for as long as possible, not even revealing it to Ms. Joseline.

"Well, we thought she was having a boy," Loriana said to Projex.

"It's all good. I'ma spoil the fuck out of my niece."

"Trust me; I already know. Your ass probably thinking of going shopping when we leave here."

The smirk on his face let her know he indeed was. Projex smooched her lips. "You know me so well, ma. Since she having a girl, it's only right we try for a boy."

"Now you're talking crazy." She laughed, walking away from him. He followed right behind her, unable to take his eyes off her juicy ass in those leather pants.

Advancing her, he pressed himself into her while making them still move their feet. "Am I, though? You don't wanna give me a baby? Have us a lil' mini-me?"

"Do you see you? Hell, no. Your mama already let me know you were bad as fuck as a kid."

"So, what. And you were a good kid. That's balance right there. Just say you don't wanna have my baby, and you'd rather swallow them instead."

She couldn't hold her laugh back as they made it to their table. "Please leave me alone. Nobody thinking about you or them little swimmers you be shooting out."

"Yeah, a'ight. You saying that now until you telling me to nut down your throat," he boasted with a twinkle in his eyes.

Loriana's body shivered just thinking about it. "Whatever."

That's all she could say because she knew he was right. A baby right now wasn't in her plans. Could they discuss this when she graduated, sure? She wanted to throw in his face that it was too soon to even be talking like that when he had almost been someone's daddy just some weeks ago.

Then, she remembered that they were on a clean slate, so she kept it playful. Still, that baby talk was forbidden until she was ready to stop being his little freaky bitch and letting him have his way with her.

"Excuse me. Can you bring out the check, please?" Maliya asked their waitress as she walked by their table.

"Everyone on the same tab?"

"Yes," she let her know.

"Un, un. Who said we were done drinking?" Mhyale wanted to know.

"Me. One more mimosa, and it's a wrap."

Brunch on Sundays before they hit a day party was just the vibes the friends enjoyed. At their age, having partied way too hard in their teen years, this was right up their alley. Strong drinks, good music, fire ass food, and Black people enjoying themselves were the perfect vibes. While most brunch spots in Kansas City were good to eat at, not many could handle the way Black people turned up. So, being tired of the complaints and upturned noses from other patrons, two brothers opened up a spot called *Toast on Eastland*.

They served brunch all day Sunday, with a regular menu throughout the week that kept people stopping by. With it being on the Eastside near other prominent shopping areas, the business had been booming since they opened seven months ago. The girls were now considered loyal customers, having been almost every week since its launch.

Mhyale waved her off and grabbed her glass. "Girl, please. This is what we do on Sundays. We get lit and prepare ourselves for another week of being adults."

"I know that. I'm just saying. We've already gone through four bottles and had some shots."

Amiya yawned, feeling the effects of the food and liquor. "Sis, chill. She's good, plus she's not driving."

"Sure ain't," Mhyale said, lifting from her seat to do a little twerk.

When the DJ transitioned smoothly into a song that had the entire city rapping it bar-for-bar when it came on, everyone was out of their seats. Depending on the day, Amiya was usually on the same wave as Mhyale—hype and dancing. She was buzzed and in her feelings, thinking about her man. So, she chilled and left the dancing to Rhyli and Mhyale, who didn't mind putting on a show like the rest of the restaurant.

"Nigga touch me and I'm returning wit' my pistol
Fuckin' on a scamming ass bitch named Krystal
I just got the pack in, meet me in the middle, I just
made a movie wit' a bitch like Riddle
Ballin'? Nigga you ain't ballin'."

Word-for-word, everyone in the building rapped along with *Freak Block Tales* by D-Walk. It was a must you played this at any function in the town, or it was for sure getting requested.

"He say that he love me, I know he running game," Mhyale rapped, remixing the words.

Recording her on her Instagram story, Rhyli hyped her up. "Ayyye. What you say, friend?"

"Y'all over here thuggin'."

That voice behind her made Mhyale grin and turn to face the person it belonged to. Just as fine as he wanted to be, Jasheer stood before her, looking like every bit of sin Mhyale needed to be in church repenting for. The Louis Vuitton skull cap over his locs was doing something to her, adding to the effects of the liquor in her system.

"We just having fun. What's up, homeboy?"

Jasheer smirked and gave the ladies a head nod.

"You tell me," he said, eyes roaming her frame. "You look good. I see you feeling good, too."

"Of course, I am. It's Sunday. I'm out with my girls. Life couldn't be better."

"Yeah? Without me in it?"

"Oop," Rhyli said. "Let me sit my ass down."

Mhyale snickered. Jasheer wasn't playing with her, but she wasn't trying to take it there with him. If any other nigga had said something to her like that, she would've found it corny. With Jasheer, it was different. She always contradicted herself when it came to him by getting caught up in his advances.

"I mean, I ain't say all that."

"I hear you. I'ma see if you still singing that same tune when you about to leave."

Mhyale swallowed hard. "Mhm. I'm sure I will be."

Jasheer gave her one more salacious gaze. The jeans hugging her thick frame looked painted on, while the cropped hunter green sweater showed off her tattooed side. Mhyale knew she was fine, and Jasheer wanted her bad. His insatiable craving for her hadn't wavered one bit.

Mhyale patted her neck as he ambled away. He and a few of his niggas only slid through on the humbug, peeping the scene. It was something to do and somewhere to be for Jasheer since his son was with his mother.

"Y'all ain't hot?" Mhyale asked, and the table erupted in laughter. "What? I'm hot as fuck."

"I bet you are. That nigga got you hot and bothered," Rhyli added.

"Hot and ready. Little Caesar's head ass," Amiya joked, making them cackle.

"Oh, my gosh. Shut the fuck up," Mhyale wheezed. "I ain't worried about him."

"Yeah, but he applying straight pressure to you, sooo. What you gon' do?"

"What you mean? I'm with Naaz. Ain't no leaving that."

She meant it too. They were on solid ground right now, and Mhyale liked it here.

"So, what I'm hearing is you want to fool around with both of them?" Maliya asked.

"Bitch, you did not hear me say that."

"You ain't have to. It's okay, friend. You don't have to try and be a good woman. Hoe it out for a lil' while and see how that goes."

Maliya was so serious, and that's what made it even funnier.

"Nah. I'm cool. But you know what? Hoes do be

getting the most dick. Being a good woman is boring." She pouted, rolling her eyes playfully.

"It's boring to you," Rhyli told her. "Why be a hoe for all these niggas, when you can get slutted out by one for the rest of your life like me?"

They all hummed in contemplation before laughing.

"You know what, Lee, you making a lil' bit of sense. Let me text Naaz right now so he can come and get me."

"Boooo. I thought we were going to the day party?" Maliya wanted to know.

"I mean, we still can. Let me get some dick first. A lil' burst of energy if you may."

"Girl, you so flaw. Watch you not answer when it's time to slide."

Mhyale snickered but didn't reply because nine times out of ten, she would more than likely do just that. Naaz had the type of dick to have you snoring when you had never even done that before. And she was off the liquor? Oh, they could hang her tagging along right on up.

Thirty minutes later, after the bill was paid, they walked out of the restaurant. Mhyale purposely avoided looking or walking Jasheer's way because knowing him, he'd approach her and make her forget all about Naaz being parked out front waiting for her.

"I'll text y'all when I'm ready," Mhyale told them as she strutted to his passenger side.

Climbing in, the warmth of the heated seats and coming from the vents settled the chill from the icy January wind.

"Hey, baby," Mhyale cooed, leaning over to kiss him.

Knowing she'd been drinking, Naaz couldn't help but smirk as she smooched his lips, dragging her tongue from the bottom to the top one.

"What's up. You lit, huh?"

"I'm a lil' tipsy, but I'm not drunk. Whew. Hold on. We gotta turn this heat down some," she huffed. "You got it feeling like a sauna in here."

"You just got in here. Ain't even warmed up yet."

"I don't need that heat. Them drinks were strong as fuck. What were you doing?"

"Getting ready to watch the Chiefs play. You called me just in time."

"Oooh. We better win. We going to the Super Bowl again this year, watch."

Naaz smirked. He hoped so because he had big money on his boys. While cruising through the city and heading back to his place, Mhyale rambled on, telling him about her week coming up.

"Did you see a package for me on your porch?"

"Nah. Who would it have been from?" he told her.

"Amazon. Oh, wait. They left it in the mailbox. Dang. That got here fast," she said, pulling up her order through Safari.

"What you order now? I'ma ban them from dropping stuff off."

"I wish you would." She laughed. "It's a little toy my homegirl was telling me about."

Naaz side-eyed her. "A toy? Like a vibrator?"

"Mhm. She said it makes you orgasm in like ten seconds."

"Hell nah," Naaz swore. "Ten seconds flat?"

"Yep. We gon' find out."

"Fasho. Charge that hoe up as soon as we get in the house."

Laughing, Mhyale put her phone on the wireless charger and her purse on the ground. Slipping her coat off, she lifted to her knees in the seat and faced him.

"I will. Until then, pull that dick out."

Naaz grinned. "How many drinks you have, Mhy-Mhy? You trying to be all spontaneous. We almost to the crib."

"So, what. I'ma do it real fast. You got this dark ass tint; can't nobody see me anyway."

As she talked, she was pulling the band of his sweats, forcing him to assist with moving them slightly down his legs. Mhyale licked her lips in anticipation. The only thing preventing her from whipping his dick out was the black Hugo Boss briefs he was wearing. Reaching underneath the band, she found what her mouth was waiting for.

"Mmm. You have the prettiest dick, Naaziq," she moaned, running her warm tongue up the base of his length.

His dick was two-toned. An even divide between light brown at the bulbous tip and expresso brown at the nine-inch length like the rest of his frame. Her pussy twitched as she covered him with her mouth, letting him stretch it out due to his thickness. A steady hand gripped her ponytail as she nastily sucked him off.

Taking him into the back of her throat, Naaz growled, "You bet not choke."

Obliging, she controlled her breaths and gasped when he finally let her head up. Mhyale got right back to work, making her ass cheeks clap, giving him the perfect visual. With her back arched, she bobbed, slurped, and spit like her only goal in life was to make him cum.

"Fuuuck, Mhy," he hissed, stretching his legs out. Thankfully, they were almost home.

She moaned, loving the sound of his powerful voice in her ear. It made her wetter than she already was. The ringing of her phone clashed with the sounds she made. Naaz wasn't going to glance down to see who was calling, but they came to a stop sign. Feeling the car stop, Mhyale went in as his eyes squinted at her screen sitting in the dock. The fist around her ponytail tightened, making her think he was about to nut, only for him to yank her head off of him.

"W-What? Why'd you do that?" she asked, eyes slightly wide.

Naaz licked his lips while stuffing his dick that was softening back in his briefs. "Get yo' phone."

"I'll call whoever that is back."

On cue, her phone rang again. The clenching of his jaw made her panic a bit. Slowly, she slid back to her seat. When her eyes landed on her screen, with Jasheer's name big as day illuminating it, Mhyale wanted to throw up. Instead, she clicked her seatbelt on and acted like she hadn't seen him calling.

Naaz scoffed out a chuckle. "You so full of shit."

"What! I ain't tell him to call me."

"So, the nigga hitting yo' line for no reason? I thought you were done being on your bullshit. Ain't that what you told me?"

"I am! You pressing me for no reason," she fussed.

"Nah. It ain't ever for no reason when it comes to you. Ever. Here I am being loyal to your ass without us being in a relationship, on some clown shit. I look like a clown ass nigga to you?"

"I mean if you painted your nose—"

"Mhyale."

The way he said her name in that chilling tone of voice sent a ripple of awareness through her body. She'd better stop playing with him, and quick. They sat quietly at the red sign. No cars came to disrupt the storm brewing between them. Naaz gritted his teeth, trying to locate the perfect words to say that'd make her understand how out of pocket she was. Mhyale knew it, though.

She hadn't told Jasheer to call her, but their flirting definitely led him to believe that once he hit her line, she'd answer. And she would've had she not been in the passenger seat of Naaz's ride.

"You're going to miss the game," she commented.

"If the next words coming out yo' mouth ain't an

explanation for that nigga to be hitting yo' line, I don't even wanna hear you talk."

She sucked her teeth and snaked her neck in his direction. "Well, I don't care what you ain't trying to hear. You acting like I'm the bad guy."

"Somebody has to be. I can't trust you, Mhy-Mhy. That's really the fucked-up part about all of this."

"You have serious trust issues," she huffed, folding her arms over her chest.

"If I do, it's because of you. You made a nigga this way, and I keep letting you damage a good thing."

She sniveled, hating to hear how distant his words felt. They hit her right in the gut. "I'm not trying to, Naaziq."

"You're not trying to stop doing your thing either."

When she had nothing to say, Naaz slid his foot off the brake. It didn't matter what he was saying to Mhyale right now. It was clear she had some more growing up to do, and Naaz wasn't trying to stick around for that. As much as he loved her, playing the fool again wasn't in his plans.

Chapter Fourteen

W ith graduation approaching in less than four months, Nyree was putting in overtime to make sure she walked across that stage. She was trying not to make her trips home too frequent, needing to stay focused, but it seemed every week it was someone's birthday. So, here she was on a Friday evening, pulling up to her mama's house. Her visit was unexpected, having made the decision to drive down at the last minute.

"Mama," she called out, walking inside the house with her overnight bag draping her shoulder.

"What you doing here?" Nakita asked, coming out of the kitchen.

Nyree grinned. "Trell having a birthday dinner

tomorrow, and he told me I better not miss it. You look cute."

Doing a spin, Nakita showed off her peach-colored, rib-knit sweater dress with heeled ankle boots. Whenever Nyree posted pictures in cute clothes, Nakita would text her asking her where she got it from. She didn't get hip to the affordable, fast shipping, online shopping until just last year. So, she was supporting most of the Black-owned businesses she came across.

"Thank you. I got this at that store you be shopping at. The sisters own it," she explained.

"MAG Co.?"

"Yeah, that's it. They got some cute stuff. One of the sisters, I can't place which one, said they were getting ready to open up another location."

"I think in the spring. Where are you about to go, though? I was trying to hang with you."

"Out with my boo. We're going two-stepping with some friends of his."

Nyree pursed her lips. "You ain't grown, lady."

"Child, please. Have you talked to your Uncle Chris?"

"No. Not since last week."

"You should call him. Maybe you can hang with him if he's not working. Avoiding him isn't going to erase what happened. He still loves you, and so do I, but you knew better."

Nyree sighed. It'd been a little over two months since Uncle Chris had to bail her out of jail, but Nyree was still feeling guilty about placing him in a bad position. She'd been avoiding him and ducking his calls.

Nyree had been charged with possession with intent to distribute. While her car was searched, they'd also found her gun. Thankfully, it was registered in her name. Knowing she needed a lawyer or she'd be facing at least up to three years in prison, Juice didn't hesitate to put that money up for her. After he met her family on Christmas, he knew she was solid. Plus, he was a man of his word. He wasn't going to let her take the fall.

Before the case could even go to trial, which Chris somehow got sped up, Nyree's lawyer had her take affirmative actions. She gathered letters in support of her and documents showing she was in school working toward her degree, showcasing that she otherwise had no prior record or run-in with the law.

The issues were also raised behind why she was detained in the first place. When it came out that the cop's son was indeed an addict, he was forced to take a chemical evaluation and was suspended from basketball for a semester. Her lawyer was able to negotiate a deal where Nyree pled guilty of the charge, and the court gave her a stay of adjudication. The case against her would be dropped if she agreed to be on a diversion program from six months to a year.

Nyree took the deal and was so grateful. Once she completed the program, there would be no sign of the arrest on her record. Had it not been for her uncle and the damn good lawyer Juice hired, she would've been doing some serious time. With her being in school and working, the court agreed for her to start it once she graduated. But if caught again, the charges would heighten, and there'd be no clean slate.

"I know, Mama. It's just that you and him have done so much for me, and I disappointed y'all. I still feel bad."

"Don't. You can't go through life cautiously because you're afraid to let people down. You'll lose every time. People's expectations of you are just that; theirs. You know I've always told you to live your life and experience all of it full circle. Going to jail was one of them. Hell, it ain't like I haven't been." Nakita chuckled.

"I remember that. I was boo-hoo crying when they put you in the back of that car."

She was only a little girl at the time, but Nyree would never forget that night they pulled up on her dead-beat daddy.

"And I didn't forgive myself for a long time for letting you see me act that way, but I did eventually. That's what you need to do because me and Chris already have."

Nakita pulled her into a hug and kissed her temple.

"Okay. I'll call and see what he's doing after I get settled."

"You and Jovani don't have plans?"

Nyree smirked. "His name is Juice, Mama."

"Girl, his name is what he introduced himself as. I'm not calling him no damn Juice. Now, what he got going on?"

"You so nosey, but I'm not sure. He hasn't texted me back yet."

"You kids and this texting. Y'all need to learn how to communicate over the phone."

Nyree laughed. "You be texting me!"

"Because your ass don't be answering the phone I pay the bill for. That's okay. I'ma let it get cut off."

"You love keeping up with me too much to let that happen."

"Mhm. Keep on and see."

Nakita went to finish getting dressed for her night out while Nyree retreated to her room. Nothing in it had been changed except the bed, making Nyree feel more at home. Toeing off her tennis shoes, she checked her phone to see if Juice had texted her back. When she didn't see a message from him, she took her mama's advice and dialed his line. She was trying to do pop-ups and would regret it if he was out of town or busy. When he did pick up, seemingly by accident, Nyree's chest grew tight at the sound of him yelling. The sound was so foreign to her, she wondered who had pissed him off.

"Man, get the fuck away from my car!" Juice spat.

"No! You come through here dropping money off, and I can't get shit? What type of son are you?!"

"The type that's not about to keep taking care of your ass. Now, move! This my last time telling you."

She lifted her foot to kick his car just as Juice swung his door open, making her stumble backward.

"I wish you would."

"You know, what. Fuck you, Juice! You gon' regret the day you handled me this way. Your own fucking mother!"

"You ain't been a mother to me in years," he spoke coldly, making Nyree gasp a little.

Hearing the sound, Juice's nostrils flared after seeing the call was connected over the Bluetooth inside his car. Slamming the door, he pulled out the parking spot he was in.

"Hello," he hissed.

"Um, hey."

He sighed heavily, trying to calm his nerves. His mama was truly the only person who could piss him smooth the fuck off and ruin his day. Sometimes, his entire week. *I gotta stop letting her get to me, man. Fucking negative ass,* he thought, having said those words before.

"What's up, Ny?"

"Nothing. I was in town and wanted to see you, but you sound upset so, I guess I'll see you another time."

"How that sound? You ain't ever about to come in town, and I don't see your face. Where you at?"

"Home. I just got here like twenty minutes ago," she informed him.

"Yo' mama there?"

"Yeah, but she about to leave. You can stop by."

Juice thought about it for a second and then shook his head. "Nah. Slip something on, so I can take you out. I can't sit in the house right now. Fuck around and go crazy," he uttered.

"Okay. I'm dressed. Is jeans and a t-shirt cool?"

"Yeah, that's straight. Let me make a few plays, and I'll call you when I'm on the way."

"Okay," she said and then added, "I don't know much about the relationship between you and your mama, but don't let her have that much control over you. Take some deep breaths, smoke you and blunt, and exhale the bullshit, okay?"

Juice licked his lips, busting a left at the corner before his little brother's dad's house. "A'ight, lil baby. I got you. I'll see you in a minute."

Nyree told him to be safe and hung up. Sitting with the phone in her hand, she couldn't help but wonder about the backstory of Juice and his mama's relationship. She cherished the one with hers, and her heart ached for Loriana since her mother was gone. Not letting her mind venture too far into a negative place, Nyree called up Loriana next.

She figured with it being a Friday, Loriana was more than likely just getting off work or still there. It was hard enough keeping up with her own schedule, so Nyree wasn't sure if she had a late-night class or not. When her phone went straight to voicemail,

Nyree put her phone on the charger, knowing she'd call back.

Across town, sitting on Projex's couch with papers scattered about his coffee table, Loriana had her phone on do not disturb. It was crunch time. She had a report due at midnight, while a music review over her thoughts about the Grammy's coming up was due in less than an hour. Voiding all distractions, she hoped Projex didn't wake up and come bothering her.

Upstairs, Projex was on the phone with his grandma and kept yawning in her ear. Between traveling, the late-night studio sessions, and interviews, sleep was the last thing he'd been getting. So, the five hours he was able to get in was everything he needed to eventually get his day going again.

"There you go yawning again. You better be getting your rest, Bryshon. All work and no relaxing of the body is the quickest way to wind up sick," Juanita preached, sounding just like his mama.

She'd been on his ass for weeks now about listening to his body.

"I just woke up. I'm just getting the yawns out, my bad."

"Mhm. You better be getting more than that in. Come by here and get a jar of this sea moss I made."

His nose scrunched up. "That shit is nasty."

"Bryshon Emery! I know you ain't on this phone cursing at me."

"My fault, Granny," he chuckled. "It is, though. I don't need that."

"You need something to keep you healthy and give you some energy. Sleep being number one."

"I'ma get some more sleep when we get off the phone, a'ight?"

"Don't just be saying that. Are you coming by here on Sunday for dinner? Mauriana said she was going to make the macaroni and cabbage," Juanita let him know, calling Moo by her real name.

"I'ma be there, fasho. What you want me and my plus one to bring?"

"You can bring some pop. I don't want anyone around here to get sick if you cook something," she joked, making him chuckle. "Tell my girl she can just bring herself."

"Now, you know she's not walking in there empty-handed."

"I know that, but you asked. How are y'all doing?"

Projex stretched, wincing a bit when all of his bones seemed to pop. "We straight. Busy as ever, but it's all good."

"It is. You guys are young and setting the foundation now for you guys' future. Oh, before I forget. Be sure to call your grandpa and thank him."

"He got the place situated for us?"

"You know he did. Anything for his favorite grandson," she mocked.

Projex laughed. "Aww. Don't tell me you jealous."

"Not at all. Both of our names our on the house, but of course, he tried to one-up me. That's okay. I'm going to remind him of that when he comes in town trying to wine and dine me."

"Y'all wild. Let me get off here, so I can get some more sleep. I'ma see you on Sunday."

"Okay, baby. Tell my girl I said hi."

"I will. Love you."

Juanita told him she loved him too and hung up. Getting up from the bed, Projex went to go pee and brush his teeth. He showered when he'd gotten home. As he used the toilet, his eyes involuntarily fell to his trash can. Days before, it had been occupied with Loriana's hygiene products, wrapped in tissue. When he didn't see any, Projex grinned.

Loriana's wish for him not to disturb her was granted for all of twenty minutes until he came downstairs. She had taken a break to stretch her legs and was grabbing her something to drink when he waltzed into the kitchen behind her.

"Bae," he called out, making her face him.

Loriana turned with raised brows, silently asking him what was up. Projex walked up on her.

"Let me eat yo' pussy right quick."

Her mouth fell open as she hurriedly tried to mute her phone. She was on a conference call, multi-tasking, with her AirPods in. His lips pursed outward in an O-shape before he covered his mouth, but it was too late now.

"Bryshon, I'm on the phone," she whined.

"Damn, ma. My fault. I ain't know. You got them shits in your ear. I thought you were listening to music or something."

"No, you didn't," she uttered, calling his bluff.

Projex smirked, loving how she knew him so well. He hadn't even peeped the AirPods in her ear until she was muting her phone.

"You almost off? I wanna talk to you about something."

"Yeah. I'll come find you when I'm finished," she said, turning around to face the counter.

He slapped her ass cheek. His favorite one. "Aye. Don't be dismissing me. Gimmie a kiss."

"Give me like twenty minutes; I'm a give you this pussy to kiss too. Hold on."

He choked on a laugh as she pecked his lips before shooing him away. Going to find him some business, Projex went back inside his bedroom to grab his phone. Checking his email, pride filled his chest at all the business inquires forwarded over from his assistant.

"That's crazy. I really got an assistant," he muttered before dialing her number.

"Projex, hey. Did you get my email?" She got straight to the point.

As a business affairs assistant, Kierra took her job very seriously. Projex wasn't the only person she worked with within MM Record Label, but he was indeed one of the most hardworking. It was her job to help assist him with bookings outside of actual producing jobs. If you wanted to get in touch with him, you had to go through her.

"Yeah. I got all of them. That one from BLAKC, though," he beamed, trying not to sound too hype about it.

Kierra could hear the excitement all in his voice. "I know, right. That's major. Everyone is trying to link with the mastermind behind most of the top hits on the charts today."

"I see. My schedule dumb packed right now. When do I got some availability?"

"Eh, not for a while. Let's see," she began, reading off the dates he had booked up.

BLAKC was the main radio station in Kansas City. They played nothing but the best of the best from hip-hop, R&B, and gospel music, and the urban contemporary station had to get Projex on their show. His name had been buzzing throughout their studio ever since he was locked up. Now that the Grammy's were approaching, it seemed like everyone wanted to have a sit down with him.

Projex was honored. He'd grown up listening to BLAKC all his life and still did on occasion. He remembered vivid nights calling in to read off one of the top ten songs during the weekend. Or requesting a song to be played for him and his niggas, while shouting their names out before they cut him off the air. It'd changed over the years, but one thing they still did was support their own. Laurent's music was played every hour on the hour, getting him paid as well.

"Okay," Kierra hummed. "So, you really don't have any free time until the week leading up to the Grammy's. Does that work for you?"

Projex pulled the calendar up on his phone. "Yeah. Tell him that Monday or Tuesday is cool."

"Got you. Are you still going out of town next week? I want to make sure people leave you alone."

He chuckled but appreciated that because his phone would ring off the hook for hours. "Yeah. Just got confirmation earlier. We'll be gone for like four days."

"Enjoy. Shoot me a text with the dates and what time you fly out, so I can arrange for a driver, or are you good?"

"Yeah, I'm good. I'll handle all that. I'll be off them four days, and so will you from assisting me."

"Right. I'm never not working."

"I fucks with that."

"We're like-minded. I'll email you the details for the interview, and don't forget to send me over the specific dates of your trip."

Projex told her he would, and they hung up. A surreal feeling soared through him as he stood in the middle of his bedroom. Scheduling interviews, hiring drivers, going to business meetings, and all was the life he'd dreamt of having for so long. Even when he was doing small gigs for Maine, writing lyrics for his upcoming music company, and having to pick up his money in cash, Projex always knew he'd be bigger.

Having Grandpa Joe labeled as an OG in the game didn't mean anything when Projex was trying to make his own mark and leave behind his own discography.

Figuring it'd been at least twenty minutes, Projex headed back downstairs. When Loriana glanced up from her MacBook, he looked at her ears with squinted eyes. She playfully rolled her eyes at his observation.

"Yes, I'm off the phone, nasty."

He grinned. "Shit, I was just making sure this time."

Shirtless, showing off his SAG tat along his washboard abs that led to V-cuts so ingrained she wanted to drag her tongue up it, Loriana stared him down. He was only wearing shorts with no briefs underneath, causing her eyes to hone in on his dick that was soft but still making a statement. She wanted to take her tour of his body down to his bare feet and long toes but got distracted.

Projex came and sat in the spot that wasn't occupied by her work. "You almost finished?"

"Yes. I'll be done in like an hour. Why? You need me?"

"I always need you."

Her head swiveled his way, with raised cheeks on display. "You're so sweet when you want to be."

"I'm always nice to you. Say I ain't."

She laughed as he poked her side. "Stop! You have your days, but I'm used to it."

"Speaking of days, you off that?"

"Off what?"

"Yo' cycle?"

She held her grin back. "Nope. Not yet."

Projex sucked his teeth. "It's heavy or like it's almost done?"

"Why, Bryshon?"

"Cause, ma. I need some pussy. Yours specifically."

"Well, I don't know what to tell you, sir. You can wait a few more days."

"We can lay a towel down or get in the shower. Why you acting brand new?" he asked, sliding his hand between her legs. They'd had sex on her cycle before, back when they were younger, because Projex always made her shit come down. Loriana didn't hate it, but she wasn't a fan of it either.

Loriana hurriedly shut her legs. "Oh, my gosh. Will you move. Clingy self."

"Man, I don't feel no pad. You lying, but a'ight. Remember that."

He snatched his hand back, and Loriana cracked

up. Stubborn to the bone, Projex hated not getting his way.

"You're such a baby. If you leave me alone for another hour, I promise to spend some quality time with you."

"Nah, I'ma be sleep."

"That's fine. I'll just wake you up. What'd you have to talk to me about, though? I'm sure it wasn't my cycle."

She'd distracted him that quickly.

"You gon' be busy next week?" He wanted to know. "I mean, I know you always busy, but you got some PTO or something."

"Yes," she replied with caution. "What you got up your sleeve?"

He grinned. "I booked us a trip to Puerto Rico for Valentine's Day."

Loriana faced him completely. "What? Are you serious?"

"Yeah. My grandparents own an oceanfront home out there. I see how hard you been going with yo' classes and work and figured you needed a break. Plus, we ain't really been on no vacation together."

Concern covered his face after seeing tears in her eyes. "Wait. What you crying for?"

Sniveling, Loriana removed her MacBook from

her lap and climbed into his. "Because. That's so nice. I've never had a real Valentine's Day before, and you're flying me out of town."

He wiped at her cheeks. "You so emotional, man," he said in jest. "You know it's whatever for you. We both need a break, but I know you need it more. You deserve it."

"You do too. When should I take off? Oh, my gosh. I have to buy me some swimsuits and book my hair appointment. I'm too hype," she said, dancing on his lap.

Projex grinned, loving that smile on her face. "One more thing."

Her eyes expanded, hanging on to his words.

"I got extra tickets just in case you wanted yo' friend to come. That Monday is President's Day, so I know there ain't no classes."

She gave him a squinted-eyed gaze. "Did you do something wrong?"

"What you mean?"

"I'm just trying to see because you've been real generous with the gifts lately."

He outlined the birthmark on her neck with his finger. "I ain't doing nothing I'm not supposed to do as your man. Can you let me do my thing?"

She giggled, tossing her hands up in surrender.

"My fault. I'll leave you to it. Thank you," she told him. "Nyree called me earlier, so let me call and let her know."

When Projex ran the idea by Juice last month, he was all for it. He gave him the money to get their flights booked and was ready to get the fuck out of town for a few days. With the day he had today, next week couldn't get here fast enough.

"Nyree is your only friend with a man, huh?"

"Boy," she laughed, "she's not, but don't do Candace and Trell. They're having fun right now."

"And that's exactly why they ass ain't coming with us." He laughed. "Couples only. Gon' and get your work done so we can take a nap together."

She smooched his lips. "Okay. I can get used to this."

"What? Us being a couple?"

"No. Being in your space, taking naps together, cooking us food and stuff. I kind of like it."

"If you trying to move in, say that."

"No. Not yet. Cause when you piss me off, I'm not gon' be down bad and not have anywhere to go."

"We talk shit out over here, so I don't even know what you saying right now."

She rolled her eyes. "I know we do, but still."

"Still nothing. You better go somewhere in the

house and cool off, then come talk to me when you ready. Ain't no going nowhere."

"So, you saying if I did something that had you so mad, you wouldn't go to the studio and blow off steam?"

He scratched his beard that was growing in quite nicely. "Nah, see. That's different."

She laughed. "No, it is not. You better go somewhere in the house and cool off," she mocked.

"A'ight. I see what you saying. That's my outlet. I just don't want you going to your friends and shit if we beefing. I know you gon' talk your little shit cause that's you, but what goes on between us should stay that way. Why let a mothafucka who ain't in yo' shoes tell you how to tie yo' laces?"

Projex wasn't telling her she couldn't talk to her friends or vent to them, but at the end of the day, their problems would still only belong to them when she came back home to hash things out. He learned long ago that caring too much about another mothafuckas' situation only hurt you more in the end. Especially if you loved them.

"You're right, and I hear you. You're always putting me on game."

"Got to. Can't have you out here moving blindly. You my eyes too, so I need them hoes clear as day."

Loriana couldn't do anything but agree. When Projex left her alone to finish working, she sent Nyree a voice message about plans for next week. She couldn't wait to be laid out on someone's beach, running her toes through the sand.

On the lower level of the oceanfront home, Nyree stood out on one of the verandas, listening to the waves crashing onto the shore. The view was one she wished she could capture forever, besides on her camera. The tranquility it brought her while out here was unmatched. Traveling to different colleges to party and kick it was one thing. Even though she wasn't out of the country, it put a battery in her back to want to enjoy this type of luxury more often. Seeing the world outside of Kansas City was now added to her bucket list.

If it wasn't nightfall and dark as hell, she'd go down to walk the beach. Instead, she recorded a video then headed inside the house. It was going on one in the morning, and after an eventful day of activities, they were still up, ready to play some drinking games. Thanks to Kierra, they had a full itinerary for their four-day stay and had already done so much. Today had been the most thrilling, though, as they went horseback riding on the beach and rode ATVs through the rainforest.

"They still in the room?" Nyree asked Juice as she popped a squat on one of the stools.

"Yeah. They got that music going, so you already know what's up."

Nyree tittered. "Yeah. Well, they better come on so we can play this game."

At the kitchen counter, Juice was removing bottles of liquor they'd stopped by the store to get. They asked one of the workers which was the best kind of rum to get, and he had them at the bar inside the store, sampling his favorites. By the time they left, Loriana's lightweight self was buzzed, and they'd copped four bottles.

While the couples split off to go shower, with plans to meet back up in the living room after, Juice and Nyree did just that. Loriana and Projex had other things on their mind. Projex told her to shower first, but Loriana pulled him inside with her.

The massive bathroom had a walk-in shower that opened up to the outside, with a view of the beach. Inside it sat a square jacuzzi tub, an eighty-inch double sink vanity, and a huge mirror Loriana couldn't stay out of. This was her favorite place in the house, and she was fucking Projex inside it as if he was purchasing her one next. She was putting the pussy on him in appreciation for his efforts in making her Valentine's Day one to remember.

Before he could completely dry off, Loriana forced him to sit on the edge of the tub that was positioned right in front of the mirror. In a zone, she bounced her ass on his dick, getting turned on by looking at her damn self. Projex had his hands clasped around her ankles, letting her do her thing.

"Ooooh, yes! This dick is sooo good."

She was loud and didn't have one care in the world either. With her feet planted firmly on the sides of Projex's thighs, she rolled her hips, pulling harsh grunts from the back of his throat. They looked good enough to record and get paid to view. With hands flat on his chest, she rode him to the gruff sounds of Kevin Gates' voice floating through the built-in speakers. The raunchy lyrics of *Power* took their sex to the next level.

"Yeah, this wet ass pussy got some power for real," Projex huffed in a trance, thrusting his hips. He couldn't agree with the lyrics more.

Loriana began to squirt all over him as he hit switches in the pussy. Smacking her ass, he gripped both cheeks as she tried running from his feral pounding. Slipping some, Projex maneuvered them until he was crouched low as if he were doing pelvic thrusts. She could run, but he was right on her ass.

"Where you going, huh?" he spoke directly in her ear, holding her close. "You can't take this dick?"

"I can, I can," she panted, holding onto him tightly. Her body bounced as Projex felt his balls tighten. "This my dick," she spoke against his neck.

"Act like it then."

Plunging into her wetness with a vengeance, Projex drove so deeply inside her, Loriana was coming again. His back stiffened.

"Bryshooon!" she screamed out as her pussy contracted around him, snatching that nut right from his body. He would never get enough of her shouting his name.

Loriana continued to roll her hips, eliciting a growl from him that made her body tingle.

Shiiiit," he breathed out, sliding them to the bathmat.

She rested her head on his shoulder, tired as fuck but thoroughly satisfied. Projex ran one hand down her sweaty back while the other massaged her scalp. She decided to let her hair be free while they were there, and he loved it.

"Whew," she let out, lifting her head. Projex's

eyes were closed as his chest heaved. "You know you got some good dick. I can go straight to sleep after that."

His eyes peeled open. "Nah. We about to play that drinking game. I gotta hop in the shower again. You wet me the fuck up."

Grabbing his face with both hands, Loriana commenced their tongue kiss. Slowly, they explored one another's mouth as his dick began to harden inside her again. Knowing they'd spent enough time in there already, Loriana hopped up. She stared down at his dick that was coated so beautifully in her juices. Not being able to resist, she squatted and took him into her mouth, slurping him clean—or dirty again.

When she removed her mouth, Projex gripped the front of her neck. His dilated eyes made her grin. "Mmm. We taste good together."

"You gon' make me crazy."

"You already are."

"Nah. On some next-level shit, ma. I swear. I love the fuck out of you," he declared, dropping his hand.

"You already know I love you, too. Now, come on so I can beat y'all in this game."

Projex had told her the same thing but now was ready to say fuck it so they could lay up. They held a staring contest for all of five seconds before Loriana stood up. She knew he loved her. No ifs, ands, or buts about it. When a man loves you for real and is all in, off rip, he's going to be crazier than the woman. Projex loved her first, so it was inevitable to keep the beast in him tamed when it came to anything pertaining to Loriana.

Once they were dressed, they headed into the living room. They played the game Categories, forcing them to test their ability to name things, people, places, and other words from memory. With pressure applied to their thinking skills, if any of them took too long to keep the chant going, they had to take a shot. They were on round four, and Loriana was tore up, having missed two turns already.

"Okay, okay. It's Juice's turn," Nyree said, grinning. "Come on, baby. We can't let them win."

"We competing now? Y'all cheating cause she already fucked up," Projex said as they all looked at Loriana.

She grinned. "I'm good. We don't take no L's over here, bae. What number shot are we going to until we lose?"

"I think six combined is good. We both have two, so it's tied up."

"A'ight, bet," Projex said, ready to win.

Juice started his turn as they chanted zing, zing, zing, and a one, two, three.

Clap, Clap.

"Categories."

Clap, Clap.

"Such as."

Clap, Clap.

"Names of."

Clap, Clap.

"Cereal."

"Frosted Flakes," Nyree sang.

"Fruity Pebbles," Projex answered.

"Fruit Loops," Loriana said.

"Captain Crunch," was Juice's answer.

Nyree said, "Waffle Crisps."

"Cheerios," Projex added.

Loriana's eyes scattered as she mumbled, "Um, Frosted Flakes."

Nyree hollered. "Nope! I already said that, and you hesitated. Take your shot, friend."

"That's not fair. My brain isn't working right now." She pouted, making them laugh. "Pour me a shot, bae."

Doing the honors, Projex grabbed one of the bottles and her mini red Solo cup. Pouring right to the brim, her eyes shot up at him.

"Why would you pour all of that? That's wrong."

"Want me to take one with you?"

She grinned. "Yes. Come on."

"Y'all so sickening. Let her take it on her own," Nyree kidded.

Loriana stuck her tongue out and flipped her off. She and Projex toasted and threw their shots back.

"Oh my gosh." Loriana gagged as her body shivered. "What the fuck was that, death?"

"Nah. That shit wicked. We can't drink that straight," Projex grimaced.

Loriana shook her head from side to side. "I'm good. If I keep playing, I'ma be throwing up. Y'all win."

"Awwww. You suck. I thought y'all don't take no L's, L-Boogie," Nyree taunted.

"We are tonight. I can't. I should've taken a BC powder before fooling with y'all."

Seeing how serious she was, Projex decided to call it a night too. With Valentine's Day the following morning, he didn't want her too hungover for what he had planned. After cleaning off the table, they said goodnight and retreated to their room. With the ceiling fan on, nestled under the plush duvet, Loriana was out cold the second Projex helped her in the bed. He'd gone to get her some meds and a bottle of water, and she was knocked out when he came back.

"Ma, get up and take this BC powder."

Loriana didn't even open her eyes. She sat up slightly, feeling like her head weighed a million pounds and was going to roll off her neck. "Bae, I'm drunk."

"I know. That's why you gotta take this."

"You treat me so good. Can't none of these other lame niggas out here fuck with you. They be trying, though."

His brow raised. "Aww yeah. What they be saying?"

"Dumb shit. Spitting weak-ass game in my DM, like they don't know I fuck with a straight shooter."

He chuckled, knowing she was drunk for real to be cussing like she was. "Better let them niggas know, bae."

"I do. I don't want them. I don't want nobody but you. I wanna love on you forever and have your babies. Your nut tastes good, but I'm tired of swallowing it."

This time he laughed loudly, causing her eyes to open.

"What?" she asked as if she didn't know what she'd just said.

"Nothing, ma. Open your mouth so you can take this right quick. I know you wanna lay down."

"I do," she mumbled, letting her jaw drop.

Drunkenly, she flicked her tongue out at him, while her lavish lashes and pretty ass face made Projex grin. Her bare face and glowing skin were so attractive to him. It always had been. Tearing the rectangular packet of white substance open, he sprinkled it all on her tongue before holding the bottle of water to her lips. When she was done, he helped her lay back down. Two minutes later, Projex was in bed spooning her.

"Bae," he called out as she dozed off.

"Hmm?"

"You wanna have my babies for real?"

"Mhm."

"How many?" he asked, rubbing her hot stomach. She scooted further into him, wanting to get as close to him as space would allow.

"However many you want."

"Three."

"Okay, three," she mumbled and yawned. "I gotchu'."

He grinned behind her, placing a kiss on her neck. There she was using his lingo again, coining it as hers now. Projex was cool with that. He was cool with her agreeing to three kids, too. Drunk or not, he was going to remind her when that time came that she owed him.

The following morning was rough, seeing as though Loriana had only gotten just enough sleep to not have her walking around with an attitude. There was no need to be, though, especially with the way Projex woke her up. Warm kisses trailed down her stomach, making her thighs fall apart before her toes were in his mouth. Making his way back up, Projex buried his face between her legs, skillfully licking and sucking on her clit until she came hard. Loriana's face prickled with pleasure as her eyes fluttered toward the ceiling. Catching glimpses of red and pink hues, she tried clearing her fogged brain to grasp if she was dreaming or not.

When she was fully able to open her lids, her pulse quickened, and her eyes glossed with tears. Projex came from under the sheet. With a grin on his face, he kissed her poked-out lips.

"Good mornin'. Happy Valentine's Day, ma."

"Bae," she whined as her eyes danced about their room. "When did you do all this?"

"Last night when you fell asleep."

When he was sure that she wouldn't wake up, Projex snuck out of the room and down the hall. Yesterday, he had someone deliver pink heart-shaped balloons, red heart foil ones, and a big white banner with red lettering that said *I Love You, Ma*. He had to hide everything in one of the spare bedrooms.

The entire room was filled with balloons floating. On the dresser sat a red suede heart-shaped box with pink roses that lasted for up to a year. Loriana was so overwhelmed, she couldn't do anything but hug him. Once she told him she had never gotten much of anything on this day, Projex made sure to go all out.

"You really outdid yourself, bae. Thank you so much."

"You're welcome. Let me get your card right quick," he said, climbing from the bed and walking over to the dresser.

Opening the envelope that was labeled L-Boogie, she grinned. The card stuck to the theme but had a Black couple on the front of it. Kierra had put him onto a married couple who started their card business specifically for Black people.

"This is cute," she said, opening it.

A hefty stack of neat hundreds fell out, covering her lap. "Whoa."

He smirked. "Wasn't expecting that, huh?"

"I never know what to expect from you. That's a good thing," she said as she began to read the card.

The imprinted one was nice, but Loriana loved his handwritten note more. Projex's elegant penmanship would always be her favorite.

"I love your handwriting. It's so neat."

"Thank you."

Her lips poked out as she read his words.

Projex didn't know why he felt nervous as she read the card, but he did. The money inside it didn't matter to him. He just hoped that she liked everything he'd done so far. This was his first time ever going all out for a woman, besides his mama and Joi. The little girl he gave a teddy bear and candy to in fifth grade didn't count. This was real love. So, he didn't know if he was doing too much or not enough. He popped his knuckles as she looked up at him and tossed the covers from her frame. He picked her up with ease as she wrapped her legs around his waist and arms around his neck.

"I love it, and I love you."

"You better. Got me smelling yo' breath this early," he joked, pecking her lips.

Bad breath and all, she was his.

"This only the first half of the day. I got some-body cooking us breakfast."

On cue, her stomach growled loud as hell, making them both laugh. "I'm starving. Are they coming here?"

"Nah. We gotta go to them… on a boat."

Her eyes stretched. "What?"

"Yeah. It's a little bit across the water, but on the beach still."

"I don't deserve you."

Projex smirked. "Yes, you do. Can't nobody handle me the way you do."

"You're right. That's nothing but facts. I got you something too, but it's not ever going to top this."

"It ain't got to. You know I like whatever you get me. Shit, you the only gift I need, for real."

"Say less," she giggled, sliding down from him.

Grabbing her phone off the charger he'd put it on last night, she wrapped the sheet around her and started to record the room. Silently, Projex pulled up his Instagram and recorded her walking around the room in awe.

"Bae," he called out, making her face him with a big smile. She literally lit up their room even with the curtains drawn.

His heart thumped, knowing she was it for him. Before posting to his story, he added the words *The only girl that got a nigga's heart*. And he meant that. Knowing breakfast food was her favorite meal any time of the day, Projex arranged for them to have a private brunch on the beach. This would be one vacation she remembered forever.

Chapter Fifteen

It was back to business as usual when they returned home. Projex couldn't remember the last time he'd gotten a total of eight hours of sleep. At this point, he was running off of straight hunger. Every day, he was striving to be better than him from yesterday. He wasn't even the same person from two weeks ago.

He'd bossed his life up in months and was taking no days off until absolutely necessary. With the Grammy's in five days, those days weren't included. It was midafternoon when he was on his way to the BLAKC studio for his interview with them. Knowing he wouldn't have time to stop and grab something to eat, he asked Kierra to pick up a box of his favorite cereal and some almond milk. Loriana had put him onto it, and he hadn't looked back.

"You are not eating a bowl of Fruity Pebbles right now." Loriana laughed on FaceTime.

"In the backseat of a Maybach too. This shit so player," he said, showing her the inside of the whip.

Maxwell went above and beyond for his artists and anyone who worked under the MM Record Label umbrella. When he brought it to Projex about getting him a chauffeur, Projex wasn't with it. He was cool with driving himself around. That was until Maxwell put it on the table to hire whoever he wanted, as long as he trusted them. So, of course, Projex hired Sneaks as his driver. He'd been that since they slid on niggas blocks for fun, so it was a no-brainer. Plus, he wanted anyone who came up with him to get money as well. Projex wasn't greedy at all and wanted to see his day one niggas eat too. Shit, his plate was full.

"I'm trying to be like you when I grow up. I'm about to walk into class, though. Have a good interview, and don't answer anything that'll incriminate you."

He smirked while chewing. "Look at you talking to me like you my manager."

"I mean, I could be. Keep it all in the family."

She gave Projex something to think about, considering he didn't have one at the time. Exchanging I love you, the two hung up. After posting a picture of his view to his story, Projex relaxed his mind for the rest of the ride. Fifteen minutes later, he was walking into the building with his entourage of people. Kierra was a few steps ahead of him while Sneaks and Bo followed up the tail end.

Projex hadn't done many interviews, preferring to play the back, and let his work be all that needed to be heard, but he was stepping into the role of a true businessman. He left the spotlight and serious ass questions for Laurent to answer, but this was business and pleasure. Projex didn't mind sitting down and speaking into a mic for this interview.

His presence inside the building garnered long, lustful stares from the women in their offices while the men saluted him. Kansas City was small, but it wasn't that small. Most of the office staff had either already known who Projex was or tried digging up some information on him before today. One thing was for sure, the man could dress, his smile was killer, and he showed respect to everyone in his path.

"Yo, my man," a janitorial guy called out as they walked by.

Projex pivoted. "What's good."

"It's crazy seeing you up here interviewing. My kids grew up down the street from your mother."

He grinned. "So, you from the hood, too?"

"Born and raised. Southside all day."

Projex stuck his hand out, and they slapped hands. "Straight up."

"Keep grinding, young man. All your hard work is going to pay off," the older man with a crisp salt and peppered beard declared. Projex nodded his head, receiving all that positive energy.

"I appreciate that."

As soon as he stepped into the recording room, Kent and Kapri, the two on-air personalities, greeted him with a warm welcome. They hadn't found out much about him, but they hoped to be able to change that by the time he left. Getting comfortable, Projex adjusted his Chevy chain around his neck and took a swig of his water.

"You need anything?" Kierra asked. He shook his head no. "Okay. Remember what we discussed. If at any time you feel uncomfortable, we're leaving."

"We should be good," he let her know. He hoped it was all good.

As soon as the on-air sign popped on, Kent jumped straight into it. Projex noticed a girl recording and let her rock since he'd already agreed to do the interview. He'd watch it back whenever it was released.

"For our long-time listeners, you know we here at BLAKC have to show love to the people from our hometown making a way out. We have Mr. Grammy nominated songwriter and producer, Projex in the building with us today."

Fake applause sounded off, and Projex smirked.

"Thanks for sitting down and talking with us. It's an honor."

"What's up. I appreciate y'all for extending the invite."

"Of course," Kapri chirped. She was just a grinning, looking at Projex's as if he were her son. "We had to sit down and chat with you. Your name has been ringing off the hook here lately."

"I've been busy." Projex chuckled, trying to shake his nerves a bit.

"We see. So, we already know you're nominated for a Grammy; congratulations, by the way," Kapri said.

"Yeah, man. That's huge. Congrats," Kent added.

"Thank you."

"What we don't know is how you got started. Did you always want to write and produce music?"

Now, he felt comfortable. Projex could discuss

music all day, so he wasted no time explaining to them how he grew up around it and just had a niche for it. He further explained who his grandfather was, shocking them both.

"Ah, so there's that connection to the industry," Kent stated.

"Nah. Not for real. My grandpa is well-respected in the game, but I got my shit out the mud. Respectfully."

Kapri smiled. "Okay. I know that's right. Does he support what you're doing or thought you should be somewhere else in your life right now?"

"He supports it one hundred percent as long as I'm with it."

Kent nodded his head. "That's what's up. It's a blessing to have such a strong support system behind you."

"Fasho. They're the ones that keep me going."

"Speaking of support, I just so happen to follow you on Instagram, and you always post this pretty young lady named Loriana. Is it—"

"It's Loriana," he corrected, as Kapri pronounced her name wrong.

"Oop. I'm sorry. Loriana," she said correctly. "You hear that, ladies? If that man doesn't check someone behind the pronunciation of your name, he's not the one," Kapri said, as the studio laughed. "I know that's right. So, it's safe to say you're not single?"

"Nah. I'm in a committed relationship. That's my baby right there."

Women listening in their cars and at the hair salons all cooed, Loriana being one of them. She'd snuck on the BLAKC app just to listen, not expecting for her name to be brought up. Her heart fluttered.

"It's good to have someone by your side in this industry. Shit can get crazy," Kent let him know. "Shoutout to the misses. How'd you and Laurent team up?"

Projex smiled. That was his nigga, fasho. "Aww, man. Me and Laurent go way back. We used to hustle up money together just for studio time. He always took it more seriously than me but never let me fall off my grind either."

"You from South Ave, right?"

"All day. Shout out to the guys. I know they listening." Projex smirked.

Grammy-nominated or not, Projex showed love to his hood cause they always did the same in return.

"I have some family who grew up over there. Man, it's hard to make it out," Kent expressed.

"Yeah. I ain't gone lie. It's not the safest on the

Ave, but it's home feel me? We family over there. So, even if only one of us make it, it's like the entire hood made it."

"That's true. Everybody doesn't or won't see it that way, though."

"Of course not. That's why you gotta show genuine love for yourself, not expecting mothafuckas — oh my fault," he laughed, "excuse my language, but you can't expect for everybody to move, feel, or think the same as you. That's why the big dog upstairs made us all different. My path ain't everybody else's, but it don't mean the next person can't travel their own. I see it like this," Projex said, adjusting in his seat.

"The quicker we accept people for who they show us they are, the better off a lot of us will be. I can't make somebody wanna get out the hood if they already doubt that they weren't built to survive out of it. Now, if I give back, reaching my hand out to you, trying to show you the ropes, and you drop em', that's on you. You can't ever say I ain't extend my hand yo' way cause I ain't have to, to begin with."

"Young man," Kapri began, "you are wise beyond your years. That's some of the realest stuff we've heard from a man in a while."

"Really, Kapri? I'm sitting right here," Kent said

in jest, making them chuckle. "No, but she's right. Y'all who are still tuned in, I hope y'all taking notes."

Pressing a few buttons, Kent took them off live air and went into a station break. Just as Projex went to speak, his phone vibrated against the table. Seeing that his mama was calling, he asked for them to give him a second and stepped out. He hadn't gotten to the point of giving Kierra his phone to hold yet, and he was glad he hadn't.

"What's up, Mama?"

"She's almost here!" she shouted so loudly, Kierra jerked her head his way. "We're headed to the hospital now."

Projex's heart skipped a beat. "A'ight. I'm on my way."

"What's going on?" Kierra questioned.

"My sister about to have her little girl. We gotta shake."

Nodding, Kierra went to let Kent and Kapri know what was going on. Projex thanked them for having him and promised to visit again in the future. Sneaks pushed the luxury vehicle through traffic as Projex sent Loriana a text, telling her to meet him there. He locked his phone and smiled. Kierra glanced his way.

"You nervous?"

"Nah. I'm hype. My niece is about to come into this world. I already know she gon' change my life."

Kierra smiled. "Little girls always do."

S hamari stood in awe, with his heart beating wildly in his chest. He couldn't believe he and Joi created such a gorgeous baby. She didn't look like either one of them fresh out, but she for sure had a head full of hair that traveled down her back as well. For all of the heartburn she had, Joi knew it wasn't for no reason.

"Bruh, I love her already," Projex claimed, holding her.

Joi had given birth an hour ago, and the people who she wanted there most, were right by her side. Serenity Aadya Royal had the entire room on a high and was passing around severe baby fever. She was the perfect blended complexion of her parents, with the tips of her ears showcasing she'd take after Shamari's chocolate hue, more than Joi's caramel one. Weighing six pounds and seven ounces, with a length of twenty inches, Shamari wasn't sure how he even held her at first. She was tiny, as newborns are, but fit perfectly in the palm of his hand.

"You need me to get you anything?" Shamari asked Joi as she stuffed her face with lasagna and breadsticks her mama made.

She finished chewing and said, "No. I'm okay. You wanna get up here with me?"

"Later." He smirked, already planning to do that as she slept.

"Give her here. You're hogging her already," Loriana told Projex as she dried her hands.

Swiveling his frame away from her, Projex went to walk across the room to sit down when Symir pushed his way through the door. Right behind him was April, he and Shamari's god mom. She'd been stuck in a meeting up north and had finally made it there.

For a second, Projex thought he'd have to get out of pocket with Symir when he glanced Loriana's way. *I wish that nigga would move his lips to speak to her.* Already knowing what her man was thinking, Loriana moved his way just in case Symir got bold. She wasn't surprised that she hadn't heard from him. If she was him, Loriana would've acted like she never existed if a gun was placed to her head.

Symir kept the peace, only speaking to those who he knew he could. He'd taken up the offer his dad was trying to bring Shamari in on and had moved to

Florida to expand their family business. He just so happened to be in town at his local Royal Motors location, handling a few things.

Sitting next to him, Loriana grabbed Serenity's balled-up fist and uncurled it. Immediately, Serenity curled her fingers around her index. Loriana loved when babies did that. Taking her from him, Loriana cradled her in her arms, inhaling her scent.

"I love how babies smell." She sighed dreamily. "She's so freaking pretty."

"She got that from our side of the family," Projex spoke loudly.

"Boy, hush," Joseline chastised. "You were the funny-looking baby, so I wouldn't start if I were you."

Joi snickered. "Dang, Ma. Like that?"

"Right," Projex added. "I'm handsome now, so that's all that matters."

"Yeah, until you have one of your own. We gon' have to hide y'all baby for a few months until it's ready to be shown off to the world," Joseline told them.

"You're pregnant?" Symir blurted, with menacing eyes on Loriana.

"Nigga, and if she was? Who the fuck you getting loud with?" Projex questioned, standing to his feet. "You shouldn't even be speaking to her."

"Un, un. None of that," April said, standing in front of him. "Symir, mind your business. Loriana is no longer your concern."

"She never was, fuck nigga. Know that. She always been mine," Projex boasted.

"Bae. Relax." Loriana sighed.

Symir gritted his teeth, knowing he had nothing to say. Well, he could've, but there was no point in doing so. It wasn't like Loriana was going to give him a second chance. Loriana wasn't pregnant, but like Projex stated, even if she was, that was none of his damn business.

He'd tried keeping the peace, knowing his sister didn't need all this drama fresh out of delivering a baby, but Projex was never letting a nigga come out the side of his neck toward him. It'd be a cold day in Egypt before he let that happen.

"Joi, I'ma step out. I ain't trying to start nothing," Symir told her apologetically.

Projex mugged him all the way out the door and didn't take his seat until it closed. Joseline shook her head. "At least he was the bigger person and left," she kidded.

"Whatever. He should've been apologizing to me."

"Boy, for what?"

"He got my blood pressure all high thinking this girl pregnant," he said seriously. "I was about to spazz out."

Loriana rolled her eyes. "If I was, trust me, you'd know."

"I'm glad you got that energy cause my niece got me too ready for one of our own." Projex leaned over to whisper in her ear. "We still having three, right?"

Loriana jerked her head away from him as he laughed. "Three what? I ain't agree to that."

"Yeah, you did. Off that liquor, you was making mad promises. Don't turn fraud now. You owe down."

She waved him off as Serenity let out a big yawn. "If you're the only one who can remember what I said when I was drunk, then it doesn't count."

Projex smirked. "Yeah, a'ight. I'ma make it count."

They won their first Grammy.

Projex was no longer a nominee but a Grammy Award-winning songwriter. He couldn't believe it. From running the streets of South Ave., raising hell, to beating a murder case, then coming home to this? God for sure didn't play about him.

Glancing around the private party full of everyone who made this happen, elation settled in his chest. He'd never felt more accomplished in his life, and this was only the beginning.

His entire crew had flown to California for the awards, including Grandma Juanita. With a newborn at home, Joi was sad she couldn't make it, so she sent Shamari in her place. He didn't want to leave, but she literally made him go for the both of them while April stayed with her and Serenity.

The energy in the room was nuts. Projex had never seen so many people smiling and enjoying life. It was a sight to see, and he knew there'd be plenty more occasions like this. Sauntering his way with his chest poked out proudly, Laurent handed him an ice-cold bottle of Ace. He grinned and nodded his head enthusiastically.

"Yeeeah! Gon' head and pop that bitch," Laurent told him.

Cheesing, Projex did just that. Cameras flashed while videos recorded their celebration. Two Black men from the hood had made it. They'd seen it happen for others, always thinking they'd be next, and here they were. They could've given up on their dreams long ago but didn't. They'd set the bar even higher now for little boys who looked like them.

"Aye," Laurent said, searching around the room. "Where the mic at? My nigga got something he wanna say."

Projex shook his head with his hand out. "Nah. I'm good, cuz. You speak. You're the reason we're here."

Someone handed Laurent the mic. "*We* the reason we're here. Get on this mothafucka, man." He grinned. "You ain't gotta say much. Just let these mothafuckas know what time it is."

Grabbing the mic, Projex exhaled as the room quieted down a bit. If this was the life he was about to have to live, he'd better get used to speaking in front of crowds. There was no more playing the back.

"Aye, how y'all doing," he spoke. His husky tone vibrated through the room. "Seeing all of y'all in this room means you contributed to this win tonight, so thank y'all. It's so many people who put in work to bring this Grammy home, and I don't wanna miss anybody. I been drinking." He chuckled, making the room laugh. They all had been sipping. "But, um. First, shout out to God. My man's uh hunnid grand. Him and the prayer's from my loved ones kept me covered, fasho. I wasn't supposed to be here, let alone winning awards and shit."

For those who knew him, like really knew him

and not of him, their eyes misted. Especially Loriana's and Joseline's.

"Big shout out to my grandparents. Y'all played a
major role. My mama. Lady, you already know how
I'm stepping behind you. You literally did whatever
to see me make it. I got you for life. This fool here,"
he said, tossing his arm over Laurent's shoulder. "A1
since day one. He forever kept it solid with me and
never folded. It's plenty more where these came
from," he said, lifting the gold trophy in the air.

Whistles and handclaps sounded off around the
room.

"Aye, where Maxwell at?" Projex asked, and he
stepped closer so he could acknowledge him. "From
the day I got out, you put me in a position to win and
get this money. I'll always appreciate that. Thank you.
MM Record Label ain't nothing to play with."

"We sure aren't," Maxwell cosigned.

Locating the last but certainly not the least of the
people in the room, his eyes fell on Loriana. He'd
already tried to get her out of the dress she was wearing, twice. The royal blue silk gown with a high split
up the right thigh had her looking like every bit of
royalty and thick as fuck as it clung to her curves. She
paired it with silver heels Projex couldn't wait to tell
her to keep on to fuck her in, and a silver Tom Ford

clutch was at her side. Projex rocked a black custom-tailored Tom Ford suit that did his body justice, fitting just right. Loriana couldn't wait to get her hands on him.

She blushed his way as he licked his lips.

"L-Boogie, this your award too, ma. Thank you for everything. Always my muse and my motivation. My biggest cheerleader and critic, you a real one. You don't ever have to wonder cause it's always you for me."

Everyone said aww as he openly expressed his gratitude and love for her. Blowing him a kiss, Projex smirked and lifted the mic.

"A'ight. I'm done," he said, making the room laugh naturally. "Thank you to everyone."

Laurent grabbed the mic. "The man who swore he ain't have much to say. Everybody raise ya' glasses."

"I think that's my part of the speech," Maxwell said, interrupting him. Laurent handed the mic over and wrapped his arm around Maliya's waist, pressing a kiss to her cheek.

"To one of many Grammys from these men; congratulations Projex and Laurent. This is to beating the odds and proving every doubter wrong. We coming for them all."

The party cheered and toasted. Walking over to

Loriana after taking a few more pictures, she welcomed him with open arms.

"I'm so damn proud of you, baby," she told him for what seemed the millionth time tonight. It didn't matter. She'd recite those words until her throat dried.

"Thank you. None of this would be possible without your support."

"Yes, it would've. It was already written in stone for you to win; I was just your cheerleader on the sideline."

He nicked her chin, making her grin. "Is that right?"

"Yep."

"Can this cheerleader do a split on my dick later on?"

"Whew!" she exclaimed. "I don't know about all that. You gon' have to stretch me out some."

"Shit. You already know that ain't ever been an issue for me."

Grinning, she adjusted his tie. "Of course it hasn't."

Chapter Sixteen

W hen Loriana woke up this morning, the last thing she expected to happen was to be offered a promotion. Not just any ole' promotion with a higher salary. No, baby girl was getting the works and deserved it all. Over the years, she learned to stop questioning every single thing that happened in her life. Good or bad, every situation and experience had molded her into the young woman she was today. Every life lesson and loss had matured her in ways her mother had told her about growing up.

She wasn't going to cry inside her boss' office. No, she'd save those tears for when she retreated to her own. They were happy ones, of course.

"You don't have to accept right now. Think about

it. Give it a few days and come and talk to me," Nicole told her.

Loriana sniveled. Her prayers outweighed her thoughts. She'd asked God in specific detail to expand her life in all ways, and like only He could, He came through expeditiously. Even if she didn't feel prepared for where He was taking her, Loriana's position had already been prepared for her arrival.

"I don't need any time to think. I know this is what I want to do."

"I figured that'd be your reply." Nicole chuckled. "I'll have the paperwork drawn up and sent over to you on Monday. Would you like to start after graduation?"

"Yes. That way, I'll have more time on my hands."

Nicole nodded her head. "Of course. Speaking of graduation… yours is coming up. Don't be surprised when you have tons of gifts in your office."

Loriana grinned. That was another reason she loved working for a company that actually cared about her. Nothing with them, from what she'd experienced, had been fake. From day one, it'd been genuine love, support, and good vibes. The fact that she was accelerating in her field already and before a degree spoke volumes as well.

"I've been warned more than once. Thank you again, Nicole. So much. I can't wait to embark on this journey for the culture.

"You're welcome. Like I said, your dedication to not only Aspire but to the artists we serve and our community, is beyond commendable. Is there a certain someone who inspired you most to pursue a career in music? I don't think I've ever asked you that."

She grinned a bit. That answer was easy. "I've always loved music, but a special someone from the hood, who never gave up on me or their dreams, inspired me most."

"Does this person have a name? That's a lot of inspiration behind your hard work and talent."

"He's produced a bunch of big *projects*. I'm sure you've heard of him."

The way she said the word projects let Nicole know exactly who she was speaking of. "Ah. I see what you did there. Well, kudos to him and congratulations. You can have tomorrow off. Go out and celebrate tonight." Nicole slid her a gift card to Tune Me Up, a karaoke bar.

"I sure will. Thanks. Have a good rest of your day."

"You do the same."

Before she could get entirely out of the door, Nicole was on her phone handling another operation of business. The day wasn't over because one task had been checked off her to-do list. Stepping into her office, Loriana closed the door and exhaled.

"Thank you, God," she spoke loudly. "Thank you, thank you, thank you."

Without Him, none of this would've been possible, and she wasn't afraid to give Him praise. On a high, she didn't even sit down as she grabbed her phone to call Projex. He was the first person she always wanted to share her good news with.

"You sneaking on the phone at work?" he joked once he picked up, making her giggle.

"No. I don't have to do all that. Are you busy right now?"

Projex spun the chair he was in around and held up his finger to the engineer. "In the studio with Misa and her crew. What's up?"

"I got a promotion today."

"What? Hell yeah, ma. That's what I'm talking about it. Congratulations."

His excitement made her want to be in his presence. "Thank you. It was so unexpected too. She called me in her office and was just like, bam."

They laughed at her dramatics.

"That's how it be. What was it for?"

"You remember when I was mentioning wanting to do like a webisode series for artists and their lives behind the music?"

"Yeah. I fucked with that."

"Apparently, Nicole did too. I brought it up in conversation one day, thinking aloud, and she created an entire position for it. Can you believe that?"

"Hell yeah. Not only is that shit entertainment, but it's needed. So, you'd basically be doing what you're doing now, but in person and on video?"

"Yep. I'm so hype." She grinned, walking around her office.

"I'm hype for you. I better be the first artist, too."

"Well, I was kind of thinking Laurent," she let him know.

"I'm playing, baby. I ain't gotta be the first. That nigga, Laurent, all the way up right now, so I'm sure he'd be cool with being your first webisode."

"Right. Bro gone come through like always. I won't start until after graduation, but you already know my mind is on a million with ideas right now."

"Fasho. You're an innovator, ma. It's in yo' blood. We gotta celebrate when we get off."

"Oh, we are. I'm off tomorrow and got us a gift card to Tune Me Up."

Projex nodded his head. "That's a bet. We can slide through there. I'ma have Kierra call and get the largest room reserved for us."

"Okay. Thank you."

"You ain't gotta thank me. I'll see you later. I love you."

Her stomach always fluttered hearing those three words. "I love you too."

Going to her and her friend's group chat, Loriana sent them a text with the plans for the night before texting Mhyale separately. Nyree was mad she was at school and couldn't celebrate her best friend's win, so she ordered her an edible arrangement and had it delivered to the house when she got off work.

It was the small things for Loriana. Her group of friends sent voice messages screaming, congratulating her, letting it be known that they were getting her fucked up tonight. Loriana hadn't had a super drunk night since Valentine's Day, opting to let Projex get wasted on the night of the Grammys. So, she was all for it.

"Are you recording this!" Joi yelled in Mhyale's ear, and she nodded her head.

"Yep. With her non-singing ass." Mhyale laughed.

On stage, putting on a show with Projex by her side, Loriana had tapped into her inner Beyoncé. Everyone woman had a little bit of her in them when singing her songs or going about their day. While she could've chosen a song to sing by herself, Loriana picked one for her and Projex to do a duet.

Part II (On the Run) ft. Beyoncé blasted through the private room at Tune Me Up, and Loriana was in full concert mode. Projex bobbed his head as she sang the chorus. A grin was on his face while watching her in her zone. The bright lights on stage brought out the sparkle in her eyes as she sang to him.

"I will hold your heart and your gun. I don't care if they come, nooo," she belted.

"Okay, friend! You better sing that shit!" Trell yelled. He was up out of his seat with a drink in his hand and hips swaying.

"She almost sounded kind of good there." Candace laughed.

"Man, hell no," Ayo said, sliding his chair next to her. "We going up there next."

Candace spun her head to her right. "Who is we?"

Ayo gave her a grin that made her breath hitch. "Me and you."

"Boy, please. I'm doing a solo performance."

"Ol' independent ass."

Ignoring him because the earthy aroma of his cologne and handsome face was getting to her, Candace focused back on the stage. Jay-Z's verse had come up, and Projex was coolly rapping the lyrics but let them know he meant them too. If he wanted to be a rapper, Projex most definitely could the way he commanded the stage with his presence. His long legs were covered in track pants as he strode across it, while his hands moved animatedly with each lyric flowing from his lips.

"Cross the line, speak about mine. I'ma wave this TEC, I'ma geek about mine. Touch a nigga where his rib at, I click-clack. Push yo' mothafuckin' wig back, I did that."

In the crowd, Joi was grinning, watching her brother be so in love. She thought she'd be used to it by now, seeing as though Loriana had been around for a while, but she wasn't. From watching him sneak girls in the house, to hearing them cry about him ignoring them, to having Loriana have this man on stage rapping to her was what she called a damn transformation.

Shamari leaned her way. "You gon' sing to me?"

"I can," she said, staring at him, seeing nothing but their daughter's twin.

The couple was happy to be invited tonight, needing to get out of the house. Joseline had no problems watching her grandbaby and told them to not come bothering them until she called. Serenity had everyone wrapped around her fingers already. Especially Projex, who'd gone all out and converted one of his bedrooms into hers. He didn't care that she was a baby; he wanted her to have her own room when he got her.

When the song came to an end, everyone clapped as they got off the stage. Loriana did a little twerk on Projex.

"Ayyye. We killed it. Y'all knew better than to let us go last cause it's over now." She laughed.

"Girl, bye. Up there sounding like Yung Miami," Mhyale said, making them holler.

"Caresha, please!" Trell added, causing Mhyale to fall all over him.

Poking her lip out, Loriana leaned into Projex, who was holding his laughter back. "Whatever. My man liked it."

He kissed her head full of curls. "That's right. They just hating on you."

"You sounded good, sis," Joi told her.

"Don't be trying to gas her 'cause you want a babysitter," Mhyale said, making them crack up.

"She knows I don't mind watching my little baby. Who going next?"

"Me!" Candace hopped up. "Let's get some Tink cracking in this mothafucka."

"Yeees!" all the women plus Trell yelled.

Projex shook his head and sat down. Loriana played her so much, he damn near knew every word of her latest album. While they crowded the front of the stage, singing along loud as hell to *Bottom Bitch*, the men sat back and chilled. After everyone who wanted to perform went, they all headed outside. It was a weekday, so the Westport wasn't as busy, but there were still a few people out and about.

"What y'all about to do?" Trell asked.

"You already know where I'm going," Loriana said. "The taco truck is around the corner."

"You and these tacos." Projex chuckled. "You been hooked ever since I put you on them."

Reminiscing, Loriana took a trip down memory lane. That day he came and picked her up from Nyree's house was the day Loriana knew she loved him. He'd hopped out in the middle of traffic and checked a nigga about some money they owed him, fed her some fire ass tacos, and made her enjoy parked car conversations. That was their first of many little dates, and she loved them all.

"Right. Had me sneaking out of Nyree's house. I knew then, I was in deep with you."

Projex smirked as they headed around the corner. "I'm glad you knew."

As they approached the truck that had a few people in line, Loriana put a hand on Projex's arm, stopping him from walking.

"What's wrong?" he asked, sensing her concern immediately.

With her face scrunched up, Loriana retched as her stomach flipped. "I think I'ma be sick," she uttered, breathing hard.

"You gotta throw up or something? You ain't even drink that much."

She quickly shook her head no. "No. I don't have to throw up, but I feel nauseous as fuck."

Projex gave her an intent gaze. "Yeah? Then, you don't need these tacos, then."

Loriana sucked her teeth. "Now, you're talking crazy. It was that last shot we took."

"Yeah. A'ight."

Sneaks walked up to them. "I'ma pull the truck around here."

"A'ight. Everybody headed up here?"

"Nah. They still on the corner talking," he let him know. "I'll be right back."

When he walked away, Sneaks turned back around to tell him something but was stopped mid-sentence.

"Aye, nigga," some man called out, walking in their direction, causing him and Projex to glance his way.

Peeping him reach for his waist, Projex and Sneaks both pulled their guns out while Sneaks stepped in front of Loriana. Shots rang out, making the area sound like the Fourth of July. Screaming from everywhere took over as the man ran off. Not before he'd gotten hit with a few bullets, though. Loriana lay flat on the ground with her hands over her head and heart pumping wildly. Beside her was a body, and when she went to lift up, her hand pressed into a puddle of blood.

"Nooo! No! Oh, my gosh," she cried out.

A night of fun had turned into utter chaos, and Loriana just knew this wasn't how their night was supposed to end. She prayed it didn't because the city was about to be painted red if they lost him.

L oriana hated hospitals.

The sterilized smell of them. The shivering

temperature they set the entire building to. The whole atmosphere was gloomy. Death and sadness clung in the air on the floor they were on. Her nerves were bad, eyes bloodshot red, and stomach hollow. She couldn't feel a thing besides her phone that'd been vibrating for the last hour.

The only thing that did get her attention was Moo coming into view in front of her. Confused as to how she'd heard what happened, Loriana's brows pinched as she spoke to Mhyale.

"Hey. Thank you," Moo told her before she came over to Loriana. "Are you okay?"

She shook her head no, as more tears filled her eyes. Moo wrapped her arms around her. She knew she was a bit shaken up because so was she when Mhyale called her. Sniffling, Loriana lifted her head and wiped her cheek.

"Who told you?" she asked.

"I saw Mhyale's tweet and asked her what happened. I feel like this is my fault," Moo admitted. Her voice cracked in the process.

Loriana was even more confused now. "Huh? How is it your fault?"

"Me and Sneaks been fooling around. My ex warned me about cutting the nigga off that'd I'd been seeing, but I thought he was playing. I didn't think he knew anything about us. I thought he was just talking, trying to scare me."

That news shocked Loriana more than it should've because, for one, when did Moo and Sneaks become a thing? Or were trying to become a thing? Moo was up scrolling Twitter when she saw Mhyale's tweet that said *I can't believe this* 🌑. Moo wasn't trying to be nosey, but she hit her DM's anyway. They pretty much ran in the same circle, so seeing that had her wondering what was wrong. Or who was hurt because this was Kansas City. Anytime anyone tweeted something about being sad, people's antennas went up, and they were on standby to see what was going on.

Never did she think Mhyale would be telling her Sneaks was shot. She gasped so loudly and dropped the phone when she read the message. Unable to type out an entire message to reply, she told Mhyale to call her and sent her number. Not thinking anything of it, because Moo was Projex's cousin, Mhyale gave her the run down, and now here she was.

"Are you serious?" Mhyale wanted to know.

Moo nodded her head yes. "Yeah. I just… man. I feel terrible. He didn't deserve that. What're the doctor's saying?"

"We haven't heard much yet. We're still waiting."

Sighing, Moo finally took a seat. Her eyes immediately fell to the blood on Loriana's pants leg, and the tears fell. Guilt consumed her entire body as Loriana rubbed her back. This wasn't fair. She was single and didn't belong to anyone. The jealousy her ex, Don, had bubbling inside him had just gotten him a certified death certificate.

Across the room, the wheels in Projex's head were already spinning with what he'd do to the nigga who shot Sneaks. Even if he hadn't been shot, niggas were on his head. Projex wasn't aware Moo had anything to do with it all yet, and even when he did find out, his plans would still be in motion. Sneaks little brother, Armon, sat in a chair across from Projex, talking lowly. Bo and Ayo already knew the police would be swarming once they arrived, so they ducked off.

With Sneaks shooting back as Projex's security detail, he had every right to shoot back, and the police didn't stick around for long once they realized that. They weren't getting any questions answered today or the next. Projex was so deep in conversation and lost in his thoughts that he too became confused when he looked up and saw his cousin crying.

Standing up, he walked over to her. "Moo, what's up?"

"I don't even want to tell you because I know you. You don't need to retaliate."

His nostrils flared. "You know the nigga who had something to do with this?"

She nodded her head, yes, and Projex knew without her saying that it was Don. Projex didn't have time to get a clear view of his face because he was busting back and trying to make sure Loriana didn't get hit. Don had got his little shots off but had there not been some people in the way, he and Sneaks both more than likely wouldn't have made it. Don had run while shooting, too, so he was almost out the clear before getting clipped by a few of Projex's bullets.

Shaking his head, Projex scratched his scalp. "Damn, cuz. You already know how this shit is about to go."

Moo's heart broke. She did, and there was nothing she could do about it unless she asked him not to. "I know, but can you hold off? At least let him admit it to me. If he doesn't snitch on himself before Sneaks recovers, then go ahead. I just hate it had to be this way."

"Before he recovers?" That was all Projex heard. "You know some details we don't?"

"No. I just know he's a fighter. Sneaks gon' pull through; trust me.

459

Her words were spoken with so much confidence, they had no choice but to believe her. Loriana prayed he pulled through. Too much good was going on in their lives for them to take a hit like this. As strong as they were, they wouldn't have been able to handle this one.

Chapter Seventeen

"I wish you'd quit reading that shit," Projex grumbled, walking into the living room.

Loriana looked up from her phone. "You don't even know what I'm looking at."

"Them fucking blogs and Instagram pages. They don't know shit about what's going on over here. That's all you been reading since that night."

It'd been three weeks since Sneaks was shot, and the blogs still had his, Projex, and Loriana's name in their mouths. He was irritated as fuck because he couldn't publicly speak on the situation. There was no case pending, but he knew the police were watching. Projex hated that he couldn't get back at Don on his own. Even putting some money on his head wouldn't have been satisfying enough.

Sighing, she locked her phone. "I know that, but I can't help it. Every time something goes on with you, they bring up the situation, and then I fall into a rabbit hole."

"Well, climb yo' ass out of there," he said seriously but made her chuckle. Projex smirked at her. "Man, I ain't playing. Stop reading that shit. It's bad for yo' mental. You know it best that mothafuckas gon' run with whatever story and drama hot at the moment."

"I do, and I wish it wasn't about us."

Projex couldn't agree more. Even when he thought the buzz behind the shooting had died down some, there'd be a blog post or messy ass commentary about what people assumed happened on social media. It was crazy to him how people he'd gone to high school with were speaking on him like he knew them. Fame was a mothafucka for sure.

It didn't help that Projex was in the middle of helping promote Misa's new EP. This one meant a lot to her, and Projex wasn't about to half-ass his duty as the producer of it because of some clout people were chasing. Business still had to be taken care of.

"I do too but fuck it. We can't control what they're doing. Only what's going on over here.

Enough of all that, though. What you making for dinner?"

"I want some jerk chicken pasta, but I gotta run to the store for some bell peppers. We ate all the other ones," she let him know.

Projex scratched at his bare stomach. They were at Loriana's for the day and had been knocked out on this good Sunday, thanks to it raining half the day. He'd woken up to an empty bed and gone searching for her.

"A'ight. That's cool. Let me throw something on real quick. That rain had me in a coma."

"I know. Soon as we laid down, you were knocked out." She snickered. "And all over me."

"So. I get the best sleep that way. Nah, don't roll your eyes. I can't lay on you now?"

"You can. I was just saying, dang."

He walked over to her. Leaning forward to where she was on the couch, Projex put his face up close to hers. Their noses brushed one another's.

"You been real funny acting lately. You good? Something you need to get off yo' chest, cuz?"

Loriana hated how he always made her grin even when she tried being serious. "Move. I'm not your cuz."

"You something 'cause my L-Boogie wouldn't be

handling me like this. You stressed? Need Daddy to suck on them toes and pussy?"

"Bryshon!" she squealed, then laughed.

"What? That shit normally relaxes you. I'm just trying to help you out. Be the good boyfriend I take pride in being."

Warmth spread throughout her chest as her eyes locked in on his. "It's just one of those days, but leave it up to you to make me smile."

Projex pecked her lips. "That's what I'm supposed to do."

On the drive to the store, they carried on in casual conversation. Mainly discussing how close graduation was and how ready Loriana was to be done with school. At first, she had plans to go straight into grad school in the fall, but with her new promotion underway, she had a slight change of heart.

As soon as they pulled into the parking lot of Target, Projex's phone rang. Whenever the caller's name popped up on his screen, relief and gratefulness filled him.

"Yo, P. What's good," Sneaks voiced in a raspy tone.

"Not shit. At this store with L-Boogie."

Sneaks coughed, and Projex grimaced. "That's

what's up. Aye," he said and paused. "I'ma need you to hold off on that."

Projex already knew what he was talking about. "For good?"

"For now," Sneaks let him know. "I'm trying to figure some shit out... put two and two together with some information I just got. I ain't trying to get ahead of myself."

"A'ight. I gotchu'. You good over there, though? Need us to bring you something?"

"Nah, man. I'm straight. My Ol' Lady here watching me like a hawk, so you know how that goes. A nigga ain't wanting for nothing."

Projex chuckled. "I'm already knowing. Tell moms I said what's up."

"A'ight. I'll hit you later."

"Fasho. Get yo' rest, my G. I need you healthy and shit just in case I go on tour with this nigga, Laurent, in the future."

Sneaks smirked. "I'ma bounce back in no time."

After having had to receive multiple surgeries after a bullet to the chest, Sneaks was happy to still be alive. Getting at Don would've been much too easy and an even easier way to get him locked up. With Moo being their connection, Sneaks wanted to lay low a bit and figure out what the deal was with them.

He'd heard her tell him more than once that they were through, but a nigga wasn't running up and shooting for no reason. Sneaks wasn't even about to play like that, so he was on standby with her. Them sneaky link-ups had finally caught up to them both.

"I'm glad he's at home and feeling okay," Loriana said. They'd stopped by the day before yesterday to see him.

"Yeah. Me too. I don't think I could've handled losing him too. That shit would've had me sick."

Loriana grabbed his hand. "You didn't. So don't think that way, okay? We're good. He's gonna get back healthy, and we'll move on and grow from this like we have with everything else in our lives."

"See. That right there is why I keep you around, ma," he said in jest, kissing her cheek. "I love you."

"I love you."

Like Sneaks, Projex had some questions for his cousin as well, but he was going to let Moo make it for now. He had enough business of his own to focus on.

Visiting her mama's grave never got easier. The pain just hurt less, while her chest always went through that familiar ache. Telling herself to breath, Loriana exhaled. She had to calm down, or she'd lose it.

It was early. Much too early for her to be up on the day of her graduation that wasn't set to commence until two o'clock. Loriana had to come and see her girl, though. She missed her terribly and knew Linette was rooting for her even though she wasn't physically here.

"I did it, Mama. I'm graduating today," she said after rearranging her new stems of artificial flowers.

"I know it was you who kept me motivated and getting up even though I didn't want to some days. On most days, honestly. I'm better now."

She was glad to finally admit that. Every day wasn't the best, but she had more good ones than bad. But on those bad ones, she tried not to stay in that space too long. Loriana didn't want to go back to when she harbored suicidal thoughts and a mild case of depression. No. She was claiming victory and healing over her life. The devil would never reside where God lied hands ever again.

"So, thank you. For everything. You taught me to face my adversities head-on. To stand up for all things I believe in and not take shit from anyone." She chuckled. "I hope I become half as the strong-willed, loving, and beautiful mother you are. Not were, because you're still here with me. I love you, lady. Keep watching over us."

Walking back to the truck, Loriana felt lighter. She always did once she visited and got things off her chest. Climbing inside the passenger seat, she exhaled and clicked her seatbelt.

"You want a hug?" Projex asked.

She smiled his way. "No. Because then I'll really start crying. I can give you a kiss, though."

Meeting her halfway, they pecked lips. "I'll take that, ma. You need to go anywhere else?"

"Nope. We can head back to my house so I can get ready. Don't forget to tell your mama to bring the cake she made me."

"Not you thinking about that damn cake early this morning," Projex said, pulling out of the cemetery.

"I'm not gonna tell you how I dreamed about then," she laughed. "Mm. I can taste it now. All that lemony goodness."

"See. Now you making my stomach growl."

"Me too. Swing by Wendy's before we go to the house. That honey butter chicken biscuit with those potato wedges? Yes. I need all of that."

Projex glanced her way. "Calm down, greedy."

She shoved his arm. "Shut up. You know how I get."

He smirked, already knowing. "Yeah, I do. Let me gon' head and feed you so we can get ready. My baby graduating with honors in this mothafucka."

Like always, when he hyped her up, Loriana blushed. Just as she was his biggest cheerleader, he was hers and had bought a blow horn to let off in the stands when they called her name.

Hours seemed to fly by after they got to the crib. Loriana hurriedly got dressed so she could be ready when the makeup artist arrived. Her apartment was packed as everyone made her spot the meet-up location. She was glad that Candace and Trell's graduation was yesterday, so they could attend hers. They all planned to have a joint dinner celebration tomorrow evening.

Before long, Loriana was splitting from her family and going to stand in line with her fellow graduates. Her nerves were bad, and she kept adjusting her tassel. The closer they got to the stage, the more her stomach rumbled.

"I don't know why I'm so nervous. I've busted my ass for this moment," she said to one of the girls in front of her. They'd been conversing since she walked up.

"It's normal. It'll go away as soon as your name is called."

She hoped so. When it was her turn to receive her empty diploma book, Loriana wiped her hands along the black gown before handing the announcer her name card. Making sure he pronounced her name correctly, she began to walk.

"Loriana Simms."

Like he promised he would, Projex blew the blowhorn, letting it be known he was proud of her.

"Let's go, ma!" he shouted as the rest of her crew clapped and carried on before sitting.

Grinning up at them in the stands, she waved and posed for a few pictures as she headed back to her seat. Her little brother, Ethan, was jumping up and down, excited as ever to see his big sister on the projection screen. Her dad and his family had driven up that morning. Nyree and some of her other family members had come into town yesterday.

Once the ceremony concluded with the class tossing their caps in the air, everyone headed out of the stadium. Loriana couldn't help but open the graduation program again to see her name. Receiving a bachelor's degree in journalism with a minor in mass communications and media studies was something to be damn proud about.

Walking outside to greet her people, Loriana's smile stayed spread across her face. Nyree was the first to spot her, and she rushed her way. With open arms, she hugged her best friend before pulling her phone from her clutch.

"Congratulations, friend. I'm so proud of you."

"Thank you. You're up next."

"Yes, ma'am. But can we get into the look, though," she said, recording her on Instagram. "My best friend is a college graduate out this hoe, huh? Get into the outfit. It's the body and real hair for me."

Nyree hyped her up as Loriana posed and laughed. Her normally curly hair had been silked pressed by Moo two days ago and was sweeping the top of her waist, holding a shine unmatched. Her makeup artist had given her a natural beat that had the comments on her page going nuts. Loriana was so organically pretty, it was hard to hate on her.

"I know that's right, niece. You better strut on these hoes," Peaches said, switching over to them. "I'm so proud of you, lil girl. You walked that stage and owned it."

"Thank you, Auntie."

Mhyale was the next to greet her with a big hug. A card and balloon were in her hand while Naaz stood behind her with a gift bag.

"Super proud of you, cousin. My little baby who's all grown up," Mhyale said, getting emotional.

"No. Don't start, or I'ma start, and we gon' be looking a mess. We look too fine right now."

Giggling, Mhyale told her okay, and Naaz outstretched his hand. "Congrats, sis. You want me to hold it until later?"

"Thank you, and yes. I don't have enough hands for hugs and all this stuff. I'm happy to see you here," she said, throwing a bit of shade, but was glad he'd shown up. She invited him and Mhyale together, but they rode separately.

"Fasho. You gon' always be lil' sis no matter what."

Mhyale rolled her eyes. "Okay. Let someone else see her now."

Shaking his head, Naaz scooted out the way. Memphis gave his cousin a hug and slipped her an envelope that was far too heavy to just have a card inside. Candace and Trell greeted her next, then her dad and his family. Everyone was trying to hand her gifts, but she could only hold so many. When Projex strolled over to her with that handsome grin on his face, Loriana blushed.

"You on a whole other level now, ma. You hear me shout yo' name?"

Loriana fell into his embrace and nodded her head. "Yes. Between you and Ethan, I don't know who was the loudest."

"Little dude was trying to compete with me and then talked my ear off the entire ceremony."

Loriana couldn't do anything but laugh because that was Ethan. When he found out Projex had won a Grammy, he asked Loriana for his number. Of course, she said no, but she did let Projex talk to him on FaceTime. Since then, he'd considered Projex cool enough to date his sister. Same with Greg. They'd had plenty of man-to-man talks that Projex appreciated from a father and husband's standpoint as well.

"I see you ain't taking nobody's gifts. You better take mine," he told her as his mama, Shamari, and Joi walked up.

"Ooh, my baby," Loriana cooed. "Is she awake?"

Peeking inside her stroller, Loriana pulled the blanket back to a very much so wide-awake Serenity. She grinned as soon as she saw Loriana.

"Hey, my girl. Looking all pretty in your yellow dress. She is too cute, y'all."

"Thank you," Shamari said. "And congrats."

"Yes. We're so proud of you, sis. You definitely motivate me to stay focused even more."

The love was overwhelming as she poked her lips. "Aww. Thank y'all. Hey, Ms. Joseline."

"Hey, honey. A bunch of congratulations are in order, huh?" she said, handing her a bag.

Loriana glanced Projex's way, and he smirked. "Yes, I guess so," she giggled, "thank you. We're gonna have to put some of this stuff in the truck right quick."

"Yours or mine?" Projex asked.

Her brows furrowed. "Um, yours. We drove yours here, remember?"

Reaching inside his pocket, Projex pulled out a key fob. "Yeah, but you gone have to drive yours home, or you want me to take it back?"

Her eyes widened. "Shut up," she whispered before yelling. "Shut up! You got me a new truck?"

"Yeah. You wanna see it?"

"Yes! What kind of question is that?" Loriana blurted, making them all laugh.

Leading the way, Projex lead them across a short walkway where Laurent was waiting for them. Loriana stopped dead in her tracks as her hands began to tremble.

"Oh, bitch," Nyree whispered close to her. "No, this nigga didn't."

"Bae," Loriana whined. "You got me a Range Rover?"

She was crying now and didn't even care that people were recording. She was overwhelmed and too damn happy. Projex had tissue on standby thanks to his mama and patted her face.

"You gon' fuck up yo' makeup." He chuckled as she looked up at him.

"I don't care. You really got it for me?"

"Yeah, girl," he laughed, "come look at it. Acting like you scared."

"Shut up. I'm not. I just… shit. I can hardly move right now. I'm shaking."

Helping her walk, Projex placed a hand at her lower back and took them over to her brand-new Range Rover with no miles on it. She'd never forget when he pulled up on her at prom with an all-white one just like this. It was her dream ride then, and Projex had made it a reality now like only he could.

"Sis, you looking a little nervous," Laurent joked. "I'ont think you gone be able to handle my gift then."

"It's from both of us," Maliya spoke up and said.

"Aww, thank you, guys. Let me just smell the leather." She laughed, opening the driver's door. Her mouth fell open, and then she turned so quickly on her feet to face Projex, she got dizzy.

"I know. That shit legit, huh?" Projex asked, already knowing the answer.

While the exterior was coke white, the interior was orange. Her favorite color. Loriana was bawling like a baby with her hands covering her face. When she heard something that sounded like a dog coming from the backseat, her head lifted slowly. Going around the back, she grabbed the orange leather Fendi shopper bag and screamed.

"Oh, my gosh! It's a dog in here!"

Laurent cracked up at her reaction, knowing that'd be it. "Get him out, sis. That's from me and Maliya."

Reaching inside, Loriana pulled out a white Pomeranian puppy. Laurent thought it'd be the perfect gift, considering how she said she didn't like being bored when Projex was away at the studio. So, he gave her some company. She hugged the seven-pound dog, then turned to face her family.

"What am I going to do with a dog and a baby?"

Every single person gasped loudly before some of them started screaming.

"Oh, my gosh!"

"Bitch, you lying!"

"You're pregnant!"

"I know you lying!"

Everyone's outbursts had Projex weak. Mhyale shot her eyes over to him.

"You knew!" she shouted.

"I mean, that is my baby. Yeah, I knew."

"That's not faaaair," Nyree whined, rushing up to her. "It's a baby in here for real?"

Loriana nodded while wiping her face. This was not how she planned to tell her family that she was pregnant, but hell, why not. She literally couldn't wrap her mind around Laurent getting her a dog, so a baby as well was just doing the most. She was overwhelmed, to say the least.

"Yes."

"Girl. I should slap you. How far along are you?" Mhyale asked.

"Seven weeks," Loriana mumbled. She looked up at Projex, who was already looking her way.

"You don't gotta explain nothing to her, ma," he joked, coming to her rescue.

Randomly, when they were out getting groceries, Projex had eased their basket into the aisle with the pregnancy tests. At first, he thought he was tripping because she was snapping on him more, requesting foods he never saw her eat, and she was mad sensitive. It sealed his suspicions the night they were on the Westport, and she claimed to be nauseous.

. . .

"**W**hat we stop in this aisle for?" Loriana asked him.

"Man. You know why. Which ones of these you wanna take?" he asked, reading the different labels on the pregnancy boxes.

Laughing, Loriana walked away from him. "None at all. I don't know why you think I'm pregnant."

"I don't know why you think you ain't. It don't matter, though," he said, grabbing one of each test he felt would give them some accurate results and tossed them in the basket.

When they got to checkout, Loriana was so embarrassed as he calmly scanned each one. He tried to make conversation with her the entire ride home, and Loriana ignored him. Walking inside the house, Projex pinched her ass cheek.

"You can pout all you want, but you taking one of these tests," he told her.

"Leave me alone, Bryshon."

"Oh, you serious." He laughed as he dropped the groceries off in the kitchen.

Putting them away, his mind ventured to how he'd act if she was indeed pregnant. Going upstairs to find her, Loriana was laid out in his bed.

"Come on, ma. I ain't playing."

"Ugh. You're so annoying. You gon' be looking silly when I'm not."

He shrugged. "That's cool. You still taking one, though."

Annoyed, Loriana climbed from the bed and trudged to the bathroom. Projex was right behind her with the bag of tests with a smile on his face.

"You gon' watch me pee?" Loriana questioned. Her voice full of attitude.

"Loriana, you done squirted in my mouth. Seeing you piss ain't shit. Now, which one you wanna take?"

Sucking her teeth, Loriana pulled her leggings down and sat on the toilet. "It doesn't matter."

Opening one of the tests, Projex handed it to her. Grabbing the box, Loriana read the instructions as her stomach churned. She heard of girls having pregnancy scares, but this was her first one. Not necessarily a scare, but the first time she thought she might've been wrong in the situation. Exhaling, it's like her body had already chosen whose side it was on, as she peed on the stick with ease.

"A'ight," Projex said as she placed it on the box, wiped, and stood to wash her hands. "Now, we wait."

At the sink, Loriana's heart was beating so fast, she felt ill. Coming behind her, Projex placed his hands around her waist. Instantly, a calm fell over her body.

"Relax, ma. We gon' be good whether it's positive or not."

"I'm not ready for a baby."

"Shit, I ain't think I was ready for a Grammy, but I got that mothafucka don't I?"

Smiling at him, he smirked back. "Always so positive."

"That's you rubbing off on me. If you are, we got time to get ready. We been practicing with Serenity anyway."

"That's not the same." She pouted, poking that lip out.

"It's practice, though."

Loriana closed her eyes as he casually massaged her frame. They stood that way until three minutes went by. Without unwrapping his arms from around her, Projex peeked at the test, and he stopped breathing for a second.

"What does it say?" Loriana whispered.

His hands slid from her thighs to her belly. He palmed it and whispered, "My baby giving me a baby."

Instantly, Loriana started crying. He turned her around to hug her, rocking them back and forth.

Projex was so affectionate with her. Loriana felt safe in his arms and protected, so even if she hadn't planned to have a baby within the next nine months, she was happy it was with him. Her first love. The universe almost hadn't saved her a baby daddy, but it came on through in the fourth quarter.

"You happy?" she asked him.

Projex smiled big. "Yeah. I ain't gone lie; I'm happy as fuck. So much weird shit has been going on and you carrying our child is a blessing. I needed this good news."

Loriana exhaled and had to agree. "I have to schedule a doctor's appointment."

"Fasho. We keeping it a secret?"

"For now. I'm still trying to wrap my head around it all."

W hether they were trying to keep it a secret or not, Loriana had spilled the beans. While her family and friends showered her with love, Projex grabbed her puppy. He told Laurent not to get her that damn dog, but Maliya had already made up her mind about it. While they were inside the ceremony, Laurent had Maliya bring the dog to meet him at the truck.

"Man, somebody take this damn dog. We don't need it now," Projex said, making Laurent laugh.

"Give me my dog! You treating him bad already," Loriana fussed, marching over to him.

"What you naming this lil' thing. It's small as hell."

Loriana shrugged. "I don't know yet. I have to name a dog and a baby? Chile," she stressed, making Projex laugh.

Kissing her lips, he pulled her closer to him. "*We* have to name a baby. This yo' damn dog."

"Whatever." She laughed, then got serious. "Thank you so much for my truck. You're getting too good at these gifts. I can't keep up. And your birthday is coming up. I have to start planning now," she rambled like always.

He palmed her belly that hadn't grown much at all. Projex knew their child was growing in her womb, though. "This is all the gift I need, ma. You and my baby."

Loriana had shamelessly turned him into a lover boy when he'd been such a ruthless savage. For her, he tried to be his best because that's who she brought out of him. Projex was never half-stepping when it came to her, and now he was about to take things up a notch for their child.

Epilogue

—————

"A 'ight, auntie. I'll holla at y'all later," Projex said, giving Jasmine, Chevy's Aunt, a hug.

"Okay, Projex. Don't forget to tell Lori to call me about the baby shower. She better be lucky y'all live too far out, or I'd pull up on her."

Jasmine was so happy when Projex told her he had a baby on the way. Anyway she could feel close to her nephew, Jasmine was for it. She didn't have to try, though. Projex was constantly checking in on her and dropping by when he could. Today was one of those days. She appreciated him more than he probably knew.

He smirked. "I gotchu'."

"You be safe out there, too."

"Always," was Projex's reply, but that was to not

have her worrying. There was no guarantee of his safety, but he wasn't about to live his life scared either. He'd always been a risk-taker. As his Air Forces descended the porch steps, Chevy's cousins, nieces, and nephews called out to him.

"Why you leaving, cuz?" Chevy's little brother asked. "I was trying to get in the booth."

"Call me next week, and I got you," Projex told him.

"I'ma call you too!"

"Me too!"

"Let me drive yo' car!"

They all shouted at him as he hopped in his Audi. It was nice out today, so he was riding with the top down. Going to his music, Projex felt like playing some Jeezy. All of his music put him in the mood to get more money and turn his hustle up. Taking it back, Projex blasted *Done It* as he pulled away from the curb.

Riding through the city, he took in where he grew up and had to thank God he made it out. Kent was right. Not everyone made it out, but he had. He was one of the lucky ones. *Nah, blessed,* he thought, hopping on the highway to head home.

Before his lease was up on the townhome he stayed in, Projex had already been looking at houses for him and Loriana to move into. When it was confirmed that she was pregnant, that had him even more anxious to get them into a home. Projex wanted to share a home with her. He wanted everything prepared to go when their baby arrived.

Pulling into their three-car garage driveway, Projex left the roof down and jogged up the steps. The door was locked, but the alarm wasn't set like Loriana told him she'd do when he talked to her earlier.

"This girl and her pregnancy brain," he mumbled, locking the door.

It wasn't a complaint but an observation. As her body grew and changed, Projex was eager to learn about what was going on with her and the baby just as she was. He'd send her different links throughout the day, curious as to if that was how she was feeling. Walking up the steps, he was greeted by Loriana's dog. He was scared to climb down all of the stairs and would wait for someone to pick him up.

"What's up, Hemi? Where yo' mama at? I told her to be ready at four."

Projex was speaking to the dog as if he could respond. For someone who was so against her dog at first, Projex was appreciative of Hemi. In the last four months between them moving, his busy schedule, and her getting adjusted to being pregnant, Hemi was her best friend. Walking into their bedroom, Projex realized why Hemi was all by his lonely.

Fast asleep with her round belly on display in the grey nightgown she was wearing, Loriana was knocked out. Projex couldn't help but grin. She'd recently hit six months and only wanted to sleep and eat. That was cool with him 'cause Projex would keep her fed. He'd already told her if she needed some time off from work to get adjusted to being a mother, it was nothing. This transition wasn't easy, but he wanted to make it as smooth for her as he could. Loriana wasn't doing that, though. She loved her job.

"Ma," he called out, leaning over the bed. Instinctively, his hand palmed her belly.

Projex never felt their baby kick, but Loriana was always telling him how he or she was in there doing the most. When she didn't wake up, Projex gently kissed her lips. Finally, she stirred, peeling her eyes open.

"You in here sleep," he said, grinning.

Loriana yawned. "I know. I was looking for something to wear and got sleepy as hell. Where Hemi?"

"Laying on my feet. You left lil' cuz all by himself."

She snickered. "I told him to get up here with me."

"He hardheaded. You still trying to go get your nails and toes done?"

Another yawn escaped her as she sat up in the bed. "Yeah. 'Cause I know you gon' be whining if we don't go today."

His mouth pursed outward. "Whining? Man, watch out."

"Yes, whining. You're still stubborn if things don't go your way."

"Okay, Loriana." He laughed. "I got the top down today, so put yo' hair up."

"Top down in the winter, that's what winner's do," she rapped lazily, making him grin.

It wasn't quite winter yet, but that didn't matter.

"Fucking right, ma. Hemi, you hear yo' mama spitting that shit? We gon' have to put her on a track."

Following behind Loriana into the bathroom, Hemi ignored Projex like always when in her presence. Giving her some space, Projex went back downstairs. Inside the kitchen, he washed his hands before looking through the fridge for something to snack on until they grabbed a bite to eat.

This was one of those rare days where they were both at home, so he was taking advantage of it. Spending some quality time getting their nails and toes done was the perfect date. Shooting a text to

Sneaks and his two other security details, Projex let them know the plays for the day. Sneaks had bounced back to an almost complete recovery. He'd have chest pains here and there, but for the most part, the bullet he'd taken hadn't done much damage.

Fifteen minutes later, Loriana descended the steps. Meeting her in the living room, Projex had her favorite snacks in his hand. In one Ziploc bag was cut-up cucumbers with ranch seasoning, while another held cheese flavored sunflower seeds. He didn't know how she ate those things, but she tore them up every chance she got until the roof of her mouth was tender.

"Thank you. Did you see my tuna sandwich in there?"

"That was a tuna sandwich? Where you get that from?"

"Your mama made some yesterday when I was over there. I ate most of it before I could even get out of the house." She laughed.

Going back to retrieve it, Projex bagged it up too. "A'ight. We good to go now, Big Mama?" he asked.

Loriana nodded her head. "Mhm. Gimmie a kiss first."

Projex tongued her down, gripping her booty that seemed to get fatter since she'd gotten pregnant. The grip she had on his shirt when he pulled away was comical. Her eyes were still closed but slowly peeled open.

"You missed me?" he asked.

Her head bobbed. "I always miss you when you're gone."

"That's why Laurent and Maliya got you, Hemi."

"Boy," she chuckled, "I love him, but he has nothing on you."

"Is that right?"

"That is."

"You really love a nigga, huh?"

Loriana blushed. "I mean, is it that obvious?"

"Like a mothafucka, ma. Promise me one thing, though, L-Boogie."

"What's that?"

"Promise to keep loving a nigga even when shit gets hard. It ain't gon' always be easy, but I want you to remember the good days. I'ma try my best to give them to you and our child."

There went that bottom lip poking out, and Projex ran his thumb across it. "You know I'm emotional. Stop it."

"Promise me," he urged.

Sticking her hand out, they did the handshake

reserved for SAG only. Loriana was a certified member at this point.

She grinned and said, "I gotchu'."

"I gotchu', too. For life. I mean that."

THE END!

Continue reading for an exclusive sneak peek and other surprises.

Sneak Peek

The Trenches – 2006

"This the last time I'm dealing with this nigga's bull-shit," Nakita hissed as her fist tightened around the steering wheel of her car.

She pushed the 1999 Buick like a bat out of hell. The big body vehicle held no weight to her anger. In the middle of playing cards with her family, a picture came through on her Blackberry of Karl and some bitch with her kids. Confused to how her baby daddy had time to be parlaying in the hood with some other hoe, while he didn't take care of Nyree, had her pissed. Usually, she'd let shit slide, but this was the last straw.

Whipping into the apartment complex of Southern Heights, Nakita only slowed down a bit because there were a few kids out playing in the street when they should've been in the house. The streetlights of the poles that did work, were already on. Making it in front of Karl's building, she jerked the car in park and swiveled her head to the backseat.

"Nyree, stay in the car and don't get out. You hear me?"

Nyree's wide, curious brown eyes peeked out the window. "Why we at my daddy's house?"

It didn't matter that she'd only been there a handful of times; she remembered where he stayed. In hopes that'd she'd get to come back over and play with the little girls next door, Nyree kept the vivid image of his building and the number on it in her mind.

"I need to talk to him, but you stay in here. Don't unlock the door for anybody."

Nyree's head nodded. "But am I going to get to spend the night?"

"Not today, baby." Nakita saw the hurt all over her face before she could complete her sentence. That alone fueled her anger even more.

Before she could let her baby girl get her in her feelings, Nakita hopped out, leaving the car running and the doors locked. The dope boy's posted up nearby nodded their heads in her direction, letting it silently be known that they'd watch her whip and Nyree, who hadn't moved her forehead from the glass. Trying to see what her mama was doing, she unclicked her seatbelt and climbed from the back into the passenger seat.

Swinging the rickety door of the building open, Nakita stomped the entire way to Karl's unit, number 113. Her first banged like she was there to make an arrest, but the boisterous sound was nothing new to the occupants. This was the hood. The mothafuckin' projects. It was loud and busy all the time.

"I know you're in here, Karl! You, that bitch, and her raggedy ass kids!" Nakita screamed.

Turning around, Nakita lifted her foot, slamming it into the door with all her might.

BOOM! BOOM! BOOM!

"Bring your ass out here!"

Behind the door, Karl was scrambling to put some pants on while Tracey, the woman he'd been laying up and taking care of, tossed her hair into a ponytail.

"See, that bitch want me to whoop her ass," Tracey fussed.

"Nah, nah. Stay in here. Make sure the kids don't come out the other room," Karl urged.

Rushing to the front of the two-bedroom apartment, Karl undid the locks and tried to make his way out of the apartment. Nakita shoved him hard, making him stumble back.

"You got me, and my baby fucked up!" she wailed, swinging on him. "You around this bitch laid up with her and taking care of her mothafuckin' kids, and Nyree can't even get a phone call from you!?"

She was on a thousand right now. There was no stopping her. The pain in her voice almost hurt him more than the vicious punches she was delivering. Bearhugging her, Karl squeezed her tight.

"Nakita! Calm your ass down, woman."

"No! I'm tired of this shit. You pop in and out of our lives then go missing for months. Nyree doesn't deserve that!"

"I know, Kita," he spoke calmly, trying to diffuse the tension. "I'ma do better. I promise."

"You always say that! Lying ass nigga. Let me go!"

While she struggled to break free from his grasp, Tracey decided to make her presence known, stepping into the living room. All Nakita saw was red.

"I don't know why you coming over here starting trouble. It's clear Karl is with who he wants to be with," she said.

"Bitch! This ain't about his bum ass. Oooh! Let me go!" she screamed, clawing at Karl's arms with her sharp nails.

"Fuck!" he spat, loosening his hold.

That was all Nakita needed. Full speed, she ran up to Tracey, not giving her an inch to swing as she punched her in the face. Tracey was from the hood too, so of course, she naturally didn't fight fair. They went head up for some seconds before Tracey pulled a blade from inside her mouth.

"Ol' bitch, you trying to cut me!" Nakita yelled, picking up a candle that was nearby.

Hurling it in her direction, the glass smacked Tracey dead in the forehead right above her eye. The blow knocked her to the ground while blood began to pour from her head.

"Nakita! That's enough!" Karl belched as she stomped her out, not giving a fuck about the blood on her brand new K-Swiss.

Picking her up, Karl placed her on the other side of the small living room before going to check on Tracey. The second bedroom door opened, and one of Tracey's four kids peeked their heads out of the door while the other three followed suit.

"Mama!" the oldest one screamed, seeing her laid out on the floor.

Rushing out of the room, Nakita got a clear glimpse of how he was over here moving. She hadn't seen it with her own two eyes until now. The rumors she'd been hearing were true, and Nakita couldn't front; she was hurt. Not hurt for her, but for Nyree. She was disgusted with herself for having made him her baby daddy in the first place.

"We call the ambulance," one little girl said, not pronouncing the B in the word.

"Tracey, can you hear me, baby?" Karl spoke soothingly.

"Fuck you and her! I hope I knocked some sense into her ass," Nakita spat.

Outside of the building, one of Tracey's friends who lived on the third floor of the building stopped to talk to Cream. He was one of the top go-getters in the neighborhood.

"Who car is this with they lights on?" Gabby wanted to know.

"That ain't even my business to tell, but you better go check on you homegirl," he told her. "You know Karl keeps her in some bullshit."

"Oh, hell no," Gabby hissed, just as police sirens echoed from the entrance of the complex.

Tracey was walking out of Karl's apartment when Gabby came storming her way. With her adrenaline already pumping, she hoped like hell that she didn't have to whoop her ass too, but she would. Thankfully, Gabby rushed by her.

"Gabby! That lady did this to Mama!" Tracey's oldest yelled.

"Oh, my gosh, T! Un, un. I'm 'bout to fuck her up."

Rushing back out of the apartment and down the hall, she pushed the door open just as Nakita was on the last step. Hearing Gabby approach, she spun around. The two went blow for blow until Gabby slipped on the unbalanced concrete steps. She kicked her legs and feet as Nakita dragged her to the sidewalk.

"You gon' try to run up on me!" Nakita was out of her body.

She didn't hear Nyree screaming for her to stop or the police cars that whipped into the yard, damn near crashing into the building. Nyree's heart thundered in her chest seeing them yank her mama like a rag doll.

"Stop! Get off of her!" Nyree yelled, banging on the window.

She was obedient and hadn't gotten out of the car, but she wanted to. Rolling the window down, she kept yelling.

"Get off my mama!" she cried angrily.

Hearing her baby's voice snapped Nakita back into reality. Their eyes connected, and Nakita shook her head as she was cuffed.

"Nyree, I love you."

"No. No! This wasn't her fault! Let her go!"

Her pleas fell on deaf ears as she was placed up against the back of the car. Looking toward the building, Nyree became a bit hopeful when she saw Karl, but her face fell when she saw who he was carrying in his arms. Tracey's kids were right behind him while coming out of the building.

"Daddy! Daddy! You gotta help Mama!" Nyree screamed.

Karl glanced her way with wide eyes before ignoring her and rushing Tracey over to the police.

"She needs help. She's losing consciousness," Karl stressed.

"Who did this to her?" a policeman asked.

Gabby didn't hesitate to point her finger directly at Nakita. "She did! Look at my friend's face!"

Chaos broke out as Tracey's kids cried as she was placed onto a gurney. Nyree's screamed crippled Nakita as she was placed in the back of the squad car under arrest, and Nyree's hatred for Karl was set in stone right there in her mama's Buick. At only seven years old, she'd gotten her heart broken by the first man who was supposed to love her.

Juice's eyes bounced back and forth as he sat outside of their apartment. The hallway reeked of an odor he'd become accustomed to. What was left of the fluorescent lighting in the ceiling flickered, making his leg shake. He was always nervous sitting out here, but it was better than being in the dark. He hated the dark.

His back was pressed against their apartment door, and his legs bent at the knees. This was where you could find him at least once a month for more than a few days straight. Only at nighttime, though. The navy-blue pajama pants he had on were too small, stopping at his calves while the shoes on his feet were too big. He was supposed to bed in the bed he and his two-year-old brother shared, but Juice had priorities. At ten years old, he'd already deemed himself the man of the house and stood firmly on that.

"Dang. What's going on over there?" he mumbled, hearing the sirens and noticing the flashing red and blue lights coming from across the courtyard.

He wanted to be nosey but wouldn't dare move from his spot. The window he noticed everything coming from was way at the opposite end of the hall. Their apartment was right by the staircase, making them an easy target for the drug addicts posted up inside it. The sickening stench of them lighting their pipes seeped through the door, making Juice crinkle his nose.

Hearing the locks to their apartment turn, Juice quickly stood to his feet. Light filtered through their pitch-black home, giving him a clear view of his younger sister, Asha. She was rubbing the tears from her eyes as her little chest heaved.

"What's wrong, Asha?" Juice asked, squatting to be at her level.

"I-I'm scared."

The trembling of her bottom lip let that be known.

"Where the flashlight I gave you?"

"It's not working. Can I sit out here with you?"

Juice scratched his arm. "No. It's not safe. If you go to sleep, you won't be scared."

Her head shook from side to side, forcing her huge puff at the top of her head to bounce. Juice knew there was no getting through to her.

"Please," she begged, making him give in.

Making her way through the door, Asha plopped right down beside Juice after locking the door back.

Stuffing the key in his pocket, he stretched his legs. Just in case he fell asleep on accident, he never left the door unlocked. Mothafuckas around there wouldn't think twice before running in their shit.

"What were you doing?" Asha asked, snuggling against him.

She'd been the baby for all of three years until Celeste had her fourth child. So, she was used to being babied by Juice. She was the youngest girl.

"Just sitting. Somebody called them people across the yard."

Her eyes lit up. "Ooh. The police?"

Juice nodded his head. "Yep. I bet somebody going to jail."

"I wanna go see," she said, about to stand up, but Juice pushed her shoulder down.

"No. You can't run down the hall by yourself this late."

Whenever they'd come in from that side of the building, they'd post up in the window and watch what everybody was doing. It was their entertainment when they couldn't go outside or if the rigged cable Celeste finessed every month wasn't working.

When the door to the staircase creaked open, Juice pulled Asha closer to him. His hand instinctively went to the hammer tucked between the folded, small cover near him. Juice's teeth gritted as the man approached them, yet he felt no fear in his heart.

"What y'all doing out in this hallway?" the man spoke.

Juice stared him down. The man's eyes went to his hand under the cover, and he smirked.

"I see what it is. You holding little dude?"

Still, Juice didn't bother to utter a word. His menacing eyes roamed over the man, who was dressed way too nice to be hanging around the hood this time of night. Juice was surprised the long chains hanging from his neck hadn't been snatched on the staircase. You only walked those during the day, and sometimes not even then.

The Jordan's on his feet were fresh out the box, having just dropped the prior weekend, while the navy-blue Dickies and crisp white tee still had creased iron lines in them. Juice's eyes fell to the gold watch on his wrist. *Damn, that's nice.*

The man peeped him looking and unclasped it. "Here. You wanna try it on?"

Juice shook his head no. Had this been under different circumstances, he would've taken his shit and ran off with it before pawning it for some cash.

"That's a nice watch, Mister," Asha spoke in an airy tone.

"Sssh. We don't talk to strangers," Juice told her, keeping his eyes on the man.

"I ain't no stranger. Well, to y'all, I am. Yo' mama named Celeste, right?"

Juice spoke then. "Yeah, why?"

"Just asking youngin'. I'm Kano. Now, let me know what y'all doing out here. I ain't leaving until you do."

"Our lights cut off," Asha mumbled. "It's scary in there."

Juice nostrils flared. "I told you to be quiet."

Her lips poked out. "Okay."

"It's a'ight, baby girl. You don't gotta talk to me. Your big brother seems to be the man around here."

"I am." Juice's words were firm.

"I like that in you," Kano acknowledged, now understanding why they were posted up outside the door.

He knew who they were, thanks to Cream. He'd done his run-through of the building collecting his money from the workers when one of them let him know Juice was posted outside their apartment again. This wasn't new to the folks who lived in Southern Heights, but to Kano, it was. He didn't like it one bit either.

"How long the lights been off?" Kano questioned.

"A few days."

Kano nodded his head before digging in his pocket. The knot of money he pulled from it was as thick as a softball. Juice's eyes widened a bit before he relaxed them. When Kano peeled off five hundred dollars and stuck his hand out, Juice looked up to him.

"What's this for?"

"Tomorrow, have yo' mama pay the light bill. Spend the rest on some food cause I know the shit y'all had in there bad now."

It was. Most of it had already been on the last day before it expired, or already was. Licking his lips, Juice eased his hand from around Asha and grabbed the money.

"Thanks," he mumbled.

"You welcome, young buck."

"I'ma have to pay you this back?" Juice wanted to know.

That question stunned Kano for a second. "Nah. That's y'all's to keep."

Juice nodded his head, and Kano felt like he'd done his due justice for the evening. He'd slide through next week to see if Juice had been sleeping in the hallway and if so, he was going to have a talk with Celeste's ass.

When Kano made it just halfway down the opposite of the hall, Juice stood up. "Don't move," he told Asha before jogging behind him. "Aye," he called out, making Kano turn and face him.

"What's up?"

"This money," he said, holding it in his hand. "How can I make some more of it?"

Kano knew what he was asking but didn't want to be the one to place him in that position. As soon as you started hustling, it was hard to stop. The rush it gave you was addictive. The money made or lost fueled you in a different type of way. You became too hungry, never knowing when to stop overindulging. Juice didn't care. He was starving.

"You too young for a job," Kano let him know.

"I'm trying to work for you."

Juice didn't know who Kano was at first, but his iced-out K chain gave him away. His friends raved about getting them a chain just like his when they got some real money. Kano's name was spoken highly of through Southern Heights. Not by all, but by the majority. There wasn't a drug being pushed through the low-income housing buildings that he didn't know about. He knew when the last bit of cocaine had been snorted, rock had been smoked, and flame lit to melt heroin.

Kano peeped the hunger in his eyes. It wasn't one of desperation but one of survival. One of protection. Juice was asking with an open mind. A young mind that had matured way before its time. Peeping over his shoulder to check on Asha, Kano made his decision.

"Meet Cream in building twelve tomorrow at seven. Y'all lights should be on by then, right?"

"Yeah. They will be."

Kano nodded his head. "What's your name?"

"Juice."

"A'ight, Juice. Keep holding shit down."

He waited until Kano pushed through the door before walking back to his spot in front of their door. Taking the cover, he spread it over Asha's frame as her head lay in his lap.

"What you say to him?"

"None of yo' business. The lights will be on tomorrow," he told her.

"What about the next day?" she asked, not fully understanding how getting them cut back on worked.

Juice wasn't either, but he knew this would be the last day he or any of his siblings slept in the hallway or in a pitch-black apartment.

"They won't get cut off again."

"Good," she yawned, "no more sleeping with the flashlight on."

Being the oldest of six kids, Juice would forever protect them the best way he could. Even if that meant going against his mama's wishes. Living deep in the trenches wasn't for everybody, and Juice made an oath to get them out of it.

Made in the USA
Las Vegas, NV
22 August 2024